Man Shark

The Legends of Ḷainjin

Book One

Man Shark

The Legends of Ḷainjin

Book One

A novel of historic literary fiction by Gerald R. Knight

IGUANA

Published by Iguana Books
720 Bathurst Street, Suite 303
Toronto, ON M5S 2R4

Publisher: Meghan Behse
Editor: Shelley Egan
Front cover design: Daniella Postavsky
Front cover image: "Marshall Islands Canoe (C19)" by Herbert Kawainui Kāne, with permission from Herbert K. Kane, LLC.

"Knowledge of the past gives us a rudder to navigate the present."
— Herbert Kawainui Kāne

ISBN 978-1-77180-228-4 (paperback)
ISBN 978-1-77180-329-8 (epub)
ISBN 978-1-77180-330-4 (Kindle)

This is an original print edition of *Man Shark: The Legends of Ļainjin*.

I dedicate this series to author Kim Echlin, whose inspiration made these writings possible, and to the waitress who told me I looked like a writer and reminded me who I was.

Author's note

There is a single story in the extensive oral literature of the atoll-dwelling Marshall Islanders that, uncharacteristically, has no ending. This is the story of Tarmālu and her son, Ļainjin. In accordance with legend, she leaves her baby in the care of others as she leads her fleet of proas[1] from the shelter of the Wōtto Atoll lagoon into the open ocean to save their craft from the certain destruction of an oncoming typhoon. She is never heard from again. When her son grows up, he goes on an epic search to recover her story and creates a renowned navigational chant to record the seamarks along the way. It is never told if he finds her. These are tales told in many versions betwixt islanders dispersed across an inviting yet harrowing ocean that has long since washed all prehistory into its depths. The footnotes are necessary only for those who wish to delve below their surface into the environment, language, and culture from which they spawned.

---

[1] Outrigger canoes rigged with sails.

Foreword

Greetings to you all, my sisters and brothers in Christ. I, Deacon Alfred Capelle, would like to sincerely thank Mr. Gerald (Jerry) Knight, the author of the book named *Man Shark* (*Ļōpako*), for this excellent accomplishment he has achieved not only for himself but especially for all Marshall Islanders. I first met Jerry when I worked with him for the Alele Museum from March 1996 to October 1991. Jerry was then the Chief Executive Officer and Director of Alele Museum.

Iọkwe kōmiwōj ro jeū im jatū ilo Christ. Ña, Deacon Alfred Capelle, ikōṇaan kaṃṃoolol Mr. GeraldKnight, (Jerry) eo eaar je bok in bwebwenato in etan *Man Shark (Ļōpako)* kōn jerbal ṃōṃanṃōn in eaar kōṃṃane ej jab ñan e wōt ak eļap tata ñan kōjwōj ri-aelōñ kein ad. Ikar jino iioon Jerry ke iaar jerbal ippān ilo Alele Museum jān Ṃaaj 1996 ñan Oktoba 1991. Jerry eaar Chief Executive Officer im Director eo an Alele ilo tōre eo.

Man Shark (*Ļōpako*) is a legendary folklore about Tarmālu and Ļainjin, her son. You can read the story and enjoy it yourself. It is quite appropriate for Jerry to have authored the book, being as keen on listeing to island folklore as he was as a young man ri-pālle. Jerry came to our islands when he was nineteen, as a member of the Peace Corps in 1967. Before joining the PC he was in college majoring in literature, where he learned the required skills for one wishing to be attentive to recitation, to understand and question our morals, and to learn the effective methods of listening and writing a legend or a story as told. And so when he came to the islands he already possessed the keen interest and skills necessary to help him listen, understand, and write the legends and stories the elders in those days related to him. Jerry also deepened his local language-speaking ability to that of native fluency and developed his understanding of the local culture from his interactions with the older members of the communities on atolls and islands such as Namdik (Namorik), Roñļap (Rongelap), Arņo, Mājro (Majuro) and others where he was able live at length on. The time well-spent in the atolls and islands benefited Jerry with the knowledge, skills and deep interest in the stories and words that are the information foundation of our language and culture. The combination of knowledge, awareness and love inspired Jerry to write the stirring and valuable storybook *Man Shark* (*Ļōpako*). Therefore, on our behalf, again, "Thank you kindly, Jerry, for this your wonderful gift to us all, people of these islands. May God bless you and your family!"

Man Shark (*Ļōpako*) ej bwebwenato kōn Tōrmālu im Ļainjin ļadik eo nejin. Koṃ maroñ make liñōre bwebwenato in im itokļimoimi kake. Elukkuun kōkar bwe Jerry en kar je bok in bwebwenato in kōnke ej juon likao in pālle eo ijeļā bwe ekanooj itok limoin im kōņaan roñjake bwebwenato in aelōñ kein. Jerry eaar itok ñan aelōñ kein ad ke 19 an iiō, tōre eo ke eaar uwaan Peace Corps ilo 1967 eo. Ṃokta ļọk jān PC, eaar jikuuļ ilo college im katak kilen im wāween roñjake, meļeļe kake, kajitkini im jeje bwebwenato kake. Innem ke eaar itok ñan aelōñ kein ededeļọk an wōr itok limo ippān im an jeļā rāpōļtan ko raorōk ñan jipañe kāroñļọkjeņ, meļeļe, im jeje bwebwenato ko rūtto ro ilo tōre ko raar bwebwenato kaki ļọk ñane. Jerry eaar bareinwōt kaṃwilaļ ļọk an jeļā im meļeļe kōn kajin im ṃantin aelōñ kein ke eaar mour ippān rūtto ro ilo tōre ko ke ej Peace Corps Volunteer ilo aelōñ in Naṃdik, Roñļap, Arņo, Mājro im aelōñ ko jet eaar maroñ mour ie. Pād eo an ippān armej ro ilo jukjukin pād ko ilo aelōñ kein eaar kōjeraṃṃan Jerry kōn jeļā im meļeļe ko rōṃwilaļ ilo bwebwenato im naan ko rej pedpedin im kōmletin ṃantin aelōñ kein ad. Kobain in aolep jeļā, kapeel im iọkwe kein ippān Jerry ekōṃṃan an ellowetak bwe en je bok in bwebwenato kōbbōkakkak im aorōkrōk in: *Ļōpako*. Kōn men in, ilo etamwōj ri-aelōñ, "Koṃṃool im jouj, Jerry, kōn menin letok aiboojoj in aṃ ñan kōṃwōj aolep, ri-aelōñ kein. Anij en maroñ kōjeraṃṃan eok im baaṃle ņe aṃ!"

At this point I would like to take this opportunity and encourage all Marshall Islanders who will read this great book to keep a keen interest for our language and culture, our most valuable gifts from our Creator, God Almighty, our

Father in heaven. We have reached the tides in which our language and culture are being threatened, and so let us be very watchful together and wholehearted as we tighten our belts in solidly maintaining our language and culture to prevent their fading and lost. In reading the *Man Shark* (*Ļōpako*) story we are inspired to be gratified and to want to help do what we can to keep our language and culture healthy and lively as long as our republic breathes. I would also like to urge the heads of the department of education for our islands to recognize and use this as a textbook in the public and private schools. If the public school teachers adequately review this book it will help open their eyes and make them aware of the importance and the need to teach their students properly via the means of the language and culture. I end my words with the following adage: "It was not accidental that a wandering tattler (bird) should alight on the beach rock!" So long to you all and may God be with everyone.

Ilo tōre in ikōņaan bōk iien in im kōlowetak aolep ri-aelōñ kein bwe en itok limoidwōj kōn kajin im ṃantin aelōñ kein ad, menin letok aorōkrōk kein adwōj jān ad ri-Kōṃanṃan, Anij Ļapļap Jemādwōj ilañ. Jebuñūt tok tōre kein rōkauwōtata ñan kajin im ṃanet kein ad, innem jen kanooj mejmej karruo ippān doon im bōro wōt juon ilo ad kūkkim dāpij im kōmājojoik kajin im ṃanet kein ad bwe ren jab mājkun im jako. Bok in bwebwenato in *Man Shark* (*Ļōpako*) ilo ad liñōre ej jipañ kōllowetak kōj bwe en jubūruōd im kōņaan jipañ kōjparok kajin in ad im ṃanet kein ad bwe ren emmourur wōt toon wōt an emmenono rūbablik in ad. Ij bareinwōt rōjañ jeban jerbal eo ej bōk eddoin im loloodjake jeļāļọkjeņ ilo aelōñ kein bwe ren kile im kōjerbal bok in ilo jikuuļ ko an kien im bareinwōt ilo jikuuļ ko jet. Eļaññe enaaj jejjet an ri-kaki ro an jikuuļ kein liñōre bok in enaaj jipañ kōpeļļọk mejāer bwe ren meļeļe kōn men in eaorōk bwe ren aikuj katakin ri-jikuuļ ro ilo kajin im ṃantin aelōñ kein. Ij kōjeṃļọk naan kein aō kōn jabōn kōnaan in me ej ba: "Ekar jab jirrilọk bwe kōtkōt en jok ioon bar!" Iọkwe kōmiwōj im Anij en pād ippādwōj.

Alfred Capelle
Chairman, Customary Law and Language Commission
Republic of the Marshall Islands

The calm

Peck. Peck. "He must be thirsty," Ļainjin thought as he awakened from the day's deep, lonely slumber. He glanced out from beneath the shade of his worn woven pandanus-leaf sail. He had draped it like a tent to shade his boat, and there in the blazing sunlight was the Chief himself, with his coat of iridescent black feathers and his red neck-sack drooping in regal splendor. He was pecking on the outrigger deck yet again, breaking the quietude as if to summon Ļainjin's attention. By default, silence had invaded his being. He had experienced the unthinkable. Now, truth be told, he preferred to stow his thoughts as much as possible and, like the bird before him, simply observe and instinctively react. At this moment, all he wanted was to stuff his gut. He had crossed the ocean and lived to tell about it. Yet he had nothing to say and no one *not* to say it to. He and the bird had both been snatched from their mothers' warmth too young. Both had braved the same skies but only one of them carried sadness, reflection, regret.

The bird straightened his neck and pointed his long, hooked beak to the light blue sky. Then he lowered it and belched up a freshly caught silver mackerel five knuckles long and dropped it before the commoner.

"*Kommool.*"[2] Ļainjin chuckled as he grabbed the fish and rinsed it in the calm, clear sea below. He had not eaten fish for several days and sorely needed the energy. He was about to pop the nourishing treat into his mouth when the bird pecked him to stop. Suddenly, the surface of the water erupted into a chaotic battle of shiny mackerel baitfish chased skyward by rapacious tuna into the beaks of swarming, screeching, and diving terns. He was not ready for this! Or was he?

---

[2] Thank-you.

The bird, swept up by the excitement, flapped his long, elegant wings, nearly as long as Ḷainjin's arms. He rose upon the breathless air and quickly climbed through the terns to the top of the flock, where those whose gullets were full were likely to be found gliding upon the faint thermal breath reflecting from the ocean's shiny surface. His keen eyes observed the various circles of fish below. At the center of the various engagements were circular clumps of confused and panicking bite-sized baitfish broken apart by speedy, black-backed fish with the delicious, bloody hearts that his worker liked to rip out and feed to him. Ringing these encounters were much longer fish with their sails up, their spears raised, and their gluttonous mouths open wide. Twisting through the translucent blue, now and again, were the somewhat slower-moving big-mouths ready to eat him, his worker, his *kubaak*,[3] or anything else they could crunch with their pointy teeth. Unlike the white-and-black flappers about him, he sensed that these same weightless wings that allowed him to glide and sleep among the clouds would prevent him from rising off the rolling but dangerously flat surface below, particularly in this nearly breathless calm. Were it not for his perch and the commoner's ambitious paddling, he knew he could not survive these doldrums that caused death to his kind under these moons in this part of the ocean.

From the Chief's perspective, Ḷainjin served as his one and only worker, but Ḷainjin, unlike his sole companion, now had no one to depend upon but himself. The sky about them had crept into their spirits as they had flown from one place to the next — he on the surface, his Chief at times so high he was out of his sight — yet one of them held trapped inside him the story of his mother, his dead friends, the bloody battle beyond the *kāleptak*,[4] and all he had seen and done before his search for her and since then. Surely, this untellable tale would color his perspective wherever they traveled.

"Ak!" the Chief squawked as he surprised a tern and clamped onto its tail feathers with his strong, light bill. As though commanded, the frightened bird emptied its gullet into the air. Instantaneously, the Chief released his captive,

[3] Outrigger float.

[4] Swell that "slaps from behind"; the countercurrent of the Intertropical Convergence Zone, which periodically streams through the islands just north and south of the equator.

converted into diving mode, and plucked most of the fish ball from the sky long before it could splash into the ocean, boiling with activity below. Then he landed carefully back on his platform just in time to encourage his commoner to get fishing for one of those satisfying hearts. "Ak!" he commanded.

Though Ļainjin had eyed his bird from time to time, he had raised the butt end of his mast from its resting place within the deep, narrow hull of his proa onto its sailing position in the yoke at the boat's center. This prompted the sail's booms to swing outward in balance with the outrigger, and he propped them there with his paddle before securing their sheet. His decks were now clear. He had not bothered to furrow his mat sail but uncharacteristically allowed it to drape down and dip a bit into the sea. He had grabbed his fiber trolling line from its place below and, time being critical, had not even bothered to remove its precious mother-of-pearl lure. He had tied the Chief's baitfish to one of the prized hooks, tediously ground from the shell of a giant clam. The hook, of course, was strong, but the line was fashioned to troll for a fish thirty *ñeñe*[5] behind his sailing rig, not to hold a tuna racing a few lengths beneath his boat. Therefore, he tied a netted sinker ball of the dense shell onto the very end of his line to cause it to descend all the faster. He inspected the baited hook one last time. He had tied it about three knuckles below the shiny, pearl-shell lure and about half a ñeñe above the sinker ball. He held the end of the line between thumb and index finger for a moment, weighing the baited line of carefully crafted implements with an up-and-down motion as if to judge the risk of their loss against the hunger pangs in his gut. Then, caught up in the excitement all around him, he released the line, letting it slip freely over his palm. He watched as its sinker led the descent into the transparent blue water below, followed by the twirling, flashing lure, and finally, by the gently swirling silver baitfish.

The terns hovered and flopped onto the volatile surface of the sea surrounding them. The ravenous flocks plucked some of the hapless baitfish from midair as they jumped before the mouths of the charging predators below them. The screeching birds shaded the sky and showered him with cool seawater flicked from their fluttering wings. Bits of baitfish rained

[5] The length across the breast from fingertips to fingertips; one fathom.

down. In a commanding voice, he chanted, "*Tartok im kein liitiō, bwe? Ijañin eoļōk! Ellok im toto wōt!*"[6] He allowed the line to play out to what he judged was a depth of about twenty ñeñe, or about a fifth of his coil. Then he abruptly began yanking his baited line back up from the depths in one violent skyward motion after another, letting the line fall haphazardly over the outrigger platform and forcing the bird to hop to a perch on the forward deck, out of the way. "*Tartok im kein liitiō, bwe? Ijañin eoļōk! Ellok im toto wōt!*" he chanted, but still no strike.

Abruptly, he stopped and let his line slip back down over the palm of his right hand until it played out a second time. His throat dropped as the feast's center of intensity began randomly drifting away. Was this his last chance? He chanted yet again as he repeated the violent skyward yanking, and this time, his reward was a most satisfying resistance, followed by forceful pressure in what seemed to be the opposite direction. He turned his head skyward, shook his locks, and squinted to drain the burning sweat that had crept off his deeply furrowed forehead into his eyes. His sun-blackened face blossomed into a magnificent grin that soon broke into a hearty laugh. "*Kook! Kook! Kook! Kook*," he cried, as though calling chickens. "*Wōde im ajoļe!*"[7] he chanted, enticing the fish to crunch down as he would on a kernel of pandanus. Ecstatically, yet ever so gradually, he squeezed the wet line as it slipped, hurtfully now, between his calloused thumb and fingers until he judged the hook set and the body of the fish parallel to the boat. Then he began, hand over hand, to coax the fish gradually up to the surface. When the fish charged upward, he was quick to keep the line taut. When the fish turned in retreat, he allowed the line to slip, ever more firmly, through his fingers. One abrupt tug and all could be lost! As soon as he felt the first break in the tuna's strength, he began pulling more and more energetically, hauling his catch toward the boat to keep it from the jaws of any shark attracted to the struggling prey. As the fish broke the surface, Ļainjin raised it up by the line with one hand and resolutely snatched its throat between the gills with the other. Lastly, he raised the energetic and vibrating mass of

---

[6] "Rush here and yank back at me because the others have twitched me not! Relax and hang yourself!"

[7] "Chew it and gnaw at it!"

muscle out of the water, dropped the line, and clubbed the fish's forehead, crushing its skull and releasing its spirit into the fray about them.

He laid the dead fish across the deck of his stern hull and slit its silver belly from throat to anus with one effortless swipe of his unusual shark-tooth ring. The ring, when worn, encompassed nearly two digits of his middle finger. It was laboriously fashioned from mangrove, and it featured a single, large shark's tooth with holes drilled through its base, lashed into a slit between its two ridges. He sometimes looped the ring through a length of twine that attached to his trochus wristband to prevent it from slipping forward. He usually cut with the tooth turned perpendicular to the flat of his hand, the ring held in place by the incredible grip of his outermost digit. He tossed the gut into the sea and tore out the still beating, bloody prize.

The Chief had hopped, meanwhile, back onto the outrigger platform, the better to supervise the commoner's activity. His beak had grown longer than Ļainjin's hand over the past eighteen seasons since he was but a white and vulnerable ball of innocent, downy fluff. His beak was slender and light as a feather, like his other bones, but very strong and hooked at the tip. Truth be told, beneath all the feathers, less than a handful of tough, black flesh surrounded these perdurable bones, yet he had become veritably insatiable.

Ļainjin carelessly tossed the heart in the Chief's direction. The always alert bird caught it as it fell, straightened his neck to the sky, and swallowed the bloody lump in one quick motion. Ļainjin filleted the tuna into small, red strips and discarded the carcass. He and the bird ate nearly half of these. He ate his half with a wedge of *jāānkun*[8] stored below and placed the remaining strips of flesh on the deck to dry in the sun. Then he reseated the butt end of his mast back down into the stern hatch, recovered his boat with the sail, and eased himself back down through the forward hatch into the narrow hull, into which he barely fit. He unhooked one of several remaining netted and hanging coconut shells filled to their holes with rainwater. Sparingly, he drank half, lay down, and quickly fell back to sleep.

The Chief watched the minnow feast move from here to there, and finally disappear as quickly as it had appeared. The terns quieted and dispersed.

---

[8] Sun-dried sheets of pandanus pulp rolled into a log and wrapped in a sheath of pandanus leaves.

The sunlight poured down mercilessly, unencumbered by a single cloud. The rays reflected off the smooth surface of the cool ocean water and further heated the listless air above, causing it to rise skyward and provide the terns with a faint lift on the island-bound leg of their daily journey.

The boat slowly rose and fell atop the lazy rolling swells used by Ļainjin and his ancestors as navigation tools to locate islands beyond the horizon, and the chief of all birds sat perched, satisfied, and ever watchful upon his platform at the center of it all.

As youths, they had gone to Anbōd,[9] the famous shark-hunting reefs off Jālwōj Atoll, to take teeth. It was on the way back that they had stopped at the great bird island of Kōle. Never had he heard such a din. The birds shattered the silence of the sea. The boys' revenge for suffering these peace-shattering cries was to feast upon them. Before departing, he realized they had eaten the Chief's parents. He brought the fluffy chick back to Namorik,[10] where it was to become his ward and constant companion. Yet because of this sequence of random events, the Chief was forever associated in his thoughts with the good luck of that trip, the fortune they had fought for that had promoted all his subsequent adventures. Yes, having to feed the bird's enormous appetite was a distraction, but he welcomed it. And as he came to learn, a bird can follow a man where no other companion can.

These relentless doldrums had made Ļainjin nocturnal. To conserve water and energy, he waited daily for the sun to set and the air to cool before resuming his nightly passage. His shoulders and legs ached from the labor of numerous nights past. Still exhausted and now with a full tummy, he slept soundly through the afternoon. As twilight approached, he awoke and peacefully began to wonder, "Was this their fourth day without wind?" No. He counted five. He recalled that the first rule of drift was to conserve water, food, will, and strength, in that order. But did the order matter? True, he was low on water, but the sky under this moon would bear water sooner than later. Surely, amid all this calm, a rainstorm was forming somewhere close. Ļainjin

---

[9] Jālwōj islet; an area along Jālwōj Atoll's western reef known for shark hunting.
[10] Literally, "small lagoon"; an atoll in the southern Rālik Chain of what is now the Republic of the Marshall Islands.

was adept at collecting rainwater off his lowered pandanus-leaf sail and funneling it into the mouths of his coconut-shell vessels or if necessary, channeling it into his hull. He still had half of one huge log of *jāānkun* stored below, and the ocean always offered him something of sustenance. Conserving his will was tricky, and yes, it was more important than strength. Was "will" just the desire to preserve his life and that of any crew? No, "will" required the proper temperament, and it required the confidence that his story would survive and he would one day discover happiness out there somewhere below the horizon.

If his destination were farther away, he would be tempted to stay hunkered down and rested to preserve strength. The tailwinds from the storm he expected should be enough to land him at his destination. Yet he was confident he felt the faint *buñtokrōk*,[11] and the even fainter *kāleptak*, rolling beneath him unmistakably — first one and then the other, from perpendicular directions. His grandfather had told him, "The first rule of navigation is to know your orientation." That was the easiest part. "A Rālik[12] proa left to drift in the open ocean always ends up pointing roughly north and south." Understanding why distinguished a navigator from a fisher or a day sailor traveling by outrigger canoe from one islet to another along the necklace of an atoll. Understanding why went to the throat of why the dimensions of the canoe were so precisely what they were. It was why the proportions of the length of the kubaak to its hull were what they were. Everyone understood that the kubaak supports the platform deck and adds to the proa's stability. Yet only its hull maker or its navigator knew the secrets of why a bigger or longer float, while it might increase stability, was not necessarily better. Everyone knew that an outrigger craft is, by necessity, sailed with its outrigger booms to windward. Yet his grandfather had said, "Only a navigator knows that, without a sail, the proa will still drift on its own with its outrigger booms turned to windward. Only a navigator knows that, even without wind, the proa will still drift with its float facing the direction of the predominant swell."

---

[11] Swell that "falls from the south."

[12] The western chain of atolls of what is now known as the Republic of the Marshall Islands.

In the open ocean, that predominant swell came from the east — unless, of course, you had approached an atoll from the west and the swell from the east was blocked by the atoll. East was the direction from which the sun and the stars rotated, from whence were generated the incredibly strong salt storms that began at the beginning of the season of *añōneañ*[13] and churned the ocean into a daily turmoil of wind, waves, mountainous westward-rolling swells, and salt spray. It was because this swell was so strong and had obviously traveled westward for so long, over such an uninterrupted distance, that Ļainjin assumed the world was mostly water. He also thought of the world as round, like the sun and the moon. For why else would the islands he sought lie below the horizon? Legends and many actual stories were told about the islands to the west from which he now realized his ancestors must have originally come. He had been to those impressive places. They had tattooed their nightmares upon his soul, leaving him damaged inside with no wish to return.

So Ļainjin had noticed these swells from both the south and the west growing gradually more pronounced as he had paddled northward, and this could only be so if there was an atoll to the north and east starting to block the much stronger *buñtokiōñ*[14] from the north, and the always predominant *buñtokrear*,[15] from the east. As they had taught his mother before him, his maternal grandfathers had shown him how even a rock on the reef bent the current sweeping by, changing the wave patterns surrounding it and making itself distinguishable to anyone trained to feel the changes. His first memories were of his two grandfathers taking turns leading him about in a large *jāpe*[16] they had made for him. They would take him again and yet again to the immense coral rock called Daij, on the western fringing reef of Namorik Atoll, where he had grown up. As the tide swept in from the ocean — or reversed and swept out from the lagoon — they would push or pull his little boat all about the rock. They taught him to distinguish the difference

---

[13] "Call of the north"; the southern solstice, which annually coincides with winter in the northern hemisphere.
[14] Swell that "falls from the north."
[15] Swell that "falls from the east."
[16] A wooden, trapezoid-shaped vessel carved from breadfruit wood and used to knead breadfruit; the constellation Delphinus, the dolphin.

between waves generated by tidal currents sweeping across the reef — like swells from the quadrants rolling across the ocean — and surface waves generated by the wind coming from whichever direction it happened to blow. They would put a blindfold over his eyes and say, "Point to the rock." Then they would turn him around again and yet again until the disorientation forced him to feel his position by the rock of the boat amid the convulsion around it. And again they would ask, "Where is Daij now?"

They would stand waist deep in the tide on the reef, *wapepe*[17] held high, teaching the lesson that the strong, normally predominant swell from the east, like a tidal current, would bend — or at least cause a sort of current that would fall in phase with and enhance — the much fainter swell from the south. Because the atoll cut off its somewhat stronger counterswell from the north, this swell from the south would naturally grow more distinctive as he approached the yet unseen island. Its northern counterswell would likewise bend or cause a current that would likewise fall into phase to strengthen the swell rolling from the west that, on its own, would be enhanced as the atoll cut off its otherwise predominant counterswell — and so forth around the four quadrants. Ļainjin had learned a logic that allowed him to determine the direction of an unseeable atoll through a combination of reasoning and feeling that raised his awareness of the ocean environment.

He had learned these signs from boyhood. Now, in his isolation and amid this vast divide about him, his grandfathers were quietly speaking to him: Where is Daij now? Beyond, he sensed an atoll to the north and east. It was probably a two- or three-night paddle away. It could be Ujae or it could also be Lae. No matter, it was there. He was certain of it. He would stake his life on it. True, its footprint, amid the enormous open ocean of water surrounding him, was very slight, but as he approached, the signs would become clearer. He was confident of that. He had learned these simple rules of this world of islands and water. More importantly, his grandfathers had taught him to feel these four swells depicted in the *wapepe* rolling from the quadrants under him amid every imaginable weather condition. The currently calm surface of the sea, uncluttered by local wind conditions, made

---

[17] Literally, "boat floating." The symbol represents the four swells, one from each quadrant, converging upon an island in mid-ocean.

it the easiest to navigate. The old men's teachings had long ago become more than a theory. He was unblindfolded now, and they had become his very sense of reality.

The islanders probably called him Ļōpako[18] because of all the sharks they thought he killed. But those who knew him had given him that nickname when he was a boy because of his constant movement and his patient circling of whatever goal he had in mind. Who has not seen a shark circling? You imagine it is carefully planning an attack. It captures your attention. Then you see it swim away, and you imagine that the shark shrewdly weighed its odds of success and determined they were against it. In truth, the shark was just habitually moving, not thinking. Yet you remain on the lookout for it. You anxiously expect its return because you know that it could be there instantly to snatch the next fish you spear away. Perhaps that was why they called him Pako — because he was tenacious, always ready to seize the moment.

His trip to Anbōd had been a perfect example. He and his friend Kalbōk — his young yet fearless friend for life — had circled that idea for seasons. It was his friend who crushed the enormous noses of all their catch, usually with one swift blow of his long and heavy hardwood club. Ļainjin could see him there now, standing with one foot braced on the floorboards of the hull and the other propped up on the outrigger deck, his club held skyward above his head, ready to land a single fearsome blow the instant the thrashing beast's terrifying mouth, with its rows of crooked teeth, lunged up from below. He could hear the thud of the club as it invariably landed on the very tip of the monster's nose, driving the soft bone back into its brain and causing it to spasm dangerously to and fro, rendering it unable to muster much of a counterattack. The shark's lack of forward momentum would result in its death.

His destination was Wōtto. It was the next atoll along the string north of Lae. That was where his story began, and in a sense, he had set his course there, as a seabird would one day return to the island of its birth. More importantly, he should go there to maintain her myth. He could not remember his mother as she was then although there were many stories

[18] Literally, "man shark." "Ļō": the male prefix; "pako": "shark."

about her. Yet he grew up with a melancholy about him — a throat sickness, so to speak — for he was but a baby when she scrambled off in the night and left him there. As a youth, he had visited countless islets up and down the coral atolls of the Rālik and Ratak[19] strings. Everywhere they spoke well of her, and this added to his pang of not knowing her. People told tales of how she had brought a new variety of *Bōb*[20] from there to here and then from here to there, and brought this to cure that — and how she had introduced every variety of breadfruit to just about everywhere. The upshot was that she *had been* everywhere, several times, but no one knew what she had been up to! From what he gathered, that was what every *irooj*[21] had wondered, especially since they all distrusted each other and often sent their workers to battle over seemingly insignificant items of dispute. There were no stories of her being involved in any fight, just stories of her sailing around under this moon to that atoll and under that moon to another, passing around all this stuff to taste and to plant. She rewarded each irooj with what she brought, but they were jealous of what she may have given others and always wanted something else. Surely, most men felt it was a difficult enough task just getting from one atoll to the next. To think that she had led a whole fleet of — no one seems to have counted how many — boats and she had left tales of her adventures on nearly every islet of every atoll of both the Rālik and Ratak strings… Yes, she had left a glorious and widespread story of the name Tarmālu behind her. But to what end? Everybody wondered. Nobody but he knew.

When he had first tried to find out what happened to her, it quickly got too complicated for him to track it all. Her adventures were widespread, and he became the youngest seafarer any navigator had ever met — and his goal was to meet them all. He lived to listen to their stories and was good at retelling them. He would sit late into the night with the navigators and others, listening and asking questions, and because they knew he was the legendary Tarmālu's son, he would get accurate answers. She had invented

---

[19] The eastern chain of atolls of what is now known as the Republic of the Marshall Islands.

[20] Edible pandanus fruit cultivated predominantly on coral atolls in the central Pacific; pandanus tree: *Pandanus tectorius.*

[21] Chief.

chants to memorialize the various currents, circles of fish, flocks of birds, and seamarks around and between the atolls. He would pick up one here and another there. He would memorize them and then venture out to locate them for himself. Knowledge — rarely shared with those who were unproven, unrelated, or otherwise not respected — was a man's true fortune. Yet as a youth, he had often wondered if he was perhaps the only one not being told the best parts of her story. Was the sadness in his eyes keeping him from being told dark or sinister parts that might be clues to what had happened to her? One part he knew did not fit; they had all repeated the same proverb: *Emejjia wa iḷọmeto.*[22] How could she have gotten lost if she could always figure out how to get home? And how could she have lost her boat if it was safe out there? This conundrum was what had compelled him to voyage from island to island at a young age and to ask many questions, and everyone had treated him with deference, as though he was an irooj or other high person and not the humble *pejpetok*[23] that he was in his own eyes.

At first he had felt obligated to develop his mother's land on Namorik, for unlike Wōtto and the other northern atolls, his mother's land, on the more southern atoll, was fertile, devoid of coral rocks, and plentiful with taro and bananas. Yet ultimately, he had left this work to others. He had taken up the gatherer traditions and had no more interest in growing things than his insatiable companion. The old women teased that he had contracted the disease they called *ṃōjọliñōr.*[24] That fit him perfectly. He was afflicted with it and would take it to his story's end. He had probably inherited it from his mother. He preferred sleeping under the stars, and when on land, slept under thatch only if it rained. He had lived to watch islands rise from below the horizon, knowing that they were there beforehand. He had decided at an early age what he would have to become if he were ever to unwind the mystery of what had happened to her out there.

The sun had set, so it was time once again to stow his thoughts, prepare his rigging, and move forward. He instinctively began to transform his floating raft into a spear that was as sharp as possible, to penetrate the

[22] "A boat dies slow in the open ocean."

[23] The spent core of a pandanus kernel drifting about in the ocean; a drifter.

[24] Too much sky inside; sickness caused by sleeping under the moon too often.

atmosphere as easily as possible. He needed to conserve as much water, food, will, and strength as he could. First he raised the butt end of the mast he had lowered into the hull and placed it in its seat between the upward-sloping outrigger booms, where they were lashed at the yoke of the hull. Then he stabilized his forward-sloping mast by tightening its forestay and backstay. And then he began with his sail of woven pandanus leaf, which was no longer needed to shade and protect him from the sun. He compacted it as tightly around its two booms as he possibly could, until it resembled a fatter version of the leaf-wrapped log of *jāānkun* stored below. He propped the rolled sail with his second paddle again, this time sheeting it in closer to the hull to reduce wind resistance. Finally, he cleared everything from the deck — except the Chief, of course. He was already in his place as far out on the outrigger booms as possible. As likely as not, he would poop his chalky goo straight into the water. He had long since passed into his nightly trance, and Ļainjin imagined he was already busy amid his bird dreams.

Lastly, he sat his fiber-kilted rear on the edge of the stern deck with his legs braced within the hull for advantage, and almost from a standing position, he plunged his oar as deep as possible into the sea. Digging first on the right and then the left, he viewed the bluish-green iridescent bubbles streaming in the wake of his paddle's blade. There, again he felt it, as he plunged his blade and dug into the seemingly living water beneath him again. He felt *kāleptak*'s ever so gently slap on the flat side of his hull and watched his kubaak sink as the swell from the west lifted his hull, tilted the outrigger booms down, and then swamped the float and nearly submerged it. "What else could cause that but an atoll to the east?" he asked himself. He would paddle north and watch for *kāleptak* to grow in prominence as confirmation.

The stars showed brightly, without flicker in the cloudless sky. It was the night of no moon, the night of the highest tide, when lobsters crawled like ants on the flooded fringing reefs and the reefs' edges teemed with big-eyed, sharp-toothed predators. For the past nights, even as he had paddled, he had imagined mother turtles searching the beaches from beyond the reef's edge of the islets where they were born. They would have popped up at dusk from the usual coral caves, where they would have inflated themselves and slept during the day. They would have watched the tide recede from the reef until it became the flat, puddled, and rock-strewn landscape upon which they feared exposing themselves. Then, as the tide turned, they would have carefully bobbed their way landward as it ever so gradually reflooded the reef to the sandy shore. There they would have climbed up under the brush at the islet's edge, dug their nests, laid their eggs, covered them with sand, and returned to the still-flooded reef before the receding tide could leave them stranded and vulnerable in the morning sun.

Had they seen fires, they would have swum along the atoll necklace to what they perceived as safer environs. "The pathetic things did not know that we knew they were looking for us," he chuckled. The islanders knew the exact nights of the moon's cycle that the mother turtles would be watching, and so they avoided using fire those nights. Did the turtles think the islanders would not observe their distinctive tracks in the sand, which clearly led shoreward into the brush above the high-tide mark? The islanders even knew not to disturb their nests for two more nights, because they knew the turtles always came back thrice to unload all the eggs in their bellies. They also did not know that the islanders cherished the mother turtles, ate only a small number of their eggs, and could turn them on their backs only during the most festive or hungriest of times — and only after the irooj gave permission.

All the other creatures of the ocean required the islanders to study their habits, create schemes to hunt them down, and sometimes exert massive amounts of energy to catch them. Only the extremely cautious mother turtles walked ashore, stood at their feet, shed their sad tears, and practically begged the islanders to eat them. "It took a certain type of man," he thought, "to turn one of them over and cut off its breastplate, to look at that kindly thing with tears in its eyes and cut its guts apart." He had never done that, and he knew he could do that only once — and only if he used up a powerful inducement, or "fire starter" as he called it. He learned to think of every fearful or difficult thing he was likely to encounter and to have a fire starter ready to launch himself into action. To be positively certain the fire starter would successfully motivate him, however, he must promise himself to use it only once. He had a good source of inspiration for such a task, but he certainly did not want to use it up. It was the memory of a drowned boyhood friend.

His name was Jiañ and, strangely, he looked a bit like a turtle himself. He was so stocky that his arms and legs looked short. He could hardly swim a boat's length above water, but he loved to dive and was better at it than everyone else was. He saw well under the water, and when he exhaled, he could sink like a stone and stay under longer than anyone thought was possible. He would cut clams, spear fish, grab lobsters from their crevices, and coax octopuses from their holes on the bottom when most others would have to give up for lack of air, and he loved to wrestle papa turtles from their coral caves.

They would be out diving on the reef's edge burning *pāle*,[25] and if he spotted one while hunting other things, he would come up immediately to warn the others on the boat to be ready. Then down again he would go. Eventually, he would surface with the thing next to him, one flipper immobilized over his broad shoulder, his arm over the turtle's back, and his stubby but powerful fingers clutched onto the turtle's other flipper, if not the outer edge of its shell, turning it away from himself for all he was worth to keep its beak away from his face. The turtles, on their part, always tried to exhale and scull their tail flippers to prevent themselves from rising to the surface, but that is not what killed his friend. One such night, Jiañ grabbed onto a great-grandfather of countless turtles. He must have been in the process of guiding the monster around toward the mouth of its cave and must have grabbed onto its shell at the nape of its neck. That proved to be a fatal mistake. When the old boy retracted its neck, Jiañ's thick fingers must have been trapped between its bony, stubborn skull and its hard, perhaps even coral-encrusted, shell. The last they saw of him, Jiañ was dangling helplessly, looking back toward the light from the turtle's immense back, being dragged down deeper and deeper into the black abyss below. They lit one torch after another till, finally, they spent the last of them, and they never saw him again.

Ļainjin shuddered at the thought and dug his oar hard into the water to distract himself from these abhorrent thoughts. Like many others that

[25] Dried, braided coconut leaves used as torches for fishing; a coconut frond.

came tapping from time to time, they lingered over his shoulder. Looking up at the sky, he resolved to identify a star and name it after his stocky friend. His eyes searched for Liṃanṃan [26] as he paddled. He was trying to keep her left of his course. The immensity of the uncountable, unnameable points of light above astounded him. There, pointing in her direction, was the great Jāpe. That was the perfect group of stars to name after his friend because he was always looking there for direction and could watch them as they rotated above and then gradually disappeared below the horizon. There, trailing and dangling forever from the intrepid turtle, was Jiañ's arm. What a tremendous thought, to name these stars to commemorate his friend. He felt Jiañ's spirit emerge from the ocean and engulf him. Shivers climbed the nape of his neck. He promised himself that he would teach his future son to watch the pointy turtle slowly sink into the sea, dragging Jiañ's arm with it. He would explain his fatal mistake. His son would pass on the story of Jiañ, and people would tell the story generations hence. The swells continued to roll and rock his craft methodically as he paddled, keeping Liṃanṃan to his left. The stars continued to rotate. He continued to imagine the mother turtles playing their serious game of hide-and-seek among the atolls. Feeling contented and not quite as alone as before, his mind wandered over it all, and he dug in his oar again and yet again.

By this point, Ļainjin had gotten himself into a rhythm, and his proa was cutting through the water with good momentum. He had worked the pains in his shoulders and arms from the previous nights' exertions down to a dull soreness that he would be careful to preserve by not overresting. He would stop only briefly to snack or drink before the dawning of the fresh day. As he paddled, he searched for Tūṃur,[27] and there he was in the western sky, where he would set and be out of sight long before dawn. "It is true," Ļainjin confirmed again as he had before. "He would never see his youngest brother, Jebrọ,[28] who would rise in the east that morning, just before first light.

---

[26] A name: "woman beautiful." "Li": the female prefix; "ṃanṃan": "very beautiful." The north star, Polaris.
[27] Antares, the brightest star in the constellation Scorpius.
[28] The constellation Pleiades.

"*Ñaijuwe!*"[29] he cried out across the rolling, gleaming vastness surrounding him.

He was imitating Tūṃur's mother, Lōktañūr, who — as the story went — cried out to her eldest son from ashore. The story told of a great race between the opposite islets of Aelōñļapļap Atoll. The first of her sons to reach the easternmost islet, Je, would become chief. They were all to paddle, because this was supposedly during the time before they knew about sailing.

"But if they didn't know how to sail," he asked himself, "how did the ancestors get to the islands of Rālik and Ratak in the first place? Paddle?

"Not likely," he answered himself. "This was probably just another story to teach the children about sailing."

So Lōktañūr had woven the first mat-like sail, but when Tūṃur looked at it on shore, it looked to him like a heavy bundle of wind resistance. "*Etal ippān Mejdikdik*,"[30] he cried back. Mejdikdik[31] was the name of the next eldest brother, who was busy paddling to catch up. He in turn told her to go with the next eldest. It went on like that until Jebrọ, the youngest, approached. Being the last of twelve brothers, he had no choice but to obey.

"So that was probably the moral of the story," he thought, "that everybody should respect his mother's call."

Still, there was more. The descriptive, instructive part for the children to sleep on came next. Jebrọ beached his canoe and watched as Lōktañūr rigged her mast and triangular lateen sail with its upright yard attached to the forward-slanting mast and a sheet attached to its boom. The mast, rigged with a forestay, a backstay, and a stay to the outrigger, had as its main support the upright yard that attached to it. The weight of the woven pandanus-leaf sail stabilized the fourth quadrant. It luffed in the wind and held the whole contraption in balance unless the sail became back winded. When that happened, the whole setup fell with a crash, causing onlookers to laugh.

That was the perfect point in the story when Ļainjin — or better yet, another listener — would feign stupidly and knock something over, causing the children to giggle.

---

[29] "Take me aboard!"

[30] "Go with Mejdikdik!"

[31] A star name: "Little death."

Jebrọ, the story went, was skeptical at first, especially since they could not sail directly eastward into the wind but had to sail off at an angle toward the islets on the northeast edge of the necklace. Once there, Lōktañūr cried, "*Diak!*"[32] She loosened the sheet until the sail began to luff, unlashed the sail's clew where its yard and boom joined, loosened the forestay, and began walking the clew to the opposite end of the canoe. That caused the mast, attached to and suspending the vertical sail boom, to change its arc as she brought the sail forward and lashed it in place at the other end. During the process, the kubaak stayed to windward and the sail continued to luff until she resecured the backstay and cried, "*Ṇatọọn!*"[33] At which point she sheeted in and the boat moved swiftly toward the southeast.

As a boy, Ḷainjin had heard this story repeated so many times that he and most other children had involuntarily memorized it. He remembered wanting to be one or another part of the canoe that he had to act out as the shunting was repeated, and the various parts switched among the children as the story continued. They would all mimic Lōktañūr when the time came to shout "*diak!*" and "*ṇatọọn!*" Did he believe, as he looked up at Tūṃur's stars, that they were once a man who became a group of stars in the sky? No, although whoever told the story would make him wonder, when they'd point to the stars and say, "And there he is tonight, and he will set in the west and not see his brother Jebrọ rise in the east, and that's proof the story is true!" That's proof, he thought, that the stars don't cause the weather to change as the story would have them believe but instead mark the moon's thirteen cycles — and by memorizing the weather of these cycles, the children would be better prepared to survive the weather they foretell. Because of Jiañ, he was unlikely to get his hand stuck between the nape of an old turtle's neck and its shell. Likewise, because of Tūṃur's story, he was unlikely to find himself caught adrift in the dry and sunny salt storms that come under the first moon of añōneañ season, when he rises just before dawn.

---

[32] To tack or, more specifically, shunt. The tack of the sail is transported from one end of the canoe to the other, keeping the outrigger to windward.
[33] Sheet in or trim the sail.

"Elladikdik iuṃwin Tūṃur ekūtañtañin eṃṃaan!"[34] He chanted loudly.

As the story went, Jebrọ sailed by each of his eleven brothers as he shunted back and forth on his way eastward to Je, and each brother he passed wished he had hearkened to his mother's call. Finally, he passed Tūṃur, who, being the eldest, became so ashamed he turned around and paddled back westward, followed in order by each brother. There they are, lined up in a row across the middle of the sky from west to east, the story's authenticity proved repeatedly as each brother causes some sort of mischief with the weather when his stars rise just before dawn. When Jebrọ rises under the first moon of the season of *añōnrak,*[35] he brings calm waters, prosperity, and peace. "*Ej kōkōṃanṃan eoon aejet. Eeọkwe armej,*"[36] chanted Ḷainjin, as he took another mammoth stroke. He felt a pang of guilt that he had rushed through the story. He needed to learn to speak or think slowly through the story and to take more pride in his storytelling. Had there been children around him, he would have gone into detail about the parts of the boat and the various sailing techniques Lōktañūr deployed to win the race.

Then came the remainder of the story's weather-related details that he liked the best. These details related to the characteristics under each moon of each of the two seasons. He knew that survival conditions among the low sandy islets of Rālik and Ratak were more difficult than on the more fertile islands with mountains that lay to the west, so his ancestors must have created these stories to warn their descendants what to expect. Tūṃur's rising was always the most dramatic and always occurred at the very beginning of añōneañ, when the sun rose in the morning and set in the evening at its most southern arc, rising south of east and setting south of west. The Rālik Islanders called this añōneañ (call of the north) because the winds blew from more north of east, and they blew very hard and very consistently but without rain. They blew every night and every day until the ocean churned into mountainous rolling swells. The sky would turn hazy with salt from evaporated droplets whisked off the powerful waves that

[34] Proverb: "Under the windstorms of Tūṃur, a man is an inchworm at sea."
[35] "Call of the south"; the northern solstice, which roughly coincides with summer in the northern hemisphere.
[36] Proverb: "He calms the roughest waters. He loves all people."

crashed in a constant, thunderous roar upon the islands' fringing reefs and salt coated the tattered leaves of all the plants and trees, turning the islands amber and then a haggard brown.

Under the next moon came a brief reprieve from the second-eldest son, Mejdikdik. Sometimes he brought a little rain and a few days of lighter winds, but then the salt storms resumed in full force. There was no rain, no breadfruit, and no pandanus, and they would be a long time coming. Then, when Mājlep[37] arose, life became even harder. There was no rainwater to drink, and the only food was starch from the *m̧akm̧ōk*[38] root. This was a pleasure to eat but difficult to dig and time-consuming to make. There would be water from wells on the big primary islets of the atolls but none on the small islets that ring the periphery. Freshwater floated on top of the seawater at the bottom of the wells, and as añōneañ wore on, that freshwater layer would get thinner by the day. At that point, migrations from northern to southern atolls — and often fighting — could ensue. Jāpe was the last star of añōneañ, just before Jebrọ, the first star of *añōnrak*, arose to bless the waters. However, the treacherous storm *kapiļak*[39] would sometimes appear before him. Although kapiļak brought a violent but welcome rainstorm, the gale that often preceded it could appear so suddenly that uninformed sailors risked their lives — their masts broken, their sails torn, or worse, their outrigger canoes flipped and set adrift. However, the storm rarely coincided exactly with the first rising of the star, and on rare occasions, it fell after Jebrọ had also appeared. So the fisher must watch other weather signs carefully during this period, and that was now!

Ļainjin's mind wandered over these things and others as he powered his proa forward along the endless bulging and ebbing swells from his right. His boat's length was longer than three ñeñe. They had warned it was too long and too deep for one man to paddle comfortably. His oar was too large and heavy for paddling yet he toiled on, paddling without resting, methodically and deftly penetrating the shimmering water with his blade without a splash.

---

[37] The star Altair.

[38] Arrowroot; a nutritious starch processed from the rhizomes of the dryland, knee-high plant *Tacca leontopetaloides*.

[39] A gale sometimes associated with the first morning's sighting of the constellation Aries.

He moved through the water with the endurance of a shark, pivoting his paddle one-quarter turn, pushing the stern of his boat opposite the direction he had just thrust its prow, and finally, raising his blade parallel to the water and swaying it forward for another plunge.

From youth, he was never allowed to choose his own oar. One by one, his maternal grandfathers selected them for him, and the oars were always purposefully too big to comfortably fit into his hands, let alone light enough with which to paddle. Season after season, as he grew, they would make him even larger oars, until his arms and shoulders bulged and his hands gripped with the strength of an eel's clutch.

They built his proa for the four of them — one to steer with the oar; one to secure the sheet attached to the yard; one to *ņatọọn*, set the course, trim the sail, and bail if necessary; and the fourth as ballast, to move weight out onto the outrigger booms as far as necessary for stability in strong winds. They rotated positions often so monotony would not dull their concentration. Extra hands at the prow and stern came in handy when it came time to *diak*. Often he would look about him at the crew members who were no longer there. With a pang in his throat, he would ask for and listen with his imagination to their confident advice. And always he would remember their personalities — and their adventures — as sharply as though they were yesterday's.

They were boyhood friends and competitors — from Namorik all. As they grew, each of his four friends became a *ri-katak*[40] under his father's lineage, and each made himself and his family proud by outcompeting the others at his skill. Ļainjin, fatherless and unadopted, would otherwise have gone untrained were it not for his maternal grandfather and his grandfather's brother, who were master navigators. Kalbōk contracted the *ṃōjọliñōr* early in his boyhood. He fished night and day and never slept inside. He caught more fish than anyone knew because he was always giving his catch away to girls on the ocean side before returning home.

Kalbōk, he remembered, liked to fish in the middle of a rainstorm. Well, he liked to fish anytime, but particularly if it caused him to stand out among the other young men, who, during a rainstorm, usually huddled around a fire in their grandmother's cookhouse or curled up in their sleeping mats.

[40] Understudy; apprentice.

He had trained with the relatives on his father's side to grind hooks and lures of *kapwōr*[41] and fishing spears of the hardwood *kōñe*.[42] Kalbōk's fishing spears were very thin and no good for battle, but when he would scrape one on the reef as he ran, it would vibrate and cause terror in the fish he was attempting to encircle. He had divulged this secret to Ļainjin but to no other man. Most just thought he was faster or luckier than they were.

He would prepare his boat in the middle of a storm during a half-moon tide like this one, which would never reach an extreme. He would set sail in whatever gusts the storm brought or paddle in the rain if it brought none. Off he would go, slowly disappearing into the dim gray haze, and his course was always the same — to the *me*[43] across the lagoon on the northern fringing reef of the atoll that the ancestors of his clan had built and maintained for generations before them. Word of his departure would travel like lightning from the young women of his family to those of their neighbors and to those of others up and down the village, and all the young women would begin a guessing game of which among them he would choose to feed with his delicious catch when he returned.

On such an occasion, Ļainjin would quietly slip away and set sail, knowing where he would find Kalbōk, and though he had no rights to fish with these traps, his friend for life would be happy for his companionship and would gladly share his catch with him. He would stand silently outside the apex of the funnel-shaped barrier of rocks the ancestors had gathered, laid out, and piled into shallow walls, for perhaps thirty ñeñe on the lagoon side of the reef flat. The funnel-shaped, knee-high blockade ended in a circular wall a mere two ñeñe wide that formed a pool with an entrance but no other exit. Ļainjin's part was to stand motionless in the rain, bearing whatever cold breezes the storm imparted. Then, with the tide constant at his knees and the roar of the ocean breaking on the reef's edge in the murky distance echoing beneath the low gray clouds, he would silently watch as Kalbōk searched out a circle of *ellōk*[44] that

---

[41] Giant clam: *Tridacna gigas*.

[42] Ironwood: *Pemphis acidula*.

[43] A fishing weir; a permanent V-shaped fish trap built by piling stones on the reef.

[44] Literally, "it pricks"; a species of rabbitfish highly prized for its flesh that schools in a line and is characterized by its venomous spines. Streamlined spinefoot: *Siganus argenteus*.

had meandered up from the lagoon to graze upon the reef flat. Using his spear, his swiftness, and his angler's instincts, he would herd them toward Ḷainjin as he stood motionless. Ellōk had a peculiar habit of grouping, one after the other in a straight line, and Ḷainjin would watch as they passed one by one through the narrow channel at the apex of the funnel. Then he would fill the channel with two or three boulders, and the fish would be trapped, confused, and ready to be speared. The vibrations of Kalbōk's spear as it scraped the reef frightened the fish, and he claimed he used the rain to his advantage, preventing the fish from spotting him and defeating his maneuvers to flank them. Yet Ḷainjin had seen him do just as well during these half-moon tides on sunny days. This fish's long dorsal spines were sharp and filled with a mild poison, so they had to be careful, once they had speared one, to grab it securely by the eye sockets. They strung them through their gills and unusually small mouths with the midriff of a young coconut-tree leaf, being careful not allow the fish to *lik*[45] them back. This fish had no scales, only a smooth skin that the girls peeled back with their teeth before devouring the fish raw.

Later that evening, Kalbōk would show up, usually in the still-pouring rain, at their grandmother's cookhouse with his catch. With gratitude, she would send her granddaughters off to the lagoon to clean them, and that was when he would make his famous choice. If he chose well, the rain would make it all the easier for Kalbōk and the eager girl to scamper away unnoticed amid the haze of the downpour. They would soon disappear into the cold, gray dusk, where, perhaps backed against a tree, each would, in turn, devour the heat of the youthful body of the other until their passion sparked a release, a final embrace, and then a casual return to the grandmother's cookhouse. There, he would be offered food and hot, pungent *nen*[46] tea in a half-shell cup.

Yes, the women all loved Kalbōk because he never stopped fishing. Depending on the tide and the time of day or night, he knew which type of fish to chase and how to catch it, and just as important was that he had the skill and the patience to make the fishing implements necessary for success.

---

[45] Prick.

[46] Fruit from *Morinda citrifolia*, a small tree prized throughout the islands for its medicinal properties; a tonic thought to promote health. Also called "noni."

So naturally, when the young friends hatched their plan to seek their fortune, they asked Kalbōk to fashion the tackle necessary to capture the monsters and extract the jaws. They needed hardwood hooks as wide as a man's spread hand and as thick as the eye of the large bonito tunas they would use for bait, and braided lines of twine strong enough and long enough to recover the beasts from whatever depths they might attempt to escape.

Ļani made the fishing line, not from coconut husk but from the inner bark of the *arṃwe*[47] tree. Taknoļ was a *ri-jekjek wa.*[48] The others laughed at him, a small boy, for engaging in woman's work. He cooked breadfruit, gathered and processed pandanus leaves, and woven pandanus-leaf matting. At first Ļainjin thought Taknoļ was the kind of boy who was more like a woman. However, after a while, he came to realize that engaging in these chores was not a choice — it was part of Taknoļ's responsibility as a *ri-katak*.

Ļainjin loved to *bwilbwil*[49] with the other children, racing toy outrigger canoes up and down the reefs and along the lagoon shore. On such occasions, he would stop and watch Taknoļ, all alone, grinding broken pieces of giant clamshell into adze heads for his craft and sharpening the heads of adzes that belonged to his uncles. It did not look like a lot of fun. Taknoļ explained that he knew how to read the coral shapes fused together at the reef's shore, how to choose the best surfaces to grind his pieces of giant clamshell, and how to distinguish the best grade of sand to use as the abrasive. Ļainjin would watch him sit for an entire morning, pushing and pulling with shoulders and arms and clutching onto the shell fragments with his battered fingers until he had ground enough away to receive an uncle's approval. Later, Taknoļ explained to him that the first rule of the hull-maker's trade was to respect the adze's blade for the time devoured in its making and thus become careful to strike a clean and accurate cut with each thump into the breadfruit wood.

Next, Taknoļ's studies turned to the breadfruit tree. He learned each variety in detail. He learned to estimate each tree's current and future

---

[47] A small tree: *Pipturus argenteus*; the bark (or "ōr") of this tree is stripped and twisted into fishing twine.
[48] Literally, "person who hacks hull"; boat builder.
[49] To make and race toy proas on reefs or along the shoreline.

ability to produce fruit based in its location, and the location of trees surrounding it. One breadfruit could feed one person for one day, and yes, he learned the various methods of preparation, cooking, and preservation of the fruit. Finally, he learned the attributes of its timber — easily shaped by adze — strong, buoyant, and less likely to split than other wood when seasoned properly, and resistant to rot when kept drained and dried. He grew to know every tree, including its age, its fruit-bearing capacity, and its pace of growth. He would sit in one tree all afternoon and carefully count the breadfruit into the hundreds. He fashioned the longest harvesting tool on the island, prided himself on knowing exactly which fruit to fell next based on its point of ripeness, and desired method of cooking. Then he sat listening to his elders deliberate about which tree to sacrifice to produce the next hull based on size and purpose of use. The second rule he learned from Taknoḷ was to respect the resources sacrificed to produce the hull. Each hack of an adze blade was a sacramental task made only after much deliberation, forethought, and anticipation, and such was Taknoḷ's early education.

Later in childhood, he began to study how to make matting from pandanus leaves. This was the period when he followed the women to the various pandanus patches. Not to the pandanus trees where men went to twist the large fruits and fell them to chew or prepare for cooking or preservation, but to the fruitless pandanus bushes where the women cut the still-green leaves, singed them in their fires, and dried, rolled, and otherwise prepared them for shredding and weaving into sleeping mats, skirts, and kilts. Taknoḷ explained that a hull maker needed to understand the whole matting process to make the strong, finely woven lateen sail. Were a sail to tear on a voyage, the hull maker must be prepared to make any necessary repairs. And the hull maker studied the women's important roles in Rālik society to master their skills to become a self-reliant voyager.

As he grew older, Taknoḷ's lessons turned to the coconut tree. The hull makers required him to study the fiber of the coconut husk. They loved, planted, and attended to the types of coconut trees that every other man hated. These trees produce long and skinny nuts that are light and difficult to husk. They bear small, oblong nuts with very little water inside. They loved these because the length of husk fibers made the ropes they twisted from them all the stronger and quicker to make. Therefore, Taknoļ's responsibility started with protecting and gathering the nuts of these trees, and he was no sissy at safeguarding them! Ļainjin proudly watched him fight with tenacity many times. Taknoļ would often follow a boy right up the tree to prevent him kicking down the immature nuts for the others to steal. When a standoff occurred, Ļainjin would intervene. He would call up to the thief and threaten to climb up and throw him off if he did not immediately climb down. That always worked because they were all afraid of the *ṃaanpā*[50] skills he learned from his maternal grandfathers. He could slap a boy three or four times before the boy had a chance to step back or otherwise retreat.

Because trees were scattered, almost hidden around the island for greater protection against violent storms, it was difficult to protect them all, and his uncles would punish him with more grinding if the nuts went missing. Once he was successful in collecting a sizable pile of nuts, he would remove the husks by spearing them on a sharpened hardwood stake. Next, he would enclose the husks within large coconut-leaf baskets and immerse them beneath piled coral rocks at the lagoon's edge for several moons until the outer strands separated easily from the inner layers of useless fiber. Then Taknoļ would take these strands to the eldest hull makers of his father's lineage. This was the part where Ļainjin loved to tag along, because these men sat day in and day out beneath their children's stilted, thatched houses making twine, arguing about all manner of things, and telling stories that gave him shivers.

Yet it was later in their childhood, once Taknoļ had learned the symmetry, proportionality, and dimensions of the proa and lateen sail combinations, that his young friend became more useful to him and their friendship bonded like hull to keel. Ļainjin loved to race toy proas and Taknoļ taught him how to win. He had learned that, for a hull of a certain length, the height of the mast should be this, the distance to the kubaak should be that, and so on. Ļainjin loved asking him questions because Taknoļ's responses were so exact, and he knew any toy boat built by Taknoļ would be faster than his because of his skill as a *ri-jekjek wa*. Nevertheless,

---

[50] Literally, "before the hand"; traditional fighting using quickness and distraction.

he played more often than Taknoļ did and so earned a reputation for being first among others. During that period, especially during the day, Taknoļ was learning to lash. He claimed it was due to their lashings that the Rālik and Ratak proas were so indestructible in the open ocean. Of course, any boat is at risk of destruction among the reefs of an atoll. The renowned saying *Emejjia wa iloṃeto* was used to emphasize that a boat is safer outside the reef environment than within it, but it also lent confidence that the ancestors had spent hundreds and hundreds of seasons perfecting its design. Taknoļ practiced these lashings to the point where he could tie them blindfolded or — his favorite — repair them from below, in the water in the lagoon or even out in the open ocean. When Ļainjin thought about all the things Taknoļ had taught him and how many lives his friend had given him, his throat thickened and his eyes glossed over with gratitude.

He looked at the boat Taknoļ always referred to as his peerless achievement. He remembered the tree sacrificed and the seasons of tribute that they paid for it. He remembered the block of wood that Taknoļ had cut into with his adze, one deliberate hack after another. He remembered the gathering of the nuts, the husking, the soaking, the making of the twine, all the stories, all the parts fashioned, all the lashings, the sail making, and the enormous gathering to commemorate the boat's launching. But most of all, he remembered his friend-for-life's character, as well as those of the other men sitting there in his imagination, and tears crept into his eyes now and then as he realized what those boys, over the seasons, had collectively become to him — the father he had missed and now knew he would never know.

He paddled on through the night like this, his mind swirling with stories and chants and proud and sad thoughts of days and nights past until at last, the small kite-like stars of Jebrọ arose above the eastern horizon. He knew that dawn was about to break, and then his throat sank into his chest as he peered desperately into the distance ahead. Two boats, silent as the night, appeared — as though from nowhere — directly in his path! He stopped, sat quietly listening, and peered ahead. He searched the horizon in every direction to see if there were other boats about him but detected nothing. The unsettling part was that the two boats were either moving toward him or not moving at all. Perhaps they had seen him and were now waiting for him to close the distance before making their move. He waited to see if they were closing on him. No, they were not moving, and they were silent. Might they be drifting? Sleeping? Or pretending to be? At this point, if they had ill intent, it would be a big mistake to try to paddle away. The main rule of combat: Never allow your opponents to run you down! Then you end up fighting exhausted with your back turned into the helpless target of a shot from a sling or spear. It was always better to attack and allow their fear and the element of surprise to assist you. Since he was alone, surely, they would have enough crew to paddle him down. In addition, he was tired and they were probably rested. But might they be asleep and drifting, and should he attempt to skirt them and paddle by in the night? There was not much chance as dawn was about to expose him, and if they decided to attack him, he could end up trapped like a mother turtle on the beach.

Likely, they were friendly islanders from Ujae or Lae, but not knowing for sure, only a fool would approach them unprepared. Tame islanders, if lost, could become mad from thirst, hunger, or fear of the unknown. A retreat in any case would be unwise and cowardly. As the faintest glimmer of dawn broke in the east, Ļainjin cut a short length of his trolling line, quickly tied six slipknots that would function as little nooses along its length, and tucked it under the belt of his fiber kilt. He fastened his ring, reached into his hull below, and grabbed his shorter, hand's-length *rajraj*,[51] placing it on the shelf under his outrigger platform. Then he grabbed his oar and paddled forward with calm deliberation. If they were proas from Pit,[52] he would board them, and if he found weapons he would scatter them, cut their sails, and string as many of their paddles as possible before diving and swimming them back to his boat. He would only be vulnerable until he reached the water. No man could approach him there and live. "If they were asleep," he thought, "so much the better." If they had no weapons he would have nothing to fear and would leave them to their own devices.

As he closed upon them and as light began to illuminate the darkness, he realized there was only one mast. "Might one of the boats be disabled?" he

[51] A knife or sword-like weapon uniformly edged with shark teeth.
[52] A chain of thirty-three atolls south of Rālik and Ratak; currently the Republic of Kiribati.

thought. No, there was only one boat, and it was anchored onto a *kājokwā*.[53] He was relieved when he saw *ak*[54] feathers hanging from the boat's fore- and backstay. It was a Rālik proa. He would proceed with caution but would not attack them. This could prove interesting.

The Chief awoke and glided almost effortlessly off the boat into a faint morning breeze. Even a whiff of a breeze was more to his liking than the heavy air of recent days past. He rose like a kite, up and up with hardly a flap of his wings. He saw the island in the distance but then became disturbed by a more panoramic sight before him. The entire southeastern sky, yet again nearly void of clouds except along the horizon, was slowly turning from yellow to a bright, transparent red color. In his short life of eighteen or so seasons, he had never seen a sunrise that shade of red, and some instinct within did not like it. Red in the morning was usually a signal of rain. Unlike most seabirds, his feathers lacked oil and did not shed water as easily. He hated rain and usually soared above the clouds to avoid it, but he had only rarely viewed a sky that frightened him. Full of energy from yesterday's catch, he quietly circled the large object to which the other proa anchored. He remembered that these drifting things were good for fishing. The light was not yet right for him to see deep into the water below, but he could see circles of slow-moving fish congregating beneath the floating object. And here and there, a big-mouth twisted ominously through the water like a bitter lizard, hunting insects along the strand. He spied, scattered about on the dead, barkless tree, carcasses of fish used for bait, and delicious bite-sized heads here and there. He saw three humans sleeping on its dry surface. It was too bad he was afraid of those lying things, or he would flop down and gobble all those tasty tidbits! It would be a grand gesture were the commoner to get busy and collect them for his breakfast! After all, he had not eaten a thing all morning!

Below, Ḷainjin had been distractedly observing the magnitude of the cloudless red dawn, and he knew what it signified. He paddled vigorously

---

[53] A tree trunk adrift in open ocean or washed up on the shore.

[54] The frigate bird: *Fregata magnificens*; tied feathers used as telltales to confirm wind direction.

toward the *kājokwā* and adjoining proa. Surprise was the mark of his fighting prowess. The boat was somewhat larger than his, but its hull appeared weighed down to a dangerous degree. He guessed they had filled it with fish they caught the day before, during the night, or both. He felt poised and confident, and ready for the encounter. If he raised his sail in this faint breeze, they were so overburdened they could never catch him. Nevertheless, they were probably friendly and from one or another of the atolls about him — and probably from the closest. Otherwise, why catch so many fish only to have them rot? Per tradition, because women were aboard, there was a tiny, hastily thatched hut upon the proa's outrigger platform. Sitting cross-legged in the open doorway was a woman with wild, gray-streaked hair, attentively observing every stroke of his approach. When he got close enough for each to distinguish the other, the smiling woman, as though she were Lōktañūr herself, jokingly called out, "Ñaijuwe," harkening back to the story of Jebro̧.

"You can go along with kapiḷak," he joked back, continuing his approach. She appeared to glance furtively at the deviant red dawn, and laughed as she acknowledged his clever and timely response.

"You think that's kapiḷak?" she inquired, pointing her finger eastward.

"You know the legend. Kapiḷak's storm comes before Jebro̧ rises, but some say not always. I put trust in what I see."

She stood and lifted a half-eaten stalk of pandanus kernels from inside the doorway. Demonstrating considerable strength, she hurled the stalk of orange fruits at him as she responded. "Well said, Jebro̧!" Then she sat down again, pushing her wild, graying hair away from her face.

The stalk landed halfway between their vessels with a splash, submerging but then popping up and floated there invitingly. Now Ḷainjin was a man of little weakness, but like his ancestors before him, he had an irresistible penchant for gnawing pandanus. Ḷainjin's large mouth and pronounced square jaw, perhaps born from ages past, left him well suited for it. Disregarding the red dawn, the threatening ring left exposed on his finger, any possibility of an ambush lurking from inside the hull or hut, the whereabouts of the Chief, or anything else that would normally encourage him to be attentive, he paddled forward and grabbed the weighty, floating stalk by its stem. Then he broke off a gigantic ripe kernel, bit off the piece of the inedible stalk attached to it, and crunched and twisted the fibrous fruit until his mouth was filled with the sweet, satisfying flavor he had missed over so many seasons past. It was the taste of home.

At that instant, from the corner of his eye, he noted a slight figure escape from the hut behind the woman and then jump onto the *kājokwā*.

The Chief, who had mustered the courage to land on the floating tree, was in the middle of gulping down a fish head when he was surprised by the spent pandanus kernel the female human hurled at him. She had excellent aim, and had she not eaten away most of the projectile, it might have clobbered him good. All feathers and little flesh, he escaped with only a minor loss of plumage and, spreading his wings, rose quickly atop the light breeze above the *kājokwā*. In a nasty temper, he viewed the commoner, still loafing with the others below. "When is he going to start fishing?" the Chief wondered. In the interim, he warily eyed the young female, who had decided to stick a foot beneath the leaves wrapped about the waist of one of the three sleeping males and jiggle it with a squeal.

"Grandma, his mast is hard as he sleeps!" Ļainjin heard her shout faintly above the sound of his mandibles chomping.

"He must be dreaming of me!" the older woman laughed back.

"Grandma, I can't wake him up!" Ļainjin turned to see one of the men wake up and try to grab her foot, but she was too quick and rushed to wake the others.

She kicked his foot. "Wake up! A stranger has arrived."

Ļainjin, who had seen the Chief rise from the *kājokwā* as he broke off a second kernel, continued crunching and twisting the pulp free from its fibrous core. He saw three men rise, menacingly perhaps, from where they had been sleeping. He nodded at them and continued his pleasurable chewing and twisting. Finally, the men from the *kājokwā* and the young woman who had awakened them one by one hopped aboard their vessel and stood on either side of the sitting woman's hut. They had a name for this chewing, twisting eating of the pandanus fruit. They called it *wōdwōd*,[55] and they appeared, to a person, to be disarmed by the look of absolute ecstasy he felt on his face as he continued to chew. How could he have forgotten the

[55] To chew on a pandanus kernel with a twisting motion that crunches out the pulp and minimizes the fibers caught between the teeth.

aromatic flavor and distinctive citrusy juice of this variety that swirled pleasantly now in his mouth and ignited so many memories of days long past?

The young woman, the apparent leader of the group, had casually begun to ask Ḷainjin questions. What was he doing all by himself out here in between the atolls? Continuing to eat, he had shrugged both shoulders and his eyes laughed a bit, as if to intimate he had no particular reason for paddling around in the open ocean.

Next, she asked where he had come from. Continuing to *wōdwōd*, he responded with an abrupt turn of his head over his shoulder, as if to say, "Back there."

"Aelōñḷapḷap?" she asked.

He responded by raising his eyebrows as he chewed and quick-canting his head back, as if to say, "Yes, I've been there."

"Naṃo?" she asked.

He responded similarly, as if to say, "Yes, I've been there too." He continued to *wōdwōd*.

"Ellep?" she asked.

"Yes." He canted his head again, continuing to *wōdwōd*.

"So where was it that you were headed?"

Pointing his nose toward where he assumed the island was, he tossed the wasted fibrous core of the kernel into the water and tore another from the stalk that was still floating in the water next to him.

"Lae?" she asked. "That's where we are from. Why are you going there?"

He scrunched his nose, lifted his shoulders as though to say he was not sure, and continued chewing, so engrossed in his pleasure that he must have made the young woman feel ignored.

"Enough!" he heard her say just as she dived headfirst into the water. He had not paid her much attention until then. The men in the proa stood to watch her submerge and stroke under water several times before popping up and grabbing the pandanus stalk from the water next to him.

"*Daō*,"[56] she said, tearing loose a kernel and biting into it. Now that got his attention. He dipped his hand in the water and rinsed the pandanus juice

[56] Literally, "my bite" or "my food"' often used by a child to declaratively assert the intention to eat or to demand food from an elder.

that had run down into his scraggly beard from the corners of his mouth. Removing the wasted core from between his teeth, he examined it, dropped it in the sea, and reached for another, but she held the stalk playfully away from his grasp. The men were all shouting at her to swim back into their protection, but she appeared to relish the attention she was receiving and hung onto the bulwark of his boat playfully, as though she was a child with no need to ask permission to do so.

However, there was. In Rālik and Ratak culture both, you could sit yourself down by a man's fire, enter his shelter, grab onto his fishing line or his kilt, or even throw pandanus fruit at his bird, but you could never touch his boat without permission. To board another's craft uninvited was an act of aggression, and he nearly reflexively slapped her. However, an alluring smile broke across her lovely face. The pandanus fruit stuck coquettishly between her large white teeth as she held onto the boat with one arm and extended the pandanus stalk teasingly away from him with the other. Then she lunged her head forward, daring him to snatch the kernel from her mouth. Instead of slapping her, he twisted the bait from between her clenching teeth, put the kernel into his mouth, and crunched down into the crisp pulp as she puckered her full lips in response.

Suddenly he realized she had hooked him. She had used his greed and succeeded just as surely as he had hooked that tuna the day before. They had all watched it, and without amazement because, as he was soon to learn, she was the irooj's daughter and always got her way! She was the most enticing thing he had ever witnessed. Her long, straight hair carried the aroma of flower-scented coconut oil. The ebony tattoos covering her bare auburn shoulders, arms, and hands — right up to the little squiggles that led to her short, clean nails — were of masterful quality and exquisite in detail, but the woman's nearly childlike personality was what captivated him. She scrunched her nose, imitating his response to her grandmother's question, and he could not help but stop his munching to laugh at himself as she turned to the others to let them see her comic clowning impression of him. They all broke into laughter together. As he laughed, she deftly reached up and began pulling at the fiber line he had tucked into the belt of his kilt. There was something sensual in the way she popped each noose — with which he had intended to steal their paddles — from between his belt and his muscular, tattooed stomach that prevented him from staying her with his free hand as he crunched. Treading water, she wrapped the line ridiculously about her neck as though to create a necklace of it.

"Okay, it's settled. I'm going with Jebrọ," announced her grandmother.

One of the young men, perhaps her grandson, began to protest vigorously.

"Your boat is too full!" she told him. She explained she did not want to be on his boat when the storm hit. "You'll throw me overboard to save your precious catch!" She used the word *eakpel*, which means to discard ballast into the ocean to create more freeboard, but in more serious and life-threatening situations, it could also refer to discarding people — usually the eldest first!

"Grandma, you don't know anything about this stranger. How do you know you can trust him? Look at that thing eat! He looks as useful as a baby sucking its mother's tit!"

All the men, including Ḷainjin, laughed, although he continued to chew.

"Well, he knows more than you do! He is obviously a man of the ocean. He is a seafarer and not an irooj's spoiled son. He's used to being out here," she said. "You're used to life on shore, and you're going to panic when the storm hits. Today I trust him."

"Jebrọ," she requested, "paddle over. *Ñaijuwe!*"

"What storm? What's she talking about?" her grandson asked. The three men huddled in discussion.

Ḷainjin had been preoccupied with trying to grab another pandanus fruit. Every time he stood up to reach over the young woman in the water, to grab what was left of the stalk that she kept extending away from him, he risked exposing everything under his kilt to her, and she kept coaxing him to do so. Meanwhile, treading water, she had managed to move his vessel over to theirs. But of course, her grandmother could not board until Ḷainjin invited her to do so, and the three men were standing on the deck between her and his boat, as if to prevent the elder woman from reaching it.

At the same time, since the Chief had been given full rein over the *kājokwā*, he had eaten the last of the fish heads. Now he glided back to claim his place and dig his claws into the lashings on the outer cross-booms of the outrigger. The bird's eyes peered at the young woman holding onto the pandanus stalk. She repeatedly teased him by pretending to throw another pandanus nodule at him, but the bird's sharp gaze saw through her ruse and he remained calm.

Finally, the young woman, perhaps feeling that the center of attraction had gravitated away from her, announced she was ready to make an exchange. They would give the stranger *all* their pandanus if he would give her his ring and agree to take her and her grandmother to Lae. As Ḷainjin considered her proposition, he wondered what he had to lose. Additional crew would be helpful in the storm, but he knew he could never control this vivacious animal in the water next to his boat. That probably broke some rule, although at that moment he couldn't remember which one. And he was aware that time was running out for all of them!

He tossed the ring, with the loop of line that had secured it to his wristband, into the water, where it floated next to her.

The men were clearly surprised that the stranger had surrendered his weapon so willingly. Caught off guard, they permitted the grandmother to board Ḷainjin's boat. Then, at her command, they began loading his pandanus stalks. The young woman, still treading water, removed her necklace of twined fiber, slipped its loop through that of the ring, and dangled the ring as a pendant around her neck. All stopped motionless as they watched the stranger, pandanus kernel clenched between his teeth, grab her under her outstretched arms and lift her effortlessly over the bulwark into the hatch beside him. And then they all watched as he allowed her to playfully extend her necklace, put the ring's shark tooth to his neck, and ever so gently prick his skin.

A small trickle of blood ran down his neck. She caught it with her finger and, with elated eyes, held it up to him and then jubilantly put it to her tongue. Perhaps such trust was better shown than said, and all at last agreed.

Except, of course, the Chief, who continued to scrutinize her every move and was unlikely to ever trust her.

The storm

The cool morning air had long since dissipated and the sun was in their eyes as Ļainjin, still distractedly biting a pandanus kernel, paddled his proa over to the *kājokwā* before launching on the next leg of his journey. He could not bring himself to leave such a towering thing without researching its history, the signs of which only he among the others in the small group could decipher the significance of. He quickly found what he was looking for. The surface of the smaller end of the trunk appeared to have been smoothed by the friction of towing ropes. Finally, at the base of the massive trunk — perhaps three times the length of his boat — he found a hand-sized *wapepe* symbol carved unmistakably into it. That drew an emotional shiver that emanated from his throat and extended down his spine to his extremities. This was one that had gotten away from his Seeker friends. A swell of emotions that he had long ago taught himself to ignore overcame him, and memories of those for whom he had never properly grieved promptly swamped his soul. Yet he stolidly turned his craft about to face the wind and asked his new crew to hoist their sail.

A faint but steady breeze allowed them to set a course a little north of due east. Gone was the smooth face of yesterday's ocean as myriads of ripples now covered the surface of the rising and abating swells. Wondrously, the proas began to glide slowly across the water, and a feeling of relief to be in motion without having to strain his aching body lifted his spirit, coupled with the elation of no longer being so unimaginably alone. How long had he been by himself out there? He had long ago lost track. He sat at his place, his legs dangling through the stern hatch into the hull at the edge of the stern deck. He had tied his oar and was now lazily using it as a tiller when the young woman clambered around him, grabbed onto his shoulders from behind, and pressed her bare breasts against his back. She settled there, arms around his neck, straddling him. He had glimpsed her left knee as she crawled on all fours around him and immediately felt a pang in his throat and a rise in his manhood.

The elder woman had noticed his glance and responded playfully, "She likes you! Pretty soon she'll grab your fish!"

"Shush up, turtle!" the young woman responded, her chin resting on his shoulder. "You want to eat his fish!"

At this, they all broke into laughter. It felt good to laugh with others.

"I'm going to test him," she announced, and with that, she put her hands over his eyes.

"Father says a true navigator can steer blindfolded. I'm going to test him!"

Ļainjin turned his head a little to the left and the right until he heard the faint breeze equally in both ears and then set his course accordingly. He could feel the wind in the sail by its pressure on the tiller. It was an easy game to play. Her father, of course, was correct.

Once she was convinced he could steer just as easily with his eyes covered, she announced, "All right, my turn!"

She crawled back over him, stood in the hatch between his legs, and forced him back onto the stern deck, straddling the hull as she had. Taking control of the tiller, she said, "Okay, cover my eyes."

Through all his seasons, Ļainjin, as the serious navigator that he considered himself to be, had never done anything quite so silly. If he had, perhaps as a boy, it was too long ago to remember. After incessant pleading on her part and embarrassment on his, he complied, and she proved to be as good a steersman as he was. As soon as she would let him — and not until he repeatedly praised her ability at the helm — he dropped the silly game. Crossing his feet behind her, he lay back on the stern deck and turned his face to the sun, enjoying the opportunity to relax. He had slipped off to sleep several times when she shook him and insisted he go below to rest.

"It's good, it's good," the elder repeated. "She knows how to sail. Her father taught her. And I taught him." She laughed. "After you get your sleep, I'll take over and you two can play *ṃōṃaan ṃaj*."[57] The old woman laughed, and laughed again.

"Be quiet, old turtle. You want to hide his eel in your stinky well!" her granddaughter bantered back.

As Ļainjin ducked below, from the corner of his eye, he saw his bird rise off the outrigger booms where he was perched. He effortlessly soared skyward, no doubt wondering as he rose why his worker would be so foolish as to pass command of his perch to the pandanus-pelting pest, oblivious to who was actually in charge!

Ļainjin lay down on the narrow bow floorboard that Taknoļ had fashioned to fit perfectly to the contour of the concave hull at each end. The high, narrow hull kept a single sailor on his back dry and comfortable at each end, even when rain seeped into the triangular bilge beneath the floorboards on which they slept. From below, Ļainjin could tell if the boat was on course by its rocking motion, the slapping of the waves against the hull, or any gradual or drastic change in either. Yes, he was apprehensive about turning his beloved craft over to such a willful spirit, but he needed to conserve his strength for what he assumed was coming, and having paddled the night through, the need to sleep had overwhelmed him. After all, how much harm could she do? He reflected on how she had cajoled him into the girlish game that ended up with her in complete control of his boat.

Ļainjin was a little surprised by the constant banter between the young woman and her paternal grandmother. It demonstrated a degree of endearment that Ļainjin had observed only rarely among women in this relationship in the past. It meant that the mentoring had become so informal it took on a sisterly nature. This was not surprising because, as her father's mother, the elder could not pass her lands to the younger, who was outside the matrilineage. The elder could only give knowledge and love, so the younger woman had no need to pander. Among men, although humor was also an important element, the relationship between *ri-katak* and mentor

---

[57] Literally: "a man is an eel," which means that he always develops a relationship with a hole.

was more differential and never brotherly, but he had noticed that women always had a way of turning things around to suit their fancy. He had long ago stopped trying to understand them, sensing it was easier just to accept their cunning, persuasive ways.

From where he was lying, he could study her legs as they dangled. Surely, she was purposefully exposing her knees and parts of her thighs to him, because it was uncustomary for Rālik women to expose these parts of their bodies to the view of men, and he had never experienced such familiarity from a woman he had just met. Her legs were unscarred and of a light, almost reddish color. That meant she did not toil in the pandanus patches with the other women. Yet she was smart and experienced on a boat, and she was brave. Typical of a strong Rālik woman. The men truckled in her presence. Even her older brother capitulated quickly under her gaze. Ļainjin watched as she lowered the toes of her left leg down even farther, showing him even more of the still lighter skin of her inner thigh. Did she send him below to sleep or to lie there and observe the depths of her underside? He turned on his side. After a cloud of pleasant feelings that seemed to soothe the difficult memories of all he had endured passed over him, he fell into an unusually peaceful and contented sleep.

After what seemed a very long and restful period, she woke him as she slowly wedged herself next to him, holding a pandanus nodule. He suddenly felt cramped and claustrophobic. The hull was too small for two. *The déjà vu image of the two of them lying against each other, struggling to swat the hordes of sucking mosquitoes torturing each other's blood-smeared bodies, flashed before him.* Finally, her smile a hand from his face disarmed the memory, calmed his struggle to breathe, and forced him back into the present — their bodies touching, the long braids of her thick hair smelling of flower-scented coconut oil, her bushy eyebrows raised with excitement, and beads of sweat forming on her forehead and among the fine hairs on her upper lip. Once situated, her head propped on her elbow, she teased him with one of her flirtatious glances and then smiled at him with wild, wide-open eyes. She put the fruit to her mouth, then crunched and chewed. Glancing at the fruit, she said, in a matter-of-fact manner, "I found the island!"

His first response might have been to peek through the forward hatch, but she had him pinned down in the narrow hull, and the exit was at their knees. They lay in such a way that it would not have been easy for either of them to get out. That was when she pulled back at the slit of her pandanus-mat skirts and placed her knee against his aroused manhood. He raised his leg slightly, and she slipped her bare leg between his. He felt strangely as though he had just disembarked onto the shores of her island. He could grow old like this, in complete happiness.

"Rest awhile. Let Grandma steer!" she said, laughing. "She told me not to tell you!"

"About the island?" he asked.

She began chewing and crunching the pandanus fruit until half-spent and then stuffed it into his mouth. He remembered that lovers chewed pandanus to freshen their breath so he complied, but neither hand was currently free. This amused her greatly, and she began twisting the nodule in his mouth by its core end as he attempted to crunch down. This she made into a game of timing that she purposefully altered from moment to moment to keep him frustrated.

With much effort, he freed one hand, clutched onto the nodule between his teeth, and chewed it until he extracted the remaining pulp. Then she followed her first game with a second, playful demand: "Pick the fibers from my teeth." She opened her large mouth wide. The orange fibers of the fruit stuck between her teeth in little clumps, and she had pulled back her lips into such a silly face he could not help but laugh uncontrollably and loudly.

The old woman chimed in from the stern hatch, where she was at the helm and had only their feet in view. "*Ṃōṃaan ṃaj.*"

"Shush up, Grandma! Keep your eyes on the sail, please!" She opened her mouth again, but neither could control their laughter. Finally, he began picking at one clump and then another. Her teeth were complete, unbroken, and otherwise very clean from all the pandanus flossing. He was thankful his fingernails were clean from so many days at sea. They were too thick though, and he had trimmed them too short with his secret supply of greenstone to get the work done properly. He drew quickly to the intimacy of the task, glad that her knee was compressing his very firm manhood, beneath his fiber kilt, to keep it from popping out.

"Enough," she announced, taking the spent core from between his teeth and sticking it into her mouth again. Then, after sucking the last of its juice, she dropped the core to the floorboard between them and ordered him to open his mouth — it was her turn. Her fingers were dainty and her fingernails longer than his, and she seemed to delight in things meticulous.

"Grandma told me not to tell you, but I can't help myself," she whispered. "You are the most handsome man I have ever seen … also, the stinkiest." She giggled.

"Well, out here … I didn't expect to meet—"

"The woman you will choose?" she asked. Then, to cut off his stumbling response, she kissed him on the mouth, jabbing him with her tongue and then retreating, as if to say, "What did you think of that?"

He desired her but realized he was staring at her with a look of confusion on his face, like that of an inexperienced boy. She had maneuvered him back into his youth. For the first time in a long time, he realized he was uncertain how to proceed. If she were a fish or a cloud or an enemy about to attack, he would be better prepared. He hated not knowing what to do. He found her so … disarming. He needed fresh air. He started to sweat. He felt cramped. Then she broke into that face, as she had done earlier when she mimicked him scrunching his nose, and they both laughed and laughed again as she continued to tease with yet another rendition and then another.

Speaking in a whisper so only he could hear, she said, "I think you are afraid of me. Do not be. I am nothing special. My father is the irooj, but all his islands pass through his sisters to their daughters. My mother was from Ujae and my lands are there, but father is very powerful and fierce, so all the men are afraid of him. He taught me to choose for myself, and I do not want any of the men from Lae or Ujae. I choose you, Jebrọ! When we arrive on the beach, you must take my hand. When my father comes forward, you must keep holding on to me. No man on Lae or even Ujae would have the throat to do that! Can you do that, Jebrọ?" she asked, looking down and then flashing her eyes up at him to study the face of his response.

Surprisingly, he heard the boy of his past — without an instant of consideration — say, "Yes!"

"You must stare him down until he smiles, and I will be yours. He will bring me to you before the darkness falls, and all those little boys will wish they were you. I have never done it with anyone. My father told me none of the men on these islands were good enough for me and asked me to save myself for a truly great man that he promised would come along. I flirted with a couple of men on Ujae who were good dancers. Did they teach you to *jebwa*?"[58]

She continued without waiting for him to answer. "We came from a *keemem*.[59] The men performed and a few of them caught my eye, but when I prodded them, there was nothing inside. Oh, they had answers for everything. They boasted they had done this and they had done that and soon they would go here or there. Not like you! 'Where did you come from Jebrọ?' 'That way...'"

He laughed, not at what she said but the way she said it — and mostly at the way she laughed with her eyebrows up and her eyes and mouth wide open.

She continued her parody softly. "Where are you going?

"That way." She motioned with a flick of her head.

"Why are you going to Lae?"

He knew what was coming next as she scrunched her nose into that silly face again. "I don't know," she replied to herself.

"Well, why are you out all by yourself in the middle of the ocean?

"Well, why not?" she mocked. "It's as good a place to paddle as any other! I can tell you are just like my father. You do not meet a woman and spill your story all over her like a shell of water. She must draw it out little by little from your deep well. You must be the man I have waited for. You could surprise me with a different story every night, and you are a great lover!" she joked.

"What makes you say that?"

---

[58] A battle dance; a fierce reenactment of a classic fighting style passed along from previous generations.

[59] The first birthday feast after the passing of two seasons or thirteen cycles of the moon.

"Don't laugh! I can tell if a man is good at it by how many fish he catches. A good lover is very patient with his woman, just like a fisherman. Look at that line of yours. I bet you have caught hundreds of fish on that lure! You are very patient. It is in your eyes. I can read your eyes. Grandma taught me."

"What else do you see in my eyes?" he asked.

"Sadness and wisdom ... and you have to pee!" she kidded. "I can see that you want me more than anything else on the ocean," she boasted.

"Your mast," she teased, jiggling her leg between his, "is ready to break from your desire for me. You are in agony for me. A little bit more and you'll drench me with a wave of passion."

"*Wōjjej!*[60] Did your grandma teach you to say those things?"

"Oh, shut up!" she whispered. "That old turtle has had a hundred men grind her into the sand! She surely knows how to talk to a man and she knows a lot more. She taught me everything about men — twice! I am ready to make you crazy with desire for me!" she joked.

"That will definitely make me stink even more."

"Don't worry, I'll give you a bath every morning after your breakfast," she said. "But you will have your revenge. See this?" She tugged on his little finger. "You will torture me with this during our first night. Then this one will torture me deep inside on our second night! Then this big boy" — she was holding onto his thumb — "will gently scratch me where I yearn for your touch the most and then plunge inside me until I scream with satisfaction. But nobody will come to save me because I will be all yours to torture until blood spurts from my eyes!"

"*Wōjej!* Maybe you have some of this confused," he said, laughing. "I'm afraid Grandma has overcoached you!"

"On the fourth night, there will be no sleeping! I will wrap my legs around you and squeeze you like an *inpel.*[61] We'll do it ten times or maybe even more!"

"Girl, you've got a few more things to learn."

---

60 An idiom used to express surprise.

61 The fibrous cloth-like outer sheathing of the coconut flower buds found at the crowns of coconut trees; used to squeeze milk-like oil from coconut gratings.

"You'll teach me! You will show me all the tricks you learned in all those stinky wells you fell into! How many? I bet you've been with over a hundred women."

"No! Definitely not that many!"

"Tell me how many then?"

"I'm not saying!"

"Just like you!" She scrunched her nose into that silly face again and laughed affectionately.

"Kiss me, Jebrọ!"

He glanced into her eyes and wanted to laugh, but held back.

"Come on, your turn. You kiss me this time!"

He inched toward her. She opened her mouth. He forced air into it to make the sound of a fart.

"Oh, you are a funny man! I can see I must train you like a bird. When I wiggle my tongue like a fish, you will open wide, and I will stick it down your throat till you gag!

"Here, here's the fish. Open your mouth wide!"

He turned his head, and she stuck her wiggling tongue into his ear instead, tickling him until he ached from laughter. They played that silly game again and again, and then she invented others that caused more laughter and giggles. They began listening to each other's breathing and the beat of each other's hearts, and then they fell into and out of sleep in each other's arms for the rest of the afternoon.

Above, the elder sailed on. Ḷainjin had sensed her listening to them speak just as she had watched the powerful strokes of his oar as he had approached them that morning. He assumed she knew that any fool could sail on a day trip directly west from Lae to Ujae or back again. The young men who escorted them had made the trip so many times without incident that she probably feared they had become careless. Their stopping to fish and the overloading of their boat may have been the latest example. She was obviously grateful they had drifted upon him. He would, she no doubt hoped, safeguard their lives in the storm they expected, and she revered him because he knew what she knew, but unlike her, appeared unafraid.

He felt she had been helming a straight course to Lae Atoll. Its islets probably loomed across the eastern horizon now, and she had been making good progress toward its most southwestern islets. She would have had no trouble keeping up with her son's larger proa due to its overburdened condition and the superior speed and maneuverability of his boat. Its balance, he thought, must have surprised her, and it required very little pressure on the helm. As she guided them toward their destination, the sun moved into the western sky behind them, and he imagined her searching the horizon in all directions for any sign of the storm they anticipated.

Above, the chief of all birds had probably hardly noticed the everchanging splendor beneath him as he glided back and forth over the ocean water above the two boats. He was searching for potential circles of flying fish, his usual prey away from his worker's confines. Now and again, one of these sleek, winged fish, surprised by one of the rapidly cruising proas, would launch itself into the breeze and glide a hand's length or so above the waves, unexpectedly exposing itself to the Chief's swift flight and the hook of his long, agile beak.

When he soared, he could view the entirety of the tiny atoll they were approaching in all its magnificent, transparent hues of blue, which corresponded to the various depths of water outside the atoll, inside the lagoon, along the lagoon and ocean edges of its encircling reefs, and within the various passageways between them. There was one large islet with bright green foliage that hosted a village of humans spread along a white beach of coral sand on the southeast edge and another one that the boats were approaching to the west, at the opposite end of the atoll's islet-strewn southern fringe. Along the wide, multicolored reef that skirted the lagoon's western perimeter, there were no islets, but there were several passageways into the lagoon. And there was another substantial islet with a small village at the northern tip of the atoll, and then a string of islets of various sizes and shapes along the eastern, contiguous fringing reef that separated the brilliant deep-blue ocean water from the glistening lighter blues of the lagoon, bordered by sun-bleached coral sands. Several of these smaller islets appeared to be inhabited only by birds, and numerous scattered flocks of white terns were fishing here and there about the atoll. The tide was high, and swells methodically rolled over the reef's edge of the islet they were approaching. These swells broke into white water and rushed in curvy lines across the reef flat, swamping the shoreline and then rhythmically reflecting, retreating backward across the reef and tossing up more glimmering froth as they slapped into the next series of waves.

No human and few other birds could have viewed this stunningly colorful sight from his vantage. The Chief probably assumed the sun's evening rays had illuminated the spectacle for him alone. Yet that was probably when he noticed he was not, in fact, alone. Attracted to him and following at a distance as he glided back down was another, even larger, black bird. It had the white throat of the same species but was of a different sex. He had probably spied the female glide by one of his boats and suspected she was trying to poach on his territory. That was when they both would have felt a distinctive pressure change in their ears. An instinct would have spoken to both at the same time, suggesting that they glide on the oncoming breeze toward the safety of the atoll.

Down below, the elder woman must have shivered at the sight of what she had been expecting.

"Jebrọ!" she called. Then she chanted with an eerie scream. "*Kapiļak ej buñ!*"[62]

Ļainjin awoke from his contented half nap and immediately began tearing himself from the cozy octopus who was clinging to him, insistently shaking her head, and whispering, "No, no."

"Liṃanṃan! Let him go! I need him on deck!" the elder commanded.

"So Liṃanṃan[63] *was* her name," thought Ļainjin as she obediently went limp and allowed him to squirm his way out of the hull. Before he stood, he could not resist glancing at her face one last time. She had transformed it into a ridiculous pout, like that of a little girl disappointed by a parent's stern refusal to provide the object of her desire. Then quickly, before he glanced away, she broke back into tongue-wiggling mode and he laughed. He stood and took in the enormity of the thin line of gray clouds across the entire southern and eastern horizons.

---

[62] "Kapiļ ak falls!"

[63] A name: "woman beautiful." "Li": the female prefix; "ṃanṃan": "very beautiful." The north star, Polaris.

"Liṃanṃan is certainly a fitting name for her. What should I say is my name?" he asked himself.

The wind had freshened slightly during the afternoon, and he felt quite pleased that the elder had gotten them so close to their destination. The green island ahead looked inviting.

"Can we make it?" asked the elder.

"No. Look at how quickly the dark spirit rises."

"We don't have to make it to the passageway. It is high tide, so we can go right over the reef to the shore of that island," she said.

"Thank you, Grandma. You are a good helmswoman, but we won't make it. That thing will have its chance to crush us first. We are better to get to flatter water over there," he said, pointing north, farther into the atoll's lee.

She relinquished the helm to him. He changed his point of sail and started closing the gap between them and the other boat. By the time he was alongside them, they too had noticed the quickly rising band of gray. Ļainjin warned them that trying to reach shore before the storm struck was futile, that they should instead take advantage of the storm's foregusts to follow him north as far as possible, deep into the atoll's lee. Under whatever circumstance, they should keep their eyes on his boat, lower their sail upon his signal, and then tie down quickly and drift until the storm passed.

"And dump those fish! They are sure to spoil now anyway!

"*Emejjia wa iloṃeto!*" he chanted. When they chanted back, he sheeted in and headed north. The wind freshened a bit, and crisp waves began slapping up against their starboard hull. Their kubaak began to glide across, rather than dip into, their crests. His strategy was to resist the temptation to head directly to the island from the southwest, but rather to make better use of the firmer wind to head straight north, so as to be more in the island's lee and sheltered from its wrathful wake of choppy waves as the storm struck and passed over them. With the atoll sheltering them somewhat from the wind and storm waves — and hopefully they would be out of the current at its south end — they should drift away more slowly and comfortably during the night ahead.

Liṃanṃan had absorbed all of this without speaking. Although she had demonstrated some boat skills, Ļainjin assumed her father had mostly taken her out in fair weather. She exhibited an innate braveness tinged, due to lack of experience, with naiveté, and her current situation was clearly out of the realm of any prior experience. She was no complainer. She did not question his strategy, but he could see fear growing in her eyes as she watched the gray, billowing wall approach. It was not the amorphous, ugly gray of a normal rainstorm but something distinct, despite its approach from more than one quadrant. The burnishing light from the sun setting on the clear, western horizon ensured that every aspect of the furious beast was illuminated in such manifest definition that its awe-inspiring fearsomeness would be almost hypnotizing were it stationary. It was the astonishing rapidity of the beast as it swept toward them that they found so increasingly self-diminishing. He watched her face as the spirit of the thing drained the natural liveliness from her eyes. He waited patiently for her furtive glance.

"Liṃanṃan, now that is a perfect name for such a beautiful woman," he commented in his calm way, almost as though they were strolling down one of the stone-lined paths on her father's island. "Grandma, how could her mother have known that such a slimy little octopus would grow into such a perfectly formed body as to guide a man's journey through life?"

The elder seemed to realize and appreciate the distracting and calming effect of his words amid the impending danger and rose to the occasion with appropriate eloquence. "Every man out there" — she tilted her head toward the atoll — "would forfeit his house to sit on a boat next to her, and to think she crawled into that hull with you! Why, you must be so invigorated by her scent that you could suck up the spirit of that ugly storm and spit it out as a fart from your butt!" At that, the three of them managed to laugh in the face of the impending gale.

"I just might decide to do that, but the two of you can help me. Grandma, when the time comes to eat this thing, you must give it warning. When I give the signal, I want you to turn the boat straight into the wind, hold it there, and then count aloud very slowly to twenty. Like this, *juon ... ruo ... jilu.*[64] The timing is very important.

"Liṃanṃan, as Grandma counts, I want you to loosen the halyard there and lower it, three hands per count, while I flake the sail as it falls. By the

[64] One ... two ... three.

time Grandma gets to *joñoul*,[65] we should be wrapping it up with these sail ties. By the time she gets to *roñoul*,[66] we should have it securely propped and sheeted down and the two of you should head below, one to each end."

"Let me know when you intend to fart so I can hold my nose," quipped Liṃanṃan.

However, the time for jokes was over. The gray wall was swelling toward them like a wave about to curl onto the reef. Ļainjin turned the helm back over to the elder woman. The strongest point on the proa was where the two skyward-rising outrigger booms were yoked and tied onto the hull at its middle, or point of harness. He had long lifelines neatly coiled below, and he unstrung one for each woman's ankle. Then he had two other lines attached at the yoke point that he readied to secure the sail, once furrowed. Taking one in each hand as a safety line, he scooted himself out onto the outrigger platform and sat, legs astraddle, at the point where the two upward booms began to rise. The wind was now filling their sail with such force that he needed to add his weight to windward by crawling out even farther on these outrigger beams to add ballast to the kubaak, which was now flying well above the surface of the water. It was particularly intoxicating to fly an outrigger like that on the lee side of an atoll, where there was a lot of wind but where the wave action had yet to catch up.

He looked at the elder woman at the helm. She was now standing with her legs braced against the inside of the hull, both hands grasped onto the end of the oar tied to the bulwark. The oar was levered beneath her arm, and her ragged black-and-silver hair flew unremittingly in the wind. She glanced back at him with a wild look of exuberance in her confident eyes that showed him she could still handle the tiller. He looked over his shoulder at their companion craft, and their outrigger was flying high as well.

The two boats glided like two birds before the impending clouds. It was for but a few moments, yet it seemed an exhilarating eternity of excitement that no doubt carved an impression into their souls that would seal their friendship and instill confidence in one another to their lives' end. Then, as the color of the beast's edges turned amber from the setting sun, as the

---

[65] Ten.

[66] Twenty.

whiskers of its nasty beard fell almost to the water's surface, and just as it was about to exhale the first burst of its cold breath, Ḷainjin gave the elder the signal to turn their craft into the wind. On cue, Liṃanṃan began to lower their sail as he stood at the boat's yoke to flake it. They accomplished the task in perfect harmony and just moments before the first fierce arrows of rain were about to spear them.

Not everything, however, had gone as planned. The crew of their companion craft had not turned into the wind to lower and secure their sail as instructed. Instead, they had shunted and foolishly headed off on an opposite tack, back toward the passageway into the atoll. By the look of their boat's rise upon the waves, he could see it was still overburdened by its cargo of fish. That, however, would be the least of that crew's worries. Ḷainjin watched as a second fierce gust of the dark spirit's breath overwhelmed the sail of the misguided craft, raised its outrigger booms vertical, and catapulted its crew, leaving the boat flipped like a turtle — hull up, flat upon the sea.

He glanced into the face of the elder woman, whose jaw had dropped. She stared back in bewilderment, eyes pleading for his help. At this point, uncharacteristic of his careful and deliberate manner, Ḷainjin suddenly transformed into his warrior mode, where instinctive action would henceforth precede careful thought. His plan of hunkering down for a warm and cozy, if rocky, drift had altered. He planted the elder woman on the outrigger platform and told her to point at her grandson. "Do not blink, Grandma, or you may never see him again!"

Then, taking his ring back from around Liṃanṃan's neck, he deftly cut the ties they had just used to secure the sail and, defying the teeth of the storm, took the helm. Just as the first needles of cold, horizontal rain began to sting her shivering shoulders, he ordered her to hoist it. That proved to be a difficult task, and he could not help but admire her determination as she struggled against the force of the storm to raise the sail and then secure it.

"*Kipeddikdik!*"[67] he chanted. This was the type of sailing that such a situation called for. He sheeted in tight and pointed the yard so close to the wind it allowed most of the gust to spill from the sail. There was a downside

---

[67] To sail close to the wind.

to this point of sail. It was very difficult and very hard on the material of the sail, and progress was very, very slow, with a lot of lateral drift. But there was no other choice. Were he to point the vessel more than a fraction off wind, they could share the same end as the other craft. So the elder woman pointed as all were blinded by the cold, stinging rain, all warmed by the ocean water as it splashed off their prow. The proa bobbed and then plunged into wave after wave, and all heads ached with tension from the cold and the tortuous, tedious lack of progress. Finally, by wind shift, by chance, or by fate — or part suprahuman inspiration — and long after the sun had set, they could begin to follow the shouts of the young men to the location of their overturned craft.

They heard the words "hurry" shouted several times, and "*pako*." At this, the shark hunter grinned. Amid the gusting winds of the gale, he was more worried about anchoring his craft, in its *kipeddikdik* sailing mode, to theirs, and about timing the anchoring with the dropping of his sail. If the connection was mistimed, his boat would drift rapidly away from their raftlike, upside-down proa in the storm, and they might never find them again. The men, faces turned away from the wind, had surely seen Ļainjin approaching long before he could see them, and all three men, in cowardly fashion, quickly swam from their overturned boat toward his as soon as, or even before, they judged the distance safe. Were they not so afraid of sharks, they might have begun swimming toward him earlier. At any rate, there they were in the water beneath him — pleading to come aboard, impeding his progress toward their craft, mumbling about sharks, and distracting him from his mission. He grabbed the club he had used to crush the skull of the tuna the day before and threatened to beat anyone who dared touch his boat without his permission.

"Which one of you decided not to follow my plan?" he demanded.

The irooj's son quickly admitted it was he.

"All right, take this line and tie it to the middle of your kubaak when I tell you to — not before!" Ļainjin tied the other end of the line to the yoke of his craft.

The irooj's son did not swim. "But what about the sharks?" he asked. "I felt one rub against me."

Ļainjin was in no mood to hear shark tales from the young man who kept defying him. "Well, did you empty the boat of fish like I told you to do?"

"The fish are still good!"

"Well then, call to the women on shore to come and clean them!" he shouted. There was no response so he continued. "Now take that line and swim back while you still can! You two swim with him! Stay by your boat, and don't come back here or I'll thump your skull like a fish!" he said, shaking the club fiercely.

The net result of the men holding onto the boat and dangling in the water before he threatened them — combined with his lack of concentration at the helm — was that they had drifted back, farther away. Nevertheless, the elder had been doing her assigned task. She had kept the boat in her sight. She kept pointing to it amid the driving rain, fierce wind, and growing waves. After another period that seemed longer than it should, they were on top of the stranded men again, all three of them sitting like birds on a branch atop the upside-down hull. Ļainjin surrendered the helm to the elder woman again.

"Ok, tie us up!" he shouted.

After some discussion, one of the men reluctantly slipped into the water and tied the line to the outrigger. The line grew taut immediately, and Ļainjin's boat swung directly into the wind. Liṃanṃan had been through her tasks once before, so she knew exactly what he wanted, and they dropped, furrowed, and secured their sail as they had previously. He had accomplished his first goal. Although he had successfully anchored to the relatively stationary overturned boat, he realized he had anchored to the wrong spot, but this was only the first step in his plan. He would next secure a much-needed second line to the other boat's yoke, beneath the water but over its upside-down hull. Then he planned to secure the other boat's mast, which he must first detach, and tie onto its kubaak at the point where the boats were tied. Though much preparation was necessary, the final step in his plan was to simultaneously cut this line tied to the other boat's kubaak, have the men "climb" the mast, forcing its float to submerge vertically, and let the force of the wind pushing on his boat help rotate the yoke of the other, flipping its hull upright. At that point, they should be able to bail the water from the capsized boat and tie the bow of one to the stern of the other. With both their outriggers to windward, they would be prepared to drift together till the storm passed. It was a solid plan, but it would need the participation of all to succeed.

Ļainjin ducked down below to find a second line. By the time he popped up, he found all three men straddling the overturned hull again.

Liṃanṃan had observed all this from the prow deck, fully exposed to the storm. She shouted through the wind at Ļainjin. "You speak to them as men, but they are scared little boys! Forget about them! They are useless! Tell me what to do and I'll do it!"

He thought for a moment but decided not to put her at risk. "Here, hold this and play it out little by little as I swim. I am going to tie on a second line, unsecure their mast, and tie it to their kubaak. Then I'll be back."

With that, he secured his ring, lowered himself into the water, and began swimming. He heard the elder woman gasp "Jebrọ!" but there was no time for further discussion. He swam around the other boat and had the men string the line between them over the hull as planned. He then grabbed the loose end, exhaled, and lowered himself down to tie it at the submerged yoke. He immediately ran into the sand-like surface of a shark that had its head poked up into the overturned hull, probably trying to dislodge a fish that was somehow still within. He let go of the line, and still submerged, backed off a bit, touching it but gently to get his bearings on the thing next to him. Then he deftly inserted the shark's tooth on his ring into the soft spot under its belly fin and punched it in the stomach with his free fist. The monster ripped open its own thick hide by its agitated motion. It backed out and turned away as his knife cut loose. When Ļainjin surfaced, he was half gasping and half laughing, quite pleased with himself for getting the better of the hungry shark, and especially for the story he would be able to tell about it.

However, he was surprised to find that the men were no longer straddling the overturned hull. His fingers searched the hull above him for the line that he had temporarily draped there, but he could not find it. When he swam around the prow of the upside-down hull, he saw that something had gone wrong. His boat was no longer there but some distance away. He swam to the upside-down kubaak and took the anchor line, which had gone limp, tracing it to its end. Even in those few moments, his boat had drifted a great distance. There was movement on the boat, and he could see that one or all of the men had climbed aboard, but any sounds being made were carried downwind. The boat was drifting so swiftly that he judged he could never catch up with it. He inspected the line's end in his hand. It had snapped. Caught in the gale winds and now in the high seas, his craft and crew had drifted out of his sight even as he wondered how to catch it. Gone! They had simply vanished, like the stuck shark, into the blackness. Now it was not the shark's stomach but *his* that seemed ripped open. *His* insides could now end up as the bait that the sharks would trace to his story's end.

What could have possessed him to leave the safety of his boat? There was a rule for that. A navigator never, ever leaves his boat. He must have been drunk from the scent of that woman, and now he would never see that intriguing creature again.

He climbed onto the underside of the boat's outrigger platform, his legs spread wide and his back against the submerged hull. It had righted its drift with the outrigger now turned back toward the storm. The ocean water that crashed over him felt warm compared to the stinging rain and the cold air of the storm on his face. He struggled to master possession of his thoughts and recover from the shock. He quickly resolved that he would just have to stick it out like this until morning. Yet he knew that, no matter how warm the gale made the ocean water feel, it could be too cold for too long for his body to survive.

He realized he was a trapped turtle. He could never turn the boat upright by himself, but could he withstand the cold or would it slowly lull him to sleep and to death? Now it was he that this storm had diminished, but he had faced worse, and as the old woman advised, he was determined to soak up the spirit of this thing and grow stronger for it. Tomorrow would be bright and calm, and surely, the irooj would set out to search for his boat. He could tie the mast upright and tie his kilt as a flag. If not, and if it was calm enough, he could try to unlash the kubaak, right the hull, and retie the complicated lashings.

"If only Taknoļ were here," he thought. No, on second thought, Taknoļ would have excoriated him for being so foolish! Ļainjin was glad he was not there, but he remembered his friend's instructions. Tying the very end of the boom to the perpendicular float was the most complicated lashing on the boat. Taknoļ had taught him that, to retie the outrigger in the water, you must retie all four booms simultaneously by tying off each phase progressively as you continue. It was as though Taknoļ's spirit came to him now to provide the strength and knowledge he would need to overcome his predicament. His thoughts drifted back to the day they returned from their great shark-hunting adventure at Anbōd. After the heroic trip, Taknoļ announced he would never again leave his beloved Namorik Atoll. Taknoļ freely admitted the rest of his story would be simple and easily forgotten by others, but he was proud to have been a part of Ļainjin's great adventure and vowed to repeat his story often. Ļainjin envied him, sleeping on his mat next to his chosen and among his children, warm, safe, and wise.

Then, amid his thoughts, like a fish taking flight from the water, Liṃanṃan scrambled up onto the overturned hull and sat there straddling it, gasping for breath, hugging it, and crying at the same time. Unable to speak a word, she kicked at him again and yet again, as though to reassure herself her nightmare was real and not imagined. He looked over the hull past her and there was nothing.

She must have swum to him from his boat when the line snapped even as the others had swum in the opposite direction, toward it, he thought.

He quickly straddled the hull facing the brave woman. Her chest was heaving uncontrollably. She would have been swimming for her very life. He embraced her trembling shoulders to warm her as best he could, and he rocked her as one would a frightened child. She appeared severely shocked by the situation in which she found herself. As she sat there, speechless in the elements tossing them back and forth and with only his warmth to comfort her, Ļainjin realized the depth of the nightmare into which she had cast herself. He could only imagine her panic, as she would repeatedly have lost sight of the overturned craft as she sank into the trough of each passing wave. She would have had to time her breathing to avoid inhaling any of the deluge of water that engulfed her at the crest of the next. He imagined she must have started to swim faster and faster as panic gripped onto her and then begun to take control, especially when she turned to see that the boat she left had disappeared into the blackness of the storm.

They sat there, exhausting the muscles of their thighs as the waves rolled beneath and splashed up against them. They squeezed each other, each struggling to join the other as one, amid the stinging rain and cold wind that sucked from their bodies energy that he knew, in these conditions, they could not replace. He needed to coax her down into the sea or they would get tired and useless from the cold, but from the way she had flown up from the water despite her exhaustion, he sensed she was afraid of the sharks.

He began speaking into her ear. "They call me Pako because I am a shark hunter. Did you notice the walls at each end of my boat? Well, they wall off compartments at each end that I have filled with shark's teeth like this one in my ring. This evening, I injured one shark that was trying to drag one of your brother's catch from the hull beneath us. I cut him with my knife from here to there" — he traced his fingernails from under her arm a finger's length down her side — "and when it swam away, its scent attracted all the other sharks and they swam away chasing it.

"Let me tell you a secret that few people know. Sharks are very stupid. Have you watched them swimming around you in a circle while you swim? Do you know why they swim in a circle to keep an eye on you?"

She shook her head once abruptly as she shivered.

"Because they are afraid of you," he answered. "They do that because they instinctively know that, once they turn away, they will forget they ever saw you, and at that point, they are vulnerable! The sharks that your brother saw are all gone and have already forgotten they were ever here, and all the fish from the boat are gone except one big one that we are going to eat right now. Then we will throw the rest away so there will be no reason for any more sharks to come. Wait here, I'll be right back."

With that, he sank down into the water and soon popped up again with the better half of a large *koko*.[68] He stooped beneath her on the underside of the outrigger platform that he wanted to coax her onto, then sliced off a chunk and began eating it.

---

[68] Mahimahi; common dolphinfish; *Coryphaena hippurus.*

"Want some?" he asked. She nodded and he gave her a piece. "Come down into the water and warm up. You are too exposed to the wind and rain there."

She climbed down with her supper hanging from her mouth, stooped with him on the underside of the outrigger platform, and braced her back against the overturned hull to stabilize herself against the warm, oncoming waves. She did not speak. She appeared nearly drained of energy. She was in quiet survival mode.

"How happy is your father going to be when we sail up tomorrow and he sees I have rescued both his beloved daughter and his boat?"

She shielded her eyes from the rain with one hand and squinted into his eyes up close, studying them to see if he was speaking the truth as he saw it or the story as he hoped it would turn out.

"The only problem," he continued with mock seriousness, "is that I'll be squeezing your hand so tight it will turn black and your grandma will have to cut it off and throw it in the banana patch."

He finally got a smile out of her.

"You know, we can flip this boat over, just the two of us, anytime we want." This was a lie, as he knew it would be an almost impossible task in the storm.

She responded with her first words. "What do I have to do?"

"I'll show you!"

He jumped into the water again, this time with the strip of fish still dangling from his mouth. He swam to the line previously anchored to the middle of the kubaak and swam it around to the opposite side of the upside-down hull she had been sitting on. Then he reached up and gave it to her. The line was now in direct alignment between the middle of the upside-down hull and the kubaak. For now, it provided something secure for her to hold on to amid the tumult. Later, it would become a critical part of their endeavor to draw the outrigger vertical beneath them and flip the boat upright. Then, the fish still dangling from his mouth, he came back around to sit where he started. As he finished eating, he said, "My task is to detach the tip of the mast there from the sail," and pointed to the woven-pandanus sail. It was drooping a little below the surface of the waves but still attached to the boat with several lines.

"Then I will tie the tip of the mast to the kubaak at the same spot where your line is attached. I will force the kubaak down into the water by climbing up the mast that I will have attached to it, getting it as close to vertical as possible, and that will turn the hull nearly horizontal. Your task will be to grab that line with both hands, put your feet flat against the horizontal side of the hull, and lean back with all your weight. That might pull the kubaak just a little past vertical, and its own buoyancy should cause the boat to right itself.

"Here, eat some more," he said, as he cut another large chunk for each of them. "Eat up. The more you weigh the better," he joked. "I'm going to tie the mast to the kubaak now."

Tossing the head and the remainder of the fish as far away as possible, he slid into the water to accomplish the first part of his task. First he cut the masthead lines free from the sail. Then he tied each to the kubaak, secured the partially submerged sail, and placed the pole end across the partially submerged hull. She was better able to brace onto that with one hand while keeping the line over her shoulder taut with the other. When all his preparation was accomplished, he returned to her. Stooping on the overturned platform and bracing himself against the hull in the waves, he managed to rub each of her shoulders and arms with a free hand as he held on to the mast, angled from the kubaak to the upside-down hull. The skin on her bony body felt colder than the water. The storm had long since swamped the fire inside her. She might not last till sunrise. He explained to her one more time exactly what he wanted her to do. Then he encouraged her not to be discouraged if they were unable to turn the craft on the first try.

"Some of this task depends on catching the oncoming wave just right. We need you to lean back and pull just as the boat sinks into the wave trough after its crest. Otherwise, the oncoming wave will work against us. Do you understand?"

She nodded that she understood.

"Okay." He turned away. Then he turned back.

"One more thing. Our 'fire starter,' our kindling inspiration for this task, will be the memory of my best friend, Taknoļ. He is the hull maker who built my boat and who taught me everything about a proa that a seafarer needs to know. Have utmost confidence in what he taught me. It will not fail us! *Emejjia wa ilọmeto!*"

With that, he began climbing the mast he had attached to the upside-down kubaak. He simultaneously reeled in on a line he had attached to the yoke of the hull to keep the mast perpendicular as he climbed and forced the float down into the sea beneath him, and just as the next wave was about to rush upon them he shouted it was time for her part. At this, she stooped flat-footed upon the hull as it turned nearly level with the sea. She wrapped the line around her upper back and clasped onto the loop this made with both hands. When she had adjusted the line perfectly taut, she stood straight as a spear and leaned back. This forced all her weight into the loop just as the boat tipped into the following trough, and Ļainjin watched her hit the water on her back like a fallen tree as the craft righted itself and its outrigger popped up from beneath the water on the opposite side.

He rushed to her as she surfaced, surrounded her with his arms, turned her back to the cresting waves, and lifted her as high in the water as he could. "You did it! You did it!" he said. "Now we have one more task for you. Do you know where your father's *lem*[69] is secured?" She nodded. "Reach into the hull when I lift you and grab hold of it. Untie it if you have to." He lifted her by the thighs as she scrambled into the swamped hull and submerged herself to find the *lem*, which had been secured below. After a few moments, she reappeared with the *lem* and immediately began using it to scoop seawater from the swamped craft. Ļainjin realized she was exhausting herself to no avail. The cresting and splashing was causing the seawater to fill the boat faster than she could bail it out again.

At that point, he realized that, in their haste, they had begun to bail before the boat had righted itself to the wind. The outrigger had not yet turned to windward. Once he removed the mast tied to the outrigger, physically turned the boat, and got the outrigger to windward, she was gradually able to make progress, but it was not an easy task. He showed her how to bail downwind to conserve her energy.

---

[69] A wooden scoop, sometimes attached to a handle, used to bail water from a hull.

"Don't toss it wildly into the air. You only need to move the water a small distance from inside here to outside there." So she sat and bailed in the wind and rain as the boat bobbed and the waves crested around them, sloshing water into the hull even as she bailed. Undiscouraged, she bailed relentlessly with energy that surprised him and slowly made progress. Once progress was made, less water came in and more water went out, and soon she had emptied the boat. She sat there in the stinging rain, breathing heavily but more alert and in better spirits, no doubt warmed by the energy she had expended. He realized she was probably more exhausted than she realized.

Ļainjin knew that he needed to protect her from the cold sickness, but he had one final task for her first. Prudence dictated they refill their water containers. To this end, while she had been bailing, he had untied the mast from the sail, untied the lines securing the sail, and draped the sail over the boat like a tent, to allow the rain to wash off the sea water. Luckily, some of the coconut-shell containers still hung in their nets within the hull. She emptied the brackish water they contained and began filling them again from water Ļainjin had funneled from the sail. The water was still too salty to drink but not too salty to rinse the hull, so he channeled all the water there instead. She splashed it around as it poured in and then bailed it out again.

Then, as they were working to flush the hull of saltwater, the storm broke with the first flash of lightening and a loud clap of thunder.

"Nan Sapwe!"[70] he shouted back to the sky triumphantly. This was a sign that told him the worst was over, and he knew that by surviving, though exhausted, each would be stronger for the experience. Yet again, more lighting broke the darkness about them, and then again, more thunder. He shivered, not from cold this time but from exhilaration at the sound from the throat of Nan Sapwe. He felt the spirit of the storm enter the lower extremity of his spine and tingle up into his throat and out of his tearing eyes as he tried to consider hers. Had they become one, fused together by the hardship they had just endured? *Had he finally saved a loved one rather than let her slip, cold and lifeless, between his fingers into the sea*?

[70] Pohnpeian spirit of thunder.

Finally, the wind began to abate. The rain began to pour straight down upon them, and the water poured pure from their sail into their coconut-shell containers. One final time, they bailed their hull empty. Then they covered it with their sail and crammed themselves up into the bow of the rocking hull. Her naked body clutching onto his drove away his thoughts of horrors past, and once intertwined, one with the other, they warmed themselves into an exhausted, wave-tossed sleep.

The island

When the Chief awoke, he restrained himself from taking flight but looked down at his pathetic, pink feet grasping the sturdy limb of the *kōņņat*[71] tree. Surviving the storm had been a lot easier for the brown, black, and white terns, which all share the handy seabird characteristic of webbed feet. That and their oil-coated feathers allowed them to float on waters out of the storm's path, such as those off the lee shores of the windward islets, like the bird island upon which he awoke. The Chief and his kind lacked both these characteristics. They had only two more limited and dangerous choices for surviving such a storm: fly up to an altitude above the rain or land. In winds or even light breezes, he could effortlessly glide — even sleep — above the clouds for days. But landing on the water like a tern was never an option. Once wet, his gigantic wings would prove too heavy to lift his skinny body into flight.

Normally, the Chief would have just landed on his platform and trusted his worker to handle the details. But alas, that jealous bird hater had captured the commoner. This time, therefore, he had followed his new companion to one of the bird islands on the atoll's southern fringing reef and had landed prostrate in this tree. True, the landing had not been one of his most heroic or graceful moments. His companion had landed gracefully on the sandy beach and then hopped onto the branch next to him. Why hadn't he thought of that?

The Chief was soaking wet and out of his element now. It appeared he was trapped on this limb until he dried out. However, there was no hurry to

---

[71] A short, sprawling tree that grows next to the shore; beach cabbage: *Scaevola taccada*; "*naupaka*" in Hawaiian.

fly anyway. Usually, he avoided these bird islands, where the longed-for butt bumping took place. Something had always made him persona non grata to all the beautiful and much larger, white-breasted females. They always went for the puffer boys, who knew the secret of blowing up their throat, or gular, sacs into bright red, jellyfish-size attraction devices. They melted the pure white throats of these females. Their knees weakened, and their tail feathers twisted away from their puckered backsides. After several fruitless experiments, he had learned to avoid these butt-bumping orgies by staying away from these bird-infested islets. After all, what self-respecting male would want to sit around and watch others doing it? Too embarrassing!

This time, though, he had met a gigantic cuddle-poop of a female who seemed attracted to him. Even now, she was nuzzling up to him as though he was the only bird there. So why should he fly away even if he could? Once those beautiful eyelids retracted, he imagined that endless, wanton butt bumping would surely ensue. He wanted to gobble just thinking about it! As he did, his bright red gular pouch suddenly began to inflate until he looked exactly like one of the ridiculous puffer boys he had hated over the many seasons past. In short order, he had inflated the sadly wrinkled red sac that hung beneath his beak into a gigantic red bubble that was several times larger than the tiny breasts beneath it. This sexual spectacle — seen by some as stunning and others as simply silly — was so debilitating that it prevented his head from tilting forward.

The female on the branch next to him must have been thrilled, because she jumped down onto the coral sand and turned her wet, droopy tail feathers aside. To his excitement, she exposed her pink, puckered backside to his view. He belly flopped onto her, dug his toenails into her back feathers for traction, and tried to give her the most satisfying, if instantaneous, butt bump she had ever had. From that point forward, they had eyes only for each other. They cuddled and butt bumped throughout the morning, intermittently preening their feathers dry.

Later, they flew off together and began circling two sparsely forested bird islets off the colorful fringing reef nearby. These bird islets had their beginnings in the sunken coral forests along the reef's edge. Here, parrot fish incessantly crunched the coral and excreted the sand. It later washed up, along with storm-broken chunks of coral, onto the reef flat. Hundreds of storms later, small sandspits began to form here and there. They were forced to migrate up and down the reef by one storm or another until, by happenstance, a seed or two was blown or dropped or pooped out of some wandering bird's butt and something began to grow.

By that time, seabirds resting before their next foray into the multiple feasts that punctuated the surrounding waters had pooped and fertilized the growing islet well. The trees took root and the sands held firm. Then more and more birds landed, and the process accelerated. And there they were with their expansive white beaches, green clumps of shrubs and trees, and hundreds of birds of different kinds — flying and gliding and landing and taking flight.

Thus, the birds and the islets of the sandy atoll grew in harmony. This was not lost on the humans, who allowed them to thrive in their own realm. When the birds flew over the kidney-shaped island at the southeast edge of the atoll, they observed numerous females picking up leaves, branches, and immature breadfruit, casualties of the evening's storm. Then the females carried these remnants of the wind toward the interior of the island, where broad-leafed fruit trees with bunches of green-and-yellow fruits grew, and discarded them in piles.

The islanders had studied the island-forming process and, like the birds before them, had mastered it. They protected the bird islets by enforcing customs that prevented indiscriminate bird killing and the eating of eggs during the seasons they bred. The islanders studied the birds and used this knowledge to fish more successfully. They referred to the Chief and his kind as the irooj of all birds, because of their size and because they took their tribute from the other birds by making them regurgitate their catch.

As the Chief and his companion glided over the island that morning, he hardly noticed that the women who looked up at them were amused by his inflated, bright red gular sac. They pointed at him and called out to the others to look. They all sang out, "*Lale ej rōrōñ!*"[72]

As the two birds glided higher, they gained perspective on the groups of flappers coming and going. Various fishing feasts sprung up here and there, around the agitated, white-waved perimeter of the reefs encompassing the

---

[72] "Look, he has an erection!"

peaceful azure lagoon. The Chief saw numerous outriggers under sail, but his worker's boat was not in sight. As the morning wore on and the tide receded across the reefs, they saw male and female humans alike wading at the reef's edge to gather snails and other morsels from the sea.

After a while, the Chief's throat sac gradually deflated, making flight and hunting more practical. But inflated or not, there was no way he could outcatch his fishing companion. She made it embarrassingly clear that she was not a bullying vomit eater! She fished right along with the flappers, only instead of diving into the water to catch the swarming silver tidbits below the surface, she caught them as they took flight to escape the tuna below. Or more often, she plucked them from just below the surface with the hook of her bill. He was getting hungry just keeping up with her — that is, until she started flinging fish his way. Of course, he was always able to catch them in a dramatic, manly fashion. He had learned long ago to dive faster than a falling fish.

For his first two seasons, his worker had fed him on his branch first thing in the morning and again every evening. And children would bring numerous treats as tribute during the day. Then, once he began to fly, his worker began to play a game, tossing his fish into the air to allow him to perfect his flying skills. If by accident he missed his treat, he still had a second option — to pluck the prize from the water's surface with his bill before it sank. Ah, happy fate, to have attracted the perfect female to replace the suddenly lazy and distracted commoner.

* * *

Overwhelmed by the events of the day before, Ḷainjin and Liṃanṃan slept late into the morning. They had stripped off their wet pandanus wrappings during the night and clutched onto each other's damp bodies to absorb the other's warmth within their dark, endlessly rocking enclave. Later, as the sun rose and the rocking turned less violent, they had separated their sweaty bodies ever so slightly to better feel the pleasant, fresh breeze, some of which penetrated beneath their sail-covered craft and circulated the air within the hull. When Ḷainjin awoke, light was diffracting from here and there into the hull and partially illuminating her face, in front of his. He became lazily engrossed by the features of that lovely face. Her magnificent tattoos ran over her shoulders in perfectly straight lines ending in triangular patterns, the bases of which formed a straight horizontal line across her upper chest, above her pointy, unsuckled breasts. She consumed his every thought. What luck had brought them together, and had his mother's spirit guided their drift toward each other? Was she out there somewhere, still guiding his fate? Tears welled up in his eyes at the thought, and a moment later, Liṃanṃan's opened and met his.

"Why do you cry?"

"Well, I heard you snoring, and I was thinking, 'How unlucky to have chosen a woman who snores louder than the thunder that dampens the strength of a gale.'"

With that, he felt a firm downward yank on his manhood. "Too late — it's me or the banana patch for this fish!"

"Okay, okay!" He laughed.

She kissed him on the mouth and then wiped the tears from his beard with both of her thumbs. "You are crying because you'll never revisit any of those old holes again! You are my *ṃaj*[73] now! I am going to take your knife and trim all this hair off your face so I can see how handsome a ṃaj you are, and so all the women on the island immediately adore you and become so envious they rush to their bathing pools to view their images and cry, 'Why not me?' But first tell me why you cried."

"I was thinking of my mother. You make me think of her. I was wishing I could..."

"Tell me about her. Why not? What am I going to do with you? You are just like my father. He has never talked to me about my mother! I had to have Grandma tell me how she died. He blames himself, I suppose.

"You men are all the same. You keep your thoughts rotting inside your throat until it explodes and the stink comes out like a bloated, dead fish on the shore. Where is your knife? I'm going to cut deeper into that neck this time and sniff what terrible stink comes out!"

"Then I'll smear blood all over your skirts, and everybody will think I only chose you because you threatened to kill me," he responded.

"I'll just tell everybody I cut your throat open because you wouldn't give me the names of all the stinky holes you've known! They will say, 'Serves

---

[73] A general term for eels of all varieties.

him right.' Because everybody knows you men don't talk. You men must all take some secret vow of silence once you become of age and promise never to talk about anything inside ever again."

"We're silent like good fishermen."

"Oh, that explains everything," she continued sarcastically. "Two men are walking down the village path to the ocean side and neither has a word to say to the other. The ocean is still a long way off, but they are silent because they are stalking a big fish! That explains everything, except why you were crying. Tell me!"

"I promised her I would never tell."

"That's just like you! You hide your story inside. Then you break off one kernel and toss it out there, but only if you have to," she teased. "'I'm called Pako, the shark hunter who's killed a hundred sharks. I've got their teeth to prove it, so don't worry about all these ones circling, these ones who want to eat you! Just jump into the water with them, and I will fill in the rest of the story later!'"

"Ṃanṃan, I have many stories stuck like fish bones in my throat. Trust me, I would have coughed them up long ago were I able."

"Then hurry up and kiss me! I will fish them out with my tongue" — she raised his ring, which hung around her neck — "and no farting this time, or I vow I will really cut into that thick sharkskin throat of yours!"

He kissed her on the mouth and then covered her face with kisses until she giggled contentedly.

"Oh, that's right, I forgot. You are not an eel wanting to intertwine your tail and clutch onto your hole on the reef's edge. You are a shark who is afraid of me, so you circle, watching me, because as soon as you turn away, you know you'll forget you ever saw me! And that's when I'll attack and cut off your manhood and throw…"

"…it into the banana patch," they said in unison.

One thought must have led to another. Suddenly she became anxious about her brother and decided to crawl out and look for his sail on the horizon. His gaze fixated on her naked body as she pushed aside the sail covering the open hatch between the outrigger yoke and the foredeck and emerged into the sunlight. The thought that, soon enough, she would ask her father to bring her to him was enthralling, and he was captivated as she untied her woven skirts from the rigging and began securing them with her belt.

"Ļōpako, I don't see your sail! Could they have already arrived back at the island?"

"Not likely," replied Ļainjin. He stood naked, searching the horizon, and then stepped off the outrigger platform and plunged deep into the water below. When he surfaced, he grabbed onto the craft with one hand and drifted next to it. Liṃanṃan dropped her skirts again and followed him into the water with a splash. She put her arms around his neck. He felt her naked body against his and, for the hundredth time, felt intractably aroused.

"You're peeing, aren't you?" she asked.

"I'm not saying."

"Just like you. Here, feel this!" She took his hand and cupped it between her legs. He felt the warm water pass from her body.

"I was ready to burst!" she said.

He held onto the boat and she wrapped her legs around him. Then she took his knife from around her neck and began trimming his beard to her liking.

He launched himself out of the water, reached down into his hull, and returned with a piece of greenstone. "Here, use this."

"What is this?"

"*Dekā maroro.*"[74]

"But it's black."

"Hold it up to the sun."

"It's green inside."

"And very sharp. Be careful not to drop it."

"Where did you get such a thing?"

He smiled and flicked his head back, as if to say, "Out there."

"I knew it! You are like the black clam too bitter to eat. You keep your shiny, round stone tucked inside, all to yourself. Ļōpako, I will pry open your shell ever so little, a bit at a time. Before you know it, I will have all your secrets. Wait and see!"

---

[74] Greenstone; obsidian; a naturally occurring volcanic glass found in Melanesia.

"That stone can scrape the hair off my face if you want."

"No, you would look too much like a boy, and my father might not accept that. Besides, you would look even more handsome, and I'm starting to worry about the reaction of the women ashore. Why do you keep your hair so short, and why do you have no holes in your earlobes?

"My grandfathers refused to allow it. They were not from Rālik or Ratak. They taught me such things were vain and were a liability to a warrior in a fight."

"So you like to fight?"

"No, I hate fighting, but they taught me how to protect myself!"

"Father will never forgive Ļōbōkrōk for abandoning his boat in the storm."

"Is that your brother's name?"

"Yes."

"If you don't want your father to know, don't tell him."

"I thought your plan was for Father to know you saved me and his boat, to get his approval to choose me."

"Trust me, your father will know this boat flipped over whether we tell him or not. He must retie all these lashings before it sails again. He will know I must have been of help, but I do not need to impress your father at your brother's expense."

"But where are they?"

"Last night they were *on* the water, and they drifted away in the storm, very far and very fast. We were *in* the water and drifted slowly. We should see my sail soon, and when we raise ours, they will see us and we'll meet them halfway."

"And switch boats again?"

"Yes."

"So we'll tell Father everything but the part about switching boats?

"I wouldn't tell him the part where you ripped off your skirts and peed in my hand."

"What about the part where you tried to feed me to the sharks?"

"Or the part where you pretended to feed me like a bird, with your tongue!"

They bantered on like two children until she had him trimmed the way she wanted. Then they got back into the boat and saw the sail of Ļainjin's boat on the horizon. That was when they raised theirs in the modest breeze and set a course to meet the other boat midway between themselves and the atoll.

As the boats approached each other, they dropped sails and the helmsmen paddled toward one another. Ļainjin had told Liṃanṃan what he wanted her to do. He approached the other boat head-on, each boat's outrigger to windward, each boat's lateen sail dropped and suspended to lee. As their prows were about to ram, Ļainjin backpaddled as she grabbed onto the forestay of his boat. Both prows were naturally turned into the wind, with their dropped sails bumping and mingling into each other. Liṃanṃan's grandma, who had been sitting on the foredeck, moved forward to help her keep the boats attached by grabbing the *rojak ṃaan*[75] of the companion craft.

The boats firmly attached, Ļainjin crossed from one prow to the other. The first man he faced received two nearly simultaneous slaps that caused his head to swing from one side to the other with such force that Ļainjin's foot punch, which launched him backward into the sea, seemed — in hindsight — almost merciful. On the outrigger platform, he met the second man, who tried to defend himself by swinging one of Ļainjin's oars at him. But Ļainjin's forward momentum was such that he arrested the oar at its shank in midswing and butted the man's nose with the crown of his head. Blood burst onto the luckless man's face. Ļainjin held firm to the oar, stepped back, and likewise kicked him overboard into the water. Then he turned to face Bōkrōk, who was standing on the stern deck with terror in his eyes. Ļainjin did feel pity for the hapless youth but had already let fly with the oar, which darted straight as a spear, hitting him with the tip of its blade on the top of his scalp and peeling it back at the hairline as he, too, fell into the sea.

He saw the women looking at each other, both in complete astonishment. At first Liṃanṃan appeared unsure about what she had unleashed on her companions, but Ļainjin sat down defiantly in his place at the stern of his recaptured vessel. Anger spent, he seemed more intent on fishing his lost oar from the water and munching on a pandanus fruit than further assaulting the sorry trio. One by one, each man, sporting a battered face,

---

[75] Literally, "spar man" or "spar in front"; the vertical boom or yard of the triangular lateen sail.

shaken and in awe of what hit him, popped up from the sea and climbed aboard their own vessel.

Liṃanṃan crossed to her father's vessel and spoke with them at length. Her grandmother gazed back at Ļainjin, her face saying that she could not approve of what he had done. When she finished speaking to them, she crossed onto Ļainjin's prow and her grandmother let go of the other vessel's forestay. The boats slowly separated. Next, Liṃanṃan raised the sail and they embarked on the final leg of their journey, leaving the others behind to nurse their wounds.

She approached Ļainjin, leaving her grandmother on the foredeck. "That's my brother you just attacked. What happened to you?" she asked.

"Sorry, I forgot who… I mean, I lost…"

"He's going to wear that scar for the rest of his life."

Embarrassed and searching for a response, he replied, "Scars are good for a man. They add character and remind him of his mistakes." With that inadequate reply, he sheeted in and set a course for the passageway next to the southwest islet of the atoll.

Liṃanṃan appeared skeptical. "You're just saying that because you couldn't resist showing me what a warrior you are."

"No, I told you I hate fighting. I learned to fight only as a last resort, and always to give an opponent an alternative. I learned that would make him aware he could have avoided the fight and would cause him to blame himself for the result. I made it clear to them that climbing onto my boat was not an option. Remember, I got into the water to help them save their boat. They should have stayed there."

"Okay, so tell me about these two mistakes here." She touched each of two scars on each breast muscle. They looked like small wounds that he had allowed to fester. "Why?"

His eyes roamed the horizon, the sea ahead of them, and the bulge in the sail that was gliding them toward the green-forested islands on the horizon ahead… *He said nothing, but his thoughts were crowded with terrible remembrances of that night of vengeful blood — yes, fateful mistakes — broken bodies, and of course, the belated scream he would never forget. "That is your sister!"*

"Ugh." She responded to his silence. "How about these mistakes here?" She touched the ugly scars on his right forearm, which clutched the shank of the oar he was using to helm the craft. "Were these made by a shark?"

Ļainjin smiled at her ability to soothe the more disabling scars trapped inside and, for the first time, appeared engaged by one of her questions. "*Dāp*[76] made those scars! That's the hand I use to tickle them out of their holes!"

"Did you cut his head off to get your hand out?"

"There are other methods."

"Like what?"

"I'll tell you one day."

"Ugh! Grandma, you see how impossible he is! He will not tell me anything! He keeps all these secrets."

"He's not a man to boast. You must empty his throat one word at a time. After you sleep with him, he'll start singing to you like a bird perched on its branch after a day of filling its gut."

"Your grandmother is very wise. What's her name?"

"Her name is Taknaṃ."

"Litaknaṃ," he called, saying her name formally. "Can you come and sit here?" Ļainjin pointed at the spot in front of him, at the yoke just behind the foot of the mast. "I have questions for you."

She crawled toward the stern and sat in front of him.

"Litaknaṃ, we've decided to choose one another. What's your advice?"

"Stop beating up on her brother! Did she tell you her lands are on Ujae?"

He nodded.

"Well, one day, she will need her brother to accompany her there and work the land for her."

"No more beating up on him," he agreed. "That's an easy thing to keep in mind. What else?"

"You should ask her father to bring her to you."

"What will convince him to do that?"

"That's Liṃanṃan's task, but he'll be watching you carefully to see if you have desire in your eyes for her."

---

[76] Moray eel; marine eels of the Muraenidae family.

"That's even easier. Advise me, please. What will be the most difficult?"

"The most difficult will be resisting my niece, Likōkkālọk.[77] She will do everything in her power to get onto your sleeping mat. She is very cunning, and she will not respect Liṃanṃan's choice or yours. If you're not careful, she'll pluck you out of the water like a fish and swallow you before you know what's happened!"

"*Wōjej!*" he said.

"Many wanted her because of our lands. When I die, the entire atoll will be hers to control. The man she chooses will be very powerful, but she fears no man will step forward because they all fear Paratak."

"Well, that's easy too, because power is a sickness I avoid. So, who is this Paratak?" Ļainjin asked, as his eyes followed a flying fish *kapiknaklok*.[78] That reminded him of the Chief. "Where is he?" he thought, tilting his head upward and looking to and fro.

"He is the father of Likōkkālọk's daughter — a very large man from Pohnpei[79] who arrived on our shores in a small fishing canoe and immediately succumbed to her charms. Desire has always been her downfall. She offered herself up to him without thinking that his customs and way of life would be strange. He does not understand how to feed the bird and let it fly, confident it will return when it is hungry. He has strangled her with jealousy. The more he clipped her wings, the more she rebelled. She has gotten more and more desperate to find the right man to run him off. The women of the island hate her because she hunts their men, yet no man steps forward after she takes them because all are afraid of Paratak. Her latest tactic is to prey on newcomers. For the last two seasons now, she has taken every man who has set foot on our shores. She appears irresistible to them until they realize they must fight Paratak; then they flee for their lives. She has seduced him so well he is crazy for her. He follows her everywhere, so she has forbidden anyone to bring food — to force him to gather and go fishing — and this gives her time for her

[77] A name: "woman to make fly." "Li": the female prefix; "kōkālọk": "to make fly."

[78] A term associated with flying fish of the family Exocoetidae; to take flight from beneath the surface of the water, flutter, spread wings, and glide.

[79] Currently one of the principal island groups that make up the Federated States of Micronesia, located in the Eastern Caroline Islands.

exploits. Half his life is rushing around trying to find her. He shows no respect for her or for himself."

Talk about mistakes. He had made many. Like those of any man, they would pass before his mind's eye from time to time to temper his self-pride, but most involved coming to shore and dealing with islanders. He had to ask himself whether he was he ready for this. He found the way people of these isolated low islands got themselves all tied up in lovers' quarrels half-amusing, half-annoying. If they had only seen all that he had seen! Nevertheless, the vision they were giving him was just what he was looking for. He was a planner and confident that, given enough information, he could think his way through any problem. Life, he had learned, was so much simpler on the sea, where he could predict and be ready for what came. Life on the island was complicated by people who could be foolish, unpredictable, and on occasion, dangerous. He would prepare for that as best he could. Now that he had met this incredibly brave and lovely creature, who seemed to soothe his spirit and provide hope that his long journey might one day end in happiness, he had a reason to overcome these obstacles and fight to adjust his life to theirs.

When he looked at Liṃanṃan now, he saw a look of fear like the one he had observed the evening before the storm. Was she worried that her grandmother had told too much? Did she fear he had heard something that would diminish her in his eyes? Would he think her forwardness was motivated by worry that she would lose him to this woman once they went ashore? Truly, she was a woman of the island and knew nothing else, while he was a creature of the sea and must learn to adapt accordingly. He scrunched his nose to squelch her thoughts and make her laugh, and he realized that the happiness of someone else had suddenly become an important element in his life again. Was she about to replace the quest of his youth to solve the mystery of his mother's whereabouts? That would be exactly what his mother would have wanted.

He saw a white tern dive into the water ahead. "Enough talk, I'm going to show you how to fish." Ļainjin reached below and gave Liṃanṃan his trolling line.

"I already know how to fish. Don't I, Grandma?"

"Okay, how many ñeñe?" he asked.

"Thirty," she responded, tossing the pearl-shell lure with its lashed hardwood hook into the water and uncoiling it into the sea.

"Now what's your main objective?"

She laughed. "You sound just like my father! To preserve the lure — not to allow the line to break. And to give the fish just enough line to retreat but not allow it to rush forward and cut it with its teeth."

"All right, now the most important thing. Show me you have luck!"

With this challenge, they sailed off into an afternoon characterized by kapiļak's wake — cloudy, breezy, and cooler than the doldrums of the days past, with choppy waves underlaid with rolling swells much larger than those the current conditions could have produced. After a while, they noticed their companions' canoe following along at a distance behind them. They were approaching the same ocean side of the same green islet at the southwestern corner of the tiny atoll as the day before. They saw islanders on the ocean-side shore, lugging baskets of perhaps snails, collected at the reef's edge during the earlier tide. The few who spotted their sail raised their arms to welcome them. Clearly, there would be no ugly spirit guarding the passageway into the safety of its lagoon this time. Its peaceful shades of shallow, blue water called out to Ļainjin. He felt a sense of well-being gradually arise among the three of them as each sat silent, no doubt contemplating what had transpired and what that shared experience would mean to the story each would take from it. As they approached the broad passageway into the atoll, he spotted a flock of birds diving into the water ahead.

"Okay," Ļainjin said. "I'll teach you a chant that will make you even luckier, but I can't say it for you. It goes like this: '*Kok, kok, wōde im ajoļe.*' The '*kok, kok, kok*' part is where you call out to the fish to attract them. The '*wōde im ajoļe*' part is where you invite them to chew on your lure like a pandanus fruit and gnaw like a rat."

She tried the chant several times, and each time, Ļainjin and Grandma encouraged her to be more forceful and commanding. Then, as they reached the spot where the birds had been diving, he told her to chant once more with even more determination in her voice. As she chanted this time, her arm went stiff with the tension of a large fish, her eyes grew large again, and a broad, boastful smile of satisfaction crossed her face. Taknaṃ, from the instant of the strike, began providing a torrent of commentary and advice on her every move such that Ļainjin thought she herself would grab the line at any moment. He felt a sly grin of amusement spread across his face as he silently watched Liṃanṃan struggle with the fish. Then he felt his smile ache as he forced himself to hold it, as he watched the line cut into the pink, uncalloused palms of her hands without any indication of pain on her part. He measured the size of the fish by its countervailing force against the wind in his sail and judged it to be a *bwebwe*,[80] longer than a ñeñe in size. He shot a glance back into their wake and saw no fish surfacing, confirming his assessment. A billed fish or a sharp-toothed one usually surfaced aggressively to view its enemy, often trying to offensively rush the line and slice its way free. But a tuna of whatever kind would defensively sound as deep as possible into its territory instead, perhaps pretending to itself that the more distance from its adversary, the more likely its escape from the line hooked to its jaw. Ļainjin loosened his grip on the sheet, slowly allowing the craft to come to drift and turn into the wind.

Moments passed, and the run of the fish gradually altered from the ocean's surface to deep beneath them. The amber glow of the late afternoon sunlight illuminated the beads and tiny streams of water that began to stream down Liṃanṃan's arms, breasts, and face as she pulled on the wet, tightly braided line. Her grandmother gathered the strands of her hair and bound them in a bun atop her head, preventing them from tangling into the gain from each haul of the line that she let fly and lie where it may, over her shoulders or into the hull or back into the sea. He began to sense an expression of increasing confidence grow from the vivacious, darting eyes below her thick brows. Ļainjin was in awe of the care she was taking to preserve his lure and the pain she must be ignoring from the brine-soaked line held taut by her cut palms. At the same time, he felt chagrined by his knowledge that the pearl-shell lure she was fighting to keep was but one of a collection of several hundred resting amid the plethora of sharks' teeth, pearl-shell knife blades, and greenstone beneath the prow at each end of his seasoned proa.

---

[80] Yellowfin tuna; *Neothunnus macropterus*.

Finally, the black-backed giant, stubbornly still fighting, approached on its side. Its distinctive, yellow dorsal fins were followed by a series of tiny yellow ones, each fluttering down its back and belly like the *ak*[81] feathers used as telltales along the leech of their lateen sails. The fish one-eyed them with a terror-stricken and confused stare, and Ļainjin grabbed his club with one hand, reaching into the base of its gill with the other. He gently eased the fish's head out of the water and clubbed the flat of its skull so hard that blood spurted from its eye socket into his face and onto Liṃanṃan's skirts. They watched silently as he held the fish in the water while it vibrated violently, tempting a pack of suitor sharks that had been following and monitoring its unhappy struggle. As Ļainjin lifted the heavy fish from the water and exchanged his grip on it with Liṃanṃan's, the little pack darted off hungrily into the deep blue abyss below them. As a precaution, she tied the fish down onto the outriggers where the Chief normally perched by tying a line through its mouth and one gill. Ļainjin, who had noticed their companion craft closing behind them, deftly trimmed sail and brought his proa back upon the wind.

As they would be required to tack once to get through the passage and again to reach their destination at the southeast corner of the atoll, they agreed to coil his trolling line and prepare to shunt. When they entered the passage, they were captivated by the many colors of the mysterious forest of corals beneath them. Because the tide had turned and begun to rise, the ocean level was higher than that of the lagoon's more confined waters, and the incoming tide swiftly swept them through the passageway and into the safer but choppier windward waters along its western perimeter. Children playing *bwilbwil* with their toy proas waved and shouted at them from shore at the islet's tip, where the incoming tide of ocean water swept into the lagoon. Once inside the lagoon, they could see the long white-sand beach of the atoll's westernmost islet. It was dotted with outrigger canoes. Some were being unloaded of their cargoes of breadfruit — perhaps harvested by the storm — pandanus, fish, and other provisions, no doubt gathered from other islets around the atoll. Other canoes could be seen higher up the surf-

[81] The frigate bird, *Fregata magnificens*; tied feathers used as telltales to confirm wind direction.

splashed beach under thatched pandanus-leaf canopies along the edge of the strand. Still others of various sizes were under sail, moving from one point to another about the lagoon.

The course for their first tack took them along the length of this westernmost islet with its broad, crescent-shaped beach that tapered into a southern fringing reef, which connected it to their destination islet, Lae. Along this reef lay a string of small islets, two of which were covered with birds. Looking at their flocks of inhabitants, Ļainjin hoped that the Chief had overnighted there. Their distance from either of the two principal islets at each end of the reef was short enough that Ļainjin judged he could easily walk to either and back during a single low tide. He hoped the bird had made its shelter there or elsewhere around the atoll before the storm hit. If not, he could be submerged, with his unsatisfying feathers clogging the belly of some shark, or else cruising above the storm clouds, now so far away he might never return. In fact, at that moment, the Chief was still following his lovely fishing guide along the ocean waters north of the northernmost islet of the atoll. Ļainjin asked Taknaṃ if her son, the irooj, protected the birds of these islets, and she acknowledged he had made them off-limits for gathering.

The closer they got to the reef, the lesser the chop of the waves until the lagoon waters smoothed as they sailed nearly to the shores of these twin kōņņat-forested islets. Then they shunted and headed along the lagoon side of the southern fringing reef to their destination.

Finally, they approached the western tip of Lae islet and sailed along the lagoon side of its calm shore, which sprouted stilted, thatched houses, one after the other, along the strand above its sandy beach. As they passed each house, Taknaṃ ululated in an unusually high-pitched scream to the women who lived there. Ļainjin supposed that she was announcing their arrival, and there were many ululated screams in response as they slowly glided down the shore. The island became thicker and thicker and the breeze more and more absorbed by the island foliage as they advanced toward the center of the island's curved shoreline. Ļainjin was forced to untie his oar and paddle to assist the fading force of the breeze filling his sail. Then Taknaṃ pointed to a spot on the shore where she wanted to disembark, so he gave Liṃanṃan the sign. She dropped sail and stepped back off the prow as he paddled with force to beach the canoe solidly upon the sand.

By this time, a crowd of surprisingly quiet children with excited, smiling faces had gathered, one after another, as they had progressed along the shore, to grab hold of the old matriarch's waist the moment she stepped into the water. Under her arm and on her hip, she carried a heavy, nearly full stalk of pandanus that she offered up to the children. Each broke off a fruit and then stepped back for others to take their turn.

On her part, Liṃanṃan broke off more fruit from another stalk and tossed them to the older children in the water, who grabbed them and passed them on to others ashore. Then she turned to acknowledge her father, who was ambling unassumingly to greet them, a child at each hand. Giving the pandanus to the children, she grabbed his hand with her fingers, and hands swinging, they approached Ļainjin at the outrigger platform of the beached canoe. "Father, this is Ļōpako. We met him at sea and he helped us when your boat flipped. And this is the fish I caught outside the passage."

"Flipped turtle?" responded the irooj disconcertedly. He nodded politely at Lainjen, but his eyes soon turned to his proa, piloted by his son, that was about to reach shore. He waded deeper into the lagoon to greet them, showing no regard for the handsome new kilt he wore. He spoke to the young men for quite some time and then returned to address Lainjen.

"I must thank you for your timely assistance to my son, his crew, and my daughter."

"What about me?" Taknam asked. "What am I, a cast-off, chewed-up pandanus fruit?"

"And my mother—"

"It was me who asked him to take us with him when I saw the storm coming!" Taknam continued. "Somebody needs to teach those boys about clouds and how to handle a proa in strong wind! I do not trust their sailing skills! That could have been me flying and crashing into a wave, and coming up an ugly spirit to catch these little ones and eat them!" Then she dropped her chin, made an ugly face, and turned away to chase after a group of children with her arms wide.

"Catch me, Grandma!" cried one, raising her arms into the air. Her grandmother surrounded her with her arms and blew a loud fart with her mouth on the little girl's neck.

Her father, after thanking Lainjen, stood silent in the water, straight as a spear stuck deep into the sand and wearing a warm, broad smile on his face, as if he was expressing his gratitude not with words but rather with his presence. He had tied his hair in a bun atop his head and wore a scented crown of flowers. He had tucked a plumeria flower behind his right ear. Hollow pandanus-leaf earrings filled the enormous holes stretched into his earlobes, and around his neck hung a multistranded choker of bleached white shells with four pearl-shell pendants hanging from it. His manly, well-defined chest sported the characteristic tattoos that, from adolescence, had marked his irooj status.

"Liṃanṃan, that's a fine fish, but look at these poor hands!" He turned his daughter's palms up to inspect them. "The newcomer must have trusted you with his most attractive lure." Lainjen cut the lure from his line and gave it to the irooj, who stood admiring it for some time.

"Keep it, please. It has never brought me luck. And here, this is for you." Lainjen sliced open the belly of the fish, reached inside, and tore out the bloody heart of the tuna. He rinsed it in the water and offered it in the palm of his outstretched hand.

"From my hand to yours, and should it please you" — Lainjen extended his other hand to Liṃanṃan, who, disregarding her pain, grabbed firmly onto it — "from your hand to mine."

Outwardly shocked at Lainjen's boldness, the irooj looked at Liṃanṃan and then at his mother, who had turned to hear what he might say. His eyes went back and forth, evaluating the eyes of one, then another, and back again. And then, with a smile and as fast as the Chief himself would have acted, he snatched the heart, popped it into his mouth, and slowly chewed his tasty tribute.

At that, Taknam, who had been monitoring her son's actions intently, trilled out a joyful, ululated scream that was joined by others from a host of sister islanders who had congregated at a respectful distance on the strand above. The whole hoard of them attacked Lainjen, and this was accompanied by ululated screaming and the erratic beating of *aje.*[82] They covered him with head crowns and neck leis made of flowers that, somehow, they had hastily gathered and strung. Singing in a high pitch, the women formed several concentric circles around them all — even out into the water — that advanced them ashore. Their men came from the rear to haul Ļainjin's canoe shoreward while the women rotated around them, hand in hand, and continued to sing until the entire throng advanced to the irooj's guesthouse above the strand. The men placed his proa upon logs under the thatched canopy next to the guesthouse.

There, Ļainjin braced himself against an upright post in the doorway of the thatched house. His legs were tired and painful, having just walked farther than he had under the past several cycles. He felt a bit dizzy on the solid ground beneath him. The women charged him again, and he was covered with even more flowers by more women who had now arrived and crowded around him. Then, just as suddenly, they all flopped down close around. Feeling awkward above them, he slowly slid down the corner post at his back and sat amid a circle of friendly, inquisitive feet. He felt it was time for someone to speak, but he had no idea who that would be.

It was Taknaṃ. "They call him Pako. Which of you wants to be eaten first?"

A swarm of hands waved back and forth amid the squealing women. Those close by kicked his legs and feet and pulled at his hands and arms.

"Ļōpako, you heard it from them," continued Taknaṃ. "You have your pick! And these are just the ones who've already been chosen!"

There was more shrieking and laughing as women on their knees pointed at themselves, saying, "She lies; I have yet to be chosen. Take me!"

Another woman stuck her wrist in front of his mouth from behind him and shouted above the rest, "Eat me before I die of envy!"

Taknaṃ said, "I have many, many more with their skirts down, pretending to be collecting leaves in the pandanus patch but playing with young boys instead. Ļōpako, take your pick!"

As he looked around, he saw many of the women on their knees, pointing at themselves, waving, or shaking their hips from side to side.

[82] An hourglass-shaped sharkskin drum carried by women when they accompany their men to a battle.

Ļainjin had had *kaṃōļo*[83] welcomes many times before but none quite this raucous. He was thinking either there must be a serious shortage of men or, more likely, they were all pretending and just wanted him to feel welcome.

"Now I would be amiss if I neglected to tell you all that my granddaughter Liṃanṃan wants me to announce that she has chosen this shark as her personal pet and will scratch out the eyes of any woman who touches him!"

One called out, "No experience! Pick me instead" amid more laughter. Another in the back shouted, "I'll trade my eyes for him! Liṃanṃan, come and take them!" And one from the back said, "Who needs eyes when you've got a mast like that as a guide post?"

As more laughter ensued, Taknaṃ cautioned them. "Take it easy! Each of you will get your chance at him. Don't scare him off!"

A woman shouted from the back, "I'm going to put a hole in his hull this very night!" Another shouted, amid the laughter, "I'll keep him busy while you do that!"

Then Taknaṃ turned serious and told the story of how she had first met Pako, how she had called him Jebrọ, and what they had said to each other — as well as how he had predicted the storm and helped when they flipped turtle. She then concluded that, just as sure as she was standing there, he had saved her life and the lives of her grandchildren, adding that she would take him herself in gratitude if she wasn't sure he'd be better off beating his mast on the sharkskin of an *aje*!

At that, the whole flock of them broke into uproarious laughter, and the irooj, by custom, had to turn his back and pretend he did not hear what his mother had just said. Liṃanṃan, who had been standing there holding his hand and laughing at their antics, turned with him.

That was when Taknaṃ took advantage of the moment and untied her son's choker necklace. Telling Ļainjin to bend his neck, she tied the choker around it, under the pile of flowers already there. Then she ended her speech with the following words: "When we met, you were a wild creature of the sea. With your courage, as natural to you as the stars are to the sky, you preserved those things most precious to our irooj, Ļōpedpedin.[84] And now,

---

[83] A newcomer celebration.

[84] A name. Literally, "man this reef beneath us."

in return under his rule, I give you our humble atoll — gather anything here you choose to take. Go anywhere. Stay anywhere. Take anything. Stay if you like, or like a bird of the sea, fly away and come back at will. Bury me, or let me to sea; bury my son, or let him to sea! You are welcome here until your story's end and as long as the last of these who witness my words live, so shall this promise be fulfilled."

There was a climax of ululated screaming and drum beating, and then one of the women broke into song. They all stood and sang, and counterrotated around him in concentric circles as they sang. Then, all of a sudden, the crowd dispersed until there were only Ļainjin, Liṃanṃan, and her family.

The women were so clamorous that the *kaṃōļo* had truly exhausted Ļainjin. He found it easier to fight than be honored. Truth be told, he would rather have faced the brunt of a second storm than the attention these ambitious women had rained down upon him. He had not been ready for that. Trapped by the past as he was, he was under no illusions. Their attention was seducing, yet captivating. He reminded himself how navigating the disquiet of this welcoming society had been more difficult than trading with cannibals.

Pedpedin, he noticed, had been observing him intently since their initial encounter. He had perhaps seen this exhaustion in his manner and addressed him, saying, "My mother spoke well and I was pleased with her words. In good time, I will surely offer you my daughter — from my hand to yours, as promised — but now, because you have been at sea for so long, you have become like a giant clam, strong of clutch but without legs. You are vulnerable, a little like the white lobster that has crawled from its old shell, but do not fear. You are under my protection. Tomorrow, we will walk a little and talk, and I will give you due warning about my stubborn daughter. In the meantime, take this house as your own, and I will send a lesser daughter to care for your immediate needs."

They left Ļainjin alone by his new house, and he immediately went inside to enjoy its privacy. The moment he entered the house, even in the dim light of the setting sun, he found himself astounded by the immaculate designs embedded in the interior thatch. All the stones on the floor were fresh and still sun-bleached white from the ocean-side shore. At the other end of the single sleeping room was an enclosed garden, open to the sky, with a thatch door leading out to the open-sided boathouse where his proa sat perched. At one end, by the door of the garden, was a well, and at the other end, another small enclosure open to the sky, with giant clamshells for bathing water. After so many days at sea, it seemed more than a simple refuge to the seafarer. At that moment, it seemed more like one of the elaborately constructed sanctuaries he had seen in the high islands to the west. Pedpedin, like leaders there, must have learned to treat newcomers well. He probably did so because he realized that newcomers brought new things and had new skills to increase his wealth and give his workers a sense of progress.

Ļainjin lay down on the fresh coral stones of the enclosed garden, stretched his back, and spread out his legs and arms. There above him drifted the aftermath. Dimly lit clouds were chasing after the storm that had challenged them and moved on. The sheer luxury of his circumstances compared to his cramped and perpetually rocking hull on the open sea overwhelmed him, and he was about to drift asleep when the door opened. In came a young, newly tattooed woman — a girl, really — giggling a bit and introducing herself as Liṃanṃan's sister. Raising his torso up on his elbows, he could see she was a younger, cuter version of her older sister with the same intonation in her voice. She had brought him a sleeping mat that she unfurled, covering him with it from foot to waist, and then stooped flat-footed to lay upon his chest a finely woven pandanus-leaf kilt like the one her father wore, but of a different, more common design.

"Put this on," she said. "Liṃanṃan told me I wasn't to return without the 'stinky one' you have been wearing." He stared up at her as she stooped with her knees together. She was turned away modestly with one elbow propped upon them, but her eyes looked down boldly, in a matter-of-fact way, straight into his.

"Go on, you can take it off under the mat if you're shy, or you can stand up and show yourself like a man. Better yet, let me do it for you. I know how to handle these things," she said, reaching under the mat for his waist.

Feeling challenged, he pulled away, stood, and began to untie his kilt.

"Okay then, *ṃōṃaan ṃaj*," she said, as he turned his rear to her, wrapped himself in the new kilt, and dropped the old one.

She picked up his old, tattered kilt and, looking at him, put it to her nose and made a cute face. "I guess you couldn't take a proper bath out there." Then she stood looking him in the eyes as she held the kilt in front of him and grabbed him by the bicep. "*Wōjej*, what a muscle! I just challenged you into showing yourself to me before any of the other girls got that chance," she boasted, squeezing his arm. "And you won't mind if I brag about that!"

She was lying, as she had seen nothing and they both knew it. She released her grip, walked toward the garden door, and then turned at the last minute before she exited the garden. "Your chosen one, if I know her, will be modest and not talk to the other girls about you, but I can spread your stories from one end of the island to the other. And right now, there's nothing these island girls would rather talk about than the incredible man shark and the North Star he follows! And don't worry, I'll leave them dying with anticipation!"

When she returned a short time later, he was still standing, admiring the new fiber kilt he had just wrapped around his waist. She gave him a coconut-leaf basket of grated coconut and flower petals for bathing.

"That was prepared by Liṃanṃan herself," she said, and began drawing water from the well for his bath. "She has to sleep in Father's house tonight and every night until he decides to bring her to you," she continued, walking the *jāpe* of water from the well to the bath stall.

"Until then I'm supposed to guard you as a bird guards its egg! Those are her exact words!" she scoffed, as she paced back to the well to refill the *jāpe*.

"I can't believe my luck." She had come back from the well and stopped in front of him again. She held the heavy *jāpe* proudly. "I get to guard you from the mob of women out there who want to squeeze the coconut milk out of you," she said teasingly. Then she proceeded to the bath stall again.

"You saw them out there — 'Ļōpako, eat *me*!'" she chirped from the bath stall, imitating a woman from the crowd as she poured the water into the giant shells. "No, me!" she mimicked, marching back out and stopping before him again. The *jāpe*, which was heavy even when empty, hung from her hand.

"So, I intend to sit on my egg all night!" She scrunched her nose curiously. "And if you're too bashful for that, you'll just have to take it up with her!"

"Tell her I said you're not going to sit on me like I'm some sort of baby bird."

Not giving up, she soon returned with more water and marched right up to his face. "Everybody knows, when a voyager comes ashore, that he is looking for the closest place to stick his mast. After all those days out there, you must be full to the brim and ready to overflow like this *jāpe*. The way Liṃanṃan sees it, better me to receive it than one from that mob she cannot control. After all, I am just her follower. She is the eldest so she gets the first pick of everything, but do not pity me. Being second has a big advantage. Father keeps his eyes on her every move but lets me run wild. I am the most-envied girl on the island. It is not as though *I* am saving *myself* for somebody like *she* is. I can play with as many boys as I want. I have had lots of them inside me, but only for an instant before kicking them out again. But like Grandma taught me, that just makes them tell more stories about me. The boys are all crazy for me out there." She concluded her last trip to fill the shells in the bathhouse. "They're probably talking about us right now! We might as well get started on a great story to tell them!"

"Then please tell her she has nothing to worry about. I have complete control. Don't think I don't find you very desirable because, believe me, if circumstances were different…"

Undissuaded but unwilling to hear more, she left him alone, explicating his virtue to only himself. He entered the shower stall. "Privacy at last!" he thought. After days of aloneness, the most challenging part of life on the island, he now realized, would be the nonstop human interaction, which he often found more exhausting than fighting the elements at sea. But then the luxury of bathing in freshwater would make it all worthwhile. He poured water from a coconut shell over his head. Then he piled some of the grated coconut into a ball in the middle of the *inpel*, squeezed the coconut milk onto his face and his recently trimmed locks, and rubbed the *inpel* across his neck. He methodically scrubbed his shoulders and arms and chest in the same way, the white liquid streaming down his sun-blackened body like mother's milk. As he stooped over the gigantic clamshell to rinse himself, he felt the sharp coral stones beneath his feet. His long voyage had softened his callouses. The irooj was right. He must begin walking immediately to regain strength in his legs and feet. After rinsing, shaking his hair, and rubbing off most of the water, he retied the fine kilt around his waist and stepped out of the bath stall. Liṃanṃan's sister had set out several coconut-oil shell lamps and had spread several other large pandanus mats about the house, which now had a warm, luxurious feel to it. She reentered the house, carrying an aromatic coconut-leaf basket full of freshly cooked food that she abruptly handed to him, still pouting, it seemed, over his unwillingness to accept her advances.

He thanked her, sat down in front of one the lamps, and examined the contents. She sat on the other side facing him. There were fish in the basket, but his hand went immediately to an item that was still warm. It was wrapped in a baked breadfruit leaf and smelled of a ground oven. The sticky delicacy inside had oozed out of the brittle leaf in places and had crisped on the hot stones of the oven. He tore at one of these and placed it in his mouth. It was *mokwaṇ*[85] mixed with coconut milk and rebaked in the leaf. He ate the whole thing within a few ecstatic moments. Then, becoming talkative, he turned to her and said, "This sort of thing is what I crave after so many days of eating food raw."

She watched him intently with the pleasure only a woman takes in watching her man eat the food she has prepared. "There are others," she said, "but try this."

"What's that?"

"*Pọljej.*"[86]

He had not eaten that in many seasons. She sat there like a proud mother bird watching her chick take its fill from her day of fishing, and the obvious pride he saw in her eyes endeared her to him.

---

[85] The atoll dwellers, especially the Marshall Islanders, cultivated numerous varieties of edible pandanus. Some had flavorful juice they sucked from the fibrous nodules. Other pulpier varieties were chewed like fibrous carrots or baked, and the pulp subsequently scrapped from the softened nodules. This mash or mokwaṇ was either dried into jāānkun or mixed with arrowroot starch and coconut milk and rebaked in a breadfruit leaf.

[86] Ripened breadfruit filled with coconut milk and baked in a breadfruit leaf.

"Did you make this?" he asked.

She raised her eyebrows and wheezed affirmatively.

"Well, it's very good, but I cannot eat as I used to. I've gone too many days without much to eat and am afraid my stomach has shrunk."

She got up, brought his sleeping mat from the garden, and laid it out next to him.

He had already decided he would sleep on his canoe to protect his character from this beguiling guard of his. He most certainly would not let this little … minx make a mockery of his relationship with her sister. He wanted to rest there for just one comforting moment, so he lay down on the sleeping mat, put his hands under his head, and closed his eyes for an instant to recall the moment he loved about her the most — when she plunged backward into the sea and successfully turned the canoe upright. No matter what the night might bring, he would hold that vision in his mind … and then he slipped into a dreamless but comforting sleep.

For how long he had slept, inside as he was, there was no way to tell, but suddenly Liṃanṃan's sister appeared in a panic and awakened him. "Get up! Get up!" Muddled, he managed to raise himself on one elbow and tried to wipe the blur from his eyes. "She's coming! She is coming! Likōkkāļọk is almost here! Pretend we've been doing it," she said, pulling up the back of her skirts and snuggling her bare rear into his lap. He raised himself further to peer into the dimly lit room as he struggled to recall the significance of the name.

Finally, it came to him. Kōkkāļọk was the woman he had been warned about. Still propped on his elbow, he asked the young woman snuggled before him, "What is your name?"

Bending her neck and turning her face up to his, she whispered, "Joļọk."[87]

"Ļōpako? Ļōpako? You are not asleep, are you?" questioned a voice from outside. "Can I come inside? I have a gift for you."

"Likōkkāļọk, Likōkkāļọk. Come in, cousin. Our Pako is here with his mast between my legs! Come see!" Joļọk said with sarcastic parody.

Kōkkāļọk intruded defiantly into the house with a white kilt under one arm and holding her little girl, who was just past her *keemem*,[88] in the other.

---

[87] A name: "throw away."

[88] First birthday.

"Lijoḷọk, I didn't expect to find you here. Are you aware it is my responsibility to welcome newcomers? Where's your sister?"

"She has to sleep in Papa's house one last night, so she gave me her shark to play with."

With arresting casualness, Kōkkālọk sat down gracefully in front of them. She spread the beautiful kilt on the mat before them, her little girl sleepily crawling into her lap.

"Poor thing, she's usually asleep by now. The tide held us up."

"Oh sorry, I didn't know you were coming," Joḷọk said sarcastically. "I'm afraid you're too late. His little eel has already spit at me twice. Ḷōpako, where are you hiding my pet eel?" she asked. She rested her head on her left forearm and reached her right hand between the slit of her skirts to privately handle his manhood. Caressed by her bare rear, it had popped out between the fibers of his kilt and begun to straighten. He tried everything he could imagine to stop it — except, of course, moving away and exposing himself to their visitor.

"I can't seem to find it," she lied. "Must be all shriveled up again. You know how they are, just like a baby. First they sit up, then they get angry, then they spurt a flood of tears, and then they go back to sleep again."

"Funny girl. I came to welcome him with this kilt, not to sit on him!" Kōkkālọk said. "It is his first night on shore, and the man must be tired after all those days and nights at sea — and after saving everyone in that storm. The storm frightened me, and I was safe at home. I expected the roof would blow away as that first gust hit shore. It took me all day to clean up the mess that blew down on us."

She spoke intelligently, in a soft and friendly manner, despite Joḷọk's forward and sarcastic comments to her. In the dim flicker of the burning oil, she appeared to be a voluptuous woman of much beauty, with high cheekbones and immaculate tattoos of a different pattern from those of Liṃanṃan and her sister. But like theirs, hers ended in triangular designs in a straight line above her ample breasts, which had large, elongated nipples. She appeared taller and slightly plumper than the thinner island women he had met earlier at the *kaṃōḷo*. She wore small coils of plain pandanus-leaf earrings in her earlobes and sat straight backed, with an aura of dignity. Her complexion was very light, which accentuated her tattoos, and she had no scars or blemishes that he could see. Her Pohnpeian man had obviously never hit her. Ļainjin knew these men well, understood the cultural differences, and was unsurprised by the story he had heard. Kōkkālọk sat for some time in silence, as though waiting respectfully for him to address her.

"Ļōpako, I missed your *kaṃōḷo*, but I wanted to bring you this gift that I made for such an occasion. I am the irooj's eldest niece. Please accept this, and wherever you wear it, think of me," she said, sliding her sleeping child onto the mat and bending over her to drape the kilt over Joḷọk's shoulder and back. She stared him in the eyes inquisitively. To him, she seemed pleasant, kind, and polite, not the man-eater Taknaṃ had described. He thanked her with his eyes.

Joḷọk, he would later learn, was worried that Kōkkālọk, wanting to be alone with him, was about to ask her to take the sleeping child to her father's house — a request that, by custom, she could not refuse. As instructed by her sister, she pretended to fall asleep, making her body an obstacle between them. On his part, Ļainjin was still trying, yet failing, to ignore the silent attack of her ticklish fingers and was still unable to move one way or the other.

The attractive woman continued to talk, even as Ļainjin found it difficult to concentrate on what she was saying. "I live on the next islet. A current from the ocean separates us at the highest tide, so I was slow at getting word of your arrival. I got my skirts all wet crossing," she said, as though she was about to take them off. Instead, she just sat there seductively, tempting his attention by very slowly pulling aside the slit of her wet woven skirts as though looking for something and exposing a little of the light skin of her thigh to his view. She looked at him again in silence after her last sentence, this time as though to probe the idea that there might not be an additional need for talk. He realized at that moment that she had caught his gaze and noticed that it had settled exactly where she wanted it. This, he realized, would only encourage her to proceed with her seduction, especially now that Joḷọk had abruptly dropped out of their duel. Of course, he was not as in control of the mind behind his gaze as she assumed, and she, of course, was not aware of what he was desperately attempting to keep inside himself that was about to burst out. For what she couldn't see was exactly what Joḷọk was doing to him behind her skirts — caressing him with the light touch of her fingers, coaxing from him what she hoped would dampen any fire kindled by the woman sitting there before them with lust in her throat. It was the product of countless sun-stricken days and stormy, lonely nights fighting the elements with no thoughts other than to survive and no dreams other than those forgotten in deep, exhausted sleep.

Kōkkālọk slowly relaxed her head back and untied the bun of her long, black hair, causing it to fall with a gentle slap on the mat under her and release the pleasant, intoxicating fragrance of flower-scented coconut oil. She stared into his eyes and then slowly, purposefully drew back her skirts a little more. He watched her run her single middle fingers slowly up and then slowly down the part of her thigh she was exposing to him. His mind was out of control, watching what his eyes longed to see yet jumping from one vision to the next, struggling to concentrate on anything that might distract him from what Joḷọk was secretly and tenderly trying to accomplish. Perhaps interpreting the distracted, tortured expression on his face as intense desire for her, Kōkkālọk decided to go all out and lay her story before him first so he would have no excuse for refusing her bidding later.

"Ḷōpako, I have a feeling my cousins have already warned you about my problem. I live with a man who was a bad choice. Though he is the father of my daughter, I want him out of my life — dead, chased off… I do not care. Dead is better, I suppose, but only because I would otherwise forever live in fear that he would one day return. I loathe the mat he sleeps on. My problem is that, though many men on this island desire me and though I have given myself to too many of them already, none will stand up to him. They allow me to pleasure them beyond their wildest dreams, and once they reach ecstasy, they only talk of me, but they never look me in the eyes again. I have come to think of the men of this island as cowards. Every day they rub themselves with coconut oil, bun up their hair, and peer into reflections of their ear piercings. Now you come to us, and you are a different sort of man — a seafarer, a man every woman has been waiting for, a man who can choose among us all. Yet who is the first to appear at your door? The most desperate. I know. I have no shame. If I had any pride left, I would have waited till you had already taken the best of them and then offered myself as a humble dessert after you had already eaten your fill. Ļōpako, it shall be thus if you wish!

"Oh look, your little plaything there has fallen asleep. Young girls always fall asleep before their men reach their full potential to be pleasured."

He lay there listening intently with his mind racing, hearing but not comprehending. His gaze fixated on her finger as she looked into his eyes, assuming she had him hooked as she slowly tickled the inside of her thigh, back and forth, each cycle getting closer, each cycle exposing more of the lighter and lighter skin to him. Finally, the moment came when she lifted one knee into the air, slid her hand down between her legs, and — he imagined — began to pleasure herself, believing she had him totally captivated. What she did not know was that his body, at that moment, was shuddering in complete surrender to Joļọk's expert encouragement. How many seasons of built-up pressure had come rushing out the eye of her fist as she squeezed gently again and again and again? His eyes rolled back and closed. At that moment, Kōkkāļọk must have decided he was ripe to pick, and so she stood up and extended her hand to him.

"Come, Ļōpako. Follow me into the garden while she sleeps. I'll show you everything you long to see and cause you to feel everything you long to feel."

That was when Joļọk extended her hand instead, still warm and wet with his seed, and jerked herself up at Kōkkāļọk's expense. Ļainjin sat up and covered himself with his new kilt. Then, standing there between them, Joļọk announced triumphantly, "The little ṃaj just spit on me for the third time, imagine that! He must be exhausted now. Why don't you come back tomorrow and we'll talk some more?"

"Lijoļọk, you *are* a very funny girl. Thank you, I will be back. I promise." Then, as predicted, she said, "Can you carry my daughter to your father's house now and put her to sleep? We will stay there tonight."

As soon as Joļọk left, Kōkkāļọk sat down on the mat next to him, spread her legs, and surprised him by wiping his seed from his sleeping mat with the selfsame fingers she had used to intrigue him. Then, lying back, knees up and tawny thighs exposed, she turned her face to his, puckered her ample lips, and implanted it. Seductively maintaining his attention, she resumed pleasuring herself. "It's a shame young girls are so wasteful!" she said softly, stroking herself and twisting her hips back and forth as if to work his seed deep down into herself. “She teased it out of you, but you meant it for me, didn’t you?” She was somewhat distracted, as she appeared to be concentrating on what she was doing to herself. He didn’t answer and, in fact, had not said a single word to her since thanking her for the kilt with his eyes. For all she knew, he was a gawking imbecile, but she had him totally captivated as she closed her eyes momentarily and then, apparently satisfied, smiled with unfeigned embarrassment.

As she sat up, she said, “Do I love men? I do. But do they love me? No!” Lowering her voice to a whisper, she said, “Don’t be ashamed by our little affair. I promise to keep any news of the secret soup we blended together strictly to myself. Ļōpako, please do not think poorly of me. I’m just a desperate woman who snatches pleasure into her unhappy life as best she can.”

They were sharing a few moments of silence when they heard a bit of footfall outside. Soon thereafter, Joļọk reentered and Kōkkālọk stood up to present her parting words. “I know you desire Liṃanṃan, and Joļọk offers” — she turned to her — “additional enticements. But don’t be afraid to think of me if you ever wiggle from their embrace. After all, you know what they say,” she said, glancing at the spot on the mat where his seed had spilled. “*Ṃōṃaan ṃaj.*”

As she left, Joļọk put a furrow into her brow for an extended period to show disdain for her cousin’s actions. “She’ll climb over everything to sit on top of you! Just because she admitted what she is up to does not mean she can be trusted! Do you trust your sharks? I do not think so! She is a man-eater! Ask anyone and they’ll confirm it.

“Here, take this out.” She turned her back to him. He saw that someone had slid a small, double-edged *rajraj* down her skirts in the middle of her back. “Don’t scratch me!” she said, sucking in her little tummy and making room for him to pull back on her skirts and carefully remove the short, sharp weapon. He ran his finger across the many small shark teeth lashed on both sides above the shank of the ripper’s edges.

“What am I supposed to do with this?”

She turned, her big eyes smiling. “Cut her throat if she comes back!” she joked.

He frowned in disagreement.

"Liṃanṃan sent that to you. Likōkkālọk's Pohnpeian man followed her here and watched from the far side of the path. He is crazy with jealousy and might kill you while you sleep. My brother and his friends are guarding outside."

Ļainjin snickered at the thought.

"True, they are no match for him, but they will keep fires burning in the front and at the back. I'm to snuff out all the light inside," Joḷọk continued, going from shell to shell and covering each one with another to quench the lights. Then all was dark inside save for the light of the fires burning outside and seeping sharply, here and there, into the darkened room. She sat next to him in the dim light, took the *rajraj*, and placed it under the edge of his sleeping mat. "There, that's ready for you. You can sleep now. I will sit and watch, and if he comes in, I will wake you, and you must defend yourself before his eyes adjust to the dark.

"It's a good plan, don't you think?"

Ļainjin — or at least the ocean creature part of him — was still struggling to adjust to the pretentious drama of island life sprouting around him. He had flopped over onto his back, part of him about to laugh and the other to cry. The freedom he had once felt had begun slowly fading from the moment his feet stepped ashore.

"Liṃanṃan says Father has agreed to bring her to you tomorrow, so that means tonight will be our last night together." Joḷọk's darkened silhouette whispered to him as she ran her hand over his bicep and then squeezed it as she had before. "Of course, once she gets pregnant — which shouldn't take long, right? — she will need me to watch over you again. Already she treats me with great importance! Everyone will be talking about us, Ļōpako. Your arrival has raised my stature! Now let me know when *ḷōṃaj* [89] is ready to stand and get angry again! Those things are so much fun; I cannot think of anything I would rather play with! This time, let me know if he wants me to do it fast or slow. Grandma says every ṃaj wants it different, and some want it different each time. So don't be reluctant to guide me. I am sure Liṃanṃan can't wait to get at that thing, but tonight I have *ḷōṃaj* all to myself."

---

[89] "Ļō": the male prefix; "ṃaj": a general term for eels of all varieties.

He turned away from her, too mentally exhausted to comment on her girlish gibberish. He was ashamed of himself for allowing the flirtatious prattler to dominate him so completely — and for letting the ripe, provocative one swipe his seed as he watched, captivated and unwilling to stop her. He had a mind to launch his canoe out into the peaceful lagoon nightscape, and it would not have been the first time he abandoned an entrapment his manhood had led him into.

Joḷọk left him lying there and began to quietly pace the room, probably wondering how her sister expected her to stay awake and wondering why this newcomer was different from all the boys who could not get enough of her. He, still lying there, began to wonder how much time it would take for a man's eyes to adjust to the dim, reflected light in the room. An attacker would come through the garden and pause there until his eyes adjusted. "Their plan would only work if someone outside called out," he thought. Then, as he fondled the pendants on the necklace around his neck, he thought, "Surely, as the irooj told me, I am under his protection so this madman Paratak will not attack me under this roof." Although he didn't expect to need their help, he was amused that fate had led him into a circumstance where this temptress and the very men he had punished so harshly that afternoon were now in charge of protecting him. Again he slept, but this time, his sleep was lighter, perhaps due to the threat of attack in the dark. He woke often, sometimes hearing Joḷọk laughing with the men outside, sometimes feeling her presence in the dark next to him.

Finally, toward morning, he slept much more soundly as he sweated through his usual nightmares and then, as he was wont to do, grew hard redreaming his often-dreamt tryst with Wisina on the island of Satawan. He was not sure what that name meant; unfortunately, he had never bothered to ask her father. They had been friends, and Ļainjin found his daughter to be most intriguing. The grandmothers of that place had a tradition of enlarging young women's clitorises by repeatedly funneling a *kallep*[90] into the hole of an empty coconut water-shell and placing the mouth of the shell on the spot they wanted to enlarge. Because he and the grandmothers did not understand each other's tongues, the only explanation he interpreted

---

[90] Trap-jaw Ant: *Odontomachus simillimus.*

was "hurt bad but make feel good." Hurt bad indeed. Like every other person among the islands, he had been bitten by these aggravating creatures and could not imagine encouraging one to attack, let alone in a sensitive place like that. But then he had learned from experience that each island group had found its own curious way to satisfy the lustful cravings of its men, though not always so its women.

One afternoon, Wisina had led him to a secluded spot near the ocean side of the atoll that she seemed well familiar with. He would never forget the boastful grin on her innocent face as she dropped her skirts onto a natural seat in the stone formation. Then she lay back, spread her legs, and parted herself to expose her proudly developed treasure to his view. He remembered her looking down at it, and then looking up into his eyes and then down and up again, raising her eyebrows in consent and nodding her head rapidly to indicate what she wanted him to do. As usual, he dreamt he was kneeling before her, touching the knuckle of his index finger to the moist pink gap between her dark brown lips, gently massaging the enlarged tissue between. It was their way. Every man talked about it and encouraged him to try. Every little boy jokingly pressed his knuckle into the arm or back of his playmate.

She was wet from the moment she spread her lips. As he touched her, he always wondered whether she was able, with a thing like that, to get wet just walking with a man. Though Ļainjin was well versed in this art, this was the one and only time he had the opportunity to perform the task, and as always, he started out with a very gentle up and down motion, careful to keep his knuckle moist by wetting it on his downward strokes and applying the increasing pressure she seemed to want with his upward strokes against the swollen tissue that was obviously the center of her pleasure. Wisana eventually put her hand on his wrist to make him aware that she wanted even more and even faster pressure. As he recalled, this was not a short task by any means, and one he might have been tempted to give up on except for the intriguing expression of pleasure on her face. He heard again the curious, rapid, and enticing sounds of her sucking air between her tongue and the roof of her mouth, and anticipated the expected finale, when she would burst into intimate urination.

At that instant, however, he awoke to find Joḷọk ever so gently tickling his manhood with her self-appointed fingers, causing him to erupt a second embarrassing time. Her self-satisfied, victorious grin seemingly reiterated that she, Joḷọk, was proudly — if temporarily — in control of his sexual life.

Perhaps noting the look of astonishment on his face and wanting to avoid a scolding, she rushed into the garden to draw water as though nothing of consequence had occurred, but he was sure it had. "This young one is good throated but vulnerable to the extreme," he thought. He had heard of this sort of thing practiced by younger sisters, and it always seemed to end in some sort of disharmony. A man could spill his seed as casually as his bird could poop his goo, but a woman, whether she admits it or not, could not match a man for indifference. In his simple view, he must be careful not to carve a scar inside her. For deep down in their nature — he was now thinking remorsefully of Wisina — a woman, no matter how strong, seemed to crave permanence more than any man. They alone inherited the land and they tied themselves to it. They were the holes along the reef. The ṃaj traveled freely from one to another. "But what about the hole that no ṃaj entered?" he thought. "Would that hole not crave companionship? Was she not ready to comfort nearly any ṃaj that entered?" Yet she was, by nature, unable to cling to the ṃaj. So she longed for him to sink his tail into her innermost cranny, to cling and comfort her there. But alas, he was physically unable to do so and was destined to merely scull backward or forward, maybe to abandon or maybe not. Maybe to be a good companion, maybe to be bad. To him, there was no such thing as a bad hole, only one that was lonely or jealous. But for her to feign indifference or resignation, as the proverb suggested, was to deny her very nature — or so he thought.

Ļainjin rinsed his face at the well and walked over to the boathouse. There, he grabbed his ring, looped it around the belt of his kilt, and set off along the neat, coral-stone pathway leading toward the ocean side of the island. Here and there, girls were climbing out of their thatched, stilted houses to begin their morning chores. Some were drawing water from wells while others were filling their hands with fallen yellow-and-brown leaves, from the breadfruit trees that shaded the village, and tossing them into compost piles. Perched here and there in a flat-footed stoop, they watched him pass and invariably acknowledged his passing with a multipurpose *iọkwe.*[91] Boys began to follow in a silent, respectful line behind him. He felt them quietly push and shove to establish a sort of pecking order, probably based on who would address him first should he turn to speak with them. He stopped at each coconut tree and carefully inspected its individual characteristics. He was looking for the healthiest trees, ones that enjoyed good sunlight, had a full crown of fronds, and bore heavy stalks of fruit — but the nuts with lots of water as opposed to the elongated ones with little water used to make rope. On occasion, he would glance back at the boys and catch one or another jokingly imitating his movements. He would smile and the group would break into laughter.

As they continued toward the ocean-side shore, the forest of breadfruit trees began to thin and the coconut trees became more prevalent. He noticed a curious symbol carved into the base of the oldest and tallest trees. When he asked the boys what the symbol meant, they said, in unison, "*Aorak.*"[92]

"You mean the aorak shell?" he asked them.

"Yes, the aorak shell," they repeated.

"What does it mean?"

The boys looked at each other, but none wanted to venture an answer.

"*Bwebwenato,*"[93] said one of the older boys. "Ask Ļōpedpedin."

As Ļainjin proceeded along the path, the coconut groves began to give way to pandanus trees, nearly every branch of which he found laden down at its tip with a single, humungous composite fruit of various shades of orange and green. Just before he arrived at the ocean-side shore, he came to what was obviously the last of the prime coconut trees that he wanted to inspect. He pulled the strips of pandanus that fringed his kilt through his legs from behind and tucked them between his stomach and the waist of his kilt. Then he grabbed onto the trunk with one strong hand on each side and leaned back as he hopped onto it. With his knees spread wide below his chest and his feet flat and pointed out,

---

[91] "Aloha"; "hello (or good-bye), love."

[92] A subspecies of spider conch of the family Strombidae, species *Lambis*; characterized by stout marginal digitations.

[93] Old story; fable; legend.

horizontal to the ground, he hung in balance effortlessly. Reaching upward with both arms and then, grasping higher up on the trunk, he hopped again, still hanging in balance. He repeated this until he reached the top, grabbed one of the sturdiest-looking fronds, and raised himself into the crown.

"Which one of you is coming up?" he challenged the boys.

They looked at each other again, and then one of the older lads charged the tree and began climbing. The others made fun of him because, in his hasty enthusiasm, he had forgotten to pull a tail between his legs and tuck it into the waist of his kilt, so his butt crack and dangling manhood showed there for all to laugh at. From the top of the tree, Ļainjin felt a refreshing breeze as he watched the dim yellow-orange glare of the sun peeking through the gray clouds on the horizon. It illuminated the troughs, and it gave shadow to the crests as they curled upon the reef's edge and rippled across the flat before splashing against the rocks, shorehead, and coral stones that covered the rock-strewn shore.

"That was the source of the stones covering the path and the source of the mound of stones the village rested upon," he thought. He imagined women coming and going, each carrying a coconut-leaf basket through the village, ostensibly to gather stones. This, of course, would mask their true goal, to empty their bowels at the water's edge and allow the outgoing tide to disperse the contents onto the vast reef and surrounding waters. He struggled to calculate the concept of a single basket of stones per woman per day. How many hundreds of seasons must it have taken to create the path and raise the height of the village by a hand or two? Then, of course, the women would declare "stone mornings," when the lot of them would gather and form a procession to pass the baskets, one to another, to cover over a chosen area. Yet again, how many of these stone mornings did it take to raise the village to its current height?

Meanwhile, the boy had reached the spiraled crown of the tree, tucked in his tail and maneuvered himself until he was leaning against a frond across from him. "*Iọkwe*," said Ļainjin, acknowledging the lad. "They call me—"

"Ļōpako!" proclaimed the adolescent with a laugh.

"And what is your name?"

"Etre."

"Is your mother from this island?" he asked.

The boy raised his eyebrows and wheezed in customary affirmation.

Then Ļainjin asked him, "Do any of the men of this island make *jekaro*?"[94]

The boy lowered his eyebrows, raised his lower lip, and twitched his head abruptly one time to indicate no.

"Do you know what jekaro is?"

Ļainjin got the same response.

"Good for you. That means you have the opportunity to be the first man on your island to learn how."

The adolescent beamed with eagerness.

"Okay, we've been looking for the best prospects, but there's no way to tell if a tree is a good tree for jekaro until you cut it to see if it bleeds well. Did you know that a coconut tree produces one bunch of coconuts under each moon?"

The boy, not one for words, wheezed and simultaneously raised his eyebrows in agreement.

"What is this?" asked Ļainjin, pointing, and forcing a response.

"*Jinniprañ*,"[95] the boy responded.

"Right, we call that *jinniprañ*. Once it breaks open, it has these little branches," continued Ļainjin, touching them with his finger to illustrate. "Look at all these little flowers on each branch. Some of these flowers will grow into those tiny yellow coconuts you see on this one over here.

"What's this?" asked Ļainjin, putting his hand on a green flower bud nearly as thick as his curled hand and almost as long as the boy's arm.

"*Utak ņe*,"[96] he answered.

"Right, this is the bud from which the *jinniprañ* will burst. The tree sprouts one from the base of every frond, and the little yellow coconuts begin

---

[94] Also called "tuba," "toddy," and various other names; the sap of the coconut palm tapped from the flower bud as it grows and continues to protrude between its mature frond leaf and the less-mature inner fronds of the palm's inner crown. The skill of making jekaro is practiced worldwide wherever palms grow.

[95] A stalk or composite flower from which coconuts grow and ultimately hang.

[96] "Utak": the bud sheath from which the composite coconut flower will burst; "ņe": "that there by you." In the Marshallese language, prepositions are directional, allowing for specificity when barking boat or with fishing commands.

to grow on it. Under the moon's cycles, they turn green, and after a season, the coconuts are good to drink. After two seasons, or around thirteen cycles of the moon, the coconut husk starts to turn brown. The shell inside has become hard, and the meat is ready to grate and *jiraal*."[97]

"Correct." The boy laughed as he nodded abruptly.

"Here, look at this one." Ļainjin showed him a new bud sprouting from the next of the remaining fronds spiraling up and around the crown of the tree. "Exactly after one moon's cycle, it will be the size of the other one and it will be ready to cut. In other words, we can start tapping one new flower bud each cycle of the moon. The day to start is either *maroklep*[98] or *jetñōl*."[99]

"But *maroklep* was three nights ago."

"So we are late, and the bud won't drip at its full potential. But you'll like the taste, and it will fill you up and strengthen your spirit. I was raised drinking jekaro as a substitute for my mother's milk. It's good for you," said Ļainjin, as he took his knife and cut off the top of the bud in one swift motion. "Think about this, do you know of any living thing stronger than a coconut tree? Is it not what you will tie yourself to when the *ļañ eļap*[100] brings ocean water over the island? Jekaro is the blood of this tree. Think about the strength you will get from drinking it. Okay, that is it for your first directions. I will meet you here at sunset for your next lesson. Don't be late! If the girls are still luring you to hang around the pandanus patch, I'll have to assign your tree to another lad or take it for myself."

"Not me. The girls make fun of me," admitted Etre.

"Well, just wait! They will line up to ask for a sip of your jekaro!" Ļainjin told him. The boy beamed a second time and tilted his head in disbelief.

Ļainjin climbed back down from the tree and launched himself back down the path to the next one he had decided to inspect. "Who's next?"

And so it went until they had cut a bud on all the trees that were on the new moon cycle. The others, he explained, would be ready in ten or eleven days. His legs were very sore from all the climbing, and he needed to rest.

---

[97] To eat grated coconut, usually with fish.
[98] "Big darkness"; "new moon." The islanders have a name for every night of the moon's cycle.
[99] The night the moon rises at dusk upon the waves.
[100] "Big wind"; typhoon.

Back at the irooj's dwellings, Taknaṃ was steeping *nen* fruit placed in rainwater in a *jāpe* atop the hot stones of her uncovered earth oven. She motioned to him to join her for a coconut shell of the traditional morning tea. He entered the open-sided, thatched cookhouse and sat with her before the still, smokeless hearth, slowly sipping the distasteful — yet supposedly healthy — liquid from a coconut-shell cup. He noticed that *pāle* were stored in the rafters beneath the soot-blackened ceiling, a peculiar custom that seemed to him would invite an unwanted fire.

"I'm told Jebrọ was busy shunting his mast to and fro last night," the old woman joked.

Ļainjin was not sure how much she knew about the events that had transpired the night before. He was reluctant to comment and just stared at her with the look, he supposed, of a trapped bird.

"Naturally, my son hopes you choose the eldest, if only to fulfill her wishes. Her happiness is his paramount concern, but he would gladly grant you the younger. She vexes him so. As far as I am concerned, you can take your pick of either. They are as different as day is from night. They have always been that way. One is a leader who thinks for herself, manages others, has a mind of her own, and rarely takes advice. The other seeks only to please others, does not think for herself, works hard, and always does what she must with joy in her throat. The older will spend her nights talking to you about the events of the day; the younger will spend the day talking to others about the events of the night!" Breaking into laughter, Taknaṃ said, "A man would have a much simpler and happier life with the younger one!"

"Litaknaṃ, I'm not a man to turn back. I think before I set sail. I may adjust my course, but I never turn back, because I am confident I can handle what is ahead!"

"That's why they are all crazy for you! You know how to think or not think, and they see your experience in your eyes. You come from the sea, where you had to teach yourself to not think or go crazy with fear and loneliness. Most men we sleep with — and even the sons we raise — will never venture out to where you have been. They will live their lives letting their little ṃaj control their thoughts. As you know, the ṃaj is an ugly, tenacious fish. It's too bad we women crave to be tickled by such things that have sharp teeth pointed back into their throats, making escape from their grasp nearly impossible."

"Not impossible," countered Ļainjin, running his fingers over his forearm. The old woman could not resist running her crooked fingers with swollen knuckles over his scars as well.

"The bigger they are, the more serious their grasp on us," laughed Taknaṃ. "Those are the marks of a seriously large *dāp*!"

"These marks are from many more than one."

"I'm looking forward to those stories, but who can tame things like that? It is true that most women are too willing to settle for the first man with a hard mast to sit on, but desire lasts only until you spy something more desirable walking down the village path. You are a thinker to match her. You think about what you need to say, and you think about what not to say. Maybe you *will* be happier with the older one. At least you will never be bored; you can spend your lives trying to outthink each other. Here, I'm going to get something to show you."

She went to the house and brought back a large, rolled-up sleeping mat. "This is the sleeping mat the irooj will carry under his arm this evening when he brings Liṃanṃan to you. That is right! This evening you will have her all to yourself. I want you to know that I pounded and pounded the leaves to give her the softest mat possible for this night," she said, pointing with her eyes to the *dekein nin*.[101] Have you ever felt a softer mat? This shows the deep regard I hold for my granddaughter, and for the man she has chosen for her very first night. It's big enough to cover you both under and over, and hide the unspeakable things you intend to do to each other!" She broke into uncontrollable laughter and soothed the uneasiness he felt from the night before.

"Here, eat!" She produced a small basket of the same delicacies he had tasted the evening before. He began eating with gusto.

"So, what do you think of Likōkkāļọk? You cannot say we did not warn you about her tricks. Isn't that the kilt she made for you?"

---

[101] A heavy, oval shaped club ground from the shell of a giant clam and passed as an heirloom, by matrilineal custom, from mother to eldest daughter; used to pound and soften leaves and fibers for mats, skirts, sails, etc.

"What you warned about certainly came to pass," he replied, continuing to eat. Taknaṃ seemed to enjoy watching him relish the food.

"What I didn't expect was her telling me the same story you told. I have to respect her straightforward honesty."

"Respecting her is good, but wearing that kilt is not. That is bait, to give Paratak an excuse to attack you. She is probably hoping you will kill him. He must have watched her making it and would have expected she was making it for him. If he sees you wearing that, it will turn him crazy!"

"Maybe that's why I put it on," he said, reaching into the basket and taking out another crisp pouch of breadfruit infused with coconut milk. "Why not get this over with?"

"Well, wouldn't you want to see him first so you at least know what your adversary looks like?"

"It wouldn't make any difference. A bully will taunt another man into a fight. A killer will study his prey for a long time and patiently plan the kill, but that also gives his prey an opportunity to foil his plan. One way or the other, I will be able to 'outthink,' as you put it, this Pohnpeian — whoever he is, whatever his approach. He cannot be very crafty, getting himself caught at sea in a Pohnpeian fishing canoe. As far as I know, the smart Pohnpeian does not venture out to sea. They pay us to do that!"

He thanked her for the food and retired back into the quiet of his luxurious abode, where he rested on his mat and considered the exciting prospect of the night ahead.

Early that afternoon, Joḷọk brought more food and announced that her father was ready for their walk. So after eating, Ļainjin left the house he had been awarded and appeared before the irooj, whom he found sitting on a mat laid upon coral stones spread beneath a stilted house that seemed no different from any of the other thatched abodes on the island. Ļainjin sat before him.

The irooj was admiring the lure he had given him. "I don't believe this is an unlucky lure. It appears finely crafted — designed to trail flat in the water and not spin. You gifted this to me with rare humility, considering the gift you seek in return."

"I did not offer that gift as a trade for your daughter. Had I expected you to trade, I would have gifted you more, as I have many others. I thought to myself, 'How can you trade a wild bird?' Instead, I offered you the heart of the tuna as a symbol of my willingness to serve you as my chosen's father. One day a big fish will break that lure away, and it will end up at the bottom of the ocean. Yet on that day, I will serve you still. If the lure is as lucky as you expect it to be, then by that day, my children will surround you and listen to your story of how the big fish got away with it."

"You are a quiet man, yet you have a gift for speaking," the irooj acknowledged, slipping the lure into his *alele*,[102] on the mat next to him. I will grant you my daughter because she wishes it, but first let us walk together." He led them out from under the house, and they started down the same stone pathway toward the ocean side of the island that Ļainjin had followed earlier. Perhaps judging that the distance he wanted to cover would take half the afternoon and wishing to avoid the customary hospitality his workers would extend to them, the irooj began their stroll at a strong pace, as a signal to discourage his workers from stopping them as they strolled deliberately by. It was not customary to call out to an irooj, but there was much friendly and repetitive arm waving as they quickly made it all the way to the ocean before the older man began to slow down and speak in earnest.

"I can tell from your accent you are from the Rālik string. Which island?"

"My grandfathers raised me on Namorik. My parents disappeared in a storm when I was young."

"So you lost your parents to a storm and then saved the lives of my children from one. What a strange symmetry between your story and mine. Were they caught up with Tarmālu when her fleet was lost?"

"Yes."

"And these men who raised you, they taught you to navigate?

"Yes."

The tide was now out, and the irooj looked over the expanse of puddled reef flat. He motioned with his hand to show Ļainjin a large swath of the shore to their right, which was dedicated to defecation and off-limits for fishing. At this point, Ļainjin judged the reef flat before them to be some two hundred ñeñe wide, or perhaps a fourth the distance of the path they just walked. The breeze, unobstructed by the island foliage, began to cool the

[102] A flat, pouch-like purse, woven from processed pandanus leaves, for valuables.

sweat covering his body as the irooj led him down the rocky shore onto the island's foundation.

"In this direction" — he indicated west — "the island gets more and more narrow. But in this direction," he said, heading east, "the island gets very thick, especially at the cape there." He pointed ahead. "This is the direction men go to fish."

The cape was a considerable distance away. He realized why the irooj was leading them across the reef flat. It was because the shoreline was not parallel to their line of sight to the cape, but receded away from them as the reef widened before jutting back out toward the point. In addition, the shore was slanted and rocky while the reef was flat except for the occasional coral boulder and, now that the tide was out, much easier to traverse.

"Think of Lae as shaped like an adze," said the irooj as they walked. "The long, skinny part there to the west is the shank part of the island. Think of this part to the north as the blade of the adze, with the cutting edge touching the lagoon where we can't see and the butt of the blade forming that peninsula, where the reef juts out into the sea."

The irooj headed across the reef toward the point at such a clip that Ļainjin had trouble keeping up with him. The tiny sea snails and sharp edges here and there on the reef flat hurt his soft feet, and some of his leg muscles began to pain him due to their long period of limited use at sea. The irooj looked back, periodically catching him in his struggle and indicating each time that they would rest at the point, but he kept the pace of their stride nevertheless. The sun, which had long ago reached the apex of its blinding glare, was now beating down on their backs and illuminating the whitecapped swells as they slowly curled and flashed transparent blue before bellowing down with a progressive thunder upon the reef's edge to their right.

The reef flat began to narrow as they approached the reef's point off the peninsula, and Ļainjin began to realize that swells were converging on the point ahead from three quadrants, undoubtedly flushing it at full tide with a variety of currents and likely making it ripe with sea life. He noticed that the coloration of the sea beyond the point was lighter than expected. That meant there was an undersea shoal beyond the reef's edge where live corals would attract all manner of fish about the cape. As they approached still closer, he could see that the live coral barrier on the reef's edge was unusually higher than the dead reef foundation before it. He surmised that the brine cast up by the undulating swells kept the coral alive and growing even though it was exposed directly to the sun during low tides such as this.

Finally, after walking to the tip of the island's southern shore, they reached the exact point on the reef where the eastern shore of the island appeared. From there, they could look back along the westward-pointing shank of the adze and ahead to the northwest-pointing blade and view both shores of the island from the fringing reef protecting and bending sharply around them. Pedpedin stood there with his left arm pointing westward down the shore on their left and his right arm pointing down the other shore on their right. He declared, "The islets of Kuwajleen are like a basket to catch us as we sail one day in any eastern direction off my back. Wōtto is one day's sail a little west of north to my right." He pointed in that direction with his right index figure and with absolute authority. "And of course, Ujae" — he pointed shoreward with his nose — "is over there, a little north of west, sailing from dawn to late afternoon under strong breeze."

He turned around to face the ocean that had been behind him and pointed west of north at the easternmost islet visible along the reef to his left. Then, on an even line from left to right, he pointed with his right index finger and said, in a commanding voice, "Namorik, four days south of east."

"How many days' paddle?" Ļainjin asked.

"That, I never thought to ask! You must be a better judge of that, but rest assured you stand at the center of what our ancestors called *kapin meto*.[103]

"This is where my forefathers fished," he continued, "and their ancestors before them. This is the cape of life for my people. Here, we can never exhaust the supply of fish. Look out there, off the point. The reef does not drop straight but slants down into light blue water that teems with every type of fish imaginable. As soon as the tide turns and begins to flood, every manner of ocean creature will come to feed where we now stand."

Finally, the irooj led Ļainjin over to the rocky shore, where they sat down on boulders to rest. "So how many days were you out there paddling?"

---

[103] Literally, "backside of ocean"; the westernmost atolls of the Rālik Chain.

"From the day the wind ceased. Certainly, from the first sign of Jebrọ. Too many to keep count!" he replied.

"Sometimes I like to come here with a pole at high tide and *kōbwābwe*,[104] using the bellies of hermit crabs for bait. At high tide during the day, I can fill up a small basket, but on a night like tonight, I would fill up a large one, and I would have to bring along a boy to help me carry it back to the village."

"What about *kappej*?"[105]

"*Wōjej!* There is nothing better during these moons of calm water! You will fill your basket in no time, and you can fill another one with lobsters you catch as the tide comes in on your way back!"

"So there is no path that cuts directly back to the village?"

"Yes, there are several, but they are not well worn. We use them only when fishing. Our groves of coconut and pandanus and breadfruit are well inland from this point. As you can imagine, during the añōneañ season, waves cover these rocks during high tide. The salt haze over this part of the island is thick, and there is no reason even to come here because the currents are too strong to catch fish. Allow me to go back to what I mentioned earlier because I am sure you are asking yourself why I brought you here to talk about my daughter. I have a story to tell you about the women of this island, why they are so independent and why they perceive us men as weak.

"Liṃanṃan and the other women of this island are of the clan Aorak."

"I saw the likeness of the aorak shell carved into a couple of trees along the path this morning. The boys said it was a *bwebwenato* and suggested I ask you about it."

"Those were first carved many seasons after the trees were planted, by the women who planted them. Then each generation of their clan has traced over the carvings, making them deeper. They shined the carvings with the oil of their fingers — from the time they were young girls — with their hopes and dreams for their future, and they rubbed their tears into those carvings when they became women and grieved over a death or lost love. They are bound by their clan and taught by their granddaughters to do this, generation after generation, so to never forget to be ready should *they* ever

---

[104] Pole fishing.

[105] Pole fishing from the reef edge at low tide under a full or near-full moon.

come back. Every generation will hear this story to scare them, but also to teach them to be strong and to bind them together as one. You saw an example of that last evening. Men cannot control them, and for good reason.

"It all started perhaps a hundred seasons or more before I was born... My grandfather had fought them himself many times but was unable to turn them away empty-handed."

"The women?" asked Ļainjin, confused about who he was referring to.

"No, the men!" he responded. "He had a battle scar that ran from here to here" — with his finger, he drew a diagonal line across his face — "through one bad eye and deep across his nose and cheek. He had other scars all over his body. They were from many battles, and whenever I asked him about them, he said the men were from Pit. They had come every generation. They would cross the ocean reef and beach their canoes on the ocean side at the west tip of the island, to hide their intentions. From there, they would spread themselves along the ocean shore's 'shank of the adze' and then march lagoonward to surprise the young girls and take them captive. Each man would choose a girl — not for himself, but for the man's nephew back in Pit. They treated the girls well as they desired their light skin. Our girls knew they would treat them well because, on occasion, one would return and tell stories of her adventures to the others. Therefore, some girls secretly wished to go, but those were few. Most were frightened of their battle shells and were unwilling to leave their families and familiar surroundings and way of life.

"Then would come their champion, dressed like the others, in his battle shell. Have you ever heard of the ri-Pit[106] battle shells made from fibers of coconut husk?" the irooj asked.

"No."

"Well, that's because they never took girls from the more-populated southern atolls. They would come up here because we were fewer and because there were few coconut trees."

"What did coconut trees have to do with it?"

"I'll get to that. Right now, I am telling you they were dressed like hermit crabs inside shells made of rope! That is true. I'm not sure how they made those things, but they had their legs, their arms, and their torsos completely

[106] An ancient term for people of Kiribati; literally, "people or bones of Pit."

covered in this rope shell as thick as the first digit of your finger," he insisted, holding up his forefinger and thumb to illustrate. "They must have been terribly heavy and uncomfortable, but they were impervious to small-toothed *rajraj*. Unless a man threw a very sharp spear at very close range, it was unlikely to stop one of these men. Their champion would start at the western end and walk down the shore, and the uncle would be holding onto the girl he had chosen. Unless a man there was ready to fight on her behalf, their champion would proceed down the beach to the next house and the next until all the uncles and the girls they selected were in single file behind him."

"Didn't any of the girls' fathers fight for their daughters?"

"Yes, some would, but they were never successful against such men in such shells. And their champions were big men who were chosen for their fighting ability. They say the ri-Pit had a custom of one-punch fighting for sport. The men who were most successful at this game would become champions for them.

"However, there would always be at least one man from Lae to fight for the girls. In each generation, one man would stand out from youth and would make himself and his family proud by being the one who would stand up — but he would always come away from the fight with deep scars and broken bones. Therefore, they always took the girls. No one knows what would have happened if our champion had won because no one ever did."

"In all my travels, I never heard this story," Ļainjin said.

"Well, it is not a story we like to tell, not a story we wanted to hear, and not a story we tell to others. It is one we pass on in private, only among ourselves, like a *dekein nin* from mother to granddaughter."

"So what does the aorak have to do with all this?"

"Well, you know we have lots of those things here. Sometimes we gather them and hang them upside down in the sun until the shell gets hot, until the muscle of the creature inside loosens its grip on the shell and it drips out. If you cook a mess of them in an earth oven, heat them with coconut milk, and then eat them with breadfruit, they make quite a meal! Sometimes we throw in an octopus among them for flavor.

"Anyway, the mothers and the grandmothers mourned for the girls who were taken away. First they grew despondent, and then, after how many seasons, they grew angry and defiant. One day my grandmother had cooked a mess of them. While she was sitting there among the shells, she had this epiphany. Do you know what creature is the mortal enemy of the *wōr*?"[107] he asked.

"I would say the *kweet*."[108]

"And you would be correct because the octopus, with its sharp beak, seems to have the perfect design to creep among the corals, grip onto its enemy, and crunch into its shell. My grandmother planned such a strategy to defeat these big-boned men from Pit.

"She set off with a fleet of boats to Aelōñḷapḷap, where she had land rights, and filled the boats to the brim with coconuts. They came back here and carefully planted them in the interior of the island. We had always had coconut trees, but we would eat the nuts and rarely planted more. They know us for our pandanus forest, not our coconuts. That tree you saw today with the aorak carved into the trunk was very tall and very old and may not have even have had any nuts left, but it was surely one of those trees. Now it takes a generation for a coconut tree to start bearing fruit, and the irooj, at my grandmother's insistence, forbade any more drinking of the nuts. They made oil from every single nut. They stored the oil in coconut shells by the hundreds — they were hanging in every cookhouse and every home — and that is not all they stored. They stored *pāle* everywhere. You know a *pāle* makes a great torch, but it flares quickly. It is not very hot and you can easily snuff it out. But as you know, if you pour oil on it, the flame becomes hotter and more persistent. Have you noticed how the aorak shell fits perfectly into your palm, with a series of spines that protrude only slightly between each digit when clenched? And the single longer spine — the lip of the thing — protrudes from the base of your fist. Well, every woman slept with an aorak exactly the size of her fist under her sleeping mat. That is how they prepared. They had aorak shells all around the village, and for many seasons, on days when the tide was high, a group of girls would guard the spot where the ri-Pit liked to land their canoes.

"Well, one day they came. This was before I was born, and my mother was one of the young girls at the island's end, watching for them to come ashore

---

[107] Spiny lobster: *Panulirus penicillatus*.
[108] Octopus.

with the tide. Out they bravely ran to them while others ran in the opposite direction to warn the rest. Mother and the others flirted with the men, telling them they wanted to embark for Pit with them to wrap legs with their nephews but also saying that, to save face before their fathers, they would have to pretend to run away. Mother said the girls wanted to make the ri-Pit think this would be even easier than before, but really, they wanted to get them running before the men thoroughly soaked their shells in the ocean water. The uncles from Pit took the bait and immediately chased after them, and things progressed much like the generation before — the girls in the hands of the uncles, and their champion marching confidently down the shore to the village, and the islanders making it clear to them that my grandfather was ready in the village to fight him. The ri-Pit expected the women to beat their war drums, and scream at them, and run up taunting them as they always did. However, each woman also had a shell of oil hanging from her waist beneath her skirts this time, to spill all over the fiber clothing covering the warriors' legs.

"There was Grandfather, standing on the strand waiting for their champion, whose eyes focused upon him as he muddled his way through the women taunting him. Once the fighting began, all eyes were so concentrated on the fight that none noticed the oil-soaked *pāle* being brought down the shore and lit behind them — until the uncles turned from the heat on their feet as the women surrounded them and held the *pāle* to the bottom of their oil-soaked rope shells. As they caught fire, they did not turn their *rajraj* on the women but dropped them to roll in the sand. Those who took off toward the water quickly learned that they were just fanning the flames and dropped to the sand as well, and that's when the girls and the women dropped to their knees and punched that single digit-long spike at the base of the aorak shell into the men's skulls.

"True, their champion got the best of my grandfather in their fight, but he eventually died by the same fate at the hands of the women. When he sat to cover his flaming legs with sand, my mother and her sister claim to have run at him and stuck theirs — from seasons of premeditated planning — into each of his eyes. He stood again and swung his massive *rajraj* wildly, but eventually he fell victim to the oil, the long *pāle* that lit him from a safe distance, and the fire that consumed him as it did the others. Mother still has nightmares of the fires and the stench of flesh boiling off their bones. They decided to let a few get away — to what fate, no one knows — but they have never come back. Not to say one day they won't, but these women stand ready to this day to fight for their daughters and their sisters, and they have counted on us men for very little since."

"Well, I understand now why your women are so bold."

"They are taught to be! Like the other women of Rālik, they hold and pass the land to their daughters, but they are also sworn to kill for them, which makes them more like warriors than women. In truth, they are the irooj and we are their workers. That is the true order of things here."

Ḷainjin said, "Then I promise to be a good worker for your daughter and hold her high above all others. My only problem will be adjusting to island life. As you know, I am a seafarer. I have crossed the ocean from east to west and back again. I have nightmares from memories I can never forget and stories I can never tell. I must confess I tried and failed to settle down with women among the islands I visited. I found I could not cope with the simple tasks of daily life, or take interest in the affairs of the villagers about me."

"I, too, have been there. Your ear is always turned to the wind — as was mine — and that is why I brought you here. This is our seamark, to stay or to sail away. It is from this point that we set our course through the waves and follow it unwaveringly to our destinations. My daughter Liṃanṃan has chosen you to navigate her voyage. All I am asking you now is to promise me that if, for any reason, you decide you cannot bear whatever burdens she places on you that you will return her here, where you started."

Ḷainjin readily agreed to such a simple request. Then, having told his story, Pedpedin rose and stepped back upon the reef flat to continue leading him around the island. The narrowness of the passageway between Lae and the island to the north where Kōkkālọk and her workers dwelled surprised him. It was funnel shaped, deeper than the reef flat, and rocky on the ocean side. Then it gradually became more and more shallow and sandy as it curved between the islets and approached the lagoon. There on the opposite bank, where the shorehead and coral boulders ended and the sun-bleached coral stones faded into white sand, was the beginning of a small village, where people raised their arms to acknowledge them. Facing the passageway was a magnificent-looking stilt house that he imagined was hers. It appeared curiously exposed to the elements. Finally, there on the shore, with its rickety-looking outrigger and unusually long and narrow kubaak was the pathetic Pohnpeian fishing canoe in which Paratak had somehow crossed the ocean. Its shallow, oval-shaped hull was completely open. "What an impossible trip he must have had in that thing, and what an unusual story of survival he must have wrapped up inside himself," Ļainjin thought. "How did he rest? He must have been bailing the whole time. How did he collect the water he needed to keep his strength?"

They continued along the shoreline passageway and then cut inland to avoid the hot and lengthy trek around the sandy point at the northeastern end of the unusually shaped island. Around the point where the channel flowed into the lagoon — he remembered from the day before — was the broad, sandy shoreline, but they headed instead into the cool breadfruit forest, which shaded an immense village of well over a hundred dwellings of the irooj's workers. The carefully cultivated nature of the island was impressive, and the lack of nonessential shrubbery fostered a neat and breezy openness. It reminded him of why the atoll dwellers of the many islands he had visited always preferred their habitat to the dense, cluttered foliage of the mountainous higher islands, despite their more abundant sources of water and fertile soil.

* * *

Back at the irooj's house, Liṃanṃan and her sister were again absent, but a crowd of relatives had gathered onto the mats beneath his stilted, thatched home. He politely left Ļainjin below and disappeared up into his house, through the single entrance in the middle of the floor. Ļainjin noticed two older men facing each other at a corner post beneath the house. They were rolling coils of fiber twine from coconut husk, and he sat down with them.

"*Wōjej!* What is all this? Are you two planning on rethatching the village?"

"It's about avoiding *eakpel*!" one of them joked. "In the middle of a storm, when the navigator looks for somebody to lighten the load, he's unlikely to choose the rope maker. When the navigator gets to shore, he knows he'll have to retie some of the lashings."

"I heard Litaknaṃ claim you were about to throw her overboard until her granddaughter grabbed your mast and changed your mind," said another, to uproarious laughter.

One of the women brought Ļainjin a basket of food and two coconuts to drink.

"But to answer your question, the irooj has commissioned the construction of a new house for you and his daughter," continued the first man.

"He just didn't say which daughter," interjected the woman who brought the food, to more laughter among the group.

"Choose me instead," cried an old lady with sagging breasts and missing teeth, sitting among others in the opposite corner. "Trust in experience," she continued, putting her hands on her hips and rolling them to and fro. That led to another catharsis of laughter. Then, sensing by his embarrassment that they had thoroughly integrated him into the group, they let him eat in peace.

"All this reminds me of the story of Jibke," exclaimed the first elder, whose name Ļainjin would later learn was Ļaluj.

"Ļōpako, have you ever heard the story of Jibke?" asked Ļaluj, as he took a few fibers from a clump of processed coconut husk and then rolled them between his fingers into a bunch that was a bit fatter in the middle and tapered at both ends. He then rolled the tiny bundle on the flat of his thigh into a hand's-length strand of string. Finally, he added a thinner end of this single segment to the thin end of the line he was making by likewise joining them into a line of uniform cordage. Later, he would have to twist two such lengths of cordage, with a rope-twisting device, into a single length of dual twine for lashings. This rope-twisting process could be repeated as many times as necessary if thicker rope was desired, but it all started with these single strands rolled on the hairless, calloused thighs of these old storytellers.

Ļainjin had, of course, heard the story in many versions, but he respectfully feigned unfamiliarity and asked, "How does it go again?"

"Well," Ļaluj began, "everyone knows that, when Jebrọ won the race, he became irooj of the whole atoll of Aelōñļapļap, and that atoll is second only to Kuwajleen as the largest atoll along the length of the Rālik string. After a few seasons as irooj, tired of judging disputes among his workers, the young Jebrọ decided to choose a woman, so he prepared his canoe for a voyage. But before he launched his proa, his mother, Lōktañūr, came down to the shore and placed a band of sweet-smelling flowers on his head. He sailed westward across the lagoon to the islets along the northern fringing reef. The wave from the east wind pushed him along as he sang.

Westward flow, fallow-low.
West flow north of sun — waow!
Follow down crest of wave
westward to flow.

"He came to the first islet, where he lowered his sail and slowly flowed with the current down the shoreline. The unchosen women ran down to the lagoon shoreline and, one by one, beckoned to him, singing,

What flows and smells — waow!
What perfumed oil so
bids me to beckon you?
From port side flow.
From starboard side flow.
Irooj of pure blood show
if you want me to
jump into
your boat and go with you!

"To each, he replied, 'I desire you but you're not my fate.' He hoisted his sail and continued to steer westward."

Ļaluj went on like this, enacting the story by chanting the part for Jebrọ and then raising the pitch of his voice to depict the women's parts. He repeated himself, naming all the islets along the northern reef of Aelōñļapļap Atoll. As there are many passageways between the islets there, sometimes Jebrọ searched the ocean side, sometimes the lagoon side. He was always looking for a woman to choose on his journey westward, but each time they called to him, he responded with the same answer: "I desire you but you're not my fate."

"Choose me, Jebrọ," cried the same elder woman, addressing Ḷainjin again. She put her hands on her hips and rolled them back and forth — again to much laughter.

Then Ḷaluj continued telling the story of how Jebrọ sailed on from islet to islet, dropping his sail and paddling until he came across a woman who had come down to the shore to wash off the soot from an earth oven she had just redug.

"Her name was Lenkar, and she was embarrassed to say anything because she was so filthy. Jebrọ, however, was smitten by her long, shapely legs and arms and cried, 'Do not bother to flap your mouth. Come aboard.' Realizing he was the irooj, she complied, and he hoisted his sail to turn back to Je. This time, the lagoon current was against him, so his first tack was through a passageway into the ocean, and his next tack brought him back toward a second passageway that he intended to sail through to reenter the lagoon. However, just as he was passing by the ocean side of one of the small islets strung along the northern reef, a small cloud released a very short burst of fine rain that caused the soot to streak and blotch her skin. We call that type of rain 'a shower of Jibke' because there is enough water to cover but not enough to rinse. It is not even enough water to bother gathering our sun-dried fish. This rain hexed his thoughts and compelled him to push her off into the water.

"Swim for your life. I have lost my desire for you and you're getting my proa dirty," cried Ḷaluj, enacting Jebrọ's part with much drama. He then told how Jebrọ subsequently sheeted in, sailed straight through the passageway into the lagoon, ended his search, and shunted his way back to Je. And he told how Lenkar began to swim toward the small islet where a man called Jibke lived.

"He and his mother had laid out a large sheet of *jāānkun* to dry in the sun, and they noticed the light shower that passed over. His mother said to him, 'Isn't this rain magic for your pool?' There was a pool of tidewater close to the ocean-side shore that heated in the sun at low tide, and on occasion, he would find a fish or two trapped there. So at his mother's insistence, Jibke took his spear and walked around the island toward his pool. He caught Lenkar bathing there. He was struck by her beauty and they chose each other immediately.

They had a quiet life together until, one day, Irooj Jebrọ decided to build a new house for himself and called all his workers to come and help. When the frame was constructed, Jebrọ climbed to the top among the others and began placing the thatch. Each thatch shingle was one ñeñe in length, and Jibke's task was to spear each shingle and pass it skyward to the men above. Lenkar's task was to sew the pandanus leaves to strips of coconut-leaf fronds for each shingle using the *ņok*.[109] Her thatches were so perfect that the men on the roof begin to compete for them, so she had to produce them faster and faster."

Ļaluj began to chant:

Jebrọ beguiled by skin so fair.
Young woman — ah! Pretty girl — waow!
His line is tangled, his lashing confused.
Is she woman one or
is she woman… Waow! Lenkar! Ooo!
Lenkar turn about Jebrọ,
sewing pandanus thatch — ten at a time!

Then, raising the pitch of his voice to portray Lenkar, he chanted,

Hurry you, hurry me, Jibke.
If you don't hurry you
the spirit will surely swallow you!

"When Jebrọ looked around at the men competing for her thatch, he noticed Lenkar, came under her spell again, fainted, and fell to the ground. When he awakened, he commanded Jibke to dig the corner post for his great cookhouse. Jibke dug down and then off to one side. He had not quite finished when Jebrọ ordered them to drop the coconut-trunk post. Jibke jumped off to one side just in time but dropped the coconut shell he had been digging with. They heard it crack and assumed that it was his skull. When they removed the post, he was still alive, so in desperation, Jebrọ commanded Jibke to bring him the wind. In other words, the irooj had banished him, but before Jibke left, he cut Lenkar a stalk of pandanus and promised to be back before she finished it."

---

[109] The midrib of a coconut leaflet.

Then, feigning Lenkar's voice, Ļaluj chanted,

He cut me a stalk of Ajbwirōk[110]
My lover, my Jibke — waow!
Sighing, I chew and toss
toward northern horizon — one core.
Sighing, I chew and toss
toward eastern horizon — core two.
Sighing, I chew and toss
toward southern horizon — core three.
Sighing, I chew...

"Lenkar sang on and on, counting like that to punish the irooj. His desire slipped away again, but it was too late for Jibke. His search led him into a whirlwind that smashed his boat and left him to drift up dead on the shores of Eb.[111] There, Lirukōb — the daughter of Irooj Rilik[112] — chose him and took him into her house. As the story goes, she truly loved him, but everyone on the island wanted to eat him. Every day, they cried,

Let us ba-bake him — waow!
Eat up his soul,
eat up his soul!

"Every day she refused to let them, on and on until even the small fish on the reef cried out,

Let us ba-bake him — waow!
Eat up his soul,
eat up his soul!

"When Lirukōb finally gave in to them — waow — they started a huge fire in a mammoth baking pit, but Jibke was unaware of what they were about to cook because he did not understand a word of their language. He even helped

---

[110] A particularly delicious variety of cultivated, edible pandanus fruit.
[111] Mythical cannibal isle far to the west.
[112] Chief of the west.

them gather wood and stones for the fire. Then, when the flames were spent and the red-hot rocks had sunk upon the white coals beneath, he was led up close to the pit to let the warmth of the oven entice his beaten soul. With much curiosity, he watched them cover over the empty oven, and he left, confused and sickened. When the oven cooled, Irooj Rilik divided Jibke's soul up among his people, and sent one basket to Lirukōb. She turned her back on Jibke and ate. When she finished and needed to wash her hands, she told him not to touch any of the food in the basket, but he was hungry and did not obey her.

"When she came back in, he was staring into the empty basket, and she cried, 'I told you to leave that basket alone. Don't you understand? That was your soul that they covered over in that oven!'

"Waow, suddenly he understood, and he told her they must gather flowers. He climbed up into the tree and tossed down flowers to her, but she sensed he was leaving her as he climbed up higher and higher into the tree, and she knew there was now nothing to hold him back.

"'Good-bye, my love. Good-bye, my love,' she cried as he climbed.

"Jibke said, 'You lie because you and your father

ba-baked my soul,
ate up my soul,
ate up my soul.

"Then," concluded Ļaluj, "he climbed out of sight and was never heard from again, among the islands of the living or the islands of the dead."

He had told the story well, and that was clear because the sound of his mild voice had quietly begun to dominate the gathering. The silence of the listeners hung in the air for several moments as each perhaps contemplated the story's significance to their individual life. "For who had not fallen in or out of desire, or taken one path instead of another, or challenged their fate unnecessarily," thought Ļainjin.

He said, "That story was well told, Ļaluj. Now I remember hearing it told by my grandfathers, and that part about the corner post was part of a similar story I heard on the other side of the ocean."

"Then tell us that version, please!" asked Ļaluj.

The others chimed in. "Tell us your story, please."

Ḷainjin, however, knew he could not tell his stories from out there without explaining what he was doing and why, so he cut them short.

"That must wait for another time. The story of Jibke has made me sleepy. I must rest now from my recent walk. Is it okay if I take a coil of your *ekkwaḷ*?[113] I have an immediate use for it."

"Take all you want," Ḷaluj said.

"Thank you!"

"For kindness!" said Ḷaluj.

Ḷainjin entered his house and lay down to rest. The empty earth oven, the eating of the soul… This imagery gave rise to thoughts normally left abandoned. He longed for Liṃanṃan to come to him. She alone seemed to have the patience to draw the story struggling to emerge from within him. She alone could be trusted to keep it. He felt perturbed when the others demanded to know his stories before he was ready to tell them. It annoyed him because it touched the sore that had become his life's dilemma. Of course, he wanted to tell his story. His story *was* his *soul*, and his story would live on only if others spoke of it. Yet how were they to learn the story from a man who had vowed not speak of it? After all, a man's story is all in the telling, so it must be well told — not announced like an answer to a question. It must ripen over time as a pandanus fruit hangs and slowly turns color, each kernel, from green to yellow to orange — as each kernel's nib changes from dark green to a lighter shade of green as the sun warms its surface … day by day by day. Break the stalk open too soon and its potential flavor is lost.

He had just paddled all the way from Namorik. While floating there, outside the reef in the black of night and with the patience of a mother turtle, he decided — more by instinct than reason — to turn silently away and journey on. He was not ready to tell all the things he knew his beloved Namorik companions would want to know. It was that simple. There was much more ripening to occur, and that is what led him here, where he would be unknown. *This time, he could not wipe away so quickly the memory of the upward swirl of her hair as he released her lifeless body and watched it slowly sink into the transparent blue.* He curled into a ball on his mat as though he

[113] Sennit; coir fiber line made from processed coconut husk fibers.

were Jibke, sickened by the loss of his stolen soul, yet he slept in anticipation of the night ahead.

He awoke that evening, tied his ring to his kilt, and grabbed the line of ekkwaļ Ļaluj had given him. Then he strolled down the path to the first coconut tree he had cut that morning, where a boy was waiting for him. As directed, the boy had also brought a length of ekkwaļ, so Ļainjin left his at the base of the tree and they climbed to the crown. Fortunately, the face of the once pointy utak where they had cut its flat end was still moist.

"You're lucky. This tree should produce much jekaro," Ļainjin told the boy. Then he showed him how to tie the ekkwaļ from the end of the bud to the frond below, bending it outward ever so gently. "As the moon passes, we will bend the utak day by day until it grows horizontal and drips its nectar into the largest coconut shells you can find — so start looking. Take each one to the ocean strand as soon as you can so the tiniest of the hermit crabs can crawl through the mouth into its interior and start cleaning the shell of its meat."

"What if a big coconut crab finds it and drags it off?"

"That's always a problem, so you must put out several at once. Always put out one or two small ones as decoys!"

Such was his advice to all the boys he found waiting by their trees. Some of their utak were moist and would be good for jekaro, and some were less so. Some were very dry, and he asked those boys to find another heavy-bearing tree for them to test the next morning. When he finally arrived at the last tree toward the end of the path, Etre was already sitting at the top, motioning for him to ascend. When Ļainjin reached the top, he could see from the boy's manner that something was amiss.

"Don't look now because I don't want him to know I told you, but I saw Paratak climb up into that pandanus tree just to the north of us," the boy said, slightly tilting his head in that direction. "I think he wants to kill you!"

"I think he wants his kilt back," replied Ļainjin. "Etre, remember this: the shark you must worry about is the one who comes in a rage straight at you. You may never notice it until it's too late. The shark that circles is too cautious to kill. Have you ever seen *ṃaanpā*?"

"No."

"Well, you might get your chance. Now take a piece of your ekkwaļ, make a loop, and tie it here around the utak, just below where we cut it this morning." Ļainjin cut two small notches on either side of the frond below the utak and tied a second loop with a slipknot around the frond. "Now we will bend it slightly as you tighten the slipknot to the frond below. Every day, you will tighten it just a bit. I'll shave off a little more from the end now, and we are done until tomorrow morning before sunrise. Don't be late."

He tied his ring to his waist and began to descend. "This battle must be quick and nonlethal. Why spoil the story of such a day?" he reminded himself.

"But...," began Etre.

Ļainjin considered the boy's eyes as he continued to descend the trunk. He lowered his brows and shook his head slightly and quickly to shut the boy up. From the concern in his eyes, he imagined that Paratak was probably below, but he continued his descent without glancing behind, intending to give his opponent the false impression that he had the advantage of surprise. When Paratak violently ripped his kilt from his waist even before he had reached the ground, Ļainjin turned and grabbed hold of it with his left hand. Then he swirled and landed on his feet, using the opposing pressure on the kilt to steady himself. There was an instant when both men's eyes met just before Ļainjin, stark naked, turned his eyes to the kilt and gave it a momentary tug with his left hand. That caused his opponent to assume he was about to engage in a tug-of-war, and he foolishly turned his concentration to the decoy, tightening his grip with both hands. Ļainjin pulled on the decoy with his left hand while shifting his weight to his opposite side. Then he swung the calloused heel of his right hand with tremendous force onto the left side of his opponent's chin. The powerful, unnatural sound of the slap reverberated into the forest. The slap dazed his opponent's senses and snapped his neck sharply to the right until the opposite side of his jaw met a slower-moving blow from Ļainjin's left palm. That seemed a kinder, softer stroke, but it was meant to steady his head for a final uppercut from the same heel of his right that caught Paratak on the chin and snapped his head back so violently that it sent him into a momentary but fateful lapse of consciousness.

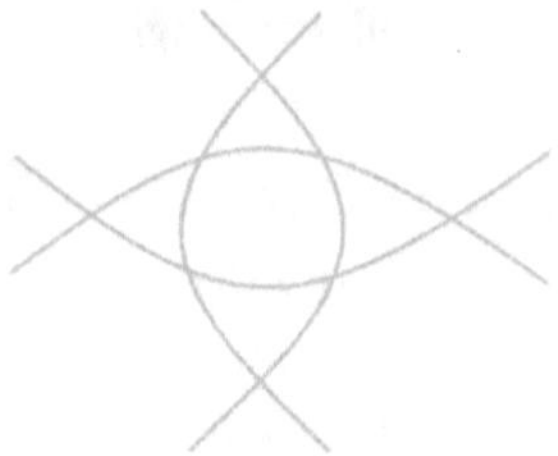

By the time he regained his senses and opened his startled eyes, Ļainjin had cut the *wapepe* image into the now-bleeding skin of his right breast muscle. His knees pinned down Paratak's shoulders and his manhood stared him in the face, and he had a length of ekkwaļ wrapped around Paratak's neck, threatening to choke the life out of him. He was about to saw the rough cord, with the intention of cutting deep into his neck when *suddenly the image of his friend sawing through the blood-spurting neck of their enemy flashed before him.* Ļainjin, remembering his grandfather's caution never to steal his opponent's dignity, abruptly and mercifully ceased. He stood above his astonished opponent — as naked and unashamed as the day he was born — and slowly tossed, up and down, the ring he could have cut his throat with. When he was convinced that Paratak had had enough of his message, he began walking casually down the path back into the village.

Etre, on his part, rushed to crowd in front of him to cover his nakedness. Ļainjin put his hands on the boy's shoulders, and they began to march in unison. Then Etre let out several sharp whistles and the other jekaro boys joined them. Shortly, other boys joined in as well until the surprised onlookers could no longer see Ļainjin's nakedness with the crowd of boys shielding him from their view. As word of the fight spread among them, the group began laughing as they marched. Then, as dusk fell, someone broke into the well-known *bọbo*[114] song, and the group began the dance before the many onlookers as they slowly pranced their way into the village, singing and pretending to swing pole nets back and forth:

A night to bọbo.
Chant and cry as
shiny-shadow fly by and
ka-pik-naaj-i-lọk.[115]
And turn around, around again,
and bọbo back across wind.

---

[114] Night fishing for flying fish with pole nets and torches of pāle.
[115] "Watch flapping wings from still water."

And tighten sail along before
silver-shadow soar.
And turn around, around again,
and bọbo back across wind.
And tighten sail along before
silver-shadow soar.

Throw me a torch, we'll
make light of the night.
Tangle up, he tangle.
Ok-kō-pooḷ-pooḷ-e.[116]
Twist pole again and
shadow catch, shadow catch, shadow catch.
Twist pole again and
shadow catch, shadow catch, shadow catch.
Tonight, our torch is burning.
The south reef flies with fish!
Tonight, our torch is burning.
The south reef flies with fish!

By the time they reached Ļainjin's house, they came face to face with none other than the irooj. He had his mother's sleeping mat rolled up under one arm and Liṃanṃan at the other. He was waiting there in the pathway, ready to deliver publicly what he had promised. Ļainjin, who had come naked to the occasion, remained confident, unbowed, and amused that all was coming together into a tale worth the telling. Liṃanṃan's long hair was tied into a bun, speared with the jagged barb of a stingray tail and topped with a crown of fragrant, oil-coated *kōṇo*[117] leaves and *wūt*[118] flowers. As his eyes met hers, such was their attraction that neither a thought, nor an action, nor an instant seemed to have passed since they were bonded by the spirit of the storm. Their throats were still as committed to each other as the day before, and their bodies drew together as she launched herself, without a

[116] To twist the pole and trap the flying fish in the net.
[117] A hardwood tree bearing orange flowers: *Cordia subcordata*.
[118] Large-leafed land taro: *Alocasia macrorrhiza*.

backward glance, into the crowd, splitting the boys one from the other as she passed, with the same determination she had exhibited diving into the water, when they first met. If surprised by his nakedness, she did not show it on her radiant face.

The group moved as one to the entrance of the house. Etre thoughtfully turned back and politely accepted the mat from the irooj, passing it forward above the throng just in time for Ļainjin to wrap it around them as they entered their sanctuary. There, he and Liṃanṃan successfully left the rest of the world behind them. As an afterthought, she turned back, grabbed a large basket of food placed inside the doorway, and handed it over to the boys, who immediately sat as one to eat at the side of the pathway. Ļainjin saw her eyes meeting those of her father as each nodded, "Well done." Then she reentered the house and burst into his arms, which quickly encompassed her. With their cheeks pressed against each other's, he twirled her off her feet, around and round, until she clung to his neck and squealed with excitement. At that point, he heard the boys outside break into laughter as they ate and surely agreed that he was a rare newcomer from whom they had much to learn.

Ļainjin swung her like that through the lamplit shelter and clear through to the open door to the starlit garden, where he scooped her up in his arms and set her down on the stone floor of the bathhouse. A sliver of moon could be seen in the western sky above the thatched wall of the enclosure. The giant clamshells were filled to their brims with water from the well, and grated coconut could be seen laid out upon smooth, green banana leaves. He grabbed a fistful, soaking it in the water, and scrubbed the bottoms of her feet with it. Then he washed himself as he had the evening before, only this time, as he stooped flat-footed on the stones, Liṃanṃan was there to scrub his back. She stood over him as she unbunned her fragrant hair, allowing it to cascade down upon him, and dried his face and neck and upper body with it. Ļainjin swept her up again and placed her wet feet on the matted floor inside. He watched them scamper across the mats from one oil-filled shell to another, quenching the lights and launching a brief puff of smoke from each. When he entered the darkening room, naked, all became secret but ripe with her fragrance and the sound of her skirts falling onto the floor beneath her.

The atoll

Peering into the room from the doorway to the garden, he stepped from the energetic noise of cooking fires and the haze that hung in the still night air above the surrounding village. With his broad, sun-darkened nose, he sniffed the smoke from the quenched lamps that curled throughout the thatched house. Then he heard her feet take traction on the matted floor of their dark harbor. The matting slid on the coral stones beneath the pressure of her dash toward him. He deftly pivoted in the starlit doorway and braced himself just in time to absorb her ecstatic leap onto his hip. She wrapped her legs about his waist, squeezed his head in her arms, and blinded him with her breast pressed into his face. Then she squealed loudly as he twirled her around again and once again, back to the sleeping mat her grandmother had given them. Dizzily, they collapsed backward, he first, she upon him as bravely as she had upon the storm-swept waters that night. The boys outside responded to her piercing cries with laughter as they politely sprang again into song, to drown the frolicking sounds of their renewed adventure.

After absorbing the falling bones, he felt the comforting weight of her slight body pressed against him as he had in the cramped hull of his canoe. However, this time, the luxurious private space about them and the scent of her long hair carried him to greater heights of intoxication as his rough hands explored the smooth skin on top of him. He was aroused but determined to follow her gently along whatever path her grandmother had taught her to lead him on, but then, as a youthful spirit might, she abruptly launched them back into the society he thought they had left outside.

"Likōkkālọk is telling everybody that you desire me so much you would not say a word to her!" she said excitedly.

"She's telling all the women they will embarrass themselves if they try to tempt you away from me. You would have expected her to lie and tell everyone she sat on you, but no. This time, she tells the truth, but she never tells the truth! How did you accomplish that?" she asked ... but went on without pausing for an answer.

"Lijoḷọk is peeved that Likōkkālọk isn't telling anyone about her part in drawing your seed to divert your passion. She is upset she will not be able to tell anyone about that now that Likōkkālọk has floated her self-humiliating story first. Who would believe her? What happened to your kilt? You did not kill Paratak, did you? What possessed you to strut down the path with no kilt on? That was the strangest thing any of us ever saw! Most men would have cut through the forest and snuck about the village. I am glad those boys were there to shield you. How did you become so popular with them?"

Patiently, he listened to her chatter, as he would the rustling of palm leaves during his jekaro regime. He repositioned her onto her tummy with her face against her grandmother's soft mat. Her injured palms were face up at her sides, and he rejoined her with her skin by poking the moist leaves covering the thick, slick ointment of fermented *nen* fruit wrapped around them and asking, "Does that hurt?"

"No!"

"Who applied the *wūno*?"[119]

"My grandmother," she answered, as he bent her leg at the knee and pressed her slim calf down hard into the back of her thigh.

"Do your hands hurt?" he asked. He slid the heel of his large hand into the ball of her small, calloused foot and inserted his thick fingers into the broad spaces between her toes, pressing down hard on her shin until she winced in pain from her stretched thigh muscles.

"No, the redness is gone, but she wants me to keep the *wūno* there tonight as a reminder."

"Reminder of what?" he asked dispassionately, as he repeated the maneuver on her other foot and leg.

[119] Medicine.

"She wants me to remember all her instructions."

"What were her instructions?" he calmly asked.

"You're joking because you already know! She told me to keep myself inside, to relax and keep my thoughts clear of everything else."

"Everything but what?"

"You know — what you want to do to me! All right, I am not going to say another word. Penetrate me!"

Ļainjin chuckled as he respectfully ignored her command, sat on his heels with his legs bent beneath him, and began firmly and deliberately massaging each bone of her foot, still moist from the coconut milk.

"How does that feel?"

"Good!"

"Does your body ache from the storm?"

"Oh, yes! Everything aches. I have been so tired too! I have been on my mat recovering this whole time! But I could hardly sleep with all the women coming and going and wanting every detail of our encounter." Then, changing the tenor of her speech to imitate the women, she said, "Is it true he chased away all the sharks as they circled about you?"

"You're probably exhausted from all the stories you made up!" he joked. She remained prone with her knees bent and her feet in the air as he systematically massaged and twisted the flesh surrounding each bone in her foot. After he finished bending, squeezing, and kneading it, he took the other foot and began the same, sensing that her tension was beginning to ease. When he had finished with her feet, he grasped hold of her legs, still in the air, below her ankles and suggested they play a game.

"I'll answer your questions, one by one, once you surrender your feet to me." He began by shaking them randomly back and forth. He would shake them and then stop, address one of her questions, and then shake them again to see if he could catch her tensing back up again. In this way, he used the competitive root of her tension against itself until he could pinch her skinny ankles and shake both feet randomly, in starts and stops, as he began to tell the story of how he met the boys, initiated their jekaro project, and rebuffed Paratak's attack. Each time she tensed up, he would stop and test her feet until she relaxed again, and then he would go on to explain why he walked naked through the village.

"I was taught to leave an enemy a reason to accept defeat. Paratak may feel satisfied by imagining he caused me humiliation. That may encourage him to consider the matter settled. If so, I will not have to fight him again. My *ṃaanpā* tricks are unlikely to surprise him a second time."

"But they'll say—"

"Does a shark..." He interrupted her, catching her feet as stiff as before they had started. "Does a shark," he repeated, "care what you say about it?"

"You *are* like a shark. Everybody agrees on that!"

"The faces in this village and the words that come out of their mouths will always be more important to you than to me because these are the people you grew up listening to. I listen to the ocean and pay attention to the moon's cycle and the way she governs all the living things about us. I have no interest in letting the people of this tiny place, or any other, determine what comes next. My story is *my* story! They will know the whole of it only if I, in good time, decide to trust them with it."

"So you don't care what they say about you?"

"I will never care what they say, but I will care that *you* care," he said, massaging her calves, "and of course, I want them to watch as our story unfolds, and to tell it as best they can when we're gone."

"They will tell a story of us! I will make it so!" insisted Liṃanṃan.

"You will be the beginning of one story but the end of another that must never be told."

"And I will dig the first story out of you … like … like Father opens the breastplate of the papa turtle and cuts out the green sack of bitter juice before baking."

"And I will cry just like the papa turtle does as you do it! And I will say to myself, 'How did I ever meet such a terrible woman?'"

Then he squeezed her calves hard, one in the grasp of each hand, and they continued the banter until he could flap her feet at will and feel the strain in her body lax, as would his proa when he eased her sheet and steered her a bit off wind.

She wanted to know everything about jekaro. So he told her, as he continued to press, twist, and squeeze her calves, how his grandfathers fed it to him as a substitute for his mother's milk. How they learned the process in Pit and then brought it to Namorik.

As the night wore on, he meticulously explained each jekaro procedure, how he would first hitch a knot at the base of the utak where it protrudes between the growing tip of the trunk and its frond, then wrap a tight spiral of twine — following the path of the moon — around the length of the utak, leaving a space no larger than a finger between each coil. How after a few days, it became necessary for him to slice away the sheath at just the tip of the utak and secure the last loop of the coil there before continuing to more tightly wrap the final three knuckles of the newly unsheathed end of the immature bud. Then how, twice each day, he would end all with a tight slipknot that held a freshly cut green leaflet, above which he would make a clean cut across the entire flat-cut surface of the soon-to-be-constricted bursting flower, causing it — after a few more days — to drip, drip, drip its clear and sweet amber nectar.

She questioned him repeatedly during his account, appearing to marvel at the idea of tapping into the immense power and strength of the majestic trees her maternal ancestors had planted — and then planted the fruits of — long before she was born. Yet, as he was earnestly describing these procedures, he was simultaneously massaging the skin beneath her thick hair, causing her scalp to shift about on her skull under the fingers of one hand. With the other, he was kneading her temples to center her thoughts inward.

"The secret of jekaro is patience. Not every man is suited. Women learn their patience from the sleeping mats that they toil to weave. First you cut the leaves off the plant, being careful not to stick yourself with the thorns that edge the leaves you will then singe in your fires, dry in the sun, and pound with your *dekein nin*. You travel many steps and plan them carefully. In the same way, a woman learns to plan her engagement with the man she has chosen, but most men are at loss for a plan. We lack patience. We are anglers who laugh at the patient one among us who sits in one spot and waits for the fish to come. Instead, we test the waters here and there, always searching out where they might be feeding. We learn the signs. We learn to evaluate the clouds, the tides. As they change, we change. We learn that the best plan is no plan. The best plan is to stay aware. So we forget to plan and choose to drift like a seabird scouring the surface of the sea for its next meal."

Then, with both hands, he seized the tense muscles in her neck where he sensed her tension was greatest, and she began to sigh in relief, "Ah, ah, that's good..." She slipped into a less questioning and more passive form of listening as — seasons ago — she had perhaps listened to Ļaluj recite his stories nightly before dreaming herself to sleep.

"Having no plan, many men become discouraged searching for the good tree. Others tire of perfectly good trees once they realize they must be climbed twice daily for nearly a moon's cycle before their nectar can be collected in full. Many cannot accommodate the early rise day after day. Others eventually suffer from boredom as their initial success turns into a daily chore demanded by others. The few who are successful drink the nectar themselves and share it with their chosen ones, and both become bonded by the gift of strength and nobility it bestows."

She lay motionless now, apparently content to listen without questioning. Her thoughts, he assumed, were concentrated on his fingers as they manipulated the muscles of her arms and wrists and fingers, and deep into the bones of her shoulders and back. Finally, he began working his way down her back by kneading the flesh surrounding each knuckle of her backbone. He continued to explain how she must rinse the rancid, white froth from the coconut shells and their nets daily, using the coral sand and stones from the seashore, and leave clean saltwater a digit deep at the bottom of each shell. He kept this one great secret to himself. He would use the saltwater to rinse the tip of the utak before cutting it. The saltwater was the magic needed to retard the fermentation process in the bound flower stems and wash away the bitter, white foam that would otherwise accumulate and burn them.

Then he reached the extreme tail of her backbone and massaged it with his thumb, deep into the crease of her buttock where he was sure she had never been probed before. She awoke from the trance he had inspired with a shriek and a giggle but soon succumbed to the stern fingers of his gentle hands.

Then he delved into the muscle surrounding the back of her thighbones, and deep into the bones beneath the ample, intimate flesh of the buttocks that bulged on each side of the intriguing crease that, unnoticed by her, was causing his manhood to stand, and sweat to begin covering his skin. He reached over her to prop open the thatched window at the head of their mat, allowing the fresh night air and its companion faint starlight, which reflected off the white coral stones surrounding the house to enter. He felt the comforting silence outside. The sounds of the village around them had long since turned quiet, and fewer words were spoken as talking was reduced to a one- or two-syllable reaction to his exploring fingers. She responded when it hurt, relieved pain, tickled, or seemed to heal a part of her body. He found bones she never knew were there, and after a while, they developed a language of their own, he with his strong hands and firm but gentle touch, and she with a painful recoil, a cringe, a sigh, or a tremble in response.

When he judged her to be completely relaxed, he straddled her, put his weight on one knee, and then deftly lifted and twisted her over in one motion. He began gently caressing her body with his mouth — slowly, deliberately, randomly, as if he were a starving man with great hunger inside but limited appetite from a shrunken abdomen. He tickled the erect nipples of her breasts with the hair on his chin that she had left. She, perhaps feeling his hard manhood caressing her thigh, clutched onto it with the eye of her injured hand. She eased it down between her legs, and clenched it tightly there between the bones of her thighs. She crossed her ankles and squeezed as hard as she could. Then their mouths met for the first time since the voyage. Her pointy tongue darted in and out against his, and each swam in the sea of the other as each soul attempted to escape from its body and creep into the body of the other.

Intoxicated as never before, he crouched on his knees, hanging hers over his shoulders, and bent her back until she was upside down. Then he began massaging her buttocks as he slowly parted her legs with thumbs burrowed deep among the bones he found there. He lifted the lips of her womanhood to his, and as she squealed, struggled, and pretentiously pounded his shoulders with wounded fists, he mixed the water in his mouth with the water of desire and passion that began to spring up from deep within her as she gave herself to him. There was no purpose for words, as his body alone attempted to convey all she wanted said. Her shrieks turned to sighs as his tongue dipped deeper and deeper into her little round well. Then her hips began to rock like a craft upon the crest of each oncoming wave until, after an indeterminable period, she uttered a final climactic sound of fulfillment.

It was a sound unique to that moment, and it reverberated out through the window into the village. However, by that time, the boys had long since returned to their parents' homes and lay curled in their mats. The night was silent, save for the occasional rustle of a palm leaf high above them or the squawk of a fishing bird returning late from far out at sea. The cooking fires had burned to embers and the village slept, so there was no one — other than they — awake to hear the raw, forever memorable sound that concluded her ardently and courageously awaited first night.

In the days thereafter, they were inseparable save for the time he was aloft among the palms with his young friends. It seemed to him that her every thought was about coupling with him, drawing his seed deep within her, and wishing to conceive. The nights were too short for his body to rejuvenate the seed she required him to provide, so they found secret places during the day to couple — amid the dense kōņņat trees that lined the ocean strand, or even hidden high among the broad, green leaves of the trees from which they harvested breadfruit.

His thoughts were more about the danger of childbirth, how to strengthen her with fish heads and jekaro. He borrowed her father's *joñ*[120] fishing pole, and she followed him in the evening to the ocean side, where her father had shown him where to pole fish. After, they would lay a soft nest of kōņņat leaves and couple there beneath the stars amid the busy chatter of the fisher birds. Then, in the early morning, Taknaṃ would gut the fish and roast them in her cookhouse on rocks still hot from the roasted breadfruit. When he returned from the coconut groves, Liṃanṃan would have eaten her fill. They would bathe and couple again in the privacy of the bathhouse — or take the chance of doing it on their sleeping mat in the hope that Joļọk would not rush in on them, as she was wont to do with fresh gossip about the upcoming battle.

[120] Mangrove: *Bruguiera conjugata.*

"Liṃanṃan! I just knew I'd catch you playing with your toy again," she would say, or "Father says Ļōpako must cut and season his spear before it's too late." Then, "He means a real spear! If that toy got cut off, you'd cry like a baby with no tit to put in its mouth!"

Everyone knew that the only place to cut a spear was in the swamp on Kōkkālọk's island. He realized this was a bone in Liṃanṃan's throat. Yet the longer he delayed, the more anxiety he would cause her father, whom he suspected was depending on him for fresh leadership.

Each night, the crescent of the moon in the sky appeared larger at dusk, and the time drew near for Ļainjin to distribute knife blades to his jekaro boys. He decided to show his treasure to her. So one afternoon, he waited for the sunlight to travel below the shade of the thatch covering his boathouse, thus illuminating the interior of the hull, which pointed inland. Then, while no one was looking, he allowed her to watch him crawl into the area where the two had first embraced. "I need to get knife blades for my boys," he told her, and showed her how to unlock the bulkhead that sealed the storage area Taknoḷ had created inside the prow of his hull, which was now somewhat illuminated. He backed out with an immense bulging *alele* that he then lugged with both hands through the garden and into the house. When he carefully emptied it onto the matted floor, Liṃanṃan appeared astonished. She had probably never imagined such wealth in one place. There were handfuls and handfuls of finely crafted fishing lures, hooks, sinker balls, stingray barbs, and immense shark teeth — as well as the pearl-shell knife blades he was about to separate out. This was obviously more than a trio of men could fashion in a lifetime. There were also broken pieces of the greenstone she used to trim his beard.

"Where did you get all this?" she asked.

"I traded for it."

"Traded what?"

"I traded sharks' teeth — mostly."

She picked up a large shark tooth. "What will this trade for?"

He scrutinized the pile carefully and began separating out the pearl-shell knife blades. After examining one carefully, he passed it to her. "That would be an even trade."

"What about this?" she asked, picking up a large, heavy lure of giant clamshell.

"That would take an eel."

"An eel!"

"You'd be surprised what Raipuinlang will pay for a large eel. The trick is, it has to be alive."

"Who's Raipuinlang?"

"The wealthiest chieftain out there."

"What does he do with the eels, eat them?"

"No, he keeps them trapped in a well on a stone islet they built on a reef."

"Keeps them for what purpose?"

"He keeps them to maintain the law."

"What law?"

"The law of the trade. It's simple. Once a man fulfills his half of the trade, the other must do the same."

"So if a man reneges?"

"A man can renege, but he has to return what he received or he faces the eels."

"How many have been eaten?"

"I asked that myself, but never found out."

"I would have found out!"

"Then Raipuinlang might have taken you to his islet on the reef, showed you the well they constructed over a cave in the reef below, and answered your question by giving you a little shove from behind. Hah!"

She screeched as he pinched her waist and squirmed from side to side to avoid his tickle, and they rolled about the matted floor as he continued. Then she put her chin on his chest, looked straight into his eyes, and in an almost peeved manner, asked, "So why didn't you tell me you had so much wealth?"

"Because then you never would have jumped in the water to save my life. You would have just drifted off with my treasure instead."

"No, I would have jumped anyway because I had already chosen you in my throat and I wasn't going to let you get away so easily."

"I think you just wanted to give me a good scrubbing because I stunk so badly."

"Well, that too, and all that hair needed to be cut off. What a mess you were! As things turned out, now I have you all prettied up and trapped in my house and I can have you anytime I want. And I end up with all your treasure anyway! See how smart I was?"

"Very smart! But a bit cocky, I would say."

"No, cocky is when you are stupid but only think you are smart!"

"No, cocky is when you are smart enough to obtain things but lack the wisdom to protect them. Wisdom comes with age, so sorry. By definition, you come up short!"

"Okay, man wiser than me. Try to obtain this!" She protruded her tongue and wiggled it at him, at which point he tried repeatedly to kiss her. But each time, upon luring him closer, she turned her head at the last instant to frustrate him.

"But is it smart to give all these valuable knife blades to a bunch of boys?"

"Yes, because they will produce a *jāpe* of jekaro! They have proven their loyalty to me twice daily. They are joyful and full of spirit, and because of their youth, they have no pretense because they have little to prove. When their jekaro begins to flow and the smart woman puts the nectar brought down from the swaying palms to her lips and feels the strength it provides, she will be happy with the bargain. Would it not be wise for the smart woman to present such a unique gift to Likōkkālọk when we ask permission to cut spears from her mangrove swamp? She will learn to crave the sweet amber nectar and become a baby sucking your tit in constant fear you might take it away. Such a smart woman can imagine the satisfaction of this type of trade."

"But you are forgetting about Paratak! He will be red with jealousy and surely attack you the moment you arrive with your jekaro."

"No *lerooj*[121] can stand by and let her worker attack another who brings tribute, especially since you will ask your father to accompany us. He needs the spears, doesn't he?"

"When will the jekaro start to flow?"

"It drips now, but not in earnest until the moon is full. Tell her we will pay her tribute on *jetkāān*."[122]

---

[121] Literally, "woman chief."

[122] The day the moon rises at dusk amid tree trunks.

"What is this?" she asked, holding a small bamboo arrow.

"That is a toy arrow that makes you sick like death. Be careful. It has a poison tip — or at least it did — and you don't want to scratch yourself to find out if the poison is still potent."

"Where did you get these?"

"Those are from a place far away, a place too ugly for your innocent face to imagine!"

"Ļaluj says you are like a giant clam deep below the reef with your mouth open just enough to allow fish to clean your mantle — but not enough to allow any man to reach inside and cut your secrets loose."

Then Liṃanṃan helped Ļainjin put his pieces of treasure back into the *alele* and sneak them back into their hiding place, and that evening, he presented the valuable knife blades to each of his jekaro boys, one by one. Each must fashion his own handle, promise to use the blade only for jekaro, sharpen it only with *tilaan*,[123] and wear it around his neck when climbing or slid into the thatch of his house when not. And each — above all — must be very, very careful not to let the fragile blade break.

That night and every night after jekaro, as the waxing moon traveled westward, he would sit on a mat with Liṃanṃan at his side and watch Pedpedin's men cross spears to the rhythm of the women's *aje* in preparation for the battle. He also watched the old man watching him, wondering why he had not cut his spear and why he was not participating in the practice. Ļainjin knew, however, that jekaro dripped from twenty trees and netted, hollowed-out coconut shells slowly collected their prize. Alliances had formed, and the impatient chief would value him even more once all the elements of his plan fell into place.

As days passed, the moon swelled by day and appeared higher in the sky at dusk. The tides were no longer right for pole fishing, so Liṃanṃan had his canoe launched and they went on nocturnal adventures. Nightly, after watching the men practice, the two of them crossed the lagoon and fished as they sailed along the submerged portions of the western reef, where there were no islets. They trolled for sharp-toothed predator fish that loved to attack his moon-illuminated lure from the darkness below as it streamed

[123] Pumice stone: a porous form of volcanic glass that drifts up on island shores.

overhead, above coral caverns teeming with competitors darting in and out of them. The lure was enticingly easy for them to intercept because of its predictably straight course. There was something spiritual about the glistening lagoon waters and the fluttering of her catch as it broke the surface and landed in her grasp. It was the competition, he supposed, which culminated in the transfer of energy from prey to fisher, that compelled the woman — and called her back again. He also loved seeing the spirit — which granted strength to the victor and swift death to her prey — well up from the depths below and shine at him through her glittering eyes. Her hands had healed and proved stronger and wiser for the scarring, and they competed to see which of them could name the fish by its method of attacking the lure, and its feel on the line as she hauled it in.

The winner of their competition — usually Liṃanṃan — would get to schedule the event and manner of their next coupling, which on some occasions occurred even before they returned to shore. She would cushion her rear with the thick mat taken from the outrigger platform and folded beneath her, resting it upon the yoke where the outrigger booms lay lashed to the hull. She, her legs spread and straddling the hull, tempting him. Her torso propped against the forward-slanted mast, feet dangling — now and then dipping into the waves, now and then desperately braced against the sides of the hull to leverage her slight body. Elbows straight bracing her torso, hands clasped to the bulwarks on either side, and her face uplifted — naked and abandoned of all modesty amid the flux about them. He, after so many seasons of standing alone at the helm, now before her, struggling to maintain his penetration, lifting his craft into the wind with his oar in one hand and determinedly clutching onto her rear to anchor himself to her with the other. Their billowing craft rising and falling with the uniformly rolling swells entering from the ocean passageway. These swells merging with the choppy, wind-swept waves that crisscrossed the shimmering lagoon and becoming one with the rhythm of their efforts. The thick, curling strands of her windblown hair flying free into their matted sail. They skipped across the water this way, he struggling to hold onto his seed until the very last moment of surrender and she maneuvering relentlessly to capture it from him and plant it deep into the damp, fertile darkness of her writhing belly.

* * *

As the days passed, one to the next, the jekaro began dripping in earnest. Ḷainjin taught the boys how to carefully guide the drip from the wet face of the utak down into the mouth of the netted coconut shell with a freshly cut coconut leaflet. Before allowing each boy to retreat from his yellow-and-green spiraled roost, he first had him drink his fill. Then he taught the boys as a group how to thoroughly wash the empty shells at the sandy shore and hang them out in the sunlight to dry. As each day passed, the boys grew stronger and all the villagers chattered about this phenomenon. Finally, Liṃanṃan visited Kōkkālọk on her island, intrigued her with a taste, and gained her acceptance of Ḷainjin's offer to bring tribute to her during the morning of *jetkāān*. All the elements of his plan were set in motion and ready in good time to be fulfilled.

On the morning of the appointed day, all talk was about the struggle that would ensue once Ḷainjin crossed the passage and set foot on Kōkkālọk's island. The boys all chattered about Ḷainjin's *ṃaanpā* skills and how they expected to see Paratak's head, slapped violently, drop into the sand as though hit by a falling coconut. Others predicted Paratak would not dare to appear. Still others repeated Ḷainjin's assessment that Paratak would not be easily surprised a second time and would have prepared a better defense. Everyone was nervous as they left the shady coconut groves and walked along the sun-drenched path between the shiny-leafed kōṇṇat trees at the island strand. They descended the canted rocky shoreline into the breeze that rushed between the islets and waded into the cool water separating them. Each, as instructed, carried a netted shell full to the brim with fresh amber jekaro in one hand and an adze for cutting mangrove in the other. They waded in single file behind Pedpedin, Ḷainjin, and Liṃanṃan. The sea level had been dropping quickly in the spring tide all morning, but the lagoon water, which recedes more slowly, was still higher than the ocean and streamed through the passageway — where it was swift and nearly waist deep — on its way to the sea.

Paratak was waiting for them, and when he stepped out onto the strand above the opposite shore, a collective gasp sounded from the jekaro boys, who now expected the worst from the furious face raging down at them. His eyes were concentrated on one individual alone — as though there was no irooj present and no tribute for his mistress. There was nothing but the hated person who had the effrontery to challenge him yet again and, this time, at the very shore of his domain. He twirled a thick spear in his hand recklessly as though he would hurl it at his opponent at any moment, but at the same time, Kōkkālọk was hustling down the sandy shore from her house, entreating him fruitlessly to step aside and let her uncle pass.

The irooj, their titular leader, appeared outraged but remained stationary and resolute. Only Ļainjin, in his shark-like manner, continued his progress through the water, unaffected by the bluster at the shoreline. He wore a confident smile on his face as he fearlessly closed the distance between them and then, just as everyone expected an eminent clash, extended his arm as only a Pohnpeian would and politely addressed Paratak fluently in his own language, in the manner of a long-separated brother. In this way, to everyone's amazement, he managed to nonchalantly disarm the surprised foreigner, cool his taciturn scowl, and transform it into a broad, childish grin. To the amazement of all, they stood with forearms embraced, in fluent, animated conversation in a language none of the others understood. Kōkkālọk's face turned from terror to relief even as she glanced at Liṃanṃan, whose anxious face turned likewise to surprise, as did those of the others, many of whom were too flabbergasted to feel disappointed at not seeing the spectacle lead to the blood in the sand they expected. Only the sage look on Pedpedin's face seemed to summarize the simple collective response that, no matter how this story henceforth might be told and whatever its end, Ļainjin appeared that day to be a man like no other.

Liṃanṃan rushed to embrace Kōkkālọk, who embraced her back, whispering, "There seems no end to this silent man's magic! We are so lucky you caught him out there!" Then she bowed as, one by one, the jekaro boys — some more intimately than others — hung their jekaro shells about her neck in ceremonial fashion. Finally, the strong woman was so weighted down that she struggled in the bright morning sun to cross the warm sand back to the food her workers had prepared for them beneath the shade of her house. One by one, she hung the shells at the corner post of her stilted, thatched home and, putting the final one to her lips, tasted the jekaro.

"Oh, it's so sweet. It's delicious," she remarked. Then she poured a shell for Paratak and another for the irooj and passed other shells around to her workers, and all agreed the drink was good to the taste. Paratak, who spoke in very broken Rālik and was used to acting out his intentions, became a bit of a buffoon, patting his tummy repeatedly after drinking and slapping his breast where Ļainjin had carved the *wapepe* symbol as if to suggest it was but a scratch between friends. With obvious self-depreciation, he then slapped his own face on either side while nodding to Ļainjin, causing laughter to explode, first among the jekaro boys and, with hesitancy, among the others. Finally, he grabbed Ļainjin by the arm again to demonstrate their new friendship. He filled a basket of food for him, sat down next to him, and engaged in frantic questioning, seeming to be a young boy at the feet of an uncle — or as one of the jekaro boys put it, "a sucker fish attaching himself to the side of a shark!"

Once everyone had eaten their fill, all eyes turned to the discussion between Liṃanṃan and Kōkkālọk. Everyone knew the purpose of the visit, and all were waiting for Liṃanṃan to request permission to cut the spears. Instead, Liṃanṃan suggested Kōkkālọk sponsor the group herself. The boys, under Ļainjin's direction, would practice nightly here on her island and represent her in the battle. Kōkkālọk, it seemed, was about to dismiss the idea. After all, they were only boys, but then — as everyone but Paratak knew — she had lain with several of them and could hardly dismiss them as such. Was she perhaps weighing the workforce and resources necessary to support such a group? How, under the circumstances, could she refuse? For a brief instant, she looked perturbed, almost angry. She peered at Ļainjin. He did not feign distraction — which would have been easy, as Paratak was blabbering at him full wind in sail — but rather had attentively focused his eyes upon hers and wore his normal curious, self-confident expression. With a lusty grin, she looked at the boys and declared, "Yes, I will sponsor these men in the battle! Go cut the spears! Let the practice begin!"

Although practice could not begin for several days, selection of the spears took the rest of the afternoon. Paratak led the way. He visited the place often as it reminded him of his native island and he had a taste for the crabs that lived there. The tide had now receded to its lowest ebb, making navigation easy. What was not easy was finding perfectly straight *joñ* trunks. Most of the easy cuts around the edge of the little swamp had disappeared over the seasons, and the hard wood was slow to grow back, but eventually each boy — under Ļainjin's direction and despite Paratak's histrionics — succeeded in finding an appropriate trunk to sever at its base. The cuttings would stay on the island. Although they were immediately useful for practice, they needed skinning, sharpening, hardening by fire, and drying in the wind — not under the harsh sun, which could cause splitting — until the sound of their clacks, one against the other, reached the appropriate tenor. According to legend, the arrhythmic clack of the spears at practice drew the women to the battle, and their frantic beating of their *aje* and their ululating cries transported their men into a detachment so fierce as to cause their opponents to cringe at the sight of them.

Late that afternoon, they returned to Lae. High in the palms above the village, each boy seemed to have his own version of what had transpired, but all boasted that, if Likōkkālọk allowed the daughters of her workers to participate, many babies would come of it! Customarily, women participating in battle often felt the need to reward one or another of the men immediately thereafter. In short, the boys were ecstatic and ready to follow Ļainjin to death in this new adventure. Word spread that their parents marveled among one another about how this man, who had drifted up but a few days ago, had affected such change and provided such direction for their sons so quickly. Ļainjin warned them to a man not to stay up discussing girls but to sleep well because there was much practice ahead. Few of them had practiced before, the spears would get sharper and harder by the day, and they would have to be ready to enter a state of absolute alertness so as not to become injured and embarrass themselves before the very women they desired.

No doubt, the days began to pass quickly for these young men, especially those who attended several trees. They got up at dawn to wash their netted coconut-shell containers, and then they climbed their trees, cut their jekaro, waded or swam through the surf to Kōkkālọk's island, practiced hard under Ļainjin's fierce direction, and returned to their homes just before having to climb again and then sleep in preparation for the following day. On occasion, one of the boys would assign his jekaro task to another, spend the night on Kōkkāḷọk's island, and surprisingly pop up in line with a grin the next morning. As each day passed, they found more trees, cut more utak, collected more jekaro, and offered more to the villagers. Not surprisingly, more boys begged Ḷainjin to join the group. Each day, the spears grew drier and harder, and the sounds of their clacks when crossed grew sharper. The young men grew stronger and more alert, and the daughters of Kōkkāḷọk's workers got trained by their grandmothers to beat the drums and ululate with more and more passion. Soon, the perusing and trysting began in earnest, and the young women who wrapped their thighs with such politeness while participating in the battle dropped their long, intricately woven skirts with abandon deep in the pandanus patch and laid them down as a cushion upon which to couple with whichever warrior they chose to entice away from the group. Thus, the young warriors would replace themselves with a new generation. Everything seemed to occur as it should, and when Pedpedin heard reports of all this, he was no doubt happy and embarrassed that he had ever doubted the newcomer's leadership.

* * *

Over time, Ḷainjin began to wonder if he would ever see the Chief again. Curiously, his companion had glided his way into Ḷainjin's very identity, and he missed wondering what it must be like to soar among the clouds. He missed him more than he did his old friends and had been remiss in not searching for him on the bird islets. The Chief might be hungry, hurt, or worse.

In his conversations with Paratak, Ḷainjin learned he had a passion for eating lobster. This creature was a delicacy on his home island. Although abundant in the maze of coral reefs dispersed about the island's periphery, they were difficult to pluck from their natural homes deep among the corals. They could only be gathered in abundance by sailing or paddling out to certain of the outer barrier reefs that encircled the island, and by custom, such catch would go only to the high Pohnpeian chiefs. Before *iieḷap*[124]

[124] Literally, "big time"; spring or extreme tides during full and new moons.

passed, Ļainjin planned a fishing trip to seal their friendship and teach him how to catch lobster on the reef flat. Ļainjin assumed the foreigner, for good reason, was rarely if ever invited to participate in fishing activities by the other islanders. Competition for environmental secrets was keen among men who used such knowledge and the success it fostered like birds that preened themselves before prospective mates. He decided that, with Liṃanṃan's help, they would sail down the reef during the darkness of *meloktok*,[125] wait on one of the farthest bird islets for the tide to ebb, and search for his missing companion in the moonlight. Then he and Paratak would walk back to Kōkkālọk's islet gathering lobsters as the reef's edge flooded and as Liṃanṃan returned the boat to Kōkkālọk's islet to wait for their arrival by foot.

That evening the three set out as the sun was setting. As they glided between the first two islets along the atoll's eastern fringing reef, Ļainjin had a lucky strike on his trolling line almost as soon as their craft picked up wind. It was an *ikaidik*[126] longer than his forearm. He pulled in the bright rainbow-striped fish just as the glow of the sun sank into the cloud-mottled horizon beyond the western passageway that they had triumphantly entered what seemed like but a few days before. Then, as the sun dropped between the line of clouds and the sea, its final glow burst, casting the happy scene in an aura of amber light. He grabbed the energetic fish from the water and killed it with a tap of his club as they glided under Liṃanṃan's tiller along the lagoon side of the northern fringing reef, which was studded with islets.

Many of the small islets passed were populated by only three or four families, and the scent from their cooking fires wafted out on the firm breeze into the lagoon. As they passed to leeward, they took turns guessing, by smell, what food was cooking.

"Ah" said Paratak softly, "That is — how to say — green breadfruit you roast until black and scrape with broken shell?"

"*Kwanjin!*"[127] answered Liṃanṃan, smiling from her place at the helm. She was naked above the skirts, as was her like, and the setting sun burnished

---

[125] Night the moon rises so late it can be forgotten.
[126] Rainbow runner: *Elagatis bipinnulata.*
[127] Char-roasted, unripe breadfruit subsequently scraped clean before eating.

her flawless auburn skin in its fading glow. She wore a tight white necklace of sun-bleached puka shells about her neck, and her hair was twisted into a haphazard bun to prevent its strands from tangling in the backstay.

"Yes, good one to dip in guts of coconut crab. I like that one."

However, there were things Paratak did not like, and he had an annoying way of comparing everything on the low islands he found himself trapped on to things he preferred on the much larger, mountainous island where he grew up. He never seemed to stop talking about the abundance of delicious crabs that lived among the vast mangrove forests surrounding the island's irregular, swampy shores. Spoiled by the abundant rainfall and freshwater streams of his home island, he hated to bathe in the somewhat brackish water he pulled up from Kōkkālọk's well, and he was constantly describing the concept of a waterfall in broken Kajin Rālik[128] to dumbfounded islanders who had never heard of a stream or seen a mountain.

"Breadfruit — good, but taro, much better. Sinks in stomach like ballast. Breadfruit — taste all right, but float in stomach. Never done eating!"

"You mean *pọljej*[129] doesn't fill you up?"

"That ripe one baked in coconut milk? Yes, that one is good, but you need to eat that with crab and not enough crab here to fill stomach!"

"He has a way of turning every conversation back to his own unhappy predicament," thought Ļainjin. He decided to press the argument he'd had many times with high-island people. Paratak was sitting on the bow deck facing them with his feet dangling down into the proa, silhouetted against the rapidly fading light on the western horizon beneath the sail behind him. The lagoon water lee of the windward fringing reef was relatively calm, and the hull jettisoned hardly a drop as it rose and fell and rhythmically cut into the gentle ripples generated by the light wind.

"Don't the crabs eat shit when your people defecate in the swamps?" questioned Ļainjin, half laughing as he leaned back across the outrigger platform on his right elbow and mischievously glanced toward Liṃanṃan at the helm.

[128] Language of the Rālik Islands, now the western chain of the Republic of the Marshall Islands.

[129] Ripened breadfruit filled with coconut milk and baked in a breadfruit leaf.

She squinted back at him like a mother cautioning her child to behave.

"Forbidden to defecate in swamps!"

"It is also forbidden for the children to pee in the streams as they bathe," said Ļainjin, "but who knows if they do?"

Paratak appeared frustrated. His persona was to appear above everyone else because he came from a bigger, more advanced place with a more sophisticated culture. Everyone had always been in awe of his tales of freshwater and endless taro pits and villages made of stone with the help of countless workers. No one had ever suggested such a place had flaws, let alone someone who had been there. The suggestion took him a bit aback. A sense of fear crept over his face as though he feared Ļainjin had lured him away to revive their grievances and kill him out there. He began glancing about as though he was perhaps looking for a weapon that Ļainjin might be ready to use on him.

"True, we have too many people to count. Lots of shit? Yes." He smiled reticently. "I agree, better to defecate on reef. Ocean surround everything and make clean." He looked at Liṃanṃan, who had her ear turned to him but was busy watching the wind in the sail. "You people of low island are lucky you are few. Much space — many fish to eat — strong women like no man has ever seen before!"

Liṃanṃan gave him a smile and a cute scrunch of her nose, and they all laughed very hard at this — Paratak especially, as he had proudly demonstrated that he was not without charm. As the tension eased, Ļainjin asked Paratak if his father was a fisherman.

"Oh yes! My father taught me how to fish beyond reef with long line for big-eye tuna."

"What did he use for a hook?"

"He had many he earned from his chief. My father never lost a hook. He was very good fisherman. Once he went into the water when big tuna pulled outrigger into air but managed to keep hook and fish."

"But what was the hook made of?" asked Ļainjin.

"The best! Same as your hook."

"*Kapwōr?*"

"Yes, that's it."

"Where did the *kapwōr* come from? Who fashioned the lure?"

"Okay, you are right! Come from people of low island. True, low island make much wealth, but no one wants to live there!"

"What did he accomplish for his chief to earn the hooks?" asked Liṃanṃan.

Ļainjin knew well the answer to this question, but he was curious to see how Paratak would respond.

"He delivered stone at appointed time."

"Just a stone?"

"Big one."

"How big?" she persisted.

Ļainjin interjected. "You have no idea," he said.

"Stone long as this boat."

"How did he carry a stone that large?" she questioned. She sounded skeptical.

Paratak looked toward Ļainjin and raised his eyebrows, deferring the question to him.

"You can't carry a stone that large. You cannot imagine how large they are. The stones have flat sides. Most have six. They are too heavy for twenty men to carry. They sort of paddle them around placing skids beneath them. It takes many days of intensive work."

Paratak followed along and demonstrated Ļainjin's words by holding up six fingers and then digging the back side of his hand into the air, smiling and nodding his head repeatedly in agreement.

"Six sides. How did they grind stones that large?"

"Nobody ground them. They are just that way!"

"Nan Sapwe make that way," added Paratak.

"Who is Nan Sapwe?" she asked.

"He make *jourur*,"[130] he replied.

"The stones differ in length and size," said Ļainjin. "Strangely, they break off from the mountains that way — with six sides. Pohnpeians say the thunder does it. You have never seen anything like them. Pohnpei is clearly a special place, but my point is that they look down on us even though we

---

[130] Thunder.

provide the tools for them to accomplish all this. We give them the adzes to cut the logs and to fashion their fishing canoes. We give them the blades for their knives, the barbs for their fishing spears, and the hooks for their lines, and we deliver all these things to them. Truth be told, they do not even know how to navigate, and their chief treats us like heroes because we cross the ocean to trade our wealth. Only the chiefs seem to realize that if it were not for us — we of the low islands — they would lose control of their people and their way of life. Yes, taro is more nutritious than breadfruit, but you will sleep all day if you do not eat fish. You can't eat crabs every day either. You need hooks and lures to fish."

"But what do they use these stones for?" Liṃanṃan asked.

"They build their great village on the reef with them."

"On the reef?"

"Yes, it is called Nan Madol. That is where we trade what we bring. At high tide, we enter the village in our boats. The village has paths of water at high tide. The stones fit tightly to enclose the mostly coral landfill, and they prevent the islet from washing away. It's a village like no other. Their houses are much larger and pitched higher than you could ever imagine. They are so large they take days to thatch, and the walls surrounding them are of stones the size of which you could never imagine. It is a trading settlement built on the reef of an island that is so high its mountains reach to the clouds. Every day, men arrive in their foreign crafts speaking different languages from all over the west and the south, and they trade and watch them lay the stones. The village keeps half of what we trade as tribute to the chief. It is the most exciting place anyone has ever seen. There is nothing like it anywhere else, you can be sure of that… Except maybe Kosrae. Paratak, have you been to Kosrae?"

"No, but Kosrae small island, no compare. Their builders came from Nan Madol. All agree no equal."

"Where is Kosrae?" asked Liṃanṃan.

"West of Namorik. If you drift off from Namorik in the windy season, that is where you end up. During these days of Jebrọ the opposite is true."

"Ļainjin, I want to see the stone villages. Take me there!"

Paratak and Ļainjin both laughed together at her request. Paratak responded first. "That trip not for women. Too dangerous!"

Ļainjin, though he knew Paratak’s statement to be untrue, nodded his head in agreement all the same to tease her.

“I’ll trade Ļainjin to a Pohnpeian chieftess! I will get a good price for him, don’t you think? Then I’ll sail home with my fortune.”

They both laughed at her joke.

* * *

Night crept upon them and its breeze dried the sweat of the day. The first stars began to appear in the clear sky. They turned silent as Ḷainjin’s thoughts drifted back to his days paddling about the canals between the stone islets at Nan Madol. Limanman concentrated on making headway toward their still-distant destination, and Paratak lay back flat on the rising and falling deck, his back cushioned by the two flat coconut-leaf baskets Kōkkālọk had woven for his catch. His legs bent at the knees, and his feet dangled through the forward hatch into the hull. He contentedly dozed off, periodically breaking the silence with a single snore that caused him to wake once or twice and peer about to remind himself of his surroundings.

Finally, their craft began to slow as Limanman steered them into the lee of the islet of their destination. The sleepy boat sounds of wind in the sail, and surging and slapping water, and the gentle creaking of their boat gave way to the chaotic squawking of the seabirds commanding the squat kōṇṇat forest of this stark, uninhabited place. It was surrounded by patches of lagoon back reef, wave-abraded coral stones, sand, and periodically outcropped shorehead. The malodorous, dank smell of fresh guano filled the air and reminded them they were but intruders upon the desolate pile of poop amassed by this horde of noisy inhabitants.

As the tide was in process of receding, they had only to beach their canoe where the shimmering lagoon water, gently rising and falling, sloshed upon the stony sand. Ļainjin loosened the halyard, lowered the yard, and carefully flaked the boat’s sail. He left the sail with its spars to hang and waft gently in the faint breeze and then inserted his fingers beneath the gill of a dead fish and lifted it off the outrigger. Paratak grabbed his baskets and slung one over each shoulder. Limanman removed her *alele* of fire-making implements from the dry place in the hull where she stored them, and the three of them left their craft and headed around the islet toward the fresh breeze of its somewhat less squawky, windward side. Ḷainjin had already asked and been told there were no *ak* to be found on these islets. If the Chief was there, he would expect to find him in plain sight, roosting amid the shore-most kōṇṇat branches. That is where he searched, to no avail, as they continued around the islet. Soon they began to hear the distant sound of the living reef crest absorbing the force of the ocean swells rolling upon it. This was followed by the rushing sound of the white starlit water swishing shoreward upon the reef flat, which assured Ḷainjin that the tide was receding. The black sky was so ablaze with countless points of light that, for a brief instant, each no doubt realized that they had indeed momentarily forgotten that all was about to change.

Then they reached a stony spot on the ocean side of the strand that was midway above the high-tide mark and well oceanward of the chalky, bird-infested forest of the interior. Ḷainjin laid the fish upon the still-wet shorehead of dead, fused coral overlooking the beach, and both men crouched beneath the kōṇṇat branches and entered the dark thicket to gather dry wood for their fire.

Liṃanṃan, on her part, sat upon the stones above the shorehead. She opened her *alele* and dug out her gift from Ḷaluj, a small ball of *bwijinbwije*[131] that she planned to use as tinder. Next, she withdrew a loosely tied fire bow of two hand lengths; a hardwood fire spindle to be inserted into a loop in the bow string; and a rounded, palm-shaped cap of hardwood with which to hold it and drill into the softer, sun-dried kōṇṇat wood that Ḷainjin had tossed upon the rocks next to her. He had split the dry branch in two with his ring, and she peeled out the soft, white center with her thumbnail and positioned it under the heels of her feet. She adjusted the bowstring — which was just long enough to create a single loop for the spindle — squatted, and began frantically drilling the dry wood beneath her feet, chanting:

---

[131] A by-product of the rope-making process; densely packed strands of coconut husk fibers too thin for rope making; used for kindling as well as washing.

Sear stick, blow coal,
fire flame, so fear me!
Eat fire, eat stick,
eat Lairi, fart!
'Where do you come from, Lairi?'
'But from your fart, my dear!'

When she could smell the scent of smoking wood, she drilled all the harder in hope of begetting a tiny coal on her first try. Soon she dropped her drilling implements, covered the smoking kōņņat branch with the ball of *bwijinbwije*, bent low to the shore, and gently blew into the fibers until white smoke began to rise from the hair-like ball. Then she placed the smoldering ball between two pieces of dry coconut husk that she snatched from the *alele* and began wafting the tinder through the air with both hands. The smoke became thicker, and the husks' cores turned red as she blew between them. When they flared, she placed them on the sun-bleached stones above the tide line of the rocky shore and covered them with the sticks the men had piled next to her. Eventually, she inserted her fire-making implements back into the *alele* and removed a dry, trimmed breadfruit leaf that she used to fan the smoldering pile of tinder until it inevitably, suddenly burst into flame.

Soon the fire was roaring. Liṃanṃan began choosing rounded stones the size of her curled index finger and gathered the hardest ones into a pile. Paratak lay down again on his baskets away from the heat of the fire, and Ļainjin took the fish out on the reef to clean it. As he crossed the reef flat and looked back at Paratak resting in the light of the fire, he chuckled to himself over the frightened look on his face when he had asked him about shitting in the swamps — as though he were a boy again and his mother had caught him squatting in the wrong place. "Should he ever start bragging about the crabs again, a little smile on my part should suffice to stop him in midspeech," he thought. He had the feared Pohnpeian eating out of his basket, which was exactly where he wanted him.

He stooped over a puddle of water, laid the fish in it, slit its belly, removed the guts, and rinsed the fish in the clean salty water. He looked across the flat to the reef crest where the live corals bathed by the breaking swells rose as shadows against the starlit foam splashing over them, and he imagined the lobsters slowly retreating into the crevices of the caverns between them. They had just started eating the green reef moss, too small for most men to notice, but had had their meal cut short by the moon that ruled their behavior. It was about to surprise all and suck away the remaining water in which they waded, and he imagined them retreating knowingly into their crevices beneath the waves and impatiently waiting for the tide to turn before crawling shoreward upon the reef as red ants would probe the strand at the scent of a dead fish cast up by the high tide.

"*Kok, kok, kok, kok!*" he chanted, to tease them. "Paratak has a big basket for you," he whispered in good humor, as he turned, chuckled, and walked back toward the firelight reflected by the reef puddles scattered across the flat. He inhaled the scent of the stark landscape about him. He had been at sea so long that he had forgotten the smell of a reef laid bare by the receding tide. "It is good to have the chance to smell that once again," he thought. Mulling the chances he had taken to fulfill his destiny, he watched Liṃanṃan covering the fire with stones as he returned with warm feelings for her and especially for his mother, whom he felt had somehow guided him to her. Now if only he could adjust to island life and all the pretense and drama that came with it, a life he was sure his mother, too, had wished she had settled for but been unable to return to.

Liṃanṃan had killed the flame of her fire with the stones, and much smoke was swirling about. Each noticed for the first time the faint glimmer on the eastern horizon that announced the moon's ineluctable rise into view. Then Ļainjin rushed up to the fire as though to warn them of some danger.

"Paratak, do you hear that?" asked Ļainjin.

"What?"

"Listen carefully! Don't you hear it?"

"Hear what?" said Paratak seriously, turning his head to and fro. He faced Ļainjin as though he was the wind and he had to immediately set his tack to escape the danger — listening intently, no doubt, with one ear turned to the roar from the reef's edge, the other to the downwind chatter of the sea birds.

"There it is again!"

"Where?" Paratak responded with a splash of fear drenching his face.

"Out there! The lobsters are calling!"

At that point, the heavy smoke of Liṃanṃan's fire broke wondrously into blaze and illuminated Paratak's face the instant his fear faded into embarrassing relief as he accepted the brunt of Ļainjin's joke. The sympathetic upward look on Liṃanṃan's smiling face erupted into laughter as their eyes met and he realized how thoroughly Ļainjin had fooled him. Jagged white stones stuck to the black of their backs as both men dropped to the beach and rolled with uncontrollable laughter.

"They are calling the name of the great Pohnpeian seafarer!" continued Ļainjin, interrupting himself in hysterical laughter as he struggled to continue. "They all want a ride in his baskets, but most are sad that only the biggest will be chosen!"

The joke was as slow to pass as the night. They continued to chuckle as the light grew in the eastern sky and gradually replaced the multitude of stars that had thus far illuminated their adventure. Their fire burned down into coals beneath the stones that cooked their savory catch as it simmered and smoked and spit its juices. Had what started in misunderstanding, rage, and fear settled into bonds of friendship? This is what they most likely pondered as the three sat silently, sharing their meal and, now and again, returning to friendly laughter. They watched the moonlight grow from the enormous oblong ball that patiently rose through a narrow line of clouds to create, as though summoned, a path of light directly toward them across a vast expanse of ocean.

"What meaning your fire chant? Eat fire, eat stick?" Paratak asked Liṃanṃan.

"We women of *kapin meto* always sing that chant when we make fire. The chant comes from the story of Lairi, who lived on the atoll over there." Liṃanṃan pointed northward toward Wōtto with her nose. Now he lives in a story our grandfathers tell us when they want to put us to sleep."

"Tell me story. I want hear."

Liṃanṃan was still picking over the head of the fish she was eating and had just loudly slurped an eye from its socket when she raised her left hand high to the sky, almost as though imploring him to stop pleading.

"Wōtto is shaped like the back side of my hand" she explained, turning the back side of the eye of her left hand toward him. "See this?" She set the fish down upon the clean stones before her and traced the inside of the cup between her left thumb and index finger with her right. "That is a lagoon-shaped reef on the northern, ocean-side edge of the islet. That's where Lairi lived because it was the perfect spot for his favorite activity, *bwilbwil*.

"Every day he would make a toy proa and sail it up and down the beach, and every which way across that reef. He hardly ever ate during the day because he was so busy running around. At night, he would light *pāle* and club fish on the reef. Then he'd cook his catch there on the ocean side, just like we are doing now.

"There is one little islet just west of Wōtto, along the northern reef where a spirit called Likoropjen lived. She was one ugly woman. Every day, she'd watch Lairi running around the reef, making her dizzy just to watch. Maybe she was a little jealous because she could not run. Her mouth was a wind trap, and she'd trip over her ears. Anyway, one night of no moon, she watches him fishing by torch light and decides to put an end to his nonsense. When his *pāle* burns out, she sneaks up on him from behind." Here, Liṃanṃan changed her voice to mimic Likoropjen's gruff tone and chanted,

Lairi, Lairi,
kupañ[132] *club in water*
next to rock.
Badet[133] *club in water*
next to shore.

"Then when he turns, she asks him politely, 'Where is your fire stick, boy?' He answers, 'Here, my dear!'

"Then she asks, 'Where is your rub stick, boy?' He answers, 'Here, my dear!'

"Then she rubs the sticks together, chanting,

Sear stick, blow coal,
fire flame, so fear me!
Eat fire, eat stick,
eat Lairi.
Fart!

---

[132] Convict surgeonfish: *Acanthurus triostegus.*

[133] Banded sergeant fish: *Abudefduf septemfasciatus.*

"When the fire flames, he sees how ugly she is. She is quick to eat him, but he is just as quick to escape.

"'Where do you come from, Lairi?'

"'But from your fart, my dear.'"

"Now Lairi has seen how ugly she is," Ļainjin said.

Liṃanṃan continued. "And she's afraid he'll start spreading rumors about her big … you know! So the next night, same as before," she said, and by tradition, repeated the tale and the song two more times with the same exact result.

Ļainjin interrupted. "Then, on the fourth night…"

"Some say the fifth…" Liṃanṃan said. "Anyway, she finally gets this epiphany—"

"Or maybe she just gets desperate."

"And she starts eating rocks. In fact, she ends up eating a large chunk out of that islet…"

"And now you should see it. It's like no other," Ļainjin added.

"And that night she's after him just like before, only this time, she's moving a little more slowly because … you know!

Lairi, Lairi,
kupañ club in water
next to rock.
Badet club in water
next to shore.

"Then when he turns, she asks him politely, 'Where is your fire stick, boy?'

"He answers, 'Here, my dear!'

"Then she asks, 'Where is your rub stick, boy?'

"He answers, 'Here, my dear!'

"Then she rubs the sticks together, chanting,

Sear stick, blow coal,
fire flame, so fear me!
Eat fire, eat stick,
eat Lairi.
Fart!

"But this time, Lairi is stuck among all those rocks she has eaten, and he can't sneak out her butt. But he is one man who knows which way to turn. He has a shell knife stuck beneath his kilt, and he starts cutting his way out!

"So she sighs,

I eat islet,
but my stomach feels fine.
I eat Lairi.
So skinny and
bony, he looks silly.
Now my stomach hurts so-ooo...!

"He cuts and cuts and by morning, she's dead and he's out playing on that reef again — Lairi!"

Paratak was amused by the story, of course, and came up with the questions most children would ask.

"Why ear so long?"

"Well because, like a reef bird, she had a long neck, of course."

"How could she eat so many rocks?"

"Well, because spirits can do all kinds of things."

After a while, Ḷainjin left the other two to carry on discussing the silly *bwebwenato*. He continued along the ocean shore and then slowly, very carefully searched for the Chief in the kōņņat branches along the islet's northern side. He belatedly returned to his boat from the opposite direction, carrying a few large *kiden*[134] leaves he had torn from a branch along the way. The tide had left it stranded on the lagoon shore of the islet, far above the gentle, incessant ebb and flow of the smooth lagoon as it sloshed restfully upon the beach. Far to the west across the shimmering lagoon, he could see a white line of Kāliptak swells breaking upon the isletless reef where he and Liṃanṃan had trolled during the nights past. He could see cooking fires — too many to count — comfortingly blinking at him from the westernmost and northernmost islets of the atoll, reminding him of the immensity of the distance he had traveled out there beyond the refuge of the coral barrier now

[134] Soldierbush: *Tournefortia argentea.*

protecting him. He nostalgically retrieved the fat log of *jāānkun*, now nearly depleted, that had sustained his latest journey and sliced off a chunk that he cut into three pieces. Then he wrapped each piece in a leaf.

Yes, it was good to be among others, but it took such effort. The simplicity of solitude was a constant enticement to him, and the Chief's companionship was so simple by comparison. Where was he?

"Ak! Ak!" Ḷainjin cried out, revealing only to himself the hidden reason for their trip. He inwardly feared he had irretrievably lost him during this recent, unexpected turn of events. "Ak! Ak!" he cried again, in a vain attempt to pierce the incessant chatter of the birds that were circling, landing, and flying in all directions about the islet. "What is all this clamor about?" he wondered whimsically. "Are they fighting over their places to perch? Are they calling to their mates and their children, or are they just announcing their positions to prevent collision as they swarm?" Would the terns respect and accept his friend into their community, or now that he no longer commanded the sky, would they treat him like a misfit? Could he assimilate on an islet such as this? His kind had their own islets that they returned to from birth, but Ḷainjin had eaten his parents, snatched him away, and disrupted his nature. "Nevertheless, he would be perched now, dreaming. He would be lost in his bird thoughts and unlikely to appear anyway," he concluded. Ḷainjin had been gone a long time, and his friends were sure to wonder what he was up to.

As he approached the fire, he launched a mysterious-sounding chant that he knew would be gradually heard by the others as he closed the distance.

U-waak tak-li![135]
Come from west to place where
they ba-baked my son there.
They cook-cooked his soul there,
under that tree called kiden.
Kiden, what kiden?"

By the time he joined them, Liṃanṃan, still preoccupied with sucking the cheeks and the brain from the head of their catch, eagerly joined in the

[135] Answer floats eastward.

chorus of the famous fable. Then she began her second tale of the evening as Paratak listened, eager as a young child.

"Story of Ujae," she began, as she tossed the inedible portion of the fish skull upon the smoldering coals of her fire. "You know, back there" — she jerked her head and pointed toward the direction of Ujae with her ear — "is one island like you have never seen, surrounded by reef. Only one narrow beach pointing toward the lagoon. The windward reef is wider than the islet, and it's not a small islet. It's as big as Lae. That reef is home to many octopus! Except octopus are not like here. A fish out there must be eating their arms and making them stubby. You catch them just like here, by jabbing a stick down into their hole until they creep out. They say you can find the sticks of our ancestors scattered all over that reef, or at least the representation of them. They call them *kina.*[136] *Kin*[137] of two old women.

"They wake up one morning, and like every day when tide is low, they walk out to gather food on the reef. And one says to the other, 'Girl, have you ever seen such a low tide?'

"That's when the women are surprised to hear Ļōppeipāāt answering them from the reef. He is one huge octopus!

So what, low tide!
I don't hide!
Two of you take me,
two of you bake me,
two of you eat me!

"Woman asks him,

'Fuel for your fire of what?'
'But marjej,'[138] *he answers.*
'Rock for your fire of what?'
'But tilaan,' he answers.

---

[136] Archaic shoals left by the old women in the story of Ļōppeipāāt.
[137] Fire sticks; the small piece of wood is used to scrub the larger piece to make fire.
[138] A spindly weed: *Wedelia biflora.*

'Leaf to cover your oven of what?'
'But atat,[139] *of course!'*

"So they take him and do as instructed, but *marjej* is only a weed and does not make a hot fire. *Tilaan* is too porous to stay hot once the flame dies, and the *atat* leaf is too small and thin to prevent heat from escaping. Once the fire burns down and the oven is ready, the women toss him in and cover him up. Then they gather coconuts and grate them, singing,

Kicking down coconut.
Many falling,
grating, grating.
Kicking down coconut.
Many falling,
grating, grating.
Too much than, too much than…

"They set a *jāpe* of grated coconut aside and sleep a bit and wait for their friend to be baked. When they estimate the time is ripe, they uncover the oven, but he is gone. He has shit in the oven and crawled away! So they take pieces of dung and eat a bit with coconut.

"Next morning, they wake up and walk, like before, to the ocean side.

"'Girl, look how low the tide!'

"But Ļōppeipāāt taunts them again,

So what, low tide!
I don't hide!
Two of you take me,
two of you bake me,
two of you eat me!

True to tradition, Liṃanṃan went through the three identical episodes of the story until even Paratak could answer when she asked, "Fuel for your

[139] A plant with small, thin leaves; the stems of this plant, *Triumfetta procumbens*, were processed to make skirts and kilts.

fire of what? Rock for your fire of what? Leaf for your oven of what?" He even joined in with the other two in the "kicking down coconuts" chorus. Then Liṃanṃan continued telling Ujae's story.

"Finally, in the fourth episode, when Ļōppeipāāt answers '*marjej*,' one woman whispers to the other, 'He's lying, better hardwood *kōñe*.' When he answers '*tilaan*,' she says, 'He's lying, better *dekā ajaj*.'[140] At last, when he answers '*atat*,' she whispers, 'He's lying. We'll use *wūt*!'[141]

"This time, their oven gets red hot, and he screams, 'I burn, I burn, I burn!'

"'Cover him,' cries the smart one.

"'Ah! I burn, I burn, I burn!'

"'Cover him!' she repeats, as they laugh and laugh and laugh and then sleep a bit while he cooks in the steaming oven. When the time is right, they uncover the oven and there he is, all red, soft, and delicious. They start to eat him with the coconut and laugh, laugh, laugh until their sides ache. Then gradually, almost imperceptibly, from a far-off edge of the reef, comes a mysterious sound of chanting…

U-waak tak-li!
U-waak tak-li!
Come from west to place where
they ba-baked my son there.
They cook-cooked his soul there,
under that tree called kiden.
Kiden, what kiden?

"One woman asks the other, 'Girl, what is that I hear?'

"'Nothing' she says, 'Keep eating. That's just the tide coming in.'

After another two rounds of chanting in which all three participated, Ļainjin asked Liṃanṃan, "Girl, what is that I hear?" At which point she jumped up, pointed toward the reef edge, and shouted, "There she is, the mother of the thing they baked! Paratak, run for your life!"

---

[140] The heaviest, densest, palm-sized coral stones.
[141] A flowering plant with large leaves: *Polyscias guilfoylei*.

Paratak laughed. "Not so easy trick second time."

"The women quickly cast lots to see where is the best place to hide. Top of pandanus tree? No. Under coconut leaf? No. Run to lagoon? No. Finally, they cast that the best place to hide is in the attic of their house. They climb up their ladder to the single entrance in the middle of the floor of their stilt house and ready their shell knives.

"When the first tentacle of the thing creeps up through the door, they cast their chant,

Arm poke through, one, two.
Saw it and saw it
and set it aside.
Arm poke through, one, two.
Saw it and saw it
and set it aside.

By tradition, Liṃanṃan went through the chorus eight times and was joined by both Ḷainjin and Paratak. All of them pretended to saw off the tentacles with their hands as they sang. Finally, she ended the story by stating that, arms spent, the thing limped back into the water, disappeared into the sea, and was not likely to return until its arms grew back — which, for a thing that size, could take hundreds of seasons.

Then Ḷainjin gave a slice of the *jāānkun* to Paratak first, then to Liṃanṃan. He hoped the sun-dried pandanus mash would round out their meal of just fish.

"Our ancestors called us people of the northern islands ri-bōb[142] because we ate so much pandanus."

"We no eat pandanus on Pohnpei. We no like," said Paratak as he pinched off a piece of the wedge and popped it into his mouth. "Waste of time to chew. But this" — the tone of his voice was changed by the gooey substance as it clung to his teeth and the roof of his mouth — "good, no core to catch in teeth! But this good! No hair! Good for voyage! I wish I had on voyage from Pohnpei, stay more strong! True this never spoil?"

[142] Literally, "bones of pandanus"; Pandanus people.

Ļainjin bit into the gummy substance that was both tart and sweet at the same time. It reminded him of the hundreds of lonely meals he had made of it out there, and of his companion who had not shared his ability to sustain himself from it. "This is … I forget how many seasons old. It has seen sun and rain and ocean water and it's still good. It was made and traded, then perhaps retraded by who knows who a long time ago, a long way from here."

"Oh, we have saying," responded Paratak. "When lips crack, you know you have drifted through Rālik, but when you drift through Ratak, you won't know because you are dead!"

"Well, that's — let's say — another difference between your people and mine. Your people don't see the wave patterns between the islands, but we do!"

"See better from eating this?" asked Paratak, curling his lips and showing the dark red substance glued to the front of his teeth.

"No," said Ļainjin, chuckling, "Know where the islands are because we recognize wave patterns they create in the sea."

"I saw only misery at sea! I will never cross ocean again! I will die dry, sleeping on mat in house with children to water my lips."

"Well," Ļainjin teased, "if you do return to Pohnpei, you must claim a high title with that *wapepe* symbol I marked on your chest."

He reached over and traced the dark scars he had carved on the Pohnpeian's chest with his index finger. "These represent the four swells that converge on an island in mid-ocean."

"What island?" asked Paratak. He was stretching his neck like a preening bird to view the clean lines with which Ļainjin had marked the symbol.

"Any island — you must imagine one. It does not appear because it is not significant compared to the immensity of the four horizons that encompass it. They are curved because they come from the four directions on the horizon surrounding the island."

"I thought this magic to kill me!" replied Paratak, grinning with relief as he fingered his scar.

"No, not at all. My friends and I tried to explain the symbol to Raipuinlang too, but he did not show any interest in the navigation symbol either. I traded under that symbol and left the island after he granted me the title Jau Areu[143] and the islet Idedh[144] in compensation for all the *dāp* I caught for him. My title is there waiting for me, but I don't care to return now that I follow this North Star, so now I give it to you!"

"Idedh? Why me?"

"Because no one knows what happened to you! Every day your father looks out at sea and wonders what happened. You must return and receive what you have accomplished."

After a while Paratak asked, "Joke like lobster, right?"

"I'm not joking, my friend! I promise. When you appear before Raipuinlang, mention my name and show him that symbol. He must fulfill his side of our agreement and either title you or cheat on his trade and — by his own law — face the eel pit."

"What law?" asked Liṃanṃan.

"Trade cast is last!" the men replied together in Pohnpeian.

"What does that mean?"

The Pohnpeian looked to Ļainjin to interpret. "Like when the *ri-kwōjkōj*[145] casts your fate. There is no recast. By their law, you cannot recast a trade. It is completed. It is over. All trades are final. No reneging allowed."

The aura of suspicion on the Pohnpeian's face began to recede gradually as he stared back at Ļainjin in the moonlight. Ļainjin saw he realized he was the recipient of an enforceable Pohnpeian bargain, but would he prove brave enough to accept it? He was no doubt studying the man shark, who had swum with the great men and spirits of the ocean only to show up by chance here, on this tiny, remote sandspit, to offer him a high title from his homeland. Ļainjin could imagine the questions in Paratak's mind.

That was when Ļainjin reached out to him again — in Pohnpeian fashion, arm to arm — and finally found confidence in the gleaming, night-black eyes that peered back in an unexpected bond of friendship that men only rarely share.

"Paratak, it sounds like Ļōpako has made you an *aḷap*,"[146] announced Liṃanṃan.

---

[143] Pohnpeian title: master fisherman.
[144] One of many man-made islets on the reef off the coast of eastern Pohnpei.
[145] Literally, "bones that cast fortune"; fortune teller.
[146] A paramount landholder who manages land on behalf of an irooj.

"I hear that word before. What mean?"

"That's one of Likōkkālọk's titles; it is something she can carry for life and can pass to her daughters. Like a little chief with dominion over territory, she is entitled to some of whatever they bring to the high chief. It is basically the same as Pohnpeian titles — you get tribute."

"Paratak, I'm jealous! He should have given me the title! Here, Ļōpako, scratch one on my tit so I can get tribute too!"

"No! No! Do not mar your beauty. Scar for old turtle like me! Ļōpako bring you tribute every day. No need scar!"

"Then I'll have him make me an eel pit, and if he breaks his bargain, I'll push him in," she responded.

"Only one problem, lucky for Ļōpako: no stones," Paratak said.

"Then I'll have him throw the eels down a well," she argued.

The men looked at each other with laughter in their eyes and then turned to Liṃanṃan and responded.

"You must build on reef," said Paratak.

"Sea eels cannot drink well water," added Ļainjin.

"Oh, so you two are in absolute agreement on this! Well, I am going to consult with Likōkkālọk. We may build it in the passageway between the islands — big enough for both of you! Ļōpako, how did you catch the eels for this high chief whatever his name? No tricks allowed this time! Paratak will be my witness if you lie to me!"

"If I tell you how I caught the eels, do you promise to grant us a pardon and not throw us into your pit with them?"

"I promise to consult with Paratak, and if he agrees you are telling the truth and if you show me, not just tell me, I will agree to spare your life. However, you must still bring tribute to me, twice a day! I need fattening up!"

The two men looked at each other with laughter still in their eyes. "If you show her how to trap eels, she can catch herself and we have big trouble," Paratak offered.

"But If I don't show her, we get no pardon and we are in bigger trouble!" Ļainjin said.

"We caught either way."

"Trapped like eels ourselves," Ļainjin agreed.

"Women of Rālik too demand."

"They give us no rest."

"They moon," Paratak cried. He laughed and pointed to the round, white ball shining at them in the clear eastern horizon.

"That is right! We are the tide forced to chase after them to and fro!"

"No rest!"

"They can't even make up their minds! They call us to shore, and as soon as we get there, they send us away again!"

"Very demand!"

"Not at all like women of Pohnpei, wouldn't you say?" Ļainjin said.

"No demand," the Pohnpeian responded.

"That's right, and they treat us like chiefs! Every night they rub us down with coconut oil."

"And bring shell of *sakau*[147] from flat stone that sing out."

"Right, and..."

"Enough! You men stick together like a circle of pathetic baitfish! That is why you are so easy for us women to catch. Now stop stalling, and show me how you caught those eels for that chief surrounded by all those Pohnpeian female sucker fish!"

"All right, I'm going to demonstrate. Here, you be my eel."

Ļainjin took one of Paratak's baskets to cushion her rear and sat her down upon large boulders on the shore just above him.

"Pretend this is the crevice at the reef's edge that you searched out and found and made into a home that you never want to abandon. You will eat every fish that enters your little domain. The waves are breaking on the reef above you, and there is much current. You sway your head back and forth as the current swishes in and out of your crevice so your prey gets used to seeing you move back and forth and is less likely to escape your lunge when you make your move to grasp it. Go ahead. You must sway your body to and fro like an eel."

Liṃanṃan began swaying back and forth, carefully keeping her legs tightly covered by her skirts in deference to Paratak as she sat above him.

[147] Kava; a drink with anesthetic properties made from the mashed roots of the propagated *Piper methysticum*, or pepper plant.

"No, not like that — put a wriggle into it! Use your shoulders more!"

Giggling, she began to sway in a slow, squirming motion, and Ļainjin rushed up the strand. He cut a stick the length of his hand and the thickness of his thumb and began to sharpen it at both ends as he watched her swaying about on the rock. Paratak started laughing at her, but that only seemed to encourage her the more.

"Come and catch me, man shark," she dared. She opened her mouth, revealing her perfect white teeth in the moonlight, and then made a ridiculous face that made both men laugh.

Ļainjin made a notch toward one end of the sharp stick. Taking the fiber cord from her fire bow and securing it at the notch, he told Paratak to stand by at the ready with his basket and resumed his instruction.

"First we need to change that mouth! You have the mouth of a turtle. It works like this." He demonstrated by hinging his large hands at the wrists and opening and closing them.

"This is your mouth talking all day with your sister," he joked. He kept his wrists hinged and clapped repeatedly as he encouraged Paratak to play the part of her sister, Joļọk. Ļainjin began imitating Liṃanṃan talking to Joļọk, and Paratak imitated him.

"Paratak, stop talking and ready your basket! Liṃanṃan! Why have you stopped swaying? You must enchant your prey with your movement, back and forth, back and forth. That's better!"

Ļainjin stood back and watched his silly-looking actors as they played their parts in his little demonstration. He laughed to himself and wondered what these antics would look like from the perspective of an onlooker. "Surely, this little play would memorialize their adventure on the reef like no other," he thought, as he glanced at the moon. It had shrunk as it rose but was now illuminating the vast expanse before them and reflecting up from the calm, glistening puddles of water spread across the desolate reef flat in both directions.

"An eel's mouth," he continued, "works like this." He demonstrated again with his hands. This time, he unhinged them at the wrists, moving one up and one down and back together again to demonstrate how an eel can grasp and hold onto something much larger than its small mouth.

"Liṃanṃan, your mouth is too small. Use your arms to extend your eel body and pretend your hands are your mouth. Do not stop swaying! Remember you are doing a little dance to mesmerize your prey."

"Paratak, you stop swaying! You are not the eel here! You must stand ready on the reef to entrap this thing once I coax it from its hole in the reef!"

"Ready now!" cried Paratak.

"All right, now both of you keep this up while I fetch my bait."

Both continued to enact their parts, with Liṃanṃan periodically pretending to lunge at Paratak and him pretending to respond by threatening to cover her with his basket. Both continued to laugh at the other's silly poses as Ļainjin rushed back up the strand to break a terminal cluster of leaves from a kōņņat branch.

"This is my delicious-looking fish," he explained, opening the slipknot at the end of the bow string. He tied it to the stick he had sharpened at both ends, slipped it over his hand, and tightened it around the wrist that held the fish of leaves.

"Now here comes the fish," he announced, holding the stick in his hand but concealing it beneath the leaves. "Liṃanṃan, keep swaying to entice the fish leaves to come closer. Now you are ready — lunge at the fish and clasp hold of it!"

She clapped her hands over the fish leaves, and at the same time, Ļainjin pivoted his hand, causing the stick to twist vertically and preventing her from pressing down upon his hand.

"That hurts!" she cried. He pulled her toward him off the rock, which she abandoned without hesitation to alleviate the pain in her hands from the sharpened stick. At which point Paratak threw the basket over her head. He hugged the feisty, squealing woman with much pleasure on his face as Ļainjin tugged on the twine and freed the pointed stick from her grasp.

"Paratak! Refuse to release her until she grants us reprieve from her eel pit!"

"Okay! Okay!" she cried, as his little demonstration came to a satisfactory end. The trio settled back down and made themselves as comfortable as possible on the cragged coral stones. Liṃanṃan kept Paratak's basket as a prize and placed it below her to soften her nest. He did the same and Ļainjin sprawled out upon the stones, happy enough, just this once, to be perched above the ocean and not amid its constant flux. The tide was almost out. The coral caverns at the reef's edge echoed the incessant plunging sounds of the swells thundering into them and then sucking the water from their shallow cliffs before flooding them once again with splashing, moonlit froth.

"Paratak, tell us the story of your journey from Pohnpei to Rālik in that tiny canoe of yours."

"That, was one big mistake!"

"A big mistake because you ended up here, or because the cause of your voyage was due to a mistake!"

"Yes!" he answered, missing the distinction Ļainjin was trying to draw from him. "Fishing was too good!"

Ļainjin had suspected such. He knew a root cause of much misfortune at sea was a fisher not heeding the weather looming about him because his attention was absorbed elsewhere. Not so the navigators, who pride themselves on planning their every move based on the surrounding sky. "Paratak's voyage was a lucky one despite the hardship, but was caused by a poor decision," he thought, and then considered dropping the inquiry, assuming Paratak would prefer to tell the story among men — suspecting, of course, that a woman like Liṃanṃan would prove incapable of keeping the Pohnpeian's admission of foolishness to herself.

"Fishing good — catching fat, black-brown fish with big mouth," he continued.

"That must be Paratak's way of describing the fish called *kūro*,"[148] Ļainjin thought, then cringed at the idea of having to sustain himself by eating such a fish raw. He hated eating the uncooked, soft flesh of fish that moped about the bottom of the lagoon, preferring the more muscular flesh, when eaten raw, of the fast swimmers or even the reef chewers.

He offered to change the subject. "You mean *kūro*. Did anyone ever tell you that you can catch that fish by the boatful in the passageways to the ocean during the moon preceding añōneañ?"

---

[148] A species similar to the brown-marbled grouper, *Epinephelus fuscoguttatus*, which spawns seasonally in atoll passageways and in lagoons close to the passageways.

"No understand añōneañ," replied Paratak.

Ļainjin was about to elaborate on one of his favorite subjects when Paratak interrupted him and returned to his story. "Bad weather all day — many cloud," he began, waving his hands above him as if drawing clouds against the background of the clear night sky. "My father warns me, no good to fish" — he scrunched his brow and shook his finger to demonstrate his father cautioning him — "but I take his canoe because my family need fish to eat." Paratak trailed both hands, palms cupped, behind him, pretending to pull a canoe by its outrigger platform across the sand. "That one is strong canoe, but not to sail." He pretended to paddle. "I paddle but wind too strong for favorite place to fish so I paddle downwind. Then I set anchor to fish. It is good to fish, that place. By afternoon many fish but wind more strong and cloud…" He pointed his index finger to the sky again and whistled as he flicked it forward repeatedly to demonstrate how quickly the clouds were passing overhead. As he held his hand out in front of him, he began demonstrating waves on the surface of the water by repeatedly scooping his fingers down and then up. "Enough fish! Time to go home," he continued.

Ļainjin recognized these signs as characteristics of a *ļañ eļap* in the making. Paratak couldn't have been directly in its path or he never would have survived, but the gradually increasing wind and the upper clouds streaming faster than the wind generating the surface waves below were both classic signs, and he knew exactly what was coming next. Paratak had trapped himself!

"But no can pull up anchor!" Paratak pretended to paddle furiously and then placed his imaginary oar at his side to pull on an imaginary anchor line to no avail.

"What was his problem?" asked Liṃanṃan, captivated by the panic Paratak was trying to demonstrate.

"His first mistake was to fish too long and allow the wind to trap him at anchor."

"How?"

Ļainjin explained. "He can't reach a vantage point to release it. Every time he paddles to where there is enough slack to release the anchor stone lodged in the coral below… By the time he lays aside his paddle and grabs the line, the wind carries the canoe back and blows his anchor line taut again. He's stuck."

"Why can't he just cut the line?"

"Well, if he loses his father's anchor line, his father will be proved right in warning him not to go fishing. He has caught many fish, so he has accomplished his goal despite the rough conditions. He wants to try once again, and then once more. It becomes a matter of pride," Ļainjin said.

Paratak nodded. "Yes, yes, I have father's knife. Father has many knife but only one anchor line. So I keep trying to free, but wind gets stronger and stronger and now my arms hurt and sky getting dark and I'm all—"

"Frustrated out of your mind," Ļainjin said.

"Oh, no, *now* he cuts the line! Now that it's too late…" Liṃanṃan said. "He should have just stayed—"

Ļainjin cut her short with a frown.

"Now too late," conceded Paratak, his head between his palms, his elbows on his knees. He'd been seemingly transported back to the instant after he cut the line and his canoe blew off, like a leaf in the storm. "I paddle hard but wind and wave push me out into ocean."

Now Paratak had reached the part of his story that Ļainjin had been curious about. He asked, "How did you ever survive in that tiny fishing canoe?!"

"Paddle into night but still drifting out to sea. Wave break on bow and make water into boat so must bail." He went on repeatedly depicting the paddling and the bailing and demonstrating increasing weariness as he continued. "So one by one, I must throw away my black-brown fish." He portrayed himself reluctantly tossing away his fish, a difficult task and last resort for any fisherman or survivor who realized they will have one less fish to eat.

"Give me one," interrupted Liṃanṃan, interjecting a little levity into the Pohnpeian's sad story. He chuckled as he pretended to throw her a fish.

"This would have made a marvelous meal for your family," she went on, pretending to bite right into the middle of the fish and then pretending to eat it.

"Then my father speaks to me and tells me to tie bailer to one wrist and my paddle to other and tie my knife to outrigger boom."

Ļainjin broke in. "Just in time," he said.

"Just in time," Paratak nodded. Next wave swamp canoe, and I jump into water to bail out and then again and same again until I realize cannot paddle. I cannot stay inside boat! Must tie wrist with loop under outrigger platform, hang in water, and let wind carry."

"Oh, Paratak, that was very, very smart! That made up for everything you did wrong. That was perfect! Liṃanṃan, do you understand what he thought to do?"

"No."

"He gave up his futile attempt to paddle back to the island, so he put his boat into a dead drift with his kubaak naturally facing the wind and his hull no longer pointing into the waves. That prevented any further swamping. Then he tied down everything he needed to survive. He got into the water next to his bailed canoe. He tied the leftover anchor line to his wrists, strapped himself to his outrigger platform with his arms slung over his hull, and just hung there. He was resting with his head suspended out of the water, but his body was drifting under his boat as the waves pushed it along. His weight lifted his kubaak and probably even helped to prevent his hull from swamping again. Very clever, Paratak! How many fish did you have left, after all the swamping?"

"Eleven."

"When did you start to eat them?"

"Right away. I ate two first night!

"During one night, you ate two raw *kūro*? That is disgusting! That's like gnawing off both your feet," Liṃanṃan joked.

"I cleaned them. I skinned them. I ate them — all of them. What would you do?"

"I'd dry them in the sun and ration them day by day," she answered.

"Next day, no sun! Only wind and rain for two days."

"He did exactly the right thing," Ļainjin said, in defense of the Pohnpeian's strategy. "He ate all he had before it spoiled. Then he collected enough rainwater to sustain him on his long journey."

"Paratak!" cried Liṃanṃan, kicking him hard on the knee with the heel of her foot. "You ate eleven raw *kūro* in one night and one day? How did you do that?"

He looked at her with a shy grin on his face, as though she was his mother scolding him. "They fit inside," he answered, holding his arms wide as if to say there was nothing else he could do. "I am hungry. I am cold." Then he smiled broadly. "So hungry I could eat your *foot*!" he joked, pretending to grab hold of it, and they all laughed at his joke.

"How many days before you got back into your boat?" asked Ḷainjin, wondering how he survived the cold sickness. "Perhaps by keeping his torso out of the water as much as possible," he was thinking.

"In, out — too many times — keep trying because cold — keep swamping because wave — day three, much rain but less wind. I clean boat, collect rainwater, and paddle for island."

"How did you know which direction to paddle?" asked Liṃanṃan.

"Only one way to paddle in big wave — keep behind!"

She looked to Ḷainjin for interpretation.

"The typhoon missed the island but set up a tailwind that generated immense eastward-flowing waves. These waves interfaced with *kāleptak*, an eastward-flowing current—"

Liṃanṃan interrupted. "I know *kāleptak*. My father is a navigator."

"Okay, so because he realized it was futile to try to fight both wave and current, he turned away from his island and followed the surge eastward." He turned to Paratak. "How many days did you paddle?"

"Two days strong — then one day weak — then too much hungry to continue... So I removed outrigger plank, lie on boat water in hull, and cover face with paddle to die." Demonstrating, he lay down on the stones with his arms on his chest and pretended to sleep.

"Boat water?" asked Liṃanṃan.

"Remember, he has filled the hull of his canoe with rainwater, but the sun is starting to drink it up, so he takes a plank from his outrigger platform to support himself above the water and shades it with his body. Eventually, he became too exhausted, hungry, and exposed to continue to paddle. He was probably drifting at a good clip anyway!"

"So what happens next?" she asked.

"The noisiest secret of the ocean," Ļainjin said. "Baak!"

"Baak!" cried Paratak simultaneously. "Baak! Baak! Baak! Baak!" The men cried together in unison with the squawking birds about the island.

"*Wūnaak*,"[149] Liṃanṃan answered her own question.

"Tuna everywhere — bird hover like cloud upon water — baitfish jump into boat — I want eat but must chance on hook," said Paratak, talking rapidly with his hands and speaking feverishly to convey the level of frantic excitement he felt after so many days without food. He pretended to hook his baitfish through its mouth, toss it into sea, and paddle as he let out his line. Then he began paddling wildly until his arm went taut — opposite the direction he had been paddling!

"You're lucky you didn't catch a shark," Ļainjin said.

Paratak acknowledged his remark with assent, as though he had been worried about the same thing.

"How did you prevent the tuna from breaking your line?" Ļainjin assumed he succeeded in catching a tuna eventually because that was about the only thing that could have saved his life in such a circumstance.

Paratak swiveled his body to face the direction the imaginary tuna was pulling his line in and pretended to hold the line with both hands.

"*Wōjej!* Whoever told of that?"

"Told of what?"

"He discouraged the thing from sounding by giving up and letting it drag his tiny boat. The drag from the shallow hull must have been just light enough to prevent the line from breaking. So the small boat served to save his life. *Wōjjej!* I would have thought the opposite…"

"How long before the next rainstorm?" asked Ļainjin.

"There were many days before rain, and then sun, and then more rain."

"How much of the tuna was left when you made landfall?"

"Nothing, I ate sun-dried bone. I ate yellow fin!"

"I'm glad I wasn't there," joked Liṃanṃan. "He surely would have eaten me, Liṃanṃan."

"How many days were you out there all together?"

---

[149] Flocks of seabirds diving for baitfish driven to the surface by tuna.

"Twenty...," he said, and then held up an additional six fingers.

"Twenty-six days?"

"Yes, twenty-six," repeated Paratak, nodding his head again to emphasize the number was correct.

"It shouldn't have taken you so long with the wind at your back like that."

"Drift west — paddle north."

"All right, that explains it. Good strategy — you knew the string runs north and south. You figured you were still drifting west and did not want your lips to crack! Paratak, I'd say you deserved to find land! You had a smart drift! Now it's time to teach you how to count lobsters!"

Ļainjin stood up and surveyed the barren reef flat. The moon had risen nearly halfway to its apex. They walked Liṃanṃan to the beached craft. The lagoon water had drained to its lowest level, and the boat was nearly ten paces from the water's edge. Without taking the time to break branches for the boat to slide upon, Ļainjin stooped to place his shoulders under the outrigger platform and began a two-part chant: "*Wūj uwaņ in!*"[150]

To this, Liṃanṃan responded, "*Jān lōļļap in!*"[151] She finished the chant and laughed as she pushed the rear side of the platform and lifted while Ļainjin nudged the boat forward a step. Paratak joined in, lifting the kubaak as they all chanted again, and moved the boat another step closer to the peaceful, shimmering water.

When they eventually reached the shoreline, the craft sank down into the lagoon. Ļainjin loosened the fore- and backstays, lifted the foot of the mast from inside the hull, and placed it at the yoke. Then he adjusted all the lines and stepped back. Liṃanṃan climbed onto the stern deck and secured her *alele* below. With a little push from the men, she glided out above the fragile corals, not far below the proa's keel. The men watched her paddle out into the light breeze, hoist her sail, and slowly glide back in the direction from which they had come. Then they sauntered back to the spent fire. Paratak grabbed his two baskets, and they began walking diagonally across the reef flat toward the ocean's edge.

---

[150] "Pull this gray hair!"
[151] "From this old lady!"

Ļainjin resolved to protect his feet no matter what and warned Paratak to do the same. His feet were still tender from so many days at sea although his callouses had begun to harden again, and with care, he knew he would be able to run again with abandon to encircle the best of the sea creatures he wished to capture. They crossed the puddled reef with determination and began wading into the surf where the dead reef flat met the live corals that had sprouted, splashed by the seawater during the lowest of afternoon tides.

The sounds of the waves tumbling onto the live corals reverberated in their ears in a slow, rhythmic refrain that was invariably followed by choirs of white water plunging up from the reef's edge. Then it rushed across the live reef crest with the intonation of an exhaled breath followed by a receding hiss of water sucked back between the corals like the sound of air inhaled between a swimmer's teeth. To Ļainjin, this was the sound of the never-tiring ocean. Its swells, having traveled in powerful silence for so long, were finally breathing a sigh of relief, gratified to snatch a taste of shore before their continuous columns carried on engulfing all in their wake.

The two men splashed their way southward along the border of the reef flat, Paratak peering to his left into the deeper water as it rushed toward them. Ļainjin was searching to his right, in the shallower water that rippled past them onto the reef. He was trying to distinguish movement among the large storm-strewn rocks that stuck somehow to the reef shoreward of the more turbid border area where they were wading. Then he stopped short as Paratak continued along for a moment before turning his face back toward him.

"Paratak, do you hear that?"

"What?"

"Lobster *juon*[152] is calling you."

"Where?" he asked in a serious tone.

"There," said Ļainjin. He stepped forward to put one hand on Paratak's shoulder, turning him around to face the gradually tapering surf as it calmed to wavelets that, exhausted of energy, sloshed upon the barren reef. He pointed to a spot that appeared to be a small rock. "Come."

As they approached the object, it glided lagoonward until nearly out of the water and then stopped. Ļainjin covered it with his foot and reached

---

[152] One.

down, grasped hold of its broad back with his strong fingers, and pulled the heavy spider-like crustacean from the water. Its eight reddish-brown legs and two sharp coral-like antennae spread in all directions, and the bristly pads that glued its feet to the reef waved in the air in a futile attempt to recover the traction it had lost. "He's hailing you, Paratak! He wants aboard your basket!"

"That's it?" Paratak was surprised the lobster had been so stupid as to trap itself by backing onto the still unflooded portion of the reef.

"That's it! Open your basket! Lobster *juon* says he wants to be carried by the strong Pohnpeian fisherman. He is tired of crawling all over the reef and he is afraid of sharks. That is why he headed up onto the shallow water, because he mistook you for a shark. If he'd known who you are, he would have jumped into your basket from the start!"

Paratak opened it with a laugh as a surge of surf covered his ankles, and Ḷainjin tossed the lobster upside down into the basket. They splashed back into deeper surf, but this time, Paratak began looking for more rock-like objects that moved shoreward in spurts and stops. Now and then, he would see one approach on his left, but once he took a step or two oceanward, it invariably retreated into the surf from which it came. Ḷainjin had to explain that the lobster would always turn to face a feared predator and by default, swim away from it with its powerful tail flipper. Its nature worked against it only if a man maneuvered himself between it and the reef's edge. After this explanation, Paratak changed tactics and caught lobsters *ruo* and *jilu*.[153] Then Ḷainjin realized that he would have to keep prodding him along or he would waste too much time chasing down the small ones and the females with eggs that Ḷainjin would make him release, and further discussion on those topics ensued.

"Only chase the biggest ones or we'll end up swimming," Ḷainjin pleaded. "We have limited time to traverse this reef."

"But they sing to me! They want come aboard my basket," Paratak joked.

"Look, can you see that islet there in the distance?"

"Okay?"

"Well, that's our waypoint. When we get there, we'll only be halfway to Likōkkālọk's island."

---

[153] Two and three.

He pointed to the islet that jutted out, blocking visual sight of the remainder of the string, and Paratak seemed to acknowledge the considerable span, given the turn in the tide.

"Now look at the position of the moon. When it gets there" — Ļainjin pointed as he explained — "we will no longer be able to walk on the reef because the tide between the islets will be too strong.

"Now we can spend our time filling your baskets with the small ones we chase down here and then struggle to carry them there, or we can fill your baskets with only the biggest ones we find along the way and make our journey easier. The decision is up to us! Small catch with much work, bigger catch with less work!"

"I understand. We keep walking."

"Likōkkālọk is singing to you too. She is hungry and doesn't want you to waste time or be swept between the islets into the lagoon when the tide comes and the ocean current begins to fill the lagoon."

Ļainjin forged ahead, chasing down the big ones and forcing Paratak, who held the baskets, to catch up. There were so many lobsters that soon his baskets started to get heavy, which discouraged him from wandering off again. Then they began moving more quickly as they progressed toward their destination. They trudged silently, their ears filled with the thump of the swells as they curled upon the reef crest, the white-water rush of the resulting surge of ocean water, and the sucking sound before the next cycle, broken only by the cry of a fishing bird as it flew white or black against the clear, deep gray of the star-dimmed, moonlit sky.

When they reached the midpoint islet, their destination came into view. Shortly thereafter, Paratak spotted a large lobster that Ļainjin had overlooked because it failed to move. When he stepped forward, it turned to face him but stayed put in the thigh-high water. He stepped on the lobster's back, but the baskets prevented him from reaching down to pry it up, and he was reluctant to release his baskets in the surf. He called Ļainjin. When he rushed back, he found that Paratak had trapped the granddaddy of them all, and both men were quite giddy over the catch.

"They call that one *bọkwōj pedped*[154] because it takes both hands to pry it off the reef." Ļainjin bent over and, submerging his face, grasped hold of the thing with both hands, pulling and twisting until he successfully unclasped the giant. Its legs spread out wider than Ļainjin's chest.

"You did not hear this one sing?" Paratak teased.

"I heard him but I took pity because he's such an old man," responded Ļainjin jokingly. Then he transferred the thing to one hand and, holding it upside down over his head, said, "Here, give me one of your baskets." He took one of the heavy baskets filled with lobsters off one of Paratak's shoulders and tossed it into the nearly waist-high water. A look of absolute panic crossed Paratak's face as he worried over the loss of so many of their hard-earned catch. Ļainjin laughed at his concern and opened the submerged basket wide to show all the prickly crustaceans embracing each other, clutched into a single, inseparable ball.

"They no swim good-bye?"

"No, when fish are scared they swim away, but lobsters clutch onto the reef. They'll hug each other like that until you get tired of watching, or until someone pulls them apart. You can set them down anytime you want," he explained, before motioning for Paratak to open his other basket. Then Ļainjin carefully set the *bọkwōj pedped* right side up inside the full basket, allowing the immense thing to hug onto the top of the pile, and grabbed the other just as it began to wash shoreward in the foaming surf. He slung it over his shoulder, set off down the reef again, and turned to Paratak. "We only have room for one more passenger like that and little time to waste, so let's find another big one or leave the rest for another time."

They headed off in earnest, soon realizing they indeed had no more time to look for others. The weight of their catch was a struggle, and the prickly legs poked through their woven baskets and scratched their arms and shoulders. Ļainjin noticed Paratak glancing nervously from time to time at the moon as it rose toward the spot where Ļainjin predicted they could no longer walk in the sweeping tide. Finally, they decided it was best to drag the baskets through the deeper surf and let the water absorb their weight as they half floated behind them.

---

[154] Literally, "grab the reef tightly"; extremely large spiny lobster: *Panulirus penicillatus.*

Shortly thereafter, with the sounds of the reef in chorus, Ļainjin broke their silence with the piercing cry of a spirit-raising chant as they trudged through the surging rollers. It was like the one he and Liṃanṃan had earlier used to muster the strength to heave their heavy canoe across the lagoon shore. This chant, however, seemed without end. It was more like a song that he may have composed and memorized on long journeys between the islands, and it went on and on without refrain, as though its intention was to record or log events as they passed.

Cut into surf onto
east reef of Pohnpei.
We sing. Stones ring! Jebu[155] *beat! Waow!*
We shake up! We wake up the
men of this western quay.
'We have come back at last!'
We drop sail. We tide wait. We
shout out to our host to
tell which way he wants us to turn.
Do we tideway our way north? Do
we tideway our way south?
We fear not the bold lot foretold today,
our last cast forecast Brave Sky!
Stones ring out and sing out,
plaything thing of Et-a-o.[156]
We drink. We fling our senses astray.
So, what does Konak say?
'Cries cut coconuts!
Go dig taro!'
They scramble, they
gang up, they gather.
They dig up that island,
bring food to our boat and

[155] A sharkskin drum used when paddling or sailing.
[156] Legendary trickster.

then he stands and smiles from on high
to end the day and teach his way.
'Trade cast is last till you return our way.
We wish you forever to cast Brave Sky!'
We heard him. We left.
We sail. We look back.
We see mountain. We beat sharkskin.
We embark on a course to death.
Our final task, our last cast — 'Do we die today?'

Ļainjin screamed this last line in a hair-raising pitch to emphasize the end of the first verse of his mother's endless chant — it incessantly recounted the names of swells, sailing directions, seamarks, and other characteristics of the surrounding archipelago used for navigation. Each verse recounted island after island as they plodded through the rising tide toward their destination.

Paratak would have understood few of his words, but the mention of his homeland must have drawn his interest, and the power of the verse was uplifting. It seemed to strengthen the spine, to make a man stand upright and muster the spirit to attack rather than accept his apparent fate, and that seemed to be just the posture their circumstance required. He was still chanting nearly a quarter of the night later when they reached Kōkkālọk's island. His timing, as always, was prescient, for by the time they made shore, the tide had reached the beach. Paratak looked exhausted by the adventure. His shoulders and thighs were scratched by the sharp and broken antennae that poked through his heavy basket, but through the course of that night he must have come to realize, as had each of the jekaro boys, that he nevertheless had much to gain in forming as close a friendship as possible with this extraordinary man they called Shark.

The next morning, Ļainjin found the boys all giggly over what had occurred the night before. Likōkkālọk had taken advantage of Paratak's absence to pleasure Etre. At her insistence, he had brought two companions. They had stealthily crossed the passageway in the moonlight. Per the story that passed between the boys, she had hovered over him "like a seabird squashing its nest." Apparently, she was renowned for tickling the very tip of her partner's manhood as she squatted over him, nuzzling it agilely between the wet lips of her womanhood until he cried out in agony and then, still hovering, plunging her squid down upon him, irresistibly provoking his seed's release. His mistake had been to bring the companions, who had secretly witnessed it all from a discreet distance yet could not keep his secret. The boys endlessly teased him, calling him "man rooster" over his quick, bird-like release.

Ļainjin was still wondering why Kōkkālọk would choose to seduce his shy friend and insist he bring witnesses to their tryst. Later that afternoon, after practice, the giggling continued as the group enjoyed the lobsters that Kōkkālọk's workers prepared for them, and he heard talk pass of which boys she might test next and who would last the longest. The group sat out of the sun in a circle beneath her stilted, thatched house, and the lobsters were served bright, steaming red from the earth oven, where they were baked next to ripe breadfruit wrapped in leaves and served in a coconut-leaf basket. During the meal, as she passed a second round of fresh coconuts, she stopped — on her knees — before Etre for a moment. She innocently punched out the mouth of his drink with her nail before passing it to him and smiling coquettishly, first at him and then the others, as she touched her tongue with a bit of the coconut custard that she had freed in the process. "Did she not realize what a dangerous game she was playing?" thought Ļainjin as he watched. Later, in overheard conversations, the boys seemed to agree among themselves that it was more than her physical ability that drained a man's seed so quickly. It must be the sensuality of her person — some said her smile and others, her look of desire. Others said her feel or her smell or the combination of all these things, or maybe it was just her inexorable passion to vanquish her opponent quickly that caused her partner to precipitously succumb to her enticement.

Paratak, who was seldom distracted from her charm, sat next to Ļainjin. He had watched his new friend observe the snickering, the provocative smile, and the blush on Etre's face. He was upset and did not eat his lobster with the relish Ļainjin expected. Later, he watched Kōkkālọk as she in turn watched the boys move their circle into the bright sun of their practice area and began playing *anidep*.[157] This was one of Ļainjin's unorthodox

[157] A game in which a foot-sized cube of woven pandanus leaves is kicked back and forth within a circle by clapping participants.

methods of readying the men for the group coordination required for battle. The anidep, a solid cube the size of a man's foot made of woven pandanus leaves, was kicked from player to player around their circle. The object was not to allow the anidep to fall to the stones upon which they pranced and clapped in unison as they played. Two claps and a kick as the square circulated about them; two claps and a kick as they launched it from one side to another. Etre was the most outstanding of the group at this sport and had evolved into the group's shy but natural leader. As they kicked the square with the sides of their feet, now and again, a man's private parts would bounce into view if his heel accidentally kicked up his kilt. Because of this, she was concentrating intently and being less than well behaved. She would turn to other women and laugh and point with her eyes, and this served to humiliate Paratak even more.

Later that evening, after the practice but before the group returned for jekaro, Kōkkālọk approached Ļainjin out of Paratak's sight with several of the netted coconut shells presented to her earlier by the boys.

"I hope you realize that I'm never satisfied by the juice of your jekaro boys," she said. "I crave only the juice of the man who teaches them. I suppose all your jekaro is going to Liṃanṃan. She must learn to share her good fortune. Poor thing would have to break her back to please you the way I would."

Ļainjin could only stare into her playful eyes as she continued more softly before turning.

"None of them can douse the coal that smolders in my belly. They are the smoke that clouds our secret, but it was your drill that sparked the flame," she said laughingly, as she turned and stepped away. Then she turned her head back once more. "Siss!" She spoke softly, as though attempting to shush a child.

Ļainjin wondered whether her aim was to get him to cheat on Liṃanṃan or to draw him into another fight with Paratak. Or was it to draw the entire group of them against his new friend? Either way, he realized she would not stop until his Pohnpeian friend met his end, and the longer the issue went unresolved, the more counterproductive it was to their battle plans. Such, in his view, was the fatuous nature of island life, and this was what had always repelled him from it.

A few days later, from the moment he left the village path, crossed the strand, and stepped down upon the rough coral pebbles leading to the ocean reef, Ļainjin felt the stiff eastern breeze he had been waiting for. As he began washing off his netted jekaro shells in the reef puddles on the ocean-side shore, he began looking forward to getting away, even if only for the day. He filled his palm with coarse beach pebbles and poured them through the mouth of each shell. In turn, he filled them half-full of clear ocean water, covered the mouth of each with his thumb, and shook each one until he was satisfied all residue from the previous day was dislodged from the inside of the shell. Then he shook out the pebbles and rinsed each shell thoroughly. During this morning ritual, it was his habit to focus on the colors as they slowly evolved and illuminated the eastern horizon. After the big storm, the wind had turned variable and light, with morning colors of pink and blue, but he had been waiting for a steady wind from the east and the orange and gray colors that promised to keep it steady. He wanted to explore the bird islets of the atoll's southern fringing reef and retrace the course that Taknaṃ had set for him the evening they first arrived.

He would need hermit crabs. Therefore, after scrubbing his shells, he walked up from the reef, hung them on a kōņņat tree — hunching low beneath its ocean-stretched branches — and began overturning the large chunks of coral rubble that lined the strand. Under the second or third coral boulder, he found a hermit crab that had no doubt recently crawled there with the intention of sleeping quietly through the sunny part of the day. The armored nocturnal creature, the size of his thumb, was burrowed inside the empty shell of a sea snail and exposed only the surfaces of its large claw and armored shoulders. These aligned perfectly with the circular wall of his cave to shield the cautious crustacean from the world outside. The sea snail had probably been caught off guard by a wave, dislodged from its spot on the reef's edge, and finally washed up on the reef flat to bake and be eaten by the hermit crab that would inherit its shell. He picked up the shell with the strange creature nestled so neatly inside and imagined it victoriously appropriating the home for itself. Then he envisioned it wading up and down the shore in the moonlight, looking for another dead carcass to pick apart, and all the while carrying its new dwelling on his back for a quick retreat in case it was accosted, for instance, by a pugnacious fish or a still-hungry night bird.

He remembered Pedpedin's story of the invading ri-Pit, who thought they, too, were safe, wrapped up as they were in their shells of tightly woven coconut-husk fiber, only to have their glorious story of female capture come to an end by the pointy shell of a different kind of snail that once thought it, too, was safe inside its impenetrable cave. He grabbed a rounded stone from the shore, placed the snail's shell on the flat of a rock, and with a firm tap, smashed it apart. His little friend immediately righted itself and tried to scramble away. It was to no avail, as Ļainjin quickly picked it up by its back with one hand and pinched off its soft, digit-like abdomen with the other. The crippled creature — minus its most-treasured body part — then scrambled for cover as Ļainjin continued to overturn other craggy-shaped boulders of sun-bleached coral that had washed up and treat the inhabitants he surprised in likewise manner until he had collected a small mound of these bite-sized marine delicacies with which he intended to catch his favorite fish. Then he stripped the leaflets from one-half of a coconut frond from a sapling he found growing above the strand, and tore them again until he had two sets of six connected leaflets. With those, he quickly wove a basket for his bait.

After jekaro, Ļainjin announced he was going fart fishing along the southern fringing reef and, not unexpectedly, Liṃanṃan announced she would accompany him. He longed for a day of solitude, yet she wanted to visit her uncle on the westernmost islet of the atoll.

As they were about to depart, Taknaṃ brought them a stalk of Ļainjin's latest favorite variety of pandanus. "Bring me a big *dijiñ*,"[158] she said, as she stuck her tongue out. She was imitating the fish whose gut, when the fish is quickly hauled up from the bottom, often protrudes through its mouth upon reaching the surface. She crossed her eyes at the same time in such hilarious fashion that Liṃanṃan and Ļainjin were still laughing as they raised their

---

[158] Fart fish; species of emperor fish: *Lethrinus variegatus*.

sail and began gliding very slowly down the long western shaft of the adze-shaped island to an islet that lay next to the passageway into the ocean that they had targeted during the storm. Ļainjin had to paddle them across the sheltered waters to make headway as only the very top of their sail caught the faint breezes that wound their way through the dense forests of the islet to windward.

He prized the *dijiñ*, or fart fish, for its firm white meat. Due to its insatiable desire for crabmeat, its thick lips, and its puckered mouth, it was very easy to catch by hook. It was true enough that the fish did invariably release gas from its anus upon landing, but he thought the ancestors should have called this the kissing fish rather than the fart fish. Sometimes, when tired, he preferred to crunch up the brittle bodies of hermit crabs, anchor his boat to a coral head, and chum the water over a period, hoping to attract a circle of fart fish. But for the most part, Ļainjin was not the type of fisherman who was inclined toward stationary activity. He did not like to wait for luck, which to him, involved a search. As he had been raised by the sea, movement seemed the natural order of things.

Liṃanṃan, perhaps sensing him lost in thought, jealously tried to capture his attention by pulling up her skirts and gently caressing his leg with her toes. Now and then, she would turn back to shore and wave innocently to someone on the shoreline. Yes, it is true he had been looking forward to a day by himself. They had intertwined their lives — with the sole exceptions being his time with the boys and with Paratak — and their private parts had become toys for each other's child's play. As usual, she was in the process of successfully turning his penchant for lonely introspection into the pleasure of being in her ever-desirous and ever-creative company.

"Remind me again why you wanted to come fishing today?"

"To pay my respects to Uncle." She responded with the playful look of someone who is providing an excuse to another who knows it is a less than complete explanation. At that point, a gust of wind caught the belly of their loosely trimmed sail and blew it taut with an eruptive flap that required Liṃanṃan to further secure the line, and *ņatọọn* a bit to restore balance to their accelerated advance across the now-rippling lagoon waters. As she did so, Ļainjin watched her deftly reposition herself as she moved her rear forward and braced herself with the strong toes of her left foot, levered against the starboard hull, and those of her right, against the edge of the stern deck upon which he sat.

"But you're probably thinking I'll cause bad luck to your fishing by breaking your concentration!" She laughed as she determinedly kicked his knees apart and further braced herself by placing the ball of her foot directly between his thighs and forcing him to scoot quickly backward to protect his hanging parts from being scrunched. The breeze had loosened her bundled, thick hair as the wind propelled them over the deep, dark corals that marked the edge of a steep drop-off into the depths below. She freed her hair, wild and tangled, with a seductive whip of her long neck as their eyes met and her toe touched him, and then she scrunched her nose and dared giggle. "Concentrate on this, man shark!" And then she mimicked the face that her grandmother had surprised them with earlier. They laughed and laughed again as each, in turn, made the silly face and attempted to outdo the other until they approached the light blue shoal that jutted out near the island's end.

This was where Ļainjin wanted to begin. He reached below for their fishing lines as he abruptly released his oar to dangle from its line tied to its windward bulwark, and then began separating the two neatly coiled lines he had prepared earlier. Their craft gently turned about in a wide, drifting arc that nearly reversed their heading and left the sail flapping and their bow pointed a bit off wind. They began their drift. Liṃanṃan released their halyard and lowered the yard until it kissed the boom, both hung in place by boom halyards on either side that ran through an eye on the masthead. She took her place in the forehatch and rested her rear against the foredeck. He placed the basket of bait within reach of each at the yoke between them.

Each line ended with valuable hooks and netted sinker balls ground from *kapwōr*. The moment he handed her one of the lines, the competition began. Each rushed to bait their hooks, drop the weighted lines into the water, and unfurrow the lines as they slipped through their fingers. Finally, as the baits approached the sandy bottom of the light blue water below, they attempted to outchant each other.

"*Tartok im kein liitiō, bwe? Ijañin eoḷōk! Ellok im toto wōt! Ellok im toto wōt!*"[159] she chanted.

"*Kok, kok, kok, kok! Wōde im ajoḷe! Wōde im ajoḷe!*" he responded, as each tried to out-energize the other.

Strikes came simultaneously, but while Liṃanṃan's hands moved slowly as she carefully nursed her catch toward the surface, Ḷainjin, having lost his, whipped his line in as fast as possible, allowing it to fly into the water behind him to reach its end again and rebait his hook. She landed her fish on the outrigger platform, where, true to form, the stomach of the thing had inverted and was protruding between its thick lips. She carefully covered its head with her palm, applying pressure to prevent it from flopping, and then slid her fingers down its back to close its sharp dorsal spines before clamping it firmly between her fingers and thumb. Finally, she steered the writhing, farting fish to her mouth and crunched down on its skull to permanently quiet it. Eventually, she glanced at Ḷainjin as she wiped her mouth with the back of her wetted hand and repeated the funny face her grandmother had taught them.

In the interim, Ḷainjin had rebaited and resunk his hook and was waiting impatiently for another strike, but he could not concentrate properly, laughing as he was at her antics.

"Don't be a sucky fish! Do not be a kissy fish! Chew down on it!" he barked good-humoredly, irritated at losing the first round. He glanced about, judging their drift and estimating where they were headed across the azure lip of the lagoon's dark blue mouth. He knew you could only catch this fish along the lagoon's reef slope, on the sandy bottom in light blue water, with the biggest ones caught along the stretch of fifty or so ñeñe before the edge of the steep drop-off into the atoll's central abyss.

Liṃanṃan placed her fish on the outrigger platform and removed a big, round basket she had earlier woven from coconut leaflets and stowed in the hull beneath the foredeck. She secured it beneath the platform but above the lagoon water that gently lapped against the hull. The dark stripes of the light grayish-blue fish had faded, and all life had passed from it by the time she flopped it into the basket.

---

[159] "Rush here and yank back at me, because the others have twitched me not! Relax and hang yourself!"

She immediately resumed fishing, and the very moment her bait hit bottom, she surprised Ļainjin with another funny face as she attended to a second suitor, this one more hesitant than her first. He in turn whipped in his line again, only to find the bait not taken, and lowered it once more with a snarl as she landed her second fart fish and carefully disposed of it. He played out his line quickly while, at the same time, keeping it as taut as possible so he could recoil it the instant he felt the slightest tug. As soon as he hit bottom, he raised his bait a few ñeñe to avoid getting his hook caught in one of the few coral heads that dotted the shoal below. "Come on," he growled again, as Liṃanṃan lowered her baited line once more. She made a face as he glanced at her hurrying to beat him yet again. Finally, his line went taut, as did hers, and they landed their fish nearly simultaneously. Then, as their current course at drift would take them into water too deep to fish, Ļainjin decided to reposition their craft.

Liṃanṃan raised the halyard, and Ļainjin sheeted in as he dipped his oar into the water. The wind quickly brought them closer to the coral at the edge of the light blue water that stretched westward, parallel to the fringing reef connecting the island's sandy tip to the first of a series of reef-connected islets and cays. They each caught a fish there, and then Ļainjin sailed them past the first islet — the shoal there had too many corals and dropped off too rapidly. They soon reached a long stretch of open reef with downward-sloping sand that preceded the bird islets where Ļainjin expected his fart fish to be plentiful. The sun was still low in the sky and the wind still cool against their skin when they began their drift. The moon had been small in the western sky before sunrise, and the time of spring tides had passed so the reef would not drain bare. The sound of *buñtokrōk* swelling upon its southern edge was less dramatic than would have been the case a few days past. They drifted three times toward the first bird islet, and the fishing was so productive they tacked back twice to repeat their drift. The light blue water where these fish circled by day and slept by night was of moderate depth. Near the end of the afternoon, their basket was full, and Liṃanṃan had many fish to take as tribute to her uncle but ended up embarrassed by a small mishap that resulted in a learning experience for her.

Fart fish liked to circle coral heads and feed close to the sandy bottom surrounding them. They had been fishing with about ten ñeñe of line in waters that varied between five and ten ñeñe in depth, and Ļainjin had been warning her to keep her bait above any coral heads over which they drifted. She continued to catch more fish than he did, primarily — as they found out — because she had been fishing dangerously close to them. Of course, she eventually ran out of luck and got her line snagged!

About halfway through the afternoon, as the wet fiber line was slipping though his calloused fingers, her sudden, frantic cry surprised him.

"Ļōpako, my hook is caught on the coral. What should I do?"

He handed her his line and told her to retrieve it. Then he grabbed his oar and quickly paddled into the wind, his immense strength easily overcoming the friction of their outstretched sail to bring them back across the rippling water to the spot above the coral head she had snagged. Once she had recovered his line, he asked her to attempt to free her line while he continued to paddle windward of the spot where it had caught. For some reason, she was unable to free her tackle and became visibly frightened by his gasping in and out for breath — like a man dying — but he had no time to explain. He untied the oar, gave it to her, and told her to keep paddling from the bow. He jumped up onto the yoke behind her and just as quickly dropped his kilt. He then dove into the water, found the line, and caught it with the thumb of his outstretched hand. He followed it downward through the blurry water, his big feet propelling him toward the white sand that surrounded the dark mound of coral on the bottom. About halfway down, the pain in his head became too intense for him to continue. Holding onto the line, he temporarily inverted by releasing half the air in his lungs. Then he pinched his nose, sneezed hard to relieve the pain, and dove again, down to the line's end. There, he released the last of his air. Without buoyancy and sitting amid the coral, he peacefully untangled her line and gave it two gentle tugs as a sign for her to retrieve it.

To Ļainjin, all this had occurred quickly and he had been below the water but a few moments. But to Liṃanṃan, who had probably never seen a man attempt such a dive, he must have been gone for an eternity, and she dried his cold face with her hands and her mouth the moment it popped out of the water.

"Ḷōpako, I'm so sorry I caused you to do that!"

"I needed to cool off anyway. It is nice and cold down there! Next time, I'll let you try!"

There would be no next time. For the remainder of the afternoon, she fished much more conservatively and, in fact, caught fewer fish. Their basket full, Ḷainjin steered them to the long but narrow bird islet they had approached that first day they had entered the safety of the lagoon. They hauled their canoe from the sparkling, clear water up onto the calm shore of fine coral sand amid the blazing colors of the afternoon sun. White and black squawking terns were flying in all directions, those of the speckled variety hovering directly over their nests on the beach above the high-tide mark. The neap tide had reached its low point for the day and had begun its patient ebb. During the morning, he had fileted two of the largest fart fish and laid them out on the platform to bake in the sun.

"Ḷōpako, can we eat now?" she asked, as she untied the basket from below the outrigger platform and placed it on top, in the area newly shaded by the still-standing sail. Not waiting for his response, she grabbed one of the fish with one hand, unfurled her matted skirts with the other, and waded naked into the glistening ripples of the cool, clear water. She rinsed the raw, scaled, and sun-seared fish and parted a strip of its serrated flesh from the limp skin with her clenched teeth. As she twisted the strip about her tongue and worked it into her mouth with her finger, she chewed provocatively and beckoned him to join her, waving the remainder in her other hand. He likewise removed his kilt and joined her. As their mouths met and he smelled the scent of her sunburned face, she pushed a piece of unchewed fish into his mouth with her tongue. And so they ate, and so she fed him in this provocative manner as each anticipated what was to come next. When they had eaten their fill of the fish, she tossed the remainder into the lagoon. He followed her through the water, prostrate as a crab, as she backed onto the sand under the shelter of the outrigger platform. He rested his chin on her thigh, and she raised the other knee and asked him to kiss her there as he had done on her first night. So, lying prone on the shore, in the shade of the outrigger's platform, with the cool lagoon water sloshing gently over him, he eagerly met her request.

Across the islet's broad beach and likewise sheltered from the hot afternoon sun, the Chief peered between the low-hanging kōņņat branches, his keen eyes focused primarily on the remaining fart fish half hanging from the outrigger platform above them. As he spied the basket of fish next to it, with the tasty-looking fins sticking through the spaces between the coconut leaves near the top, he could not help but be distracted by his inept worker struggling to bite his mate — but in the wrong place. "Maneuver her onto her knees and bite her back!" He wondered why it had taken his worker so many days to bring him fish and then hung his head in embarrassment over this pathetic display of malehood — and before the entire island! The terns must be spilling their pouches over this! He had known from the start that this female human would distract the commoner from his work. "Could it possibly take all these days to figure out what needed to get done? He doesn't even know the basics!" Then the Chief watched the female cunningly wrap her spindly legs around the commoner's massive back. Clearly, she had managed to trap him there, successfully preventing him from getting into proper position. He felt sorry for his feeble worker as he watched him pinned and unable to struggle free. And then he suddenly propped himself on his hands with a terrible look on his face, apparently writhing in pain — and gave up! Without question, it was the most embarrassing exhibition of sexual ineptitude he had ever witnessed.

The Chief watched as his worker's new mistress took his fish, his perch, and all. She was undoubtedly rejecting his worker due to his inability to satisfy her butt-bumping desires. Then he watched the canoe sail off, leaving the commoner there dejected and with but a single, puny fish. He wandered off aimlessly in one direction and returned after a long while from another, looking skyward and crying out. No doubt, he was fruitlessly apologizing to the island's considerable in-flight population for his display of sexual ineptitude. Finally, the Chief watched his worker leave the islet, fish still flopping tantalizing from his hand, and cross the reef to the neighboring bird islet to the west, where he spied him repeating the same antics and then disappearing out of sight.

The fish needed cleaning and cooking, so Ļainjin let Liṃanṃan sail their catch on to her uncle's island to the west. He was planning to walk there by crossing the relatively short distance on the reef as the neap tide slowly receded. He still held hopes of sighting his black-feathered companion but expected to find him standing out among the din of this white flock of hovering fowl, not sitting there beneath low-hanging branches weighted down with their shiny kōņņat leaves. He looked for him soaring high above, or at least perched high in the upper branches of a tree for easy takeoff, as his ilk was wont to do. When he had no luck spotting him aloft on the first islet, he had crossed the reef to the second, the last islet before the final stretch of fringing reef leading to her uncle's island. That islet was, so to speak, the last islet — or tip of the thumb — before the ocean passageway that separated it from the tip of a curling index finger, or long contiguous fringing reef, that led to a northern islet, and then all the way around again to where he stood. Like the eye of a hand, it reminded him of Namorik, except that Namorik had no passageway whatsoever to the ocean.

When he found no sign of the Chief anywhere around the periphery of this second bird islet, he set the fish on the shorehead, hoping it might yet attract his friend. He tore the crown of kōņņat leaves from a branch and sat down on the coarse sand at the water's edge of this last isletless gap on the reef to rest, wait for the tide to ebb a bit, and let word of his approach spread among the islanders before crossing. As a current will encompass a stone in its path, the breeze from the east enveloped the tiny islet and blew gently across the sweat on his back. The sun glared hot on his face and chest. He looked out toward the rippling, light blue waters at the lagoon's edge that bordered the calm, grayish-green water of the basin before him. It separated this last islet from a series of sandspits and rocky cays that led to the white sands and dark green foliage of her uncle's island, which filled most of the horizon before him.

He clutched onto a handful of sand and allowed it to pour slowly through his fingers. He pondered how many generations it would take for these incessantly screaming, ever-defecating birds, the corals, and the fish that ate them and then pooped their sand into the ever-dispersing action of the waves to expand the beaches of this string of small, sparsely wooded islets into one or two substantial islands — as had happened over the ages, he supposed, to Namorik. This atoll beneath him was slowly growing through the constant efforts of untold numbers of heroes who unknowingly, day by day, advanced its emergence into the light of day amid the surrounding abyss that threatened to swallow it up again.

Then he crossed his fingers, cupped his hands under his head, and lay back on the coral stones that led down to the shallow pool between him and the first sandspit ahead. These remaining islets had been his last hope of finding his friend, who had been a companion to his loneliness for so long. For seven seasons of Jebrọ and seven seasons of Tūṃur, they had stayed together. They had marveled together at the sight of the immense stone villages with their thatched roofs nearly blocking the tops of the mountains in the distance behind them. They had crossed the ocean from one island to another and had shared the incredible hardship, the tragedy, and the rewards of these adventures. And now, had it all to come to this inconclusive end? He clutched onto another handful of sand, and as he allowed it to pass through his palm, he wondered whether the storm had blown his friend away into the obscurity of some other, perhaps uninhabited, place. And he questioned whether he would be able to survive on his own without him. Then, as he had been taught, he trained his mind away from the fear of what might have occurred or what would perhaps occur in the future to the truly magnificent story that they had been witness to, which had made him who he was. He placed the crown of leaves over his face to shade it from the sun and decided to comfort himself with a nap.

"*Wa jab depet āne*,"[160] he thought. He had learned to live by this mariner's rule of relations. This was the strand he rolled into the only line he could use to tie it all together. This was why he had sent the fish ahead with Liṃanṃan. This was why he had brought tribute to Likōkkālọk when he crossed onto her islet. It was why he had given his valuable fishing lure to Pedpedin when he first arrived, and supposed, initially, it was why he and his friends for life had fought the sharks off Anbōd. In the absence of that wealth they had dared to earn, he would never have felt welcomed enough to begin the search for his mother. Gift giving was essential to him and his ilk. This tradition was his mother's legacy and his only inheritance. It was

---

[160] Literally, "boat does not pierce islet." This proverb means that a canoe's hull does not pierce the sand of an islet without bearing gifts.

part of who he was. He could envision Liṃanṃan arriving and presenting their basket of fish to her uncle, and him thinking, "The gifts of this newcomer precede him."

Ļainjin awoke from a dream with the image of his friends hauling his feverish, sunstroked body by wrists and ankles and floating him beneath the sun's glare into the dark hut above the sea and placing him on the slatted floor, where the beautiful, bald Ngalen splashed him with *pwentang*[161] after *pwentang* of cold ocean water. Liṃanṃan was standing at the water's edge before him, teasingly splashing water to wake him up. A second figure, a boy, shorter and even more slender — most likely a relative — stood beside her. He sat silently, and soon it became apparent the boy was wanting to lead them somewhere. Ļainjin arose, shook off his daze, and followed them around to the ocean side, to the islet he had left behind him. The boy marched quickly and without speaking, as on a mission, paying little attention to either of them. He hopped across the shorehead, then the coral rubble that led to the sandy beach along the southern edge of the strand as birds cried and hovered about them. Liṃanṃan said nothing, as though captivated by the boy's mission. Ļainjin followed, speechless, taking one step for each of theirs.

When they reached the lagoon side of the narrow islet, close to where they had landed a while before, the boy bent nearly to the sand and reached below a tuft of low-hanging kōņņat branches. After a noisy, flapping scuffle, he emerged, holding a large, black bird with a red pouch as high into the air as he was able. The long bird hung upside down, its skinny body motionless as if dead, with the head moving only occasionally from side to side, its beak opening and closing, and its eyes only periodically blinking to show it lived.

Finally, the boy spoke. "This one hasn't eaten since the full moon. It may have been abandoned by its mate."

Ļainjin looked at Liṃanṃan for an explanation. "He is my uncle's bird-watcher. He reports directly to him."

"We don't have many of its kind here. Father wants the egg to hatch. We know its mate, but we have seen no sign of her for many days now, and we are worried for him."

---

[161] A Titan word for "cooking pot."

Still hanging the bird high from his uplifted hand and balancing on one foot, the boy gently pushed aside the branch of the kōņņat with the other to expose the ragged, goo-caked nest and exhibit the single, large egg the bird had been protecting. Ļainjin bent to pick it up, but the boy snapped the limb back and motioned *no* with a quick and silent but authoritative snap of his head. Ļainjin turned his attention back to the bird dangling before him.

"Could it be him," he thought. He knew his companion by his personality, not by any particularly distinguishing features. This bird's gular sack was much larger than that of the Chief. His feathers lacked luster. They lacked the Chief's iridescent purple sheen, but then he had never seen a bird so sickly and thin.

"Can I feed him?"

The boy abruptly tossed the bird a few feet into the air. It miraculously righted itself, landed on its feet, and then waddled off to sit back on its nest beneath the tree.

Shrugging his shoulders, the boy responded, "Father says feeding makes the birds lazy."

"That's true, but if the bird dies, so will its egg, and even if it hatches, you will end up feeding the chick if its mother does not return with food."

"We will ask Father," responded the boy.

"No, we won't ask Uncle," said Liṃanṃan. "This bird belongs to Ļainjin. Only the egg belongs to Uncle. I have seen this bird on Ļōpako's boat and will vouch for that to Uncle." She turned to Ļainjin. "Can you find something to feed him?"

The Chief sat indignant upon his nest and watched his worker stumble into the narrow forest behind him. Then, as expected, he watched him burst forth empty-handed. "Did he expect to find fish there?" Then he watched him head back to the islet to the west, enter the forest there, and emerge after a few moments dragging a long, straight, skinny branch. "Octopus!" His eyes bulged!

Ļainjin waded into the lagoon. If he focused properly, he should be able to find one at the edge of the lagoon back reef between the islets in the now currentless passageway. He let the butt end of the stick dangle from one hand as he floated, allowing it to bump along the back reef in the shallow water and periodically placing his face in the water, trying to spot the identifying sign of his prey. The light of the subsiding afternoon sun angled perfectly to shadow the bottom and allow him to find what he was looking for through the cool, clear water, which gradually became less and less blurry to his sight. He cautioned himself repeatedly to relax, to search carefully so as not to miss what he was looking for along the bottom below. He searched a zigzagged path as he slowly punted his way across the channel. He breathed slowly but deeply and moved slowly to relax himself as he searched, so he could hold his breath for as long a stretch as needed once he found what he was looking for. Finally, as luck would have it, he found it and raised his face to laugh.

The Chief, nestled over his egg upon the strand above the passageway, had been watching his worker's every move, and from experience, he knew the consequences that followed from a laugh like that. His eyelids retracted to the extreme, and he waited in motionless, alert expectation with his keen eyesight focused upon the commoner, who was floating and bobbing in the water but a short bird's distance away.

The method the too-crafty octopus always used, hiding the entrance of its hole in the reef, never failed to amuse Ļainjin. Upon exiting, the creature left its stones scattered on the reef, but upon entering, it carefully gathered them again and piled them into a small mound with its sensitive tentacles, to seal the narrow entrance of its little cave. He supposed this trick worked well enough to protect it from marine predators, but to the islanders, the pile of stones not only marked its spot but also served as a sure sign that the octopus was home and vulnerable.

He began breathing heavily to prepare himself as he flipped the ends of his stick, set his face back into the water, brushed the silly pile of stones aside, and poked the slim end of the stick into the hole. He immediately felt the pliable, springy feel of his prey trapped beneath him. His objective was not to try to spear and kill it, but rather to irritate it until it crept out on its own accord. Holding the butt end of the stick, he could surface, gulp air, and periodically view the creature as, arm by arm, it attached its powerful suckers to the aggravating stick and cautiously, unwisely crept from its hole. Then, when he judged the time right, Ļainjin took one last breath, dove, and began to more aggressively jam the head of the creature still lingering in the hole.

He simultaneously slid his hand down the stick, encouraging the arms to attach themselves irresistibly to his warm hand and arm as he continued to jam it, knowing his warmth would entice it upward.

"Yes, it's me that's doing this to you! Come and stop me!" he said without speaking, and he smiled at its red, droopy-eyed face as it appeared and clung to his arm through the black cloud of liquid smoke it excreted. He knew it was on its way to his shoulder and then his back. Luckily, it was moving too quickly to take painless, exploratory bites of flesh — as its kind was wont to do — until it found the bone it would crunch into as if he were an ignorant lobster in a house that could be entered.

Ļainjin slid his fingers into the slippery pocket at the nape, at the back of the octopus's head and then, leveraging the incredible sucking force of its firmly attached arms against it, pressed its slithery face outside in with his powerful thumb until its hood tore open, its brain inside out under the sunny sky. As he surfaced, he tore its suckers off his upper arm and held the octopus as high as he could above the sparkling surface of the lagoon channel, close to the shore where Liṃanṃan was standing and bursting into her ululating scream.

"*U-waa tak-li!*"[162] A few kicks later, he was approaching Liṃanṃan and the boy on solid reef. "*U-waa tak-li!*" he repeated, as he waded slowly through the gradually shallower water toward the shore where they waited, still apparently astounded at how quickly he could achieve his objective. Once he reached shore, he had to lift the head of the dying thing high to prevent its tentacles from touching the sand, and the other two joined him in his victory chant, beaming.

U-waa tak-li!
Come from west to place where
they ba-baked my son there.
They cook-cooked his soul there,
under that tree called kiden.
Kiden, what kiden?

---

[162] Answer floats eastward.

Ļainjin broke off a branch of the kōņņat tree that was overhanging the bird, sharpened the broken limb with his ring, spiked the head of his prey from one side through the other, and hung it there to glisten in the late afternoon sun. The octopus was still changing colors from black to greenish gray to purple as if it wanted to blend itself into its background, which was its wont. Then he severed one of its slippery limbs and turned to the boy, who — still beaming at him — gently lifted the branches away from the bird. And if any had doubted if the bird was the Chief himself, all ambiguity vanished when they saw his greedy reaction. Still sitting, he lifted his head high into the tree, stretched his neck skyward, and opened his beak wide to accept the butt end of the arm's-length tentacle as it slipped quickly through Ļainjin's hand down into his throat. Still unsatisfied, the bird maintained his pose until Ļainjin managed to cut another leg free and slide it likewise into the gaping beak of the demanding bird. Finally, true to the Chief's ungrateful personality, he dismissed all three, lowered his head, squatted back down to his mission, and ignored them as though they were but chunks of coral rubble on the shore before him.

"Remember me!" teased Liṃanṃan, who had dropped on her knees to the sand to watch his gluttonous exhibition. She now flicked a few fingers of sand at the bird and stood to watch him turn, peer directly at her, and retract his head as though threatening to lunge his beak in response.

She responded, "That's it, no doubt about it! What a character! I'd roast it on hot rocks before it dies if there was any meat left on it!"

Ļainjin took the dying octopus from the limb, taking pains to bury it deep in the sand in a place the boy could easily retrieve it, and made him promise to feed the rest of it to the bird daily until he could return. Liṃanṃan teased the bird one more time, and then she and the boy retraced the steps of their mission back to her uncle's island. Ļainjin followed, his temperament revived by the events of the day and his throat warmed by the hope that his friend would survive, but he wondered what might have happened to his mate.

Soon they arrived at the pointy beachhead of coarse, brilliant sand that protruded eastward onto the reef at the island's tip. They were met by two small girls, whom he surmised were the boy's sisters. Each wore an orange *kōn̦o* flower behind each ear. They had emerged hesitantly, and approached as the three trudged up the slowly rising shore. They brought *kōn̦o* flower leis, and L̦ainjin had to bow low to allow the girls to shyly, gleefully place them about his neck. They climbed the strand together and entered the shade of her uncle's village, which, unexpectedly, was immaculately forested and conscientiously kept. There sat countless neatly thatched homes, boat shelters, and cookhouses, all resting upon individual courtyards of coral stone and strung along the interior of a path along the lagoon, beneath the shade of landscaped coconut palms and breadfruit trees. Here and there behind the homes toward the interior were neatly trimmed patches of banana trees.

They followed the path, which was lined periodically with coral slabs half-buried and turned upright and that, no doubt, traced the lagoon shoreline of the islet from end to end. From each home along the path sprang more women with flower leis to drape around their necks until neither could see the path before them without placing a hand to press them close. A cool breeze was gratefully blowing shoreward through the narrow strip of manicured, twisted-trunk pandanus trees. Their sparsely forked, gnarled limbs each ended in green tufts of long, shiny leaves and a single gigantic fruit of spiky, green nodules. Some of these were ripe, and the yellow or orange trim between the nodules' green caps caught L̦ainjin's eye. He got the impression that not a single fruit would drop without a hand to catch and process it. These had been purposefully planted along the strand above the lagoon shore, apparently to block the wind of añōneañ that, each season, would sweep the multicolored azure lagoon into a sunstorm blur of salty wind and bluish-gray, whitecapped waves. These trees had blocked his view of this magnificent village on the evening of their arrival. They had sailed past all this on their way to Taknam̧'s island. At that time, looking shoreward, he could view only the canoes and the fishermen who were unloading them along the lagoon beach.

Everyone, no matter what age, seemed to be engaged in some endeavor. Here, a woman sat softening her pile of pandanus leaves by chafing them around a hardwood stake. There, an elder was felling breadfruit with a long pole amid the branches of a large breadfruit tree. In this cookhouse, a fire was ablaze; in that one, the thin, white smoke of a soon-to-be-covered earth oven was wafting out between its walls of the blackened, upright shafts of split coconut fronds. Children were fetching this and that for their elders while others were scampering among the gentle waves as they lapped upon the lagoon shore and rushed halfway up the sandy beach. They all turned to acknowledge their presence before returning to their work or play. The bestowal of leis continued as they approached the village center, where Ḷainjin's proa miraculously sat beneath the shade of her uncle's own boathouse. Close by, in the middle of the village center, a group of young athletes had circled and were clapping and playing a game of anidep.

Liṃanṃan's uncle, Ḷōtokjān, was standing alone in front of his large, thatched house, which rested on uprights of seasoned coconut trunks. The two men nodded at each other. Tokjān was a man of good humor whose eyes seemed permanently a-twinkle, as though amused by whatever situation he faced. He also appeared acutely aware of everyone and everything in his surroundings and sought no deference from those surrounding him. He had barely begun to welcome Ḷainjin when one of the men playing in his courtyard purposefully kicked the anidep to him, unceremoniously interrupting him. He deftly responded by kicking the woven bundle of leaves straight up in the air. He then turned his back to the circle of men, carefully watched the cube fall from over his shoulder, and kicked it again — this time with the flat of his foot — back into their circle. There, they played on without skipping a beat, methodically clapping one, two, kick, one, two, kick.

"That should satisfy them for a while. They play the day away like children, but they learn to move as one circle of fish. You know because you, too, have been training with my brother's men this way."

"There is no better preparation for the coordination required in battle."

"I agree but tell me. Among which people did you develop all these skills you possess?"

"What skills?" Ḷainjin responded humbly.

"Your modesty is useless among us. Your story precedes you. Our women fly from islet to islet and chatter like birds at nest."

"I have been a fortunate beneficiary of scraps of knowledge gathered among many island groups."

Turning to Liṃanṃan, Tokjān said, "You have chosen an orator who chooses his words well — and he's a good fisherman who will keep you fed!"

With a hearty laugh and a mischievous grin on his face, her uncle turned back to Ļainjin and said, "Thank you for the fart fish. It's my favorite too!"

They both looked at Liṃanṃan, who blushed, giggled, and looked away just in time to watch the anidep, kicked astray, land close to her. Abruptly and in unladylike fashion, she punted the anidep back into the circle.

"She has always been both the lovely girl and the boy her father never had. In truth, she would rather be there among that circle of men than helping her aunt cook the fish you caught and brought to us."

Liṃanṃan, returning and hearing the last part about the fish, responded, "Uncle, if you remember, I brought the fish — and I caught more of them than he did!"

The men looked at each other's eyes, each watching the other surrender in amusement, both beguiled in their own way by her girlish charm. With mutual regard for her, they bonded with a laugh and a nod that required no other response.

"Okay," said Liṃanṃan, "I'll go talk to my aunt, and she'll tell me all your secret battle plans!" She scrunched her nose at them and headed toward her aunt's cookhouse just as the anidep interrupted them a second time.

Tokjān seemingly had not taken his awareness from the game during his engagement with them and kicked the light yet solid object back to the circle. There, it was clapped, clapped, and kick-passed from one player to another around the circle — until one innocently turned his back as a sign to all and responded to a high kick-pass by flicking the woven cube with the flat of his foot back over the heads on the other side of the circle toward Tokjān for a third time. He glanced at Ļainjin for an instant with the same mischievous twinkle in his eye. Then, simultaneously grimacing and shrugging his shoulders in surrender to the group, he deftly repelled the anidep flitting toward him with a flick of his toes high into the air straight above him. He glanced into Ļainjin's eyes again as the anidep descended and then, with the side of his other foot, gently passed it to him before moving a little toward the circle. Ļainjin, tossing aside his flower leis, likewise passed it back to him, again a little ahead of him, and vice versa. They did this repeatedly until both men could join the circle and become fully engaged in the game.

The reasoning behind why the anidep game appealed to Ļainjin as the best way to practice the art of battle is because there is much you can learn from the eyes of a man attacking you. The first rule of battle is to keep your eyes on your opponent. Once the anidep is kicked, every man in the circle senses who it was kicked to. It may be a good kick. It may be a poor one, in which case others must intervene to pass the anidep back to the player whose kick went awry for a second try. So the goal of the game is not just to not allow the anidep to fall to the ground; it is to train the group to act as one. Like a circle of baitfish surrounded by prey, the circle maintains constant motion yet keeps its integrity as a single opponent.

Once the group achieves absolute unanimity of action and exhibits such accord for an extended period of infallible play, the leader stops the action and the men reach for their spears. They are ready to begin the jebwa. And so it was that the man shark was able to merge with others who had been playing this game together since childhood, and then blend into the group and become one with it. As the circle continued to clap in rhythm with flawless play, the word spread quickly throughout the village. Men and women dropped their chores. Children scampered from the beach to watch, and the men's sisters and chosen ones gathered their spears for them — and, of course, their *aje* — and silently took their place in the first row of onlookers who gathered. At last, Tokjān grabbed the anidep and held it high as an expression of mutual triumph, and as a sign for the call of the triton shell to be blown. He took Ļainjin by the hand and led him to a mat laid out before his house. The men sat, and so did all around — except the players, each of whom was busy receiving his spear and donning his head lei to compel proper posture for the dance.

Rālik Islanders fought in groups of four that rotate so that no man's back remains unprotected and no opponent fights only one man. Their totem is the lowly stingray, which mesmerizes its enemy with its ugly face and graceful movement until attacked, when it instantaneously responds with an unanticipated, lightning-fast strike. The men contort their faces in rage induced by the ever-constant beat of the *aje* and the piercing ululations of their sisters and chosen ones. They twirl their spears and clack them one against the other, and then one man turns away to tease the opponent with a clear shot at his back, immediately defended by a twirling member of the group ready to parry or strike at any ill-timed response.

The jebwa was a fierce enactment of this classic fighting style passed along from previous generations for so many seasons that the ancient words of the chant had long ago lost their context and seemed as though of a different language. Yet the rhythms, the odd poetry of the words, and the stylized motions of the dance never failed to nourish the present and bring forth the spirit of these ancestors, their glorious accomplishments, and the heroic lives they must have lived.

The men lined up in six groups of four. The triton shell sounded once more. The women's ululation began, and the drums began to beat. Onlookers continued to rush into the opening as the auburn rays of the evening sun beamed between the inland palm leaves and splashed upon the dancers as they stood there, upon the thick bed of coral stones laid down by these spirits of the past now being called forth to mingle among them. The *du*[163] began a mysterious, rhythmic chant as they beat in unison upon their drums. In a high pitch, each called to her champion, and each man in turn responded with such a fierce clacking of hardwood spears that all anticipated one might break, and with a mysterious, lower-pitched chant in response to the *du*. As the dance commenced, per tradition, the spirits of the past began to mingle, first among the *du* and then among the dancers. All the performers began to creep out of themselves, leaving shells to be crept into by these spirits who perhaps had been wandering aimlessly from shore to shore but were now called forth to defend against unwanted intruders. The very face of the mildest woman among them became that of the fiercest warrior imaginable, seemingly capable of the bravest of deeds, with no regard for life but only for victory and the utter defeat of this foe before her. Likewise, the onlookers seemed summoned, and likewise, they responded. A handful of elders paced back and forth among the dancers, encouraging them as they would were they in actual battle.

---

[163] Women beating drums and accompanying their loved ones to a battle or supporting their chant as they dance the jebwa.

This ancient arrangement of high-pitched chant, drumbeat, responsive chorus, fierce dancing, twirling, and the rhythmic clack of sharpened spears captivated all who watched, and none turned away. Each throat shivered as its spirit slipped out, mingled among the others, and then timidly retreated, only to venture forth again and yet again to the enrapturing call of the jebwa. As the dance progressed, each new stanza brought a quickening of beat, more enraged countenances on the dancers, a more boisterous and responsive chorus from the men, and a more ferocious percussion of spears. The greater the quickening, the faster the step, and the more rapid the twirling, the more dangerous the result of a single misstep or other movement out of place. Yet the men progressed through the mesmerizing line dance with flawless, fearless, methodical execution as though they were the legs of a centipede that gracefully curls in one instantaneous motion to bite with one end and excrete its paralyzing poison with the other.

Then suddenly, in the middle of the lengthy dance, the elders' pacing came to a sudden stop. Each held his hands high to signal the pause, and from the center of the second row of the dancers facing them, two spears were flung high into the air to curl above the group and fall, one after the other, with a thud, piercing straight into the stone-covered earth toward the mat upon which Tokjān and Ļainjin sat. The dancing stopped. The chanting and drumming faded into silence. The expectation in the air was palpable. The group had summoned them to join, and two from the group stepped aside. Tokjān turned his rascally eyes to Ļainjin, who nodded, rose with him, grasped a spear, and twirled it in unison with his partner to the resumed chanting as they parried their way forward into the group. Then, as the drum beating began again, the men took their places with a violent clashing of spears, initiating a reaction that rippled outward down both sides of the lines of dancers and into the audience surrounding them — and an even more spirited pace of dancing briskly resumed.

Like his previous engagement in the game of anidep, Ļainjin sought to blend into the group rather than glare among the others. His movements, though accurate and sufficiently quick, did not equal, much less exceed, the passion of his partner or the ferocity of the preceding performance. Liṃanṃan, who had obtained a drum from someone, rushed to the *du*, voicing a piercing ululation. The high pitch of her chanting rose above the others to inspiring affect, especially upon her chosen one, who parried a particularly violent clash of spears from her uncle that served to raise the spirit of the dance to a new high. Thereafter, previous tentativeness in Ļainjin's dancing disappeared. As the pace of the dance accelerated, the awareness that she had such emotional control of him wound its way among the spirits in the crowd, and they responded by enthusiastically accepting the newcomer as one of them.

The dance continued until the sun's rays were completely absorbed by the well-planted forest surrounding them, and a welcome breeze sweeping over the lagoon had begun to cool the sweat that had sprung upon him. No sooner had the dance ended than Liṃanṃan cast herself at the feet of her uncle and begged him loudly to "overlook the embarrassing failure of her chosen one's performance" and "to spare his life out of pity for her." At this, Ļainjin dropped to one knee as though ready to receive whatever punishment his victor was about to deliver. Liṃanṃan enacted this tradition as a lesson in humility. It was for the benefit of the young girls in the audience, to teach them the proper way to beg for the life of a brother should he fail in battle. Her uncle, in response, praised Ļainjin's ability as a warrior, thanked him with a broad smile for the fish he had caught as tribute, and promised to spare his life "to dance before these children again and again until he was so old Liṃanṃan would have to parry his spear for him."

At this, the surrounding audience burst into laughter, and the captivating dance, the realistic enactment, and the ancestral lesson were over until another day. It was time for all to retreat into themselves and resume their various tasks before the night settled into the green, ever-growing forest surrounding their elegant village and crept upon the surrounding white coral beaches and multicolored reefs. Each of these supported a multitude of large-eyed nocturnal marine animals, each voraciously struggling to satisfy its seemingly insatiable appetite. It was time for the spirits that had wandered these calm shores and had, for generations, guarded the ocean passageway of this diminutive string of islets and sand cays to fade into the darkness in which they thrived. And to fade, as would the very perceptibility of these shores if not for the sometimes cloud-dimmed yet ever-astounding universe of starlight overhead, coupled with the faint flickering of the cooking fires visible mostly to the mother turtles searching for their places on the sand. Visible among these two erratic rows of atolls, each up-cropped from the depths, each an isolated pinnacle, nearly lost from the others amid the vast, everchanging expanse of deep, treacherous water separating them. Time for their inhabitants to wrap themselves in the comforting assurance that, but for the marine creatures that stirred in the darkness below and the fowl fluttering home to their nests in the starlight to feed their young or their mates at nest with their daily catch, their way of life was isolated. Thus, as they had for hundreds upon hundreds of seasons, they slept peacefully, protected in their seclusion from all but the occasional windblown fishermen or the bravest of seafarers, who had been taught their location and possessed the courage, knowledge, and fortitude to follow the secret seamarks to seek them out.

* * *

The woman chosen by Tokjān, called Lijitwa, was curvaceous and held her back straight, as does a warrior. Still of childbearing age, she brandished beautifully tattooed shoulders and chest above proud, plump breasts with long, dark nipples that had suckled many children. One or two periodically clung to the ends of her strong arms like pandanus fruits that she was ever swinging to Tokjān, to grab and try to amuse, to keep out of her way as she worked. She bore a genuinely welcoming, perpetual smile between her full, broad cheeks, and she ruled her household like a helmsman at sea. She commanded her children and man alike, and none was too busy to hear. They sat for supper in her cookhouse, where she, by her hearth, kept two or three dried coconut shells flaring consecutively in the fire during the meal. Her older daughters sat outside the cookhouse, weaving freshly stripped coconut leaflets into serving baskets. They passed them to still-younger daughters, who rushed them to her to amply fill and then deliver, first to Ḷainjin and then to Liṃanṃan, whose food sat idly before her while she held her aunt's newest-born, naked boy in her arms. Much to her amusement, she teased him with her pointy, milkless breast, but much to his satisfaction, she periodically pushed a fingertip of baked and smashed pandanus pulp into his greedy mouth.

Lijitwa was not a woman given to idle talk. As soon as she served Ļōtokjān, she got right to the point. Speaking — Ļainjin assumed — on behalf of her man, she asked, "Our son says you want him to feed one of the birds on the islets?"

The boy had explained in detail his father's policy of "no bird feeding, and no bird raising." So Ļainjin, yet to become familiar with her direct approach to problem solving, tried to politely deflect the conversation from the Chief by changing the subject to her delicious baked-in-leaf mixture of pandanus pulp and grated coconut and stating, "I always say, 'Don't be afraid to toss coconut — it's good for the skin.'"

"Well, your hide is black enough to protect you from the sun, but look at my poor niece over there, red as a hermit crab caught out of its shell. She needs to wash herself down with coconut milk, or the skin will peel from her cute little nose. Liṃanṃan, will you stop teasing that boy of mine with that pimple on your chest! Here, give him to me before he starts to cry."

She took the boy, who immediately honed in on her nipple to retrieve the last of his supper. Then she turned her smile back to Ļainjin while furrowing her brow as if to concentrate on the answer she still expected him to provide.

He ignored her gaze for an instant and filled his mouth with an enormous quantity of her cooking to give himself time to think.

"Okay," she said, laughing, "let me ask a different way. What does my son say to all the other boys on the island who want to take a similar pet?"

Ļainjin took a long drink of coconut water, sucking it loudly from the eye of a husked, immature nut of perhaps seven cycles. He inspected the empty nut, squeezing it slightly in his hand, and then a polite belch erupted from his chest as he turned to her meekly and told her exactly what he assumed she wanted to hear.

"Your son has explained his father's rule not to feed the birds. It weakens them. It makes them lazy and unable to catch their own food." Ļainjin turned to the boy sitting next to the cookhouse doorway and continued, "Children who take them as pets sooner or later tire of feeding them, so they fly away but lack the skills to flourish and die before they are able to reproduce themselves. The small birds are important to us because they nourish the soil so the kōņņat can grow, put down roots, and keep the sand from washing away." The boy raised his eyebrows in affirmation, as though he had explained all this — although, of course, he had not. "And the big birds are particularly important to us! They come down from the clouds and hover like kites over the beach to warn us to prepare for the approaching big wind. Your son explained all this to me, and I understand and agree completely with the rule. But let me ask you this: Where does a bird seek to lay its egg?"

"The island of its birth," replied Tokjān, Jitwa, and their son in unison.

There was a moment of laughter, and then the little daughters chimed in as well: "The island of its birth, the island of its birth!"

Ļainjin turned to the little girls. "That's right! That's right!" he said, as they beamed back at him. The fire's flame glistened in their black, image-reflecting eyes, as does the moon on the surface of the smooth waters of the lagoon. "My friend's mate is of this string of islets, so she is covered by your father's rule and you must not feed her. The egg that she laid is of the bird islet, and you must not feed the chick that breaks through its shell. However, my friend is not of these islets, and so he alone, among all the birds, does not live by this rule. He is a visitor and must be fed like your mother is feeding me!" To emphasize the last argument, he took another enormous bite of her cooking and grinned contentedly, not revealing whether he was satisfied with what he was eating or with the words that had just spewed from his mouth.

"Father, is it true? Can we feed the bird? Can we feed the bird?"

Tokjān looked at Ļainjin with the same amused expression and mischievous twinkle in his eye as a boy about to break his father's rule for the sheer fun of it. Then he glanced at his chosen woman, who met his eyes with the same broad smile she had worn from the moment Ļainjin had entered her cookhouse.

"Yes," he said, "you can feed the newcomer because he is not of this atoll."

"Mother, can we go feed the bird now? Feed the bird now?"

"You can go with your brother tomorrow." Then, as her smile broke into a laugh, she added, "But you must call this bird Mānnijepļā!"[164]

---

[164] A mythic bird that flew passengers from one island to another.

"Mānnijepḷā! Mānnijepḷā!" The girls had heard their mother sing these bedtime chants from the time they grew in her belly. "Mother, tell us the story again. Tell it again!"

"You two have heard that story so many times you can tell it yourselves."

"She is very beautiful. Very, very good to look at!" said the girls, in the same manner as before. Each said nearly the same thing at the same time, competing against the other for attention.

"How should we call her this time, Mother?"

"Call her after your cousin Liṃanṃan!" replied their mother, laughing. "She is very beautiful, is she not?"

Liṃanṃan had apparently heard the story, as she made a quick, funny face at her aunt that made the girls giggle as they continued. "Her name was Liṃanṃan and she lived a long time ago," said the older girl.

"And she smells good," added the younger.

"And he is a man of unusual powers," continued the older.

"How shall we call him, Mother?"

"Call him 'the newcomer,'" she replied, turning her smile to Ļainjin to let him know she intended to tease him as well but, out of respect, would not use his name directly.

"She chooses the newcomer, but he never goes fishing," said one girl.

"And she complains all the time!" added the other.

"But why doesn't he go fishing?" their mother asked.

The girls looked at each other awkwardly, each giving the opportunity to the other.

"Maybe because he loves her too much, and he is afraid someone will steal her away while he's gone," Ļainjin offered.

"That's it! He's jealous."

"He's jealous!"

Ļainjin smiled. "Well, I didn't exactly put it that…"

"You are jealous! You're jealous, jealous, jealous!" sang the girls.

"She's always nagging at him. Newcomer, why don't you go fishing? Go catch me a big fish," the older sister said, acting the part of the beautiful woman they called Liṃanṃan.

"Or even just catch me a tiny, tiny one," added the younger.

"Or even a crab off the reef."

"Or go dive for a clam, why don't you?" Liṃanṃan said.

"But he just sits there!"

"He doesn't say one word."

Lijitwa asked, "But what is he doing?"

The girls looked at one another for the answer. Then the younger one tentatively answered, "He's making rope?"

"Yes, that's it," her sister added. "He makes rope all day long. Every day, and every day, she complains! 'Newcomer, why don't you go fishing? I have such a craving for fish! Go catch me a big fish,'" she said again.

"Or even a crab off the reef."

"He has to prepare his fishing implements!" said Ļainjin, playing the part and turning to Ļōtokjān. "This is the thing women never understand."

"But surely you can catch me a tiny, tiny fish without all that planning and rope making!" the older girl argued. "Or even a crab on the reef. Even a boy can catch a crab, and I thought you were a man!"

At this, Tokjān stood, took his ekkwaļ materials from a shelf among the rafters and handed them to Ļainjin. "Just make your line in silence," he said. "No man can successfully argue with a woman. Don't even try."

He began separating the fibers and playing the part of the newcomer, sitting there in silence and listening to the little girls heckling him as he rolled twine on his thigh and kept his mouth shut.

"Liṃanṃan, how many days has it been since you ate fish?" Jitwa asked.

"*Wōjej*, it's been several cycles of the moon. My man just sits there and makes rope all day."

"Girls," Jitwa said, "how many cycles does it take for him to make all the rope he needs?"

"Three!" said one.

"Four!" said the other.

"And what does he do with all that rope?" their mother asked them.

The younger girl answered. "He anchors it to the reef."

Her mother clarified the answer. "You mean he launches his outrigger canoe and anchors it to the reef."

"Yes!"

"And what does he do with poor Liṃanṃan?"

"He takes her with him."

"Why would he take his wife fishing?" Jitwa asked, feigning surprise and continuing to lead her daughters through the classic story.

"Because he's afraid I'll run off with a man who knows how to fish," Liṃanṃan said. She looked at Ļainjin and slapped his arm with the back of her hand as though chastising him for not being a good fisherman.

"You're jealous! You're jealous, jealous, jealous!" sang the girls.

"But before he launches his proa and anchors it to the reef, he fills it with coconuts and breadfruit and what else?" Jitwa asked.

"Pandanus!" they said.

"That's right!" continued their mother. "He fills his hull with pandanus and piles it high on his outrigger deck. He anchors his proa to the reef, and they drift westward until he runs out of anchor line. And now that they are way out there, he decides to dive for fish."

"Do men normally dive for fish that far out into the ocean?" Liṃanṃan asked.

"No!" the girls said.

"Why not?"

They looked at each other. Then the older one ventured a guess. "Because it's too deep?"

"Of course, it's too deep out there," Liṃanṃan said.

Ļainjin interjected. "Maybe he's just going to pretend to dive, but he'll follow the anchor line back to the reef and fish there instead."

"You're jealous. Jealous!" the girls sang, to shut him up again.

"So the newcomer takes his spear and a long stringer of rope for his catch and prepares to dive for fish. But before he dives, what does he tell her?" asked their mother.

"Chew the pandanus!" they sang out.

She gave them a hint. "But not to do what?"

The sisters responded in unison. "Don't throw the cores into the sea!"

"And what does she do?" she asked, still leading them.

"She throws the cores in the sea!"

"Typical woman!" Ļainjin added pompously.

Liṃanṃan chastised him. "Don't make noise! You're a typical jealous man, afraid to go fishing for your poor woman!"

"You're jealous! You're jealous, jealous, jealous!" the girls sang.

Tokjān chimed in. "He might as well have been talking to his oar."

Jitwa reprimanded him. "You aren't allowed to make noise either! You're jealous too!" She was laughing with Liṃanṃan and the girls now — all delighted for this rare opportunity to be impolite to the men of the house.

"So, the newcomer dives down," their mother continued, "and Liṃanṃan starts to chew her pandanus, and she throws the cores overboard. When he does not hurry to come up, she breaks off another nodule, chews it, and throws the spent core into the sea. But he still doesn't hurry to come up, and after a few cycles of the moon, the spent cores have drifted in the current, westward to Ujae. They are found on the ocean shore by two brothers, who are attracted to them by their scent."

At this point, Jitwa changed the tone of her voice to imitate that of a man. "This must have been chewed by one fantastic woman. I can still smell her scent," she said.

Then she took the part of the other, again pretending to be one of the smitten men. "When was this core eaten?" she asked.

"Cycles and cycles ago," she answered, changing her voice to act the part of the other.

"'Let's go find her!' And so, the men launched their proa and paddled eastward."

At this point, Jitwa stopped her story, turned to her daughters, and asked, "Ready to sing, girls?" Then she led them, and the three began to sing.

Their boat they launch and paddle east,
ocean bound — waow!
Night after night,
younger brother stops to ask,
'This core was eaten when?'
'Moon and moon and moon ago.'
They track the current's westward flow,

on and on they look for her.
She someone most beautiful,
good to see — she!

The girls sang three choruses. In the second chorus, the spent pandanus core had been eaten "days and days ago." In the third, it had been eaten "tides and tides ago," to show they were getting closer.

After the singing, Jitwa continued. "So they paddled on until they found her sitting there on the outrigger canoe — still chewing, still smelling good, and still waiting for her chosen man to surface.

"'Girl, you are one whiff of a good smell!'

"'I guess I should be. That is the way of the women here,' she said, pointing with her eyes back to her island.

"'What are you doing out here?'" As she continued, Jitwa changed her voice from gruff to smooth as she changed parts.

"'I'm waiting for the man with me to surface. He's fishing.'

"The men look at each other and one whispers to the other, 'Too much sun.'

"'How long has he been down there?'

"'I forget how many cycles have passed.'

"'Okay, he must have been eaten by a shark. You better come with us.'

"So they took the beautiful Liṃanṃan back to Ujae with them, and they tried to hide her and keep her to themselves. They fed her fish night and day, but sooner or later, the irooj smelled her and took her for himself.

"Back at Lae, when the newcomer finally surfaces, he has a long string of fish and clam meat.

"'*Wōjej*, wake up, girl. Here are your fish!' He speaks slowly, pretending he's not out of breath.

"But still no response from inside the boat.

"'*Wōjej*, girl, take our line!'

"No response. Waow, he drops his line and climbs aboard. She is gone! An immense sadness overcomes him."

At this, Ļainjin covered his face with his hands, but peeked through his fingers at Liṃanṃan and the girls. They all seemed quite satisfied that he received punishment for his jealousy.

"'What to do?'

"He quickly pulls in his anchor line and reaches the beach. He runs through the village. 'Has anyone seen her?'

"'No! She is gone.'

"He returns to the ocean shore. 'What to do?'

"He finds a piece of kiden wood that has drifted up from Ujae and carves it into a bird. Then the newcomer with certain powers rattles his magic chant:

Tipen keimera? Mera?[165]
Tipen keidọọj? Dọọj?[166]

"He launches the wooden bird into the air with all his might.

Tipen kemera? Kemera?
Tipen keidọọj? Dọọj?

"Waow, his bird comes to life, turns, and flies back to him. It grows larger with each flap of its wings until the bird must hunch down on the beach so the newcomer can crawl upon its back, and with a few steps and a flap of its wings, they are off, soaring in the clouds on their way to Ujae."

Jitwa interrupted the story. "Ready, girls?" They nodded their heads twice and, on the third nod, began singing:

Mān-ni-jep-ḷā!
Search, searching off west for her — waow!
Search drifting off south for her, so
climb, climbing back north for her, go
glide, gliding on island now — waow!
Flutter, flutter past her.
Flutter, flutter past her.
Land, landing!

---

165 "Piece of what's light? What's light?"
166 "Piece of what sinks? What sinks?"

Because several islets are strung along the reefs of Ujae Atoll, and because one of the many purposes of the story is to teach the names of the islets — but also to lull the children to sleep — the bird must land on each islet looking for the missing woman. The children repeat the chorus as Mānnijepļā flies from islet to islet until, as the story would have it, they find her on the last one.

"There she is, sitting with the irooj. What is she doing?" Jitwa asked her girls.

"She is sitting behind him, picking lice from his unbound hair!"

"Mānnijepļā flutters down," she continued, "and lands on the lagoon shore close by. The bird cries 'Kook!' The newcomer hides himself under the bird's feathers. The irooj has never seen such a large bird. He impulsively announces he will take it as his pet and sends his workers to gather fish for the bird to eat."

This is where Ļainjin interjected. "Just like he impetuously snatched the good-smelling Limanman from his loyal, seafaring workers!"

Jitwa continued. "The bird eats all the fish they are able to catch.

"The next morning, the irooj is awakened by the bird, screaming to be fed.

"'Kok! Kok! Kok,' goes the bird.

"So the irooj grabbed his twine for *ekkoonak*,[167] gathered his workers again, and sailed out to a spot on the reef where they were able to encircle a large group of *ikaidik*."

At this point, one of her daughters interrupted Jitwa and turned to Tokjān. "Father, tell us again why the fish don't just escape under the floating twine."

"Because the twine makes a shadow through the water and, at first, the fish are afraid of this shadow. As the circle gets smaller and smaller, the fishermen encircle the group tightly and hold their position. By then it's too late to escape, and they all fall prey to the fishermen's three-pronged spears of stingray-tipped barbs."

---

[167] A fishing method used to catch schools of rainbow runner fish, *Elagatis bipinnulata*. A circular cord of sennit is floated on the surface around the school and gradually tapered until a group of fishermen can encircle and escort it to shallower water, where the fish are speared.

Jitwa was determined to finish her story. "No sooner had they filled their proa with the *ikaidik* than Mānnijepḷā flew up and fluttered among them, screaming 'Kok, kok, kok!' Frightened, the fishermen tossed up their catch, and the bird ate it all."

"'What kind of bird is this?' said the men. However, not deterred, the irooj announced that they should get prepared for bọbo.

"So the men went home to their villages and made torches from dried coconut fronds."

This was the part of the story that led to the famous bọbo song that the jekaro boys had sprung into on the night Paratak tore his kilt away. It was not a war dance like the jebwa but a dance to celebrate getting back to everyday life after the battle.

"Father, show us again how to bọbo," asked one of his daughters. This, apparently, was the part the girls liked the most, and Jitwa, the least.

Tokjān rose quickly, grabbed onto his pole net of two ñeñe, reached over the sitting group with the pole, and cupped the net at the end beneath his woman's two coconut shells of cooking water, which were hanging in their own nets from one of the cookhouse rafters. He twisted the net to break them away, backed the butt of the pole out the open doorway, and exited, dripping water over the lot of them. When he returned, Jitwa beat on his foot with the stick she used to stir the coals of her hearth, leaving black marks of charcoal across the top of it.

"Sit down and stop showing off!" The group roared in laughter at these antics. Jitwa seemed intent on finishing the story, but her girls were not ready.

"But Father, you said the fish would fly from all directions!"

"That's right, and that's why the men in the dance dip their poles low and then high so they can catch the fish as they fly."

"But why do the fish fly?"

"They are escaping the sharks that are rushing to eat them!"

"Why are there so many sharks?" asked one.

"At first they are attracted by the light of the torches, but as they get close, they see the flying fish there, stunned by the light. So they go for their meal, and the fish take flight to escape the sharks' bite."

After a brief silence, Jitwa returned to her story.

"That night, the men launch their proa and head out to sea, past the western reef of Ujae. The newcomer unites with Liṃanṃan, and they cling to Mānnijepḷā's feathers as it takes flight and approaches the fleet as the men fish. It flutters over them, and their torches flare as they toss up fish to feed the greedy bird. That is when the irooj sees his stolen woman. She is sitting there on the bird's back with her bare legs wrapped around the newcomer, and she is picking lice from his unbound hair. He gets a last whiff of her scent before they fly off. He will never smell her again, and she is glad she chose a man of certain powers."

When the story was finished, the younger girl said, "Mother, I'm going to take a man of certain powers."

Her older sister said, "You like Ļōbwebwe! What powers does he have?"

"I do not! But he knows how to *bwilbwil*," said the younger girl, defending him.

"And *bwilbwil* is the first step in learning how to become a great navigator," added Ļainjin, defending the girl's choice.

"What's a navigator?" she asked.

"That's a man who goes out into the ocean, sails in circles until he finds an island, and then claims he knew where it was all along!" answered Liṃanṃan jokingly. "That's where I caught this one, paddling around in circles until he stumbled upon my father's proa and followed me home."

Ļainjin's eyes squinted at her and she squinched her nose back at him.

Tokjān interjected. "The women have clearly won this evening's battle. Better to retreat than end up sleeping in your hull!" he said, departing for the big house.

"Girls, time to grate coconut and draw water for our guests," Jitwa said.

The little ones scampered. Jitwa passed the sleeping baby from her lap to one of her older daughters to take to the house and turned to Ļainjin. "Ļōtokjān hasn't heard about all the fun you two had in that hull of yours!"

Liṃanṃan, with a look of embarrassment, turned her face to Ļainjin but avoided his surprised and questioning eyes by stating it was time to draw his bathwater and then quickly exiting, leaving the two of them by themselves in the cookhouse.

Jitwa poured him a shell of steeped *nen*. He was wondering what details Liṃanṃan had given her about their first or subsequent encounters and was not sure how embarrassed he should be — but he was not about to ask.

"Just like a man," she continued. "You're so concerned about your story that you forget we women have our own stories to tell! Tomorrow, when you walk the path, ask any little girl you meet about the story of Liṃanṃan and her man shark, and they will tell you how she cast herself into the sea to die with a man she just met! She is so young, yet she is already a legend among us women! She is not cross when you tell your story of all your adventures on faraway islands. So don't be cross when she brightens our lives by feeding us landbird tidbits about her life with the glorious seafarer.

"I'll tell you a story about my sister Likeju. When Ḷōtokjān took me, he had been with many other girls around the atoll. After all, he had irooj blood, and look at him now. Even at his age, he would be a catch for any young woman! My good fortune was on everyone's lips. I was the most desirable to him, and he lay with me night and day, like a fisherman drilling the eye of his lure. It took him but a week to plant his seed, and everyone marveled at how quickly I got pregnant. Everyone was happy for me except my sister!

"She was an unusual girl who had her pride and had been with no man, and she claimed she did not want to have to please Ḷōtokjān while I was incapacitated. She told our grandmother so, and without saying another word, she took our father's proa and sailed off into a storm…" She slapped her right hand against her left palm, extending it forward to mime her sister's sail heeled over and dramatizing the depiction of her careening off into the wind.

"The next day, word came that she had made it to that northernmost islet, there" — she pointed with her face — "across the passageway. She was lucky she wasn't swept out to sea in the squall!"

"Very brave," responded Ḷainjin.

"Very foolish was my opinion at the time. I was livid!

"A few days later, grandmother mentioned why she disappeared to Ḷōtokjān and so" —she slapped her hand again as before — "off he goes!

"When he gets to the island, he sees Father's canoe in our cousin's boathouse and is told Likeju is gathering pandanus leaves. He finds her in the pandanus patch with our cousin's daughters and sits before them. He promises her that, if she returns, she has nothing to fear — that he will respect her wishes and expect nothing from her — and then he pledges before all these girls to remain celibate during my pregnancy out of respect for me!"

Continuing, she said, "What a *luwap*!"[168]

"Just like a man, he assumed she left because of him! In truth, it had nothing to do with him. It was all about *her* and me because everyone was voicing my name and she was not content to stand in my shadow. She craved her own story and that's why she left, not because she was afraid of that soft banana of his!

"The amusing thing is that, once she understood what a doting and respectful old puffer fish he was, she returned our father's proa, attacked Tokjān like a landed barracuda, and successfully planted his seed under the first moon that passed. Guess who everyone was talking about then?! Then guess what? The puffer fish got his wish because my other sisters were too young to take our place on his mat. Likeju and I became sister stars in the sky. We are inseparable. We shared every minute of our pregnancies together and have not shared a cross word since.

"Here is my point. We women have our own stories and our men need to realize this. Let Liṃanṃan tell her story any way she wants."

"Did I hear my name?" inquired Liṃanṃan from the doorway, as she grabbed hold of Ļainjin's arm and started playfully yanking him away. "Don't listen to a word she says! She is trying to get you to confess to all the private details about us that she has already tried to pry out of me with no success! It's time for your bath, little boy!"

"Well, keep the bathhouse dark," Jitwa said. "I don't want my daughters peeking at your little boy's private details! When you're done washing him, lay him on a mat in the house."

"I'm going to put him to sleep in your cookhouse," Liṃanṃan said.

---

[168] Puffer fish: *Tetraodon hispidus*; also called porcupine fish. These fish have the ability to inflate their bodies by swallowing water. Some species have a tetrodotoxin in their internal organs, such as the ovaries and liver, and are poisonous.

"Just as I thought — the poor thing has a careless mother," retorted her aunt.

Later, in the dark of the bathhouse, under the faint starlight seeping through the forest canopy of breadfruit leaves and coconut palms, they took turns squeezing the oily milk from white mounds of grated coconut upon each other and then scrubbing each other with the remaining pulp and the *inpel* used to squeeze it. The water wilted the curls of her hair, and she reminded him of the way she looked earlier that day, when she had dunked to cool herself in the lagoon — except this time, she was shivering as the well water ran cold over her sunburned skin. He embraced her with the warmth of his body, squeezed her with his arms, and lifted her high to his chest. Then he twirled her once to remind her of her first night with him. She landed on his hip with her legs wrapped about him. She pressed her breast up to his mouth, whispering the name of the little one she had fruitlessly suckled earlier. "Ļajuōn, here's your supper. Yes, here it is, here it is. What? There is nothing left? Well, you must have drunk it all. Yes, you drank it all! You are a greedy little boy! You drank every drop of my milk and there's none left," she whispered, kissing him repeatedly on the face as she had the child.

When he put her down, she wrapped her skirts about her, handed him his kilt, and led him across the stone yard back to her aunt's cookhouse, where Jitwa had left them a rolled-up sleeping mat. Liṃanṃan unfurled it, laying it on the thicker, more broadly woven mats they had sat upon earlier. Then she snuffed out the shell lamp of coconut oil that her aunt had lit, and they lay in each other's arms in the darkness, save for the dim glow of dying coals in the hearth and the starlight reflecting off the sun-bleached stones of the surrounding courtyard and shining through the slatted cookhouse walls. In the nearby house, her aunt, who commandeered her family as though they were the crew of her proa, broke the quiet periodically. There was singing and the scampering of little feet, scolding, cautioning, crying, and then orders to draw more water, to grate more coconut, to bathe, to come and to go, to lie still, and to sleep.

"Ļajuōn looked so cute dancing the jebwa."

"What made you decide to plead for my life?"

"It was a good lesson for the girls."

"I felt awkward and embarrassed."

"I wanted to embarrass you," she said, touching him, gently drawing his attention away from their discussion.

"Why?"

"Because you needed a little humbling after dancing like that." She removed her skirts and lifted her thigh invitingly.

"Dancing like what?" He rolled over, sitting on his knees and straddling her other leg.

"Your dance was too compelling," she said, fondling his bulging manhood beneath his kilt. "I saw all the women were watching you and not the others. Now when the men return home, they will be talking about the both of us and not just about you. No man wants to listen to talk about another man's dancing." She untied his kilt, flung it aside, slowly and seductively extracted her leg from between his, and wrapped it about him until he could feel her heel high upon his back.

"How do you know?" he asked, as he positioned himself.

"Litaknaṃ taught me such things." She giggled.

"Oh, Litaknaṃ again. What else did she teach you?" he asked, accepting her invitation and gently entering her.

"She told me to invert myself to plant your seed deep." Placing her weight onto her elbows, she maneuvered the flat of her feet up onto his shoulders and rolled back to accept the entirety of his swollen manhood as he hunched on all fours. He looked down into her determined face, her wet hair sprawled beguilingly on the mat beneath them. "Release it, and I will keep it warm and moist and dark within me. It will grow into a boy or a girl. Either way, we'll call it Kāmeto[169] and it will be a great seafarer like its father" — she was laughing now — "and a great fisher like its mother!"

They laughed together at her joke as he rolled her high upon her shoulders. Then he began once again his gallant struggle to master the oncoming urge to release himself into her, knowing she wanted him to rock her to satisfaction, knowing she expected him to chafe the skin of his knees red — knowing this would be the very first thing she would look for in the morning and knowing that her sister would tease him if he scabbed. He

---

[169] Name: "fly the ocean."

therefore concentrated his thoughts on the details of the things she had done or said to him. He raised his face and peered into the blackness above, searching for images of her to un-urge himself for one instant, and then another. He rejected the perennial images of the broken, ashen bodies of the friends who had lost their lives for him; the cold, dark, and putrid cave of Nan Samohl, with its single unreachable circle of light above him; the fiery sun of the doldrums beating down upon his cracked lips as though it intended to shrivel his face to the bone.

In their stead flashed her auburn face as it surfaced from the blue sea beneath him and feigned a pout as she snatched his prized pandanus and teased him by floating it away from his grasp. Here, he found her determinedly, ecstatically hauling her catch, seawater mixed with blood from her palms running pink down her forearms. There she was at the mast in the rain, releasing the halyard in the teeth of the approaching storm. One intriguing image of her led to another and then another as the moments of their short life together streamed about him timelessly, crowding away those of his harrowing, unhappy past until his desire for the noble, seductive soul striving beneath him forced him back to the faint glare reflecting off the starlit eyes peering up at him.

He, realizing she had been watching him as he had turned away to watch her out there in their past together. She, nevertheless, revealing to him, through the faintest murmur, her undaunted passion. He, realizing their heavy breathing had become one, felt the coconut-scented sweat dripping from his face down upon her, as it became his turn to watch her writhing to fulfill herself. Her face, wet with oil and perspiration, began to twist from side to side away from him, now in a seemingly solo struggle. Then, as though swimming through the waves, he watched her reach the precipice that now required her to draw herself onto it. He felt her fingers clutch onto each of his wrists as his hands were clutching the undersides of her thighs, as though she needed leverage for a final thrust. A moment later, he felt her tremble. She turned back to him, raised her eyebrows, and simultaneously inhaled sharply — and none too soon, as watching her desperate pursuit had drawn him irreversibly back to the edge of uncontrollability. His seed was now too much to bear despite his will to continue to contain it and bask in the sweltering desire that had welled up inside him. Silently, satisfyingly, he felt the storm she had so seductively brewed peak and seemingly flood her insides with its torrent.

Exhausted, they curled their naked, oily, and sweaty bodies together. They lolled in the faint breeze that had drifted across an untold expanse of waves to cross the calm waters of the reef-sheltered lagoon and then seep through the slatted walls sheltering them. They lay content that they had managed, despite all odds to the contrary, to clutch onto each other amid the boundless, unknowable universe of endless sky and sea sweeping about them, and this mutual, meditative thought lay wordless between them. After a prolonged period of silence, she covered their nakedness by folding the mat over them, and each fell separately into a deep peaceful sleep.

When he awoke the next morning and ran his hands over the smooth skin of the naked body still intertwined with his beneath the mat, he soon realized that not all was well. He could hear lagoon waves breaking on the shore. The breeze had picked up and was carrying familiar voices from the boathouse where his proa rested. Liṃanṃan protested, clung to him from the warmth of the sleeping mat, pleaded he stay, and then pouted as he nonetheless arose, donned his kilt, and emerged into the slight first light of daybreak. The air was heavy, damp, and salty. Two of his jekaro boys were talking with Tokjān. They had been sent by Etre, who had apparently hurt himself and could not make jekaro. Not till later, once he had crossed the lagoon, would Ļainjin compile the true story. Word had spread that Likōkkālọk was pregnant, and Paratak, who had seen Etre conspiring with her, now accused him of being the father. Paratak had attacked Etre, who was embarrassed that he had not put up much of a fight.

"Which of us do you want to cut your trees?" one of the boys asked.

"Neither, I will go myself. We'll sail into this weather together."

"Isn't Etre one of your jebwa leaders?" Tokjān asked, perhaps curious about the prospect of his brother losing a key combatant in the upcoming battle.

"Yes," Ļainjin replied.

"Then my brother will be concerned," Tokjān said, glancing from one man to the other. "What happened to him?"

"He hurt his leg. That's all he told us to say."

"Well, I guess you will want to launch your proa," Tokjān continued. "I will get some men to help you. Come, boys. Let's get you two fed and ready for weather." He turned back to look out over the gray face of the new day and then chanted, "*Kwe kwōjkwōjwaj jōn̄e Lan̄peran!*"[170]

When Ļainjin returned to the cookhouse, Jitwa was fanning her cooking fire. Thick smoke erupted from her hearth, forcing her to turn her head and squint as she spoke. "Naughty girl there" — she pointed to Liṃanṃan with her teary eyes — "let my fire die. She even blew the flame from the shell lamp I gave her." Then she laughed. "I can only imagine what naked contortions she was performing on you that had to be blacked out by the night!"

Liṃanṃan, still wrapped in the sleeping mat, squinched her nose at them both. Then she slid her skirts from the floor next to her and struggled to wrap herself in them from beneath the cover of the mat.

Outside, the boys ate and chatted with Jitwa's two older daughters, who had quickly donned flowers above their ears and seemed excited to receive news of who had said what about whom on the islet across the lagoon.

While they ate, Tokjān had Ļainjin's proa carried to the beach and had both boats loaded with pandanus as tribute to his brother. While the boys socialized and Liṃanṃan and Jitwa gossiped over the latest stories brought by them, Ļainjin strolled down to the shore to evaluate the oncoming weather. Though stronger, the wind had shifted only slightly from a little south to a little north of east. Yet the face of the lagoon, no longer sheltered by the length of the atoll's southern fringing reef, had changed dramatically from the serene calm of the day before. Sparkling, rippling shades of blue had changed to a frothy, whitecapped gray. The grayish blue of the shallow lagoon water just inside the southern reef was the only color that warmed the otherwise threatening shades of gray drifting about the horizon. The clear waves that had lapped gently upon yesterday's shoreline had now turned into sand-clouded breakers that thumped upon the beach and broke into sandy, white froth. Then they swept high upon the shore, lingered momentarily, and churned back into the briny tumult from which they had come.

---

[170] "You've cast the fate called brave sky."

As Ļainjin suspected, there was no boundary or single line of clouds on the horizon, nothing that foretold a dramatic change in what they would face — just a sky filled with the types of smoky-looking rain clouds that promised steady wind and periodic, annoying gusts of rain. There would be no sudden deluge of wind, and its general westerly blowing direction was unlikely to change radically. Yet each cloud would carry its own personality to them and require equal spirit and personal fortitude from each of them. And so it occurred that as Liṃanṃan and the boys joined him — with Tokjān, Jitwa and their children in tow — the cloud passing over them ejected a gust of wind and cold rain that turned their faces.

Ļainjin quickly turned to the others and swung his back to the gust, allowing its oomph to shiver up his spine and blossom into a broad smile. "*Ejaromrom utute kōj*,"[171] he chanted as he looked directly at Tokjān, who laughed affectionately with him as he faced the rain directly to receive the challenge and respond.

"*Eke eok jān Ep!*"[172] he chanted.

It was not a moment to clutter with further talk. Liṃanṃan climbed up on the proa. Standing high in the wind and stinging rain, she drew the halyard at the mast, hoisted, and then secured his matted sail. Side by side, Ļainjin and the others lifted and pushed the heavy boat through the crests of the warm, oncoming waves. It went buoyant, but although its bow rose high over the oncoming crest, it threatened to dip precariously before the next. He drew himself up into his place at the stern and used his weight to teeter his bow higher, even as the foaming crest crashed down upon it, splashed water up into the wind, and drenched Liṃanṃan with spindrift as she flopped onto the outrigger deck. She then sheeted in as he leveraged his paddle into the lagoon water. The proa heeled against the wind and angled them off into a smooth, steady glide through the tops of the whitecaps. They rose and fell as the storm clouds maneuvered about them. They teetered over each rising crest and following trough as the underlying energy marched the lagoon waves downshore from the spot from which they escaped.

---

[171] "It's lightning it's raining us."

[172] Literally, "make your veins stand out." "Inspiring you from Ep." (Ep is the western ancestral homeland.)

He looked back as they began to skip quickly from one crest to the next and saw the family launching their companions' proa. A moment later, Liṃanṃan stood, grasped the mast with one hand, braced herself upon the rocking boat with a wide stance on the outrigger deck, and thanked them with a broad wave of her free arm. Then she reset herself on the stern edge of the deck, her back to the wind and the rain. Her right foot was braced against the hull. Her right hand clasped onto the base of the mast and her left, onto the sternmost outrigger boom. Her left leg dangled bare and free, with her foot now and then dipping into the still-shallow water below. Her breasts, her shoulders, and her arms were pimpled with cold, but her face showed no sign of chill and her spirit was vibrant.

She twisted her soaking hair into a tight bun and lifted her dangling foot, exposing her inner thigh to him. Then she jabbed his shoulder with the ball of her foot. "Why such a hurry? Your jekaro buds will stay moist in this rain."

"No, just the opposite. The leaves will absorb water from the sky and not pull it through the tree from the ground. At any rate, the bud will not weep if not cut."

He looked back and saw the boys' proa rising and falling and following them on their tack to the northeast. The family had retreated from shore, and he imagined them warm and sheltered from the rain in their cookhouse, eating and drinking hot *nen* tea from shell cups.

Deciding to use her foot to cushion her rocking rear, Liṃanṃan curled her leg beneath her and sat on it. "You know he may not be there."

"Who won't be there?"

"Ḷāātre!"

"What do you mean, won't be there?"

"You know the story."

"What story?"

"The story of Ḷōkkōkālọk,"[173] she said.

Of course, he had heard the story of Ḷōkkōkālọk many times. The story ends at Anbōd, where he and his friends undertook their great shark adventure. He had always viewed the story — like so many others — as a

---

[173] A name: "man make fly."

means to teach about a place that mariners need to know. As boys, they never believed the bedtime story, yet they never doubted for an instant that Anbōd existed.

"*Diak!*" Ļainjin said.

Liṃanṃan immediately released the sheet and handed it to him. She backed herself off the outrigger deck, crawled forward onto the foredeck, released the forestay, and grabbed onto the base of the *rojak ṃaan*. Their craft rocked in the waves and drifted outrigger to windward, with the sail now flapping downwind, perpendicular to the hull. She lifted the heavy sail easily, as if it were but a kite in the wind, and brought the flapping sail back to the mast, to which the *rojak ṃaan* was attached near its top and from which it hung. Because she had loosened the forestay, the mast had begun to reverse its tilt. After she handed the sail to Ļainjin, she returned to what was now the backstay and resecured it once the reversal was complete and what had been the bow was now the stern.

After securing the *rojak ṃaan* in its new position, Ļainjin sat on the inner part of the outrigger deck beneath the mast. He sheeted in and the craft lurched into the wind on the opposite tack, now headed away from the light blue water that bordered the shore toward the darker water of the atoll's center. One of the many dark-gray clouds massed about them caught his eyes. It was spraying its vapor in a slant angled downward as it drifted over the busy bird islets abaft. That angle, a sign that the wind they were facing on the surface was stronger than the air above, was a good sign because it meant they were in no danger of a surprise drop of more forceful air streaming overhead.

"So what are you trying to say about the story?" he said. He turned his head from the wind and the rain to see her standing proudly and struggling determinedly with the paddle blade secured to the hull, cutting deep into the water. Its shaft was braced firmly in the crotch of her right shoulder, leveraging the proa into heel, raising the outrigger behind him, and flying it conservatively above the oncoming waves.

With a broad smile across a face dripping with water, eyes squinted and peering back and forth, Liṃanṃan rose and fell as the stern teetered with each wave. And as the whitecaps rushed by, she sprang gleefully into song.

Ļōk-kō-kā-lọk — waaw!
Man cause to fly so!
Sail to bring tribute from sea,
sail and cast magical wind.
I'm sleepy now so
standing up I sail — waow!
Boat to catch, boat to catch,
boat to catch, catch.
To catch me and kill...
Off wind will tilt kubaak up
windward to set to rest.

"You've heard the story?" She leaned into the wind, levering her oar into the lagoon and raising their kubaak up and over the wave as it surged toward them.

"Many times," he said, adjusting the sheet, feeling the outrigger taking flight beneath him, and noticing their companions still proceeding downshore on their original tack. So they decided to sail on this way, distracting themselves from the rain and the cold by periodically relating the details of the story to each other as they worked their vessel against the wind amid the dark, mountainous clouds floating about them.

"When Ļōkkōkālọk returns to Epoon[174] after his long voyage, where has he been?" she asked, raising the tone of her voice as though speaking to a child.

"He has sailed among the islands here in the north."

"Why would he do that? Hadn't the woman with him just given birth?" she asked.

"Yes."

"But everyone knows you never leave a woman who has just had a baby alone!"

"I guess he made a mistake. He was gathering gifts to be distributed at his son's *keemem*."

[174] A neighboring atoll seventy-three miles south-southwest of Namorik.

"Well, that was a very big mistake. What did she do while he was gone?" she asked, continuing to steer them on a close tack a little farther out into the lagoon to get a slightly wider angle off wind before their next tack.

"She became a *mejenkwaad*[175] and ate all the people on Epoon," he answered.

"Now that's a lot of people! I heard there were so many people on Epoon that they wore paths on the reef between the islets with their feet!" she said, still using her patronizing voice, as though speaking to a child.

"That's true. I've seen it myself."

"So what happened to all the people who made those paths?"

"No one knows."

"She must have eaten them!" Liṃanṃan suggested, as though doing so would be but a trifling, everyday accomplishment.

Suddenly, they sailed into an additional burst of wind and chilling, stinging rain from the cloud ahead. Their objective, of course, was to maneuver their craft lagoonward, into position for a straight shot at their destination. The cloud, which seemed to be hanging there, was in their way, so they decided they would shunt, turn back toward the fringing reef, and change places to avoid the worst of it. But the cloud's full, cold downpour engulfed them anyway, and they lost all visibility. A deluge of rain inundated them and dampened even the wind as they glided more slowly into the light blue water they had fished the day before. The rain was so heavy they could not see the bird islets they were approaching, and from inside the deluge, they could not view their companions, last seen continuing their previous tack. Their storytelling temporarily forgotten, they sailed a while, peeking intently at each other through the hair covering their faces and glancing downward from time to time onto the opaque surface of the lagoon to judge by color their distance from the back reef.

The islet appeared close by. Then, out of nowhere, flapping through the rain and seeming larger than life, a gigantic black bird with a white throat appeared and attempted to land on Liṃanṃan, who reflexively covered her head with her hands to protect herself from the screaming fowl. To Ļainjin, it appeared to be the Chief's mate, attempting to chase them away from its

---

[175] A cannibal; a witch who eats people.

nesting area. Its feathers were thick, black, and soaked, and it struggled to stay aloft in the rain with no glide to its flight, only a heavy flapping as though the bird was drowning in the drenching air.

Liṃanṃan kept one hand over her head to prevent a second attack, but the bird had disappeared as quickly as it had assailed them. Like a verse in a song, it was gone in a breath, leaving them to wonder about its meaning. Just as they assumed the rain could not be heavier, the downpour increased and drenched even the wind, which had become but a breeze that only partially filled their sail, slowed their progress, and left them idle on deck.

"What was that?" asked Liṃanṃan, her eyes opening wide with amazement.

"I think that was my bird's mate."

"What was she trying to do? I thought she wanted to peck out my eyes!"

"Maybe she was trying to scare us away from her nest."

Liṃanṃan, sitting on her feet, was laughing. "No, we were not close to her nest! Just like a woman! She is jealous! She wants to keep his pathetic little stinky butt to herself! What a vamp!" Looking straight up, she squinted into the torrent of water streaming down her face.

"Talk about Mānnijepḷā!" she said, looking at him quickly as he smiled back at her.

Then she must have remembered she was telling a different story, so she returned to that and asked, "So when Ļōkkōkālọk arrives back at Epoon, where does he tie his proa?"

"He ties it to a huge rock on the ocean-side reef they call Ļōkajaaj."

"Have you seen it?"

"Yes, it's the height of two men and maybe thirty ñeñe around."

"And where does he find her?"

"She meets him with blood dripping from her mouth, carrying her baby to the lagoon village."

"Then what?" she asked.

"*Wōjej!*" he said, taking the part of Ļōkkōkālọk. "Where is everyone? And what's that dripping from your chin?"

Ļōkkōkālọk's chosen one said, "There's a big catch of tuna in the village and everyone is gathered there."

"Okay, let's go see. You go first!" he said.

"No! You go first!" Liṃanṃan pretended to toss her baby at him and then placed her hands on her hips and pouting her lips at him.

As he pretended to catch her imaginary child, Ļainjin dropped the oar he had tied to the boat, and the craft shortly turned into the breeze. Grabbing the oar again and sculling them forward, he began to laugh at the spectacle of her sitting there all pimpled in the cold, pouring rain, pretending to be a *mejenkwaad*. Then the rain parted, and they caught a tail wind from the cloud that had finally passed. They found themselves over the slope off the back reef where they had fished the day before, so again they shunted and glided out farther into the lagoon. There, they could see their companions, evidently having outmaneuvered them, bobbing far in the drizzling distance on the opposite tack.

"Here," he said, pretending to give the child back to her. He put his hand on his stomach and pretended to have a stomachache. "I have to make ready first. Let me go behind the bushes and relieve myself."

"And what are you doing behind there, Ļōkkōkālọk?" she asked him, pretending to hold a child in her arms.

"I'm making a wind charm from coconut leaflets, and it's going 'rup-rup-rup' so you will think I'm farting, but I'm really sneaking back to the reef to retrieve my proa."

"Ļōk-kō-kā-lọk," she sang, "it's been almost a long time to finish! Ļōk-kō-kā-lọk! What are you doing now?"

"I'm placing an empty coconut shell on Ļōkajaaj to go 'woo' in the wind before I set my sail and glide away."

"Ļōk-kō-kā-lọk," she sang again, "it's been almost a long time now! Ļōk-kō-kā-lọk!"

"He's long gone!" said Ļainjin. "You better rush behind those bushes!"

Liṃanṃan pretended to be running. She teetered her shoulders up and then down, pretending to hold a baby in her arms.

Ļainjin dared her. "There's the wind charm. Eat it!"

Liṃanṃan twisted her face into that of a *mejenkwaad* and pretended to snatch the wind charm and eat it.

"He's left you with the baby! How will you ever catch him with that baby in your arms?"

She pretended to throw the baby up in the air and eat it on the way down.

"Now quickly run after him. There he is taunting you from on top of Ļōkajaaj. He is saying, 'Woo! Woo!'"

Her face still twisted, she teetered her shoulders up and down again, pretending to run.

"Oh! It is just a coconut shell singing in the wind! Eat it!"

She pretended to throw the coconut shell up in the air and gulp it on the way down.

At this point, she twisted her face and stopped to look at Ļainjin, who broke into laughter at the sight of her dripping in the rain and pretending to be the crazy, frustrated *mejenkwaad*. Then, still amused by her feigned frustration, he stood up on the stern deck, bracing himself with one hand on the backstay and the other on the tiller, and began to sing.

Ļōk-kō-kā-lọk — waow!
Man cause to fly so!
Sail to bring tribute from sea,
sail and cast magical wind.
I'm sleepy now so
standing up I sail — waow!
Boat to catch, boat to catch,
boat to catch, catch.
To catch me and kill…
Off wind will tilt kubaak up
windward to set to rest.

"And how does the story end, little girl?" Ļainjin asked, trying to mimic the patronizing voice she had used earlier.

"I brace myself on all fours on the top of that rock and stretch my neck and spear my head, screaming at you, Ļōk-kō-kā-lọk!"

"And what happens then?"

"You *diak* at the last moment. I miss and I gulp water!"

"And what happens then?"

"I have to pull my neck back in like a fishing line as you sail away."

He questioned her again in the same patronizing tone. "And what happens then?"

"I brace myself and lunge again, but this time, you've reached Anbōd. Again, you tack at the last moment, and I gulp water again."

"And what happens then?"

"Then, as I draw my head back, a shark bites it off and that's the story's end," she said, bracing herself at the mast. Yet another veil of rain slanted toward them from a second, larger raincloud. Her smile beamed bravely and she suddenly scampered at him, landing on the stern deck, sliding there, and nearly toppling them both into the water as she tried to climb onto his hip. He ended up sliding to the edge of the deck with her, her bare legs straddling his knee and her arms around him, engendering warmth amid the threatening gray, the wind, and the rain.

Then she whispered in his ear. "Well, when we women of Lae tell that story we turn it around. We say the woman's name was Likōkkālọk and she ate only the men on the island! That is why we all hate her. She ate Paratak's soul and now she's eaten Ļāātre. Go see for yourself. You will find but a shell of the man he was. You are next unless you can resist her charms."

He looked into the distance and noticed the boys. "We better *diak*," he whispered back.

When they arrived, Pedpedin and a group of men boldly confronted the increasingly heavy downpour to help them unload the boats and carry them to shelter. Visibly upset, Pedpedin gave Ļainjin the first hint that Etre's injury was caused by a blow from the hands of Paratak. Unwilling to warm and weaken himself at Taknaṃ's fire, he took his cleaned, netted coconut shells and headed along the empty path to his jekaro trees. He passed by the villagers huddled in their cookhouses, the children no doubt still wrapped in their sleeping mats, the breadfruit leaves still lying about the various courtyards where they had fallen during the night. The rainstorm had reached full deluge, and there was a flash of lightening amid the haze and then the rumble of thunder in the distance as he began to climb his first tree. His feet were secure as he placed them, one after the other, in the notches he had long since cut into each trunk with his *kapwōr*-shell adze. He reached the crown of the first tree and sat at peace, alone amid the heavy rain, his hands and fingers mindlessly going through their routine as they would have on any other day.

Then the warm colors of life — the various shades of greens and yellows about him — inspired a thought in that intense moment of heavy weather. *Emejjia wa iloṃeto!* In the storm, he sat there cradled in the immense strength of the tree, feeling protected as he had in his boat out on the water, as though wrapped in the arms of his mother. The answer to his conundrum came to him. Yes, at sea, the best plan may very well be to have no plan but to simply stay aware of one's position amid the flux. Here, landed — on the other hand — having no plan meant risking being diverted off course by random events perpetrated by pretense, ending in mishap. Either he would summon a plan to overcome the issues he faced, or he might fail to achieve the destiny he envisioned for himself and Liṃanṃan. Luckily, such a plan flashed before him, and he knew, as sure as thunder follows lightning, that he would follow it to culmination. Just as he must set his bird free to follow his destiny, so he must cut his friend Paratak free to follow his. Just as he had respected the screaming of the Chief's mate, so he must heed Likōkkāloķ's wish to be free of his Pohnpeian friend. Clearly, she would leave neither of them alone until she was free of him. He must be true to them both, though it remained to be seen who, if anyone, would understand his intentions.

He lowered himself from the tree with his vision firmly in place. He completed his rounds amid his trees and those of his friend, and then brought the brimming shells of jekaro to Ļāātre's home. Ļainjin found the boy lying on a mat, his window propped open, staring out into the surrounding, leaf-covered square. Ļainjin tried his best not to consider what Liṃanṃan had said, yet he could not help but feel the boy *had* changed. He asked him about the fight with Paratak. There had not been a fight really. Paratak had taken his spear, left among the others at Likōkkāloķ's island, and clubbed him with it as he descended from his jekaro tree the evening before. He had attacked him the same way he had Ļainjin, but the result was very different. He showed Ļainjin the swollen wound on his calf.

"He can hardly walk! He's delirious with fever but he won't close that window!" cried his mother. The family was sitting there watching over him.

Ḷāātre turned his face back to the propped-open window. The sounds of the rain splattering onto the coral stones resounded through the window and into the home. Ḷainjin wanted to ask him about his tryst with Likōkkālọk, but this was impossible with his family there. He wiped the water dripping from his face with his hand, bent low to the mat, and whispered to the boy, "Why?" Without looking away from the window, Ḷāātre raised his eyebrows and inhaled sharply. Ḷainjin took that to mean he accepted that Paratak had a good reason to attack him. "The rumors must be true," he thought to himself, as he rose and asked Ḷāātre's permission to borrow his spear, propped in the corner.

Ḷainjin left the shelter of the boy's house and walked back into the downpour, the sound of which permeated the village and the forest and eerily drowned out the everyday sounds of daily life about him. He knew what he must do. She would not stop until his friend Paratak was humiliated out of control. Had she chosen Etre as her latest supplicant because she expected that he, Ḷainjin, would avenge one friend's honor against the other?

In good time, he would learn there was a coconut tree on the ocean side of her island that they referred to as Likōkkālọk's perch. It was well known among the men and was close to that part of the reef flat where women would go to defecate in the water each morning before dawn. The tree had grown up shaded by others along the shore. Searching for light, it had grown horizontally outward from the strand across the shaded shore for seasons before finally blossoming upward into the sunlight. She would meet her sex partners there before sunrise, during her passion period of the waning half-moon. She would tell Paratak she needed to make ready and would be back shortly. Embarrassed to follow her there, he would sleep as she straddled her latest admirer, mercilessly grinding his rear against the trunk until it bruised in ecstasy. The men claimed they welcomed the pain as a distraction from the seductive nature of her control over them. Truly, she was a woman of a different sort — they all acknowledged that — but to a man, they respected her single-mindedness. They admitted that she bewitched them. They claimed they would take any risk to have her. Truly, like the aorak images carved into the trunks of the oldest trees, she had a way of burning her specter into the souls of the men she engaged in this way. He had little doubt that, one day, one of them would kill his friend Paratak in some cowardly way.

When Ḷainjin returned to the stilted, thatched house of the irooj, he stepped out of the rain and sat beneath, dripping. He found Ḷaluj, not surprisingly, rolling twine and sipping hot *nen* tea from a shell cup.

"Litaknaṃ" — he called to the cookhouse — "bring a shell of *nen*, please, for your favorite newcomer. He's as full of sky as he was the day he arrived!"

Taknaṃ crossed through the rain with two steaming shells and handed one to each man. She placed her warm hands on Ḷainjin's shoulders and then covered them with a soft mat before returning to her fire. Ḷainjin let the mat slip behind him but sipped the hot, pungent water.

"Who should I ask to hack me a new proa?"

"What's wrong with the one you have?"

"Nothing, I'd like another a little lighter."

"Well, there are several good boatbuilders on this atoll, but why not let me try?"

"Good. That way I know the measurements will be perfect."

"How long do you want it?"

"Two and one-half ñeñe, please."

"I will need to provide tribute for the tree."

"Remember the lure I gave the irooj? I have many more."

"One would be more than generous."

"Good, and I have more for you."

"One would be more than generous of you."

"Then it's settled. When can you start?"

"Can an old man wait to finish his *nen*?"

"Yes, of course" — Ḷainjin laughed — "keep yourself healthy. You have a lot of work to do. Let me know how I can help."

"I will need a *ri-katak*. Is there someone you want me to teach?"

"Yes, offer the opportunity to Ḷōbōkrōk," responded Ḷainjin, looking down at the spear next to him. "Give him this and tell him I want him to replace Ḷāātre in my fighting circle."

"He will be very happy. He has much admiration for you and even wears your scar on his forehead with pride."

Ļainjin stood, drained his cup of the warm medicinal water, grimacing at the taste, and walked back into the rain, confident in the plan he had just set in motion. He anticipated Liṃanṃan would be waiting for him, naked beneath their sleeping mat, ready to dry his wet skin with her warmth and drain the chill from his body with the yet to be fulfilled passion she had sparked earlier, which had charmed the pounding rain and brightened the gray face of the lagoon waters.

After a few days, her cousin the bird-watcher appeared and announced that the bird's mate had appeared and now sat on their egg, and that his bird had gone to sea and was nowhere to be seen. Ļainjin agreed that there was nothing else to be done. He was truly on his own now. Was that how his friendship with the bird was to pass? That he had little to say and nothing to do but, day by day, continue to twist the fibers of his former life and entwine them with those of this new one? Then so be it, and so it was that this man of notorious action must have appeared to these fellow villagers to be settling in to their normally nonconfrontational mode of island life. He was calmly able to initiate his plan as though sitting in the quiet crown of a coconut palm, making the first clean cut through the tip of a swollen utak and setting in motion a series of events that would unfold by natural order, based on a design he secretly nurtured.

So, without comment, he went about his daily affairs, progressing through his routines as his jekaro dripped, moment by moment, through the night and during the day, imperceptively faster and more abundantly. The various cycles of his day-to-day routines were disciplined by this single enigmatic purpose. He would rise before first light and wash his jekaro shells on the lagoon shore. He would meet up with the jekaro boys along the ocean path, joke with them, climb with one or another, finish his trees, and return by sunrise to Taknaṃ's cookhouse. Depending on the tide, he would either go fishing later that morning or wait until after sunset. Battle practice always started at noon and finished in time for their evening jekaro, and if not fishing, Ļainjin would visit Ļaluj's work site, where the old man had constructed a boathouse even before he had sacrificed the valuable breadfruit trunk. There, he would find both Bōkrōk and Ļāātre fulfilling their *ri-katak* duties so the two could exchange places during the afternoon, when it came time for Bōkrōk and Ļainjin to ford the passage between the islands. There, as a new member of the circle, Bōkrōk learned the art of battle from the master he followed with daily admiration and from whom he would freely harvest the invaluable fighting lessons of confident deception, repetitive and distractive grace, and abrupt attack.

As days passed, Paratak appeared among them — sometimes during, sometimes after practice. He appeared briefly and hesitantly at first but then with more boldness, even as her appearance confirmed the rumors of Likōkkālọk's pregnancy. Word spread that Paratak had boasted to her that he would surely seek out and kill its father if he found the child not to be his. Ļainjin showed no sign that he was distressed over the attack on his friend or that his concentration was set on anything other than success in the upcoming battle. Instead, as these days spun into moons and the stars climbed the night sky and, true to season, the ocean quieted even more, he spoke to Paratak about another lobster hunt and a night of bọbo — and to everyone's surprise, he began instructing him in the art of spear-throwing. Ļainjin would scratch a circle in the sand, and he and Paratak would take turns hurling a spear high into the air, judging who could land the spear closer to the center of the circle. And Ļainjin would leave Paratak there to practice by himself while he returned to jebwa with the others.

Progress on his new proa continued, and they argued out the decisions necessary to its unique design. The length of the kubaak would be the standard two-thirds of the two and one-half ñeñe of the hull he requested, but the distance from its center to the center of the hull would be its full length, which proved to be a central point of contention between the two. Ļaluj contended this critical distance should be, at minimum, a full handspan shorter per ñeñe. Ļainjin contended he wanted the greater distance for stability. Ļaluj countered that this would prevent the kubaak from rising as it should above the waves. It would be able to do so only in the heaviest of winds, making the boat slower and less able to achieve a sharp upwind angle into a lesser breeze. Ļainjin agreed, but claimed the downwind stability of the boat was more important to him.

Ļaluj countered that all the way back to Lōktañūr. "The race has always been into the wind. They raced upwind to Je from Wōjjā, not vice versa.

From the beginning, they designed our proa to cut into the wind and not the other way around. With your design, you could sail to Ujae in no time, true, but you will fight an easterly breeze for over a day when returning."

Ļainjin acknowledged his point but insisted he relished the trade-off. Ļaluj agreed to cut the outrigger booms accordingly but stubbornly stated he would cut shorter replacements in case the newcomer changed his mind once he sailed it. Then, after a moon had passed and Ļaluj had the boat nearly finished, they battled another round over the length of the mast, the sail spars, and the shape of the lateen sail. The standard is for the spars to be of nearly equal length and nine-tenths the length of the hull tip to tip — or roughly the length of the waterline. Sometimes the lateral boom is cut a hand or two longer depending on how aggressive — how much sail — its helmsman feels he can carry. Ļainjin wanted the lateral boom to be a hand shorter. Ļaluj claimed this would prevent the sail from gaining speed in light winds if close-hauled. Ļainjin countered, much to Ļaluj's consternation, that this would make his downwind trip to Ujae even faster and safer in heavy winds!

Ļaluj countered, "You sound like you are planning to sail downwind and never come back!" They debated on and on like this, with Ļaluj suggesting a more classic design that would enhance speed in a close-hauled race into the wind and Ļainjin insisting he construct the boat to be more effective on a downwind haul.

Ļainjin, Paratak, and the others continued to practice, with Paratak perfecting his spear-throwing and the rest repetitively clacking through their mesmerizing four-man motions, faster and faster by the day. Nevertheless, without the nightly interludes that replenished Ļainjin's spirit, the unaccustomed monotony of the days between might have caused him to falter and retreat to the simple solitude of the sea from which he came. He and Liṃanṃan sweated together and contorted themselves in the moonlight and in the dark or by the flickering light of a distant shell of burning oil, and after the passing of several moons, he finally began to suspect that his seed had taken root. It started with a giggle and a glance back at him as she spoke to her sister Joļọk, from whom she had become inseparable. Then she surprised him by disgorging her morning meal, much to the amusement of her grandmother. A glance and an abrupt squinch of her nose, as her grandmother laughed teasingly, was all the confirmation he needed. She was to bear his child.

Soon thereafter, the day of the much-practiced-for battle arrived. The tide was high. The night had mostly passed, and the waning moon was setting in the clear western sky when they saw the sails of the fleet approaching along the atoll's southern fringing reef. In response, they sounded the conch shell to alert all to ready their torches, their spears, and the *aje* that their women would beat as the men formed dual lines in groups of four. Their opponents beached their canoes high upon the strand at the island's southern tip. Likewise, their men lined up along the path to the village and their women began their ululations and drumbeating to urge their men onward. As they marched, their spears clacked, one against the other, in ferocious alliance, the frightening sound growing louder and closer with every passing moment.

Ļainjin and Bōkrōk stood at the head of their disciplined lines of men, which stretched eastward down the perpendicular path to the ocean. Their women formed their own groups, erratically surrounding their men on either side, and they responded with their own ululations and the beating of drums. Onlookers rushed in every direction, each carrying a dried-and-braided coconut-leaf torch, ready to flare at the appointed time. The men began to clack their spears in rhythm with their opponents as they methodically battled their way, unopposed, along the path from the south. Then, as the interlopers entered the expansive courtyard before the home of the irooj, Ļainjin and his men closed ranks on either side of his group of four until both dual lines of opponents faced each other.

Finally, at the second sound of the conch trumpet, all the violent sounds of battle ceased and the torches were flared. Pedpedin, accompanied by his niece Kōkkālọk, appeared from beneath his stilted, thatched house and entered the square. The elder had apparently appointed her to speak for him. She entered the square at the edge of the opposing lines and addressed her uncle Tokjān, who stood in the middle of the opposition directly across from Ļainjin. The men acknowledged each other with brief, barely discernible nods as the remainder of the torches flared, even as the light of the clear dawn began to glow about them. Her sky-piercing chant called out to the spirits of all their ancestors killed in battles past to mingle among them and then commanded the competition to begin.

These are the men of that west-most place,
quick tack then tack back.
They're they. Yet, we're us!

At this, the jebwa began with shrieking ululations and drumbeating accompanied by mysterious, ancient chanting by Tokjān's islanders. The disembarked group, by tradition, was the first to perform. Sly competitor that he was, even though he had invited Ļainjin to practice with his group, he had left him uninformed of the movements he had planned to use against him. His dance began with a very surprising, immediate retreat. He, with the rest of his group of four, disappeared as his lines closed in front of him. Then, in turn, the next group of four disappeared and so on, as his lines contracted and closed repeatedly and as the warriors ducked and rotated to the chant of the jebwa and to the rhythmic clashing of twirling spears. Pedpedin, Kōkkālọk, and Ļainjin's entire group were all stunned as they realized that this was *the* very movement they had themselves meticulously planned to spring on *them*.

Suddenly, Ļainjin remembered Tokjān's words to him the evening they first met: "Our women fly from islet to islet and chatter like birds at nest." Somehow, someone had informed Tokjān of the movements Ļainjin had been practicing. Sure enough, as soon as the remainder of his lines, previously horizontal to them, dwindled into two lines vertically facing them, they separated and allowed the most recently retreated group of four to battle back and reverse the movement until, at last, Tokjān's group rejoined its lines and restored all to their original positions. He had stolen their movement and now he had performed it first. The words of Ļainjin's grandfathers came to him as well. "Study your opponent. Anticipate his movements, and flaunt them to his face at the start of your engagement to defeat his spirit."

Then, without trumpet or any other sign of note, and slowly, almost imperceptibly, every other group of four battled back to form a second paired row, and the lines closed behind their retreat as they continued to dance, now four rows deep. Suddenly, again without signal, the lead circles at opposite ends of each double line began to slowly, at first almost indiscernibly, battle in opposite directions as each circle of four continued to clash spears, duck, and rotate in the jebwa's strictly stylized form. Each line then pivoted slightly inward from opposite directions with each distractive, repetitive movement until they somewhat smoothly formed a gigantic double-ringed circle just at the point in the dance where the rhythm picked up with each successive sound of the triton shell and the speed of the dance accelerated to its final dramatic end. They completed the dance to the sounds of a gasping crowd. The sun had arisen, and its soft yellow rays were flashing here and there about them as the surrounding coconut palms swayed and gently rustled in the slowly warming morning air, and it was clear to all that Tokjān had successfully developed what had always been a basic lineal dance into a more sophisticated circular arrangement.

Pedpedin could have chosen to feed his guests then and perform for them later or to press on while the emotions in the throng that had gathered were high. Kōkkālọk took her uncle's hand as they nodded to his brother's islanders to acknowledge their excellent performance. Was she squeezing his hand to stay his decision? She gave a piercing glance to Ļainjin, who nodded to indicate his eagerness to begin. His mind was racing. He took consolation in the fact that Tokjān's movement that formed the final circle was accomplished in less than flawless fashion. He was confident that, though the pattern of their movements would be similar, his men had practiced longer and harder. They could look better. By tradition, the jebwa starts with a slow, trudging rhythm that surges gradually, as would a proa at each tack if sailing into a gradually strengthening wind. He decided to challenge his group by setting the initial beat at the faster, second tack. It was a common competitive tactic to hasten the initial beat, and they had practiced for this eventuality. Thus, if all went well, the final pace of their dance should end up much faster than the pace of their competitors' performance. The risk was that, if they were unable to hold the quickened cadence, they would most likely falter at the finale. That would be a disaster by anyone's measure. The reward was that, if they failed, they would at least have set their sails into a storm rather than fair weather, which was the ancient temper of the dance. If they faced failure, they would keep their heads high until the seasons turned to give them another chance.

Ļainjin closed his eyes and recalled the battle of the aorak that Pedpedin had related, the battle that had taken place not far from where Tokjān and his men stood. He opened his throat, and conjuring the spirits of the fallen with his spine-chilling cry, he chanted the ancient words:

These are the men of that west-most place,
quick tack then tack back.
They're they. Yet, we're us!

With that, he set the temper of the dance with a mighty clash and a second timely clash of his spear against that of Bōkrōk. The accompanying *du* began the jebwa chant at the faster pace he had set. His group of four and the group of four to his left, as though doubling Tokjān's previous movements, retreated as practiced. His strategy became immediately evident as the lines closed and they disappeared into the path behind them. They would perform movements identical to those of their opponents yet mock them with greater numbers, quickness, and proficiency. To onlookers, unaware they had practiced these same movements, their performance would appear almost improvisational. He showed no mercy as he quickened the pace. The lines of the men facing Tokjān closed and shortened repeatedly as double groups of four men retreated into the path, progressively impelling Ļainjin and the others back until they reached the lines of the jekaro boys, who had remained hidden to the opposition. Then, as the *du* temporarily ceased their enigmatic chant, Bōkrōk switched places with another, who joined Ļainjin's circle next to him.

Bōkrōk, with a surprisingly loud clash of spears, then accepted the lead at an even faster pace and, with the practiced accompaniment of the jekaro boys in the lines behind him, resumed the dancers' portion of the chant at a higher pitch. Ļainjin's group of four and the group next to his split and, as practiced, immediately switched to voicing the *du* side of the chant. Bōkrōk and his jekaro boys then moved forward at an incredibly fast clip, as group after group parted before their clashing spears until they battled out into the square and demonstrated their agility to the surprised and fascinated crowd. Thus, it turned out that these same untattooed boys, previously shy and of little account, who had followed Ļainjin into the forest out of boyish curiosity, now demonstrated they had immersed themselves in his charisma. They leapt into view as accomplished young men to surprise the opposition, endear themselves to their families and adoring playmates, and elicit the pride of their irooj. Moreover, they now performed in tribute to their pregnant, scandal-prone patron who, puffing with pride, was in the process of ennobling herself in the eyes of all.

Bōkrōk and the other three in his group traced their lines as they battled and chanted — in flawless fashion — into a perfect double circle as Ļainjin and the irooj's more experienced men, with the rest of the *du*, formed a half-moon about them to chant them forward. Once the circle was formed, the chanting momentarily ceased and then began again with the angry clash of Bōkrōk's spear, and the man with the scar on his forehead led his proficient team at unmatched pace through to the finale of the spirited, skin-pimpling performance. When the dance was done, the chant completed, and the drums silenced, the boys cringed in expectation as the puffer fish himself sprang from the path and launched his spear high into the air, and all watched as Paratak managed to land it vertically in the beach stones covering the square directly in the center of their two concentric circles.

Although there were many heroes that morning, there was no talk of winning or losing. Many jokes of the great practice were told in small circles amid laughter and feasting, and many rumors spoken in low voices, and surely, the names Ļōpako here and Likōkkālọk there passed from the lips of many.

Based on past wanderlust, this would now be a time ripe for departure, time to set to sea again and leave his half-told story like the last draft draught of water upon the pretentious throats of those whose lives had intertwined with his but must now be relegated to memory. Though this option allured him still, Ļainjin had a plan to defeat his past, engage his present, and fulfill his promise to seek happiness.

In the days that followed, Ļaluj, Bōkrōk, and Ļāātre labored to lash together the canoe parts they had hacked from various live trees with their adzes. They lashed together the hallowed upper and lower hulls of breadfruit wood through holes drilled by small bows and stingray barbs. They layered pandanus leaves that would swell when wet to plug the seams, and sealed the seams with glue from the gum of the breadfruit tree. They cut deck planks fitted in similar fashion from boards previously seasoned, hacked, and sawed with coconut-fiber twine and the wet grit of crushed shell. They fashioned the rounded lower outrigger booms with identical downward curvature by hacking them from the hardwood limbs of the *kōņo* tree. The dual upward-curving booms, lashed at the hull at one end and to the outrigger stay at the other, required greater flexibility. They square-hacked these from limbs of the kiden tree. They carved the kubaak from a breadfruit log, but of course, the masterpiece that gave the proas of the islanders of Rālik and Ratak their renowned durability at sea was the lashing at the end of each lower perpendicular boom that joined the kubaak and secured it parallel to the hull. Ļaluj, amid a crowd of much-interested onlookers, lashed these himself. They were why such a canoe would prove useless in the hands of islanders not from Rālik or Ratak — because once these unique lashings rotted, how would they be replaced? It was why the mere observation of tying the lower booms to the kubaak was such a great learning opportunity for Bōkrōk, Ļāātre, and the others.

A second stylized lashing was necessary to join the *rojak*.[176] Early in the planning process, Ļaluj cut these to Ļainjin's specifications from limbs of the *kōņo* and gave them to Taknaṃ. Then, by day and on moonlit nights, she wove the finely cut strips of seasoned pandanus leaves and sewed them at the luff with fibers she made from boiled immature coconut leaves. Finally, she lashed the woven sail to the spars with Ļaluj's most tightly twined ekkwaļ.

When word passed that the boat was ready to launch, Ļōpedpedin sponsored a celebration. He called for the killing of turtles. Much food was prepared and many coconuts felled. That morning, Ļaluj and Ļainjin took the boat out for a short ceremonial cruise. Ļainjin was pleased though Ļaluj again argued that the cut into the wind should be much sharper. "Not if the

[176] The yard or lateral boom of the triangular lateen sail.

sole purpose of this boat is to sail away with the wind and never return," Ļainjin responded, mocking the old man's previous words but leaving them to dangle in his imagination.

They returned from their sail just in time for the feast. Likōkkālọk, belly bulging, came with her workers and brought food as well. The jekaro boys performed the jebwa again, much to the delight of all. Ļainjin, by tradition, spoke in honor of the old artisan who had hacked out the hull and of the titled landholder, or *aḷap*, who provided the breadfruit trunk. He thanked them all and then expounded on his favorite subject. "The proa," he said, "does not part the sand without providing food or trade or some additional opportunity to those ashore. It is an islander's most prized possession and the center of atoll life, around which all else rotates."

After speaking, Ļainjin stood next to the proa as the islanders came, family by family, and placed gifts on the boat — here a necklace, there a kilt or woven sleeping mat, or a turtle-shell comb. When the procession ended, the irooj raised his arm, and one appointed from each family came forward at once to pick one of the gifts. As the crowd massed around the proa, each politely hurrying to pick their favorite takeaway, Kōkkālọk saw her opportunity to draw close to him. She pressed her belly tightly against the back of his hand as he braced himself in the crowd and held it fast to the bulwark at the edge of the boat's foredeck. Instantly, their gazes met, hers with dancing eyes and flirtatious, puckered lips — his, he imagined, as surprised as a fish plucked up from the sea. She allowed him no escape as the ever-increasing, provocative pressure of her belly just above the edge of her skirts was such that no man could jerk his hand away without embarrassment. Therefore, he simply stood motionless, enthralled as she stood across the hull from him, wrapping her long hair into a bun and capping it off with a comb she had snatched from the deck. She leaned back to advantage her belly ever forward, glancing at his hand as though seductively tempting him to reach down into her skirts. He, feeling the child moving within her, grasped the meaning she left unsaid.

The next moment, she abruptly broke her attention. She relaxed the pressure against the back of his fingers. Her eyes steadied. Her lips formed a smile. She backed slightly away as her gaze turned abruptly to someone behind him just as he heard the nervous giggle he had listened to a hundred times and felt the familiar pressure of pointy breasts against his back. Liṃanṃan's hand reached for his upper arm, which gave him the opportunity to retract his hand, just grazing her belly as Kōkkālọk, showing no sign of awkwardness or unease, turned to Liṃanṃan and spoke.

"A boat won't part the sand!" she said, tapping the new comb atop the bun of fragrant, black hair on her head. She smiled untimidly at one and then the other, and then turned her back and passed through the distracted crowd. He wondered how much of their engagement Liṃanṃan had seen. Had she viewed the desire Kōkkālọk provoked from most men in his eyes? Could Liṃanṃan sense the infidelity she had hearkened from somewhere deep within him? He would never know unless she spoke of it. Unless of course, he asked Kōkkālọk, who could have snuck glimpses of her face moments before she approached from behind him. Not daring at that moment to face Liṃanṃan, he turned his attention to one after the other congratulating him on his new vessel as the crowd eventually dissipated. Finally, having struggled to regain composure, he turned to her and gained relief from her joyful, loving smile.

He worried she might bring the episode up as they ate. However, she revealed nothing. She maintained her lovely composure throughout the meal and then gathered leftover gifts not taken from the boat and passed them out among the feasting crowd. Her manner, of course, had changed ever so slightly since her pregnancy began, as their sexual preoccupation, by custom, had abruptly ceased. She began sleeping, as was tradition, back at her father's house. No woman of Rālik or Ratak, save apparently Kōkkālọk, would risk the health of her child to fulfill her own desire or that of her chosen, a duty often performed by a younger sister. Paratak, as rumor had it — no doubt out of jealousy — continued to play the fool by insisting Kōkkālọk sleep next to him. Ḷainjin, on his part, refused to sleep with the others at the men's house, which was a well-known ruse anyway. Those men spent their nights carousing around the island and attempting to entice girls from their father's houses. They would sleep late into the morning and then share with each other their stories of the night before. To Ḷainjin, these were men of pitiful stature. They became addicted to their nightly escapades and rarely ventured from their sexual obsessions. He ate his meals with Liṃanṃan at her father's house, and he learned to eat more slowly and to talk more. They told each other stories from their youth and came to know each other on a different level — though significantly, he continued to keep his true name and the story of his heroic search for his mother from her as promised. Some nights, he would fall asleep as they talked, but when he wakened, he would return to his house until morning unless he had planned to fish, which was often.

Battle season over, fishing became his new passion. Ļainjin took his new boat out trolling a few times to establish its luck and then eventually lent it to Paratak. The Pohnpeian had stayed away from the canoe during construction, no doubt due to unease over the constant presence of Etre, but after the launching, Ļainjin encouraged him by beaching when he spotted him on shore, offering him a fish or two, and relating the story of its catch. Soon, Paratak began watching for Ļainjin's sail, and he would find him waving from shore to receive more fish and more stories. Ļainjin first taught him the names of the fish and then the fishing methods used to catch them. Then he taught him all the parts of the boat and the sailing terminology. He taught him the important weather signs and impressed him when most of his predictions came true. Soon Paratak, under Ļainjin's tutelage, was sailing by himself and fishing with the hooks Ļainjin gave him. Their friendship grew day by day, much to the surprise of all.

On occasion, they would stop at the uninhabited islets along the reef, build a fire, and cook some of their catch. Paratak, in between his sailing lessons, was keen to hear the story of Ļainjin's visit to the stone village of his home island. He — of course — knew about the *kājokwā* and the importance of the rafts made from them in the construction of the village. However, his family did not live in the stone city. He was never part of the group that rushed out into the ocean to help tow the *kājokwā* to shore to celebrate the final day of their retrieval. So he was unaware that his own people were not the ones who retrieved them. Ļainjin explained that only the proa of the outer atolls were large enough and had hulls deep enough to tow the *kājokwā* from the *kāleptak*, the great countercurrent that streamed eastward against the wind just south of Pohnpei.

Paratak would ask, "Where do the *kājokwā* come from again?"

"No one knows," Ļainjin would answer, "but what we do know is that, during the call of the north, the wind whips up gigantic mountains of waves that must crash upon a shore somewhere and must suck all manner of flotsam back into the sea with them.

"Much about the countercurrent can be observed," he explained, "by watching water trapped at the bottom of the canoe. The water that splashes into one end as the boat dips into a trough must soon return to the other. The water from those gigantic swells that roll westward in añōneañ must stream back eastward sometime, somewhere. That is the secret of the *kāleptak* current. It is like the water sloshing back inside your canoe regardless of the direction of the wind. *Kāleptak* runs from west to east regardless of the deluge of wind and the waves that course over it. The bigger the *kājokwā*, the deeper it sinks into the countercurrent and the more difficult it is to retrieve from its stream.

"Your nature, and that of your Pohnpeian people," he continued, "is to be content with the vast resources of your high island. We of the coral atolls have a nature that compels us to venture out after such things. Your children will ask you, 'Father, how did they ever move such great stones to build this village?' and only we of the small isolated islands will remember the answer."

Ļainjin was amused at the enormous quantities of water Paratak carried with him and the way he hugged the shore or the edge of the lagoon's back reef as he sailed. This, no doubt, was due to his unhappy prior experience, adrift for so many days in the vast expanse outside the safety of their islet-encircled lagoon. But the root of his caution must have been respect and not fear. As he gradually gained confidence in his sailing master's ability to foretell approaching weather, he learned to follow him farther and farther lagoonward, from the edges of the atoll's eastern and southern fringing reefs to the more productive fishing grounds along the submerged western barrier reef, where fewer fishermen ventured. There, they could compete for larger catch, though there, they were always at risk of being swept out to sea should they get caught off guard by storm or mishap. And there, their comradery grew as, day by day, they returned home with ever-larger fish to feed their always-hungry, pregnant women.

Ļainjin usually caught more fish, and as always, he was generous with them. At the end of each day, before they left their fishing grounds, Ļainjin would maneuver his vessel to pass Paratak a few extra fish. It was a somewhat complicated movement, depending on the tide and wind, but from Paratak's perspective, better at sea than close to shore, where others could see he had not caught them himself. The hulls — with their retracted sails and booms hanging to leeward, and with their outriggers to starboard — were not designed to attach and transfer loads one to the other, especially craft that were singly manned. The only approach possible was bow to bow on opposite tack or bow to stern pointing in the same direction. He taught Paratak to drop his oar, always tied at the stern, into the water, and grab fast to Ļainjin's bow where his forestay secured the *rojak* of his retracted sail. Once he grabbed hold of Ļainjin's *rojak*, Paratak would have to work with all his might to keep the boats separated and safe from crashing into one another in whatever wave action they faced. Ļainjin, on his part, then crawled forward, dragging his large basket of fish upon the foredeck and tossing them, one by one, into Paratak's hull.

That was how their friendship grew. Day by day, one who had developed the utmost respect for the sea followed another who had seemingly mastered it. Ļainjin, whose true home was the sea and who knew its secrets, proved willing not only to share them with his friend but to share his catch as well. Each man invariably returned to his island home to distribute his catch and watch his pregnant woman cook and slowly devour the fish he brought to her. Ļainjin had received word that the Chief's egg had hatched and imagined him regurgitating his daily catch into his mate's craw as she snuggled their chick beneath her. Likewise, he took much pleasure in watching Liṃanṃan suck the water from a fish's eyes, crunch into the white, chewy eyeballs, and then abruptly invade the empty sockets with the same pointy tongue that, in prior days, had darted in and out of his mouth and teased him into elation. On her part, she must have thought of herself as puffy and undesirable, and she constantly implored him to take Joļọk to mat with him.

"Here, look at this!" she said one evening, eating in Taknaṃ's cookhouse and pulling back her sister's skirts to expose her knee to him. "Look how dark from sunlight! She has already shown these knees to every boy on the island. Soon she'll choose someone, and you'll have some ... jekaro boy standing in your way!"

Joļọk giggled and covered herself, and Taknaṃ laughed approvingly. "*Jab ālkwōj pein ak,*"[177] the old lady professed.

Yes, of course, Ļainjin stirred beneath his kilt at such a provocative sight, combined with the coquettish glance Joļọk directed his way. Yet he was a man who had searched his whole life for a mother he never knew. He had watched one moon cycle after another and yet another as he had crossed the ocean searching for her. Liṃanṃan, too, had waited her whole life for him. Why was it so surprising to her that he wanted to prove himself true to *her* too, especially now that she was about to get fat with his baby? Of course, she knew not that he had sailed beyond the farthest horizons beneath the faintest stars in search of her. How could she know in such a short time that he was not as fickle as the landlubbers who inhabited the men's house? Truly, his destiny was to be less than understood. That saddened him. Yet he accepted it — crammed it into his throat along with how many other unfulfilled desires and secrets he stubbornly promised himself never to disgorge?

So instead of distracting himself with Joļọk's beguiling ways, he kept true to his plan and companioned with Jebrọ as he led his brothers across the early morning sky, each night appearing earlier, each morning appearing higher in the sky before dawn. Ļainjin observed, in turn, each brother's rising affect the weather in its own subtle way. Then Jebrọ began to appear at sunset and cross the sky during the whole of the night. When he finally disappeared before sunrise, Ļainjin knew the call of the south was at its end, that his eldest brother Tūṃur was about to reign the skies again, and that Paratak's *kūro* had migrated from around the atoll and congregated at the bottom of the passageway to the ocean. There was a door — of less than a cycle's length — between the two seasons that allowed a man to sail pleasantly enough before the full wrath of Tūṃur's enormous seas turned the ocean to uproar. This was a period before the invariable wind of the call of the north began, before the countercurrent began returning the

---

177 Literally, "Do not bend the wing of the frigate bird"; take what is offered.

mountains of water piled high against the great islands to the west from whence their ancestors came. It was just as the fledgling winds began to huff the ocean swells of buñtokrear but before the contrary swell *kāleptak* brought the reverse current that would sweep the ocean beneath its surface converse to these forces and churn the sea to furor, tumult, and turmoil. It was the last opportunity before the torrent of sunstorms would thicken the air with salt spray and cake the leaves of the highest of coconut trees, turning them from southern green to northern brown.

It was the morning of *jetkāān*, the first day that the door of añōneañ opened, so he knew the tides would reach their extremes. And because this was the time between the seasons, these extremes would reach their ultimate. The day would be short, the sky clear, and the wind brisk and steady from the northeast. It was not to be a day like any other. He had announced to Paratak that it was time to show him how to fish for *kūro* when there would truly be "*kūro wōt laļ!*"[178] They met on the sandy shore of Likōkkālo̧k's island. Paratak's daughter was there, attended by one of her workers, and Ļainjin was joyless as he watched her wave good-bye to her proud father as they hoisted their sails and headed out across the lagoon toward the passageway.

They arrived well before noon, as the incoming tide began to pour from the rapidly bulging ocean through the passageway into the lagoon. Though the wind blew hard, the waves from the east had but a short distance to build as they crossed the lagoon, so the ocean current pouring into the passageway counteracted the push of the waves, giving their lines a straight course to the bottom, where the *kūro* spawned. Ļainjin showed his friend how to use three hooks to pull in three of the sad-mouthed, brown-and-black spotted groupers at once. The struggling movements of the fish cancelled each other. Paratak claimed he had never heard of such a thing, but he found himself succeeding at it repeatedly. His enthusiasm grew as the afternoon passed. They hoisted their sails again and again and sailed back out into the ocean, where they would lower them again and drift slowly back against the wind, fishing through the passageway with the incoming current. Their boats drifted close to one another, and the men held chanting contests.

[178] Literally, "Only kūro below!" or "There are kūro everywhere!" a saying similar to "There are many fish in the sea!"

One of them would chant, "*Jab kōrkōr ioon kūro. Bwe?*"[179] and the other would respond, "*Kūro wōt laļ!*" as they simultaneously pulled in their catch from below and competed to see which had three occupied hooks and which had only one or two. Then, at slack tide, when the water in the lagoon and ocean had leveled, Ļainjin suggested they stop and eat. With zero tide, they began drifting, with the wind slowly pushing them out to sea as they rested. Ļainjin took the opportunity to show his *ri-katak* the still-gentle *kāleptak* counterswell rolling beneath them as it lifted and lowered their boats even as the east wind, and now the current, swept them against it.

The tide had turned. The vast ocean bulge had begun to contract, and the water was now beginning to spurt out of the comparatively tiny atoll as it would through a crack at the edge of a shell cup. Ļainjin pointed at *kāleptak* and explained to Paratak that the broad swell was particularly evident because the breadth of the atoll cut off its counterswell buñtokrear and that, as they drifted westward, buñtokrear would reform and overcome the counterswell to such an extent as to make it less detectable. Then he challenged Paratak to name the other two swells of the *wapepe* symbol. He showed Ļainjin he had memorized them well. Then Ļainjin pointed out that their situation was deceptive because the wind and the tide were now moving in the same direction, so the sea appeared calmer and less threatening. Earlier in the day, the two forces were fighting each other, causing the wave from the east to crest with more intimidation. Now the wind appeared to have lessened, but it had not. He asked Paratak to drop his line in the water. When he did so, the line immediately slanted off in the direction of the passageway. This caused him to realize how quickly they were drifting seaward.

"We can no longer fish. The wind and current are doubled against us now," Ļainjin explained.

"Then we return."

"Let me give you something first!"

After some hard paddling, Ļainjin maneuvered his bow to the other's stern. Paratak immediately grabbed onto Ļainjin's proa where the two *rojak*

---

[179] Literally, "Why paddle over kūro?" This means, "Why paddle away from good fishing?" and is a riddle, the answer to which is "Kūro wōt laļ !"

met and held fast. But as Ļainjin crawled forward, straddled his bow, and grabbed onto Paratak's backstay, instead of the fish he usually swung his way, he handed him his heavy log of *jāānkun* and then several additional shells of water. Paratak grabbed onto them with a questioning look on his face just as Ļainjin let loose of his backstay, cut loose Paratak's oar where it floated between them, and used it to more quickly separate the two boats. The eyes of his Pohnpeian friend widened to such an extent they made Ļainjin chuckle.

"I'm going to teach you to sail without your paddle," he shouted at Paratak, continuing to backpaddle and further separate the two boats. "I'm going to teach you how you can use your leg as a tiller to steer. Go ahead and hoist your sail."

Paratak sat staring at him in disbelief. He turned his head back to Tokjān's gradually receding island near the passageway and then back to him several times, as though gauging the pace of their rapid drift. Ļainjin could see that he had shaken Paratak's tree of trust in him to its root. This would not be easy, but it was the best course for the Pohnpeian whom he had grown to accept as a friend.

"Paratak, you must trust me. Hoist your sail."

Ļainjin began hoisting his sail, and immediately, Paratak scrambled to hoist his. Ļainjin secured both oars below, sat in his stern, and lowered one leg into the water. He sheeted in and, using his leg as an oar, began steering his craft toward Tokjān's island next to the passageway. Paratak did the same, and Ļainjin instructed him to follow from behind and set his course on a southeast tack for the passageway. After a while, it became obvious that, although the comparably fatter leg worked as a crude tiller, their cut into the wind proved hampered by lack of a sharp blade deep in the water. The combination of current and wind, it seemed, would take them to sea south of their mark. They could not return like this, not against this current, not against this wind, but Ļainjin waited for Paratak's judgment to solidify.

"No good!" shouted Paratak. "No can go!"

Then Ļainjin told him to *diak*, and the men changed tacks and tried to sail northeast this time, using their legs as tillers. Paratak took the lead this time, but again, it gradually became obvious, more so and more quickly than before, that their course was short of target. Again, they were swept off course by the combination of wave, current, and an improper tiller. They would make neither the passageway nor the western barrier reef of the atoll, nor even the atoll's northernmost islet, but again, Ļainjin's objective was for Paratak to come to this conclusion himself.

"We can no go!" he shouted at last. "We must use paddle!"

"Okay, now sail next to me!" With that, Ļainjin released his sheet and turned his craft downwind on a course a little south of west. Paratak, who was behind him, rushed to do the same, and the boats began sailing beside each other. He turned to Ļainjin with an approving smile on his face. Now the current, the wind, and the waves were all working with them, and the boats were easy to steer, even with their trailing legs angled only slightly down into the water. So this was the last lesson to be learned — that a man who lost his oar could passably steer his boat downwind. But upwind, not so well.

After a while, as expected, Paratak, sailing next to him, shouted, "We go in wrong direction!"

"No, Paratak, this is the right direction for you!" Ļainjin shouted back to him. "This is your course to return home."

The boats were speeding along, magically skipping over the waves, sails full of wind. In that moment, in those conditions, truly it appeared they *were*, in fact, pointed in the proper direction given the current conditions.

"No go home yet! Not time yet!"

"Paratak, this is the right time!" Ļainjin shouted back, and then in short sentences amid Paratak's various protests and in between plunging into the depths of the following swells and rising on the crests of the next ones following, he continued with the monologue he had prepared. "This is the right direction for you. If Raipuinlang dies, your Jau Areu title will die with him! You must return now to your father, before *he* dies. Look at you! Remember your story! You left as a boy swept away in a fishing canoe. You were dead to them. Now you will return a hero with a title. A man traveled with knowledge of sea and sail. This is your course! Memorize your angle to this buñtokrear swell pushing us! When you get tired, take down your sail, go below, and sleep. When morning comes, put up your sail and fly just south of west at this same angle until you see the mountains of your island rise from the sea. Then you will thank me! When you see your family, you will thank me again! When you claim the Jau Areu title from Raipuinlang, you will forever remember me as your truest friend!"

"How many days?" Paratak asked, furtively glancing back at the islets diminishing amid the growing swells and darkening sky.

"Four days without rest, but you must take care to rest! You must drift and sleep when you tire! Have faith in these swells. They will continue to push you home even as you rest. It should take you no more than eight days — more likely six or even five! Think of each wave as one step closer to home. And do me one favor. If Raipuinlang asks you about my mother, tell him I did find her!"

With that, Ļainjin lifted his leg from the water, watched his boat arc back around into the wind, and leveraged his oar down into the sea. He set an opposite course before glancing back to see his reluctant friend skipping rapidly upon the westward-rolling waves like a flat stone he had cast to a separate destiny before turning away to another.

Darkness had long fallen and the moon had climbed above the trees by the time he tacked eastward across the lagoon to Likōkkāḷọk's island and beached his canoe amid the peaceful leeward waters sloshing restfully upon its shores. The tide was still receding. The sheltered lagoon glistened peacefully there in the moonlight — all in contrast to the imagined ongoing struggle of his friend at sea. "Calm yourself," he whispered into the breeze, as the palms on either side of the narrow passageway rustled in the very wind he hoped would carry his message away to the panic-stricken Pohnpeian. With much effort, he lifted two of four woven-coconut-leaf baskets of large fish by their long, braided handles and placed them on his outrigger deck. The shiny, black eyes of the unhappy groupers that still lived gleamed back at him in the brilliant moonlight as they lay nearly motionless and quietly defeated. He carried the heavy baskets to Likōkkāḷọk's cookhouse, where he met her standing in the doorway, startled by his unexpected appearance.

She immediately sensed that all had changed for her. He held fast to the baskets as she wrapped her arms around him, pressed her belly against his manhood, and looked up pleadingly. "Is he dead?"

"No, I set him off on his journey home. I doubt you will ever see him again."

"He will die at sea?"

"I don't think so. I think he will make it home!"

"Ļōpako, that is wonderful. You are truly a good man. Destiny sent you to us. I feel so … free!"

"When she grows up," he said, pointing to Paratak's daughter sleeping inside by the cooking fire, "if she wants, I can take her to him."

"She will soon forget about him. I'll see to that!"

"He will be well off. I gave him my Pohnpeian title."

"Yes, he has been bragging about that, but a title in the hands of a fool is like a spear in the hand of a woman — quickly taken."

Then, ever so slowly, Likōkkālọk began to separate herself from his body by bending her head back and shaking her bun loose, draping herself in the aroma of flower-scented coconut milk. She gazed piercingly into his eyes as though inquisitively searching for some sign there that he wanted her. She caressed his back and then his arms with her hands. She touched just one of her large, black nipples ever so slightly against his lower chest and ran her fingertips down the strong arms that held fast to the baskets. Then the grateful expression on her face flashed playfully and she began to sway her swollen belly provocatively and ever so gently against his manhood, causing it to writhe out like a fish sprung from the water. Embarrassed, he could hardly step back but instead held her gaze by gradually closing the distance between his face and her open, protruding lips.

"I will need your help," he said, feeling like a fool, his manhood slowly retracting beneath his kilt. He wondered who among her workers might have witnessed his burst of lust for her. She, disappointed at no longer feeling the point of his spear against her belly, tried to revive his passion by jiggling her tummy against it as if it had a mind of its own. Then she cupped her hands around the nape of his neck, tempting him to lower his mouth to hers.

"Anything … you want," she responded, rising on her tiptoes, pressing the enlarged nipples of both breasts against him, her lips beckoning his.

"I want you to tell them it was all your idea, that you asked me to make the proa and trick him into returning home."

"Done, but take me this once," she said, releasing him for an instant as she fumbled to untie her skirts. He dropped the baskets and, much to her dismay, stayed her hand with his as he stepped back.

"You know I am too true for that. I have already given you everything but the throat I owe to another."

"You are a magnificent man who makes us women crazy with desire. You shame me with your loyalty to my niece despite that angry one's ambition" Likōkkālọk lowered her eyes to his now-hidden manhood. "But I will keep your secret from her nonetheless. You are a loyal worker, and as your *lerooj*, I must respect that above all else. Here, I want to bring you a basket of breadfruit to take to Liṃanṃan," she said, turning away to her cookhouse.

He gazed about, looking for signs of onlookers around her courtyard. He did not want to take the basket, but how could he refuse?

"Thank you, Ļōpako! Never fear, I will keep our secret! Take this to Liṃanṃan. She will be worried by your prolonged absence, and you have much to explain."

"Then that will be our trade," he responded, as they smiled broadly at each other, and then he slowly turned and walked away. Soon, he was home, where he beached his canoe for a second time and carried the breadfruit basket and Paratak's paddle with him to the house of the irooj. He abandoned the basket by the cookhouse. Ļaluj was sitting under the house rolling twine, as he expected. Ļainjin gave him back the paddle he had fashioned and knew well. He nodded in response and chuckled to show he had solved the riddle of the boat designs that Ļainjin had insisted upon.

"So your friend is on his way home on your boat designed to return not?"

Ļainjin nodded back, and nothing more needed saying between them.

He returned to his canoe, removed the last two baskets of still-gasping fish, and rinsed them in the water. Then he placed the baskets on the wet sand at the gently surging edge of the lagoon and began rinsing his hull. He poured several scoops of clear water into the hull with his *lem* and then bailed the fishy water back out into the lagoon. Joḷọk sauntered down the beach as he continued bailing and squatted, low and flat-footed, over the fish in the baskets, teasing one of the fish with a poke as it opened its large mouth wide and then partially closed it again, as though trying to pump water through its gills.

"Poor thing, so far from its home at the bottom of the sea. *Kūro*, you definitely win the contest for the ugliest fish in the lagoon, don't you agree?" she asked, speaking as though to the fish and then to Ļainjin, and giggling as she poked one and then another with her index finger. Some, which had been caught solo and yanked from the depths quickly, were motionless and silly looking, with their stomachs inverted and bubbling out through tiny, sharp teeth. Their lips were blubbery and sad, and their eyes were small and set far too close together on their blotchy, flat faces. None were battered. They had been dehooked easily by holding on to them beneath the flap over their extremely large gills.

Ļōbōkrōk and his friends arrived and helped Ļainjin spread the butt ends of previously cut palm fronds across the sand as rollers, to slide the canoe upshore toward the shelter of his boathouse. Joļọk followed along, struggling as she towed a heavy basket in each hand. She stopped and rested, as did they, between the heaving chants that pierced the night breeze, only to be quickly absorbed by the broad and lonely expanse of sandy beach exposed by the still-receding tide stretching along the entire length of their watery home. The unsettling image of his friend alone out there, out of his usual environment like the poor *kūro*, his leg dragging through the sea, grasping for dear life onto his lunging canoe and racing toward an unknown future, loomed in his thoughts and contrasted sharply with the tranquil environs around him. Yet he chanted repeatedly and even more fiercely as they dragged and pushed the canoe through the sand and then, in three or four stints, carried it to its resting place beneath his open, thatched boathouse.

Joļọk ordered her brother to take the fish to their grandmother's cookhouse, and the two stood alone as Ļainjin patiently gathered his fishing implements. She ran her hand over one of the two spots where Ļainjin rested his rear as he steered. It was visibly worn from his many days at sea. Close by was the worn edge of the deck opposite the outrigger side where the shaft of his oar had worn into the planking. She ran her fingers across that as though searching for some connection to the man she perhaps admired but who kept himself distant despite her every effort to draw him near. She stood peering into his eyes, then lifted herself and sat where he had earlier, except that while he had placed his feet within the hull, she straddled it in unladylike fashion, exposing her knees and both thighs, which popped through the wrap of her skirts. She lifted his oar at the same time and pretended she was steering the boat through the waves.

"I drew the water for your bath, and I grated coconut and gathered flower petals to sweeten the smell of your skin. Still, I like your smell the way it is now — sunburned, sweaty, and fishy. To me, that is the true smell of a man! I would take a man before his bath rather than after. That is how I differ from my sister. I'd wrap my legs around you right now, as you stand there, but then perhaps you would rather pretend I'm my sister. After I bathe you, I'll snuff the lamps and let you drill me upside down or right side up, or like your catch" — laughing, she contorted her face by crossing her eyes and poking her tongue at him — "inside out!"

Ļainjin could not help but laugh at her antics. "Liṃanṃan has been sharing stories with her sister again," he thought. He was beginning to swell again beneath his kilt. He had not released his seed for a long time. "Can women sense such things?" he wondered. However, he had faced enough temptation for one night. "Lijoļọk," he said, you are a very desirable girl. Any man would want to drill you many ways, but a man only gets one chance to cast his story, and mine is to be" — he paused — "as loyal as possible to the one who cast herself into the sea to save me. Now I'm going to take my bath, thank you, and please… You go help your grandmother cook some fish."

"You're full of it!" she argued, still friendly. "Soon you'll be so full of seed your nose will bleed," she said, laughing at her poetic comeback.

He went straight to the bathhouse and found, as expected, that she had done as she said. His enclave was silent and lonely save for the two shell lamps Joļọk had lit for him, the rustle of the palm leaves, and the occasional creaking of the thatched framing in the wind. Inexplicably, he could not bear to spend the night by himself and, after his bath, returned to the house of the irooj. There he found Ļaluj sitting as before, his back against one of the sunken coconut trunks supporting the home above. Paratak's paddle lay next to him on the broadly woven mat beneath him.

Without speaking, he climbed the ladder into the intimacy of the sleeping family. The irooj was snoring in the corner. Ļainjin lay silently on his stomach next to Liṃanṃan and then carefully placed his hand gently upon hers without waking her. He listened again to the wind, which reminded him of his friend out there, cold and struggling, leaping down the moonlit, windblown crests and then plunging into the troughs of the dark sea all about him. He could hear voices outside as a fire was being prepared in Taknaṃ's cookhouse and conversation erupted over the surprising basket of breadfruit. He fell asleep imagining the house was sailing through the wind as it indeed whistled in periodic gusts beneath the thatched roof and, now and then, jostled its frame. He saw himself growing old, lying there for a generation or more, safe upon the stable floor surrounded by his children to be — perhaps never again to challenge the lonely vastness of the surrounding ocean.

The image of his friend's frightened face just as he turned away from him haunted his memory. "Hang on!" he called to him repeatedly amid his exhausted sleep. He wakened periodically and snuggled closer to her, rested his face on his free hand next to hers, and yet again dozed, entranced by her heavy breathing and permeated by her warmth and pregnant beauty.

Ļainjin had primed himself to answer questions about Paratak but found himself unprepared for the unplanned turn of events that occurred the following day. Upon returning from jekaro, he was told by Taknaṃ that Likōkkāļọk had arrived and requested the irooj convene the council of *aļaps.*[180] Before he could finish his morning shell of hot *nen*, he found himself parrying spears with Liṃanṃan. Why had he brought fish to Likōkkāļọk? Why hadn't he mentioned the breadfruit gift to Joļọk or her grandmother? What happened to Paratak? Where was the new canoe Ļainjin had paid Ļaluj to make? And why did he have such a regretful look on his face?

His answer to her questions and those of others was the same. He had "earned a title in Pohnpei that he was unlikely to ever use and Paratak was on his way to claim it." They had joked about the title. After encouraging him for so long, why was she surprised when she found out he had done Likōkkāļọk's bidding by nudging the Pohnpeian to sea in his new canoe? Why would she be surprised he delivered Paratak's catch to Likōkkāļọk?

[180] A paramount landholder who manages land on behalf of an irooj.

Why was she surprised Likōkkālọk would respond to the gift of fish with breadfruit?

Then Liṃanṃan asked, "What about the island Likōkkālọk has given you?"

Stunned, Ḷainjin found out that Likōkkālọk had followed him before the tide had turned that night and had told Pedpedin and their gathering of *aḷaps* that she needed to reward him for the great service he had provided her, by granting him her *aḷap* rights to the northernmost islet of the atoll under the credo of *mọrojinkwōt*.[181] He and his offspring could live there if they chose, and her workers there would pay tribute to his lineage accordingly.

Under the custom of *jab ālkwōj pein ak*, Ḷainjin could not refuse without insulting her. Everyone including Liṃanṃan knew this. Why shouldn't he accept Likōkkālọk's gift? From his perspective, he had earned the title by equitably ridding her of a problem she herself had created and could not solve. The islanders, however, seemed to be poisoning Liṃanṃan with innuendo. Rumors circled like fisher birds at *wūnaak*. Had Ḷainjin perhaps killed his friend? Had Paratak attacked him and lost? In either case, where was the canoe the man shark had given to him? Had Ḷainjin, rather than returning his body, simply set it adrift?

Most suggested Likōkkālọk's spell had captured him, and this was what he guessed troubled Liṃanṃan most. Her worry was easily explained to him by Taknaṃ: "All was likely to unfold as Likōkkālọk wanted, and it was obvious to all that she wanted the man shark! When you accept the island, she will have you exactly where she wants! She will have you bringing fish to her every night and bruising your butt on that tree of hers as she has every other man she enticed into her web and, like a spider, sucked his spirit dry!"

Ḷainjin had never seen Liṃanṃan upset before, and she seemed to grow more and more agitated as, in turn, each woman came to offer her unsolicited advice. One, he heard, suggested she leave her father's island, take him to Ujae, and raise her child there on her mother's land, where it belonged. Another suggested she stay and pluck out Likōkkālọk's eyes to

---

[181] Aḷ ap rights given for bravery in battle.

prevent her from seeing him. She appeared as though facing the vortex of a waterspout, hesitant to tack left or right to escape. Wanting to get away from it all, she pleaded he take her fishing.

"I have an idea," he said. "Why don't we go searching for *tilaan* on the bird islands of the northeastern fringing reef? The jekaro boys use it to sharpen the shell of their knives, and they are running out. You can troll for fish along the way there and back."

She seemed relieved at the opportunity to leave the island for a day. They launched his proa in the bright of the afternoon, set sail in the same brisk wind that was rushing their friend on his journey home, and left the pretentious rumormongering behind them for the moment. Liṃanṃan's spirit appeared revived, set free the moment she hoisted their sail and sheeted in. She unfurled Ļainjin's line, dropped the lure into the water, and let the line play through her fingers until she judged its distance from the boat adequate. The trip was reminiscent of the voyage they took to the bird islands with Paratak several moons prior, except that the season had changed. The tides were more extreme, the wind was much heavier, and the waves were now choppy as they crossed the fringing reef at high tide. And it was three days earlier in the cycle, so the slack between the tides would come earlier than it had that evening long ago. He related the story of what had happened the day before — told her how he had lured Paratak out through the passageway into the ocean, how he took his paddle to prevent his return and sent him on his difficult but passable journey back home. Paratak would be happy once he returned to his family. He would have a lot to boast about with his new title.

Liṃanṃan agreed that he might. "Likōkkālọk would have continued to play him for a fool until she convinced one of her playmates to kill him in his sleep. I wonder how many *kūro* he has eaten by now?" she joked, and they laughed as they each estimated.

Ļainjin thought he convinced her that he had justly solved a problem that would have surely led to unhappiness for them all. Then he reminded her that Paratak had promised to kill whoever fathered Likōkkālọk's child if it proved not to be his, and it was said to be Etre's. He regretted his duplicity the moment he spoke.

Her face turned from bright to gray as though a cloud had passed overhead. "We both know she bewitched poor Etre and got him in trouble with Paratak, and we both know her child is not his!"

At this, he felt cut to the bone by his own hand and would not, could not, muster a response. "Did she know?"

They approached the first bird islet along the string to the northmost islet Likōkkālọk was offering him rights to, and he asked her to rewind her fishing line. It was apparently not a good day for fishing. Then he laid out his plan. He knew the tide was still incoming, so once they lowered their sail, instead of beaching their canoe and circling the islet together, he would disembark at the southern tip. Then she would paddle to the northern end and wait for him there while he scoured the windward beach of the islet for any pumice stone he found washed up along the line of flotsam that marked the point of high tide. This light stone, borne of the ocean, was the magic that allowed him and his jekaro boys to sharpen the edges of their shell knives. In turn, it allowed them to cut the face of the utak with the clean, thin slices necessary to draw the nectar and cause it to drip so profusely for so long.

He disembarked into the waist-high water at the stony edge of the islet. The tide was high and cool as he felt it sweeping around the passageway from the ocean reef, and the sounds of birds squawking amid the high-tide sounds of water surging high upon the stony shore filled his ears. His lips could barely reach the skin above the back of her skirts to kiss her. Then he shoved his craft lagoonward for her mission and climbed the shore toward his. He cut through the brush at the edge of the islet and stopped to strip the leaflets from the frond of a sprouted coconut tree to weave a small basket for his finds. When he arrived at the ocean side, he found the tide perfect for his purposes. The waves had washed up a contorted, incurving line of flotsam made up of all manner of bird-nesting materials, feathers, and discarded coconut leaves and husks, and amid these scattered remains of days past, he found several pieces of pumice the size of the eye of his hand or smaller.

When he arrived at the north end of the islet, he found that, despite his orders to paddle about, she had managed — with the help of the coconut-frond skids he had cut and always carried in his hull — to beach the bow of the boat by herself. He found her there, sitting on the shore, watching the stern gently rising and falling with the remnant of the Kāliptak swell that crossed the submerged western barrier reef, swept across the lagoon, and gently sloshed upon the lagoon shores of these easternmost islets. She sat there, proud of her strength and ability to do such a thing despite her condition.

She was hungry. Unfortunately, he had given his log of *jāānkun* to Paratak the day before, so he plunged into the goo-caked interior of the islet carrying a stake from his boat. He kicked down a few fresh coconuts from one of the few palms planted on the islet and, with his stake, husked them along with several other sprouted nuts he found beneath the tree. She made do with these. He ate nothing as he watched her eat and continued to marvel that his child was growing inside her. Finally, together, they lifted the proa farther onto the shore, she rested her head on his breast, and they napped a bit upon a bed of kōņņat leaves. Frazzled from the events of the morning past, they spoke not but slept soundly, and by the time they awakened from their separate dreams, the tide seemed to be approaching its ebb. The current swept deeply and smoothly between the islets, and the colors of the back reef between them had changed from sharp to mysteriously blurry browns, and greens and grays. This was the tide where all manner of ocean and lagoon marine life could cross between ocean and lagoon with impunity.

It was time to move on. The swells from the east were rolling over the flooded open fringing reef as they sailed through the mismatch of waves and swirling currents to the next islet north. This was where he was to continue his search around its ocean side as she paddled with lowered sail along its lagoon shore toward the islet's northernmost end, where they were again to meet. Except this time, as he casually searched and casually continued to fill his basket with the precious porous stones that had by chance floated across the sea, washing up here and there at the end of their separate journeys, something unbeknown to him had happened.

Had she again attempted to land their canoe and gone inland for more fronds upon which to beach it? Had she managed to beach and then begun to search for pumice herself, only to return and find it floating away? Had she been careless, or just foiled by the currents swirling about the flooded shores? More than likely, he would later contemplate, she had been preoccupied by her thoughts of him and perhaps Likōkkālọk. That thought would bring back a pang of guilt to his throat. Yet the only thing that mattered now was that she had plunged into the lagoon in a desperate attempt to retrieve his canoe after it had somehow slipped away, and by the time he had sauntered around the islet's shore back to the lagoon, the boat had drifted so far that he initially assumed what he spotted in the distance was someone else's. Except the shore was abandoned. So, though he could not see anyone on the canoe, he realized it must be his and began waving at it, expecting her to appear from below and wave or immediately hoist the sail and come back. Curiously, there was no response from the drifting craft. His throat tightened abruptly as he spied what must be her there in the distance, swimming after it! The pang in his throat quickly traveled to his head as he began to realize the dangerous situation into which she had cast herself.

Immediately, he shifted to battle. He cleared his head of all thoughts other than the situation facing him. He cupped his hands behind his neck, faced her image swimming toward the drifting boat, and adjusted his stance so she was equidistant between his elbows. He then tattooed that image onto his mind's eye, stood steadfast, tightly closed his eyes, and slowly counted. When he reached fifty, he opened his eyes and, still at a standstill, tattooed the image again. Then he closed his eyes and again counted slowly to fifty. When he opened his eyes, he realized she was making good progress, swept by the current, no doubt. More importantly, she was not swimming toward the boat but rather anticipating where the boat was moving. It was not drifting dead in the water. Though they had previously struck sail and left it hanging properly furled, it was still catching some wind. The craft had turned to windward and was slowly making its way to the north as it drifted westward. He knew that the farther she swam into the lagoon away from the lee of the islet, the larger the waves would grow, making her return — should she be unable to catch her target — more difficult. Once again, he was tempted to leap into the water to rescue her, but how successful was he likely to be? She would be swimming away from him toward the drifting boat. She had the current and the wave behind her. He, with such a late start, could never catch up to her no matter how hard he swam. Though he could see her clearly now from his vantage high upon the shore, he was sure to lose sight of her in the troughs of the waves the moment he lowered himself into the water, especially if she tired and broke the line between him and his drifting target. Three times, he entered the water to swim after her and three times, he stepped back to shore. He realized, no matter what, it would be dark long before he could hope to catch her. She would never be downwind from him and would probably not hear his call. If she did reach the boat, she would have to tack back and might miss him, and then he would have to turn and swim back, in which case she would reach shore only to find him gone. What mistakes might she make then?

Suddenly, he saw her skirts hanging from the kōņņat tree where she had neatly folded and hung them, and was comforted that she had not impulsively dropped them in haste or cast them carelessly away. It was a sign she had at least deliberated. Her instincts must have told her she could make it! In that moment, who better to decide? Or had her "I can" attitude got the best of her? He decided he had no other choice but to remain diligently disengaged and wait for her return. He could do nothing to help her! He walked down the shore to a sandy spot, still sheltered and still warm, and lay back frustrated upon the sand. Had he lost her? Was she destined to become but another tragic and painful episode to crowd the memory of his already battered and bleeding soul? It was so comforting to have found someone to share his memories. Though he kept the darkest parts buried in his throat, at least she knew he was hiding them and periodically forced some out, as with a drowned man coughing up sea he has swallowed.

As he sat there at the water's edge, absorbing the incessantly rising and falling tidal flow, a *ļañe*[182] chased a circle of baitfish that jumped at the flooded shoreline next to him. Three of the fish landed upon the shore, one of which flipped and flopped back into the water and was gone. He watched the other two lie there on the beach, expanding and contracting their silver gills to breathe. Alas, out of water, they would surely die and soon be eaten by hermit crabs — or more probably by one or another of these noisy, flocking terns. On a different day, he might have rinsed one and popped it into his mouth, crunching down on its head to stop its wriggle and chewing

[182] Giant trevally fish: *Caranx ignobilis*; "*ulua*" in Hawaiian.

through its bones as he savored its raw, bloody flavor. If he had a line, he might have tossed pieces of the chewed fish back into the lagoon as chum, to keep the jack circling as he hooked and threw the second after the predator itself.

Just as a clear or cloudy sky would determine the color of the lagoon, so a man could see a vision of himself reflected off its surface, and so this ever-flowing sea of ever-moving participants would be the final arbiter of his destiny. He imagined Liṃanṃan settling into her own rhythm and carving her own path upon the face of the lagoon. Her ancestors, to preserve their story for posterity, had cleverly carved the image of their story into the coconut trees. Surely, the surrounding sea was swallowing her wake as immediately as she created it, so just as surely, the aorak images carved by her ancestors would disappear over time, though less swiftly. It was only their story that might survive.

Then his grandfathers again came to his aid and, in his moment of anguish, whispered their rule for the item lost. "You have not lost the thing; you have lost yourself. It is where you set it down before you distracted yourself and forgot where you left it. Learning is remembering. To cast the future, you must understand the past. Retrace your steps back to that moment you found her. Go back. Go back further into the distance of your past than comfort allows. Why were you attracted to her? Why did you pursue her? When did you last hold her in your hand? Which way, at that point, did you turn?"

As she no doubt continued her desperate chase, the horizon turned slowly orange and blue, then gray, and finally, dark red. Then, as the brightest stars projected their points of light through the deepening blue hue above, while the moon continued to traverse its arch across the night sky, shining all the brighter as the sky dimmed, it became the sole reference point for the small white clouds that drifted, one after another, beneath her majesty. The birds, gullets filled, cried out as they returned from the hunt and carelessly dropped their goo. The salty wind rustled and coated the leaves of the trees in which they returned to nest. The swells tumbled upon the ocean reef crest and thundered on into the distance. Exhausted mentally, ever so gradually, he followed their timeless advice. Cautiously, like an angler with a hopelessly tangled line, he gave up his quest, stopped all forward intention, and began retracing its circuitous path back into his past. *That*, of course, no matter how imperfect, was the one thing that truly stayed what it was. No matter how tortuous, it could never change, even as he waited for the uncertain outcome of this current contest between his chosen woman and the sea to determine what his future would be, even as he would ponder the question of the night before him. Would she succeed? There was no course of action left before him but to retreat into his past, meander there, and search for a clue.

Clearly, he had somehow led her to believe his boat and his fortune were more important to him than she and the seed she nurtured inside her. Had she known his trials and what he bore, she would never have cast herself after a mere craft and collection of shells that were in no way critical to the desperate passion he carried for her. By so carefully guarding his promise to keep his mother's story untold, he now feared he had stayed his final cast at happiness. Surely, he could have trusted her, above all others, with the secret of who he was. His past now spread before him. All the terrible experiences he had endured and struggled through cried out that her likely death would be the result of this mistake. He had already let the two women he most respected slip from his grasp into the depths of the sea. Surely, he could not withstand a third. No longer able to bear the torture of the present, he lay back upon the beach and sought relief from his past. He thought. He slept. He dreamt. Each time, he awakened sick in the gut and throat gasping as he fruitlessly sought signs of her on the horizon below the gradually setting moon. He repeated the cycle, growing more and more despondent and nauseated as each horrible moment penetrated like the first projectiles of rain driven by an oncoming, ominous storm. Each time, as instructed, he turned back yet again to seek refuge in better memories as he searched his past, desperate for direction.

Finally, in the cold dampness before dawn, the forbidding words of his mother flashed back to him. "Tell my story not! There are moments in a woman's life when her future will reach back to guide her destiny. A woman knows she must bear her child. In that moment and thereafter, she feels her future drawing her. Better to stay my story's end leading my fleet out to sea in the face of certain storm than tell its true ending — wishing for a life that could have been. Let some woman, somewhere, someday, hear of my courage and struggle forward unafraid to achieve her destiny."

He awoke and looked out with reborn confidence as the first light spread across the lagoon before him, and he believed he saw the faintest glimmer of a sail in the fading moonlight. Cautiously, he turned his eyes elsewhere upon the horizon then turned back till the same flicker caught his eye. He raced like a man possessed to the highest point above the shore. He scanned his eyes again along the horizon, and there she was with her sail blinking back at him, clear as the new day. And that is when the storm of tears he had avoided his entire life sprang forth, as he turned around and around to show his contorted, jubilant face to those in the crowd now gathered about him. Each to whom he owed love. Each of whom he had left selfishly behind, becoming but a spot on their horizon. Each of them had nourished his soul. They were all there, his grandfathers, Taknoḷ, and Kalbōk — even Jiañ and all the others who knew his story. A contrite aura of thankfulness overcame him. He happily surrendered himself to it, and as this long-awaited, happiest day of his life progressed from one event to the next, he realized it was not just a passing emotion. This thankfulness would be a new state of life for him.

She too seemed changed. He noticed it from the first moment he smothered her blushing face with kisses and she laughingly turned one exhausted cheek to expose the other. She had lost the girlish giggle he loved so much, but in its place, he found a more mature and knowing composure that he would learn to respect and similarly cherish. She was tired and, curiously, wanted him to take her to rest on that same islet ahead that Likōkkālọk had offered to give him. As they approached, it seemed large but sparsely settled and appeared to lack the manicured look of the islands of her father and uncle.

"We don't have to accept this gift if you would rather not," he said.

"Of course, we will. You are such a puffer fish! You can stop worrying she will tell everyone you are the father of her child! If she ever does, Lijoḷọk is eager as a conch shell to announce her tale of how she watched Likōkkālọk swipe your seed from her sleeping mat and impregnate herself with it! I'm glad she carries your child. It will better your chances of having a son. Mine is a girl."

"How do you know?"

Her theretofore blithe expression clouded, becoming somber. "Because the spirit out there told me so," she recalled, as though struggling to remember a dream almost forgotten. "She was the same one who calmed me. She gave me the direction to swim and the confidence to keep going. She told me that I would beget a beautiful daughter who, like her father, would attain a quiet yet heroic destiny."

At hearing this, Ļainjin wept until she shut him up.

"Stop that and look like an *aļap* or your workers will think you are weak and will cheat on their tribute! Look up! You haven't even noticed your bird circling! It perched on your boat like it was its own this morning. It was probably waiting for you to emerge from below and catch some fish for it. Imagine its surprise when I recuperated and drew myself up from the hull and chased it away! Lazy fisher, it keeps pooping its goo where it doesn't belong. You must have spoiled it!"

Ļainjin looked up and saw his friend gliding high above. He resolved not to flop their heroic story like a regurgitated fish before Liṃanṃan but to relate who they were in short, pungent sips, like those from a half shell of *nen* too hot to drink. She, of course, would marvel at his adventures as they emerged one after the prior.

Finally, after seasons in the telling, she would seem to appreciate his companionship with the Chief. She would likewise profess to respect his mother's wishes and, as far as he knew, would never speak of her, even to her closest friends.

As for the future of their daughter, his unbeknownst son, and the fall of the Saudeleurs, that story will arise in time of its own accord and prove yet again that each generation can learn only so much from history and must struggle with the past anew. As for his gift to posterity, Ļōpako would tell his future *ri-katak* that once he shadowed the wake of the man called Ļainjin, who taught him his famous navigation chant but never spoke of his mother's end. Now, after generations of silence, the story of the Forbidden Man — the prequel to Ļainjin's shelter at Lae — can finally unfold like the shifting sands from a storm are known to uncover the occasional skeleton of a long ago buried, and long ago forgotten, creature of the sea.

Glossary

Ajbwirōk — A particularly delicious variety of cultivated, edible pandanus fruit.

aje — An hourglass-shaped sharkskin drum carried by women when they accompany their men to a battle.

ak — The frigate bird: *Fregata magnificens*; tied feathers used as telltales to confirm wind direction.

aḷap — A paramount landholder who manages land on behalf of an irooj.

alele — A flat, pouch-like purse, woven from processed pandanus leaves, for valuables.

Anbōd — Jālwōj islet; an area along Jālwōj Atoll's western reef known for shark hunting.

anidep — A game in which a foot-sized cube of woven pandanus leaves is kicked back and forth within a circle by clapping participants.

añōneañ — "Call of the north"; the southern solstice, which annually coincides with winter in the northern hemisphere.

añōnrak — "Call of the south"; the northern solstice, which annually coincides with summer in the northern hemisphere.

aorak — A subspecies of spider conch of the family Strombidae, species *Lambis*; characterized by stout marginal digitations.

arṃwe — A small tree: *Pipturus argenteus*; the bark (or "ōr") of this tree is stripped and twisted into fishing twine.

atat — A plant with small, thin leaves; the stems of this plant, *Triumfetta procumbens*, were processed to make skirts and kilts.

badet — Banded sergeant fish: *Abudefduf septemfasciatus*.

Bōb — Edible pandanus fruit cultivated predominantly on coral atolls in the central Pacific; pandanus tree: *Pandanus tectorius.*

bọbo — Night fishing for flying fish with pole nets and torches of pāle.

bọkwōj pedped — Literally, "grab the reef tightly"; extremely large spiny lobster: *Panulirus penicillatus.*

buñtokiōñ — Swell that "falls from the north."

buñtokrear — Swell that "falls from the east."

buñtokrōk — Swell that "falls from the south."

bwebwe — Yellowfin tuna: *Neothunnus macropterus.*

bwebwenato — Old story; fable; legend.

bwijinbwije — A by-product of the rope-making process; densely packed strands of coconut husk fibers too thin for rope making; used for kindling as well as washing.

bwilbwil — To make and race toy proas on reefs or along the shoreline.

dāp — Moray eel; marine eels of the Muraenidae family.

daō — "my bite" or "my food,"' often used by a child to declaratively assert the intention to eat or to demand food from an elder.

dekā ajaj — The heaviest, densest, palm-sized coral stones.

dekā maroro — Greenstone; obsidian; a naturally occurring volcanic glass found in Melanesia.

dekein nin — A heavy, oval-shaped club ground from the shell of the giant clam and passed as an heirloom, by matrilineal custom, from mother to eldest daughter; used to pound and soften leaves and fibers for mats, skirts, sails, etc.

diak — To tack or, more specifically, shunt. The tack of the sail is transported from one end of the canoe to the other, keeping the outrigger to windward.

dijiñ — Fart fish; species of emperor fish: *Lethrinus variegatus.*

du — Women beating drums and accompanying their loved ones to a battle or supporting their chant as they dance the jebwa.

Eakeak jān Ep. — Literally, "make your veins stand out." "Inspiring you from Ep." (Ep is the western ancestral homeland.)

eakpel — To discard ballast into the ocean to create more freeboard. In more serious and life-threatening situations, it could also refer to discarding people, usually the eldest first.

Eb — Mythical cannibal isle far to the west.

Ejaromrom utute kōj. — "It's lightning it's raining us."

Ej kōkōṃanṃan eoon aejet. Eeọkwe armej. — Proverb: "He calms the roughest waters. He loves all people."

ekkoonak — A fishing method used to catch schools of rainbow runner fish, *Elagatis bipinnulata.* A circular cord of sennit is floated on the surface around the school and gradually tapered until a group of fishermen can encircle and escort it to shallower water, where the fish are speared.

ekkwaḷ — Sennit; coir fiber line made from processed coconut husk fibers.

Elladikdik iuṃwin Tūṃur ekūtañtañin eṃṃaan. — Proverb: "Under the windstorms of Tūṃur, a man is an inchworm at sea."

ellōk — Literally, "it pricks"; a species of rabbitfish highly prized for its flesh that schools in a line and is characterized by its venomous spines. Streamlined spinefoot: *Siganus argenteus.*

Emejjia wa ilọmeto. — "A boat dies slow in the open ocean."

Epoon (aka Ebon) — A neighboring atoll seventy-three miles south-southwest of Namorik.

Etal ippān Mejdikdik! — "Go with Mejdikdik!"

Etao — Legendary trickster.

Idedh — One of many man-made islets on the reef off the coast of eastern Pohnpei.

iieḷap — Literally, "big time"; spring or extreme tides during full and new moons.

ikaidik — Rainbow runner fish: *Elagatis bipinnulata.*

inpel — The fibrous, cloth-like outer sheathing of the coconut flower buds found at the crowns of coconut trees; used to squeeze milk-like oil from coconut gratings.

iọkwe — "Aloha"; "hello (or good-bye), love."

irooj — Chief.

Irooj Rilik — Chief of the west.

jāānkun — Sun-dried sheets of pandanus pulp rolled into a log and wrapped in a sheath of pandanus leaves; see "mokwaņ."

Jab ālkwōj pein ak. — Literally, "Do not bend the wing of the frigate bird"; take what is offered.

Jab kōrkōr ioon kūro. Bwe? Kūro wōt laļ! — Literally, "Why paddle over kūro?" This means, "Why paddle away from good fishing?" and is a riddle, the answer to which is "Kūro wōt laļ!"

jāpe — A wooden, trapezoid-shaped vessel carved from breadfruit wood and used to knead breadfruit; the constellation Delphinus, the dolphin.

Jau Areu — Pohnpeian title: master fisherman.

Jebrọ — The constellation Pleiades.

jebu — A sharkskin drum used when paddling or sailing.

jebwa — A battle dance; a fierce reenactment of a classic fighting style passed along from previous generations.

jekaro — Also called "tuba," "toddy," and various other names; the sap of the coconut palm tapped from the flower bud as it grows and continues to protrude between its mature frond leaf and the less-mature inner fronds of the palm's inner crown. The skill of making jekaro is practiced worldwide wherever palms grow.

jetkāān — The day the moon rises amid tree trunks.

jetñōl — The night the moon rises at dusk upon the waves.

jinniprañ — A stalk or composite flower from which coconuts grow and ultimately hang.

jiraal — To eat grated coconut, usually with fish.

joñ — Mangrove: *Bruguiera conjugata.*

joñoul — Ten.

jourur — Thunder.

juon ... ruo ... jilu — One ... two ... three.

Kajin Rālik — Language of the Rālik Islands, now the western chain of the Republic of the Marshall Islands.

kājokwā — A tree trunk adrift in the open ocean or washed up on the shore.

kāleptak — Swell that "slaps from behind"; the countercurrent of the Intertropical Convergence Zone, which periodically streams through the islands just north and south of the equator.

kallep — Trap-jaw ant: *Odontomachus simillimus.*

pwentang — A Titan word for "cooking pot."

Kāmeto — A name: "fly the ocean."

kaṃōḷo — A newcomer celebration.

kapiknaajilọk — "Watch flapping wings from still water."

kapiknaklok — A term associated with flying fish of the family Exocoetidae; to take flight from beneath the surface of the water, flutter, spread wings, and glide.

kapiḷak — A gale sometimes associated with the first morning's sighting of the constellation Aries.

Kapiḷak ej buñ! — "Kapiḷak falls!"

kapin meto — Literally, "back side of ocean"; the westernmost atolls of the Rālik Chain.

kappej — Pole fishing from the reef edge at low tide under a full or near-full moon.

kapwōr — Giant clam: *Tridacna gigas.*

keemem — The first birthday feast after the passing of two seasons or thirteen cycles of the moon.

kiden — Soldierbush: *Tournefortia argentea.*

kijō — Literally, "my bite" or "my food"; often used by a child to declaratively assert the intention to eat or to demand food from an elder.

kin — Fire sticks; the small piece of wood is used to scrub the larger piece to make fire.

kina — Archaic shoals left by the old women in the story of Ļōppeipāāt.

kipeddikdik — To sail close to the wind.

kōbwābwe — Pole fishing.

koko — Mahimahi; common dolphinfish: *Coryphaena hippurus.*

koṃṃool — Thank-you.

kōñe — Ironwood: *Pemphis acidula.*

kōņņat — A short, sprawling tree that grows next to the shore; beach cabbage: *Scaevola taccada*; "*naupaka*" in Hawaiian.

kōņo — A hardwood tree bearing orange flowers: *Cordia subcordata.*

kubaak — Outrigger float.

kupañ — Convict surgeonfish: *Acanthurus triostegus.*

kūro — A species similar to the brown-marbled grouper, *Epinephelus fuscoguttatus*, which spawns seasonally in atoll passageways and in lagoons close to the passageways.

Kūro wōt laḷ! — Literally, "Only kūro below!" or "There are kūro everywhere!"; a saying similar to "There are many fish in the sea!"

kwanjin — Char-roasted, unripe breadfruit subsequently scraped clean before eating.

Kwe kwōjkwōjwaj jōn̄e Lan̄peran. — "You've cast the fate called brave sky."

kweet — Octopus.

Lale ej rōrōn̄! — "Look, he has an erection!"

ḷan̄e — Giant trevally fish: *Caranx ignobilis*; "*ulua*" in Hawaiian.

ḷan̄ eḷap — "Big wind"; typhoon.

lem — A wooden scoop, sometimes attached to a handle, used to bail water from a hull.

lerooj — Literally, "woman chief."

li — Female prefix used to emphasize respect.

Likōkkālọk — A name: "woman to make fly." "Li": the female prefix; "kōkālọk": "to make fly."

Lim̧anm̧an — A name: "woman beautiful." "Li": the female prefix; "m̧anm̧an": "very beautiful." The north star, Polaris.

ḷō — Male prefix used to emphasize respect.

lōk — Prick.

Ḷōkkōkālọk — A name: "man make fly."

ḷōm̧aj — "Ḷō": the male prefix; "m̧aj": a general term for eels of all varieties.

Ḷōpako — Literally, "man shark." "Ḷō": the male prefix; "pako": "shark."

Ḷōpedpedin — A name. Literally, "man this reef beneath us."

Luwap — Puffer fish: *Tetraodon hispidus*; also called porcupine fish. These fish have the ability to inflate their bodies by swallowing water. Some species have a tetrodotoxin in their internal organs, such as the ovaries and liver, and are poisonous.

m̧aanpā — Literally, "before the hand"; traditional fighting using quickness and distraction.

M̧adm̧ad — The northernmost islet of Namorik; necklace of flowers; lei.

m̧aj — A general term for eels of all varieties.

Mājlep — The star Altair.

ṃakṃōk — Arrowroot; a nutritious starch processed from the rhizomes of the dryland, knee-high plant *Tacca leontopetaloides.*

Mānnijepḷā — A mythic bird that flew passengers from one island to another.

marjej — A spindly weed: *Wedelia biflora.*

maroklep — "Big darkness"; "new moon." The islanders have a name for every night of the moon's cycle.

me — A fishing weir; a permanent V-shaped fish trap built by piling stones on the reef.

Mejdikdik — A star name: "Little death."

mejenkwaad — A cannibal; a witch who eats people.

meloktok — Night the moon rises so late it can be forgotten.

ṃōjọliñōr — Too much sky inside; sickness caused by sleeping under the moon too often.

mokwaṇ — The atoll dwellers, especially the Marshall Islanders, cultivated numerous varieties of edible pandanus. Some had flavorful juice they sucked from the fibrous nodules. Other pulpier varieties were chewed like fibrous carrots or baked, and the pulp was subsequently scrapped from the softened nodules. This mash, or mokwaṇ, was either dried into jāānkun or mixed with arrowroot starch and coconut milk and rebaked in a breadfruit leaf.

ṃōṃaan ṃaj — Literally, "a man is an eel," which means that he always develops a relationship with a hole.

mọrojinkwōt — Aḷap rights given for bravery in battle.

Ñaijuwe! — "Take me aboard!"

Namorik — Literally, "small lagoon"; an atoll in the southern Rālik Chain of what is now the Republic of the Marshall Islands.

Nan Sapwe — Pohnpeian spirit of thunder.

ṇatọọn — Sheet in or trim the sail.

nen — Fruit from *Morinda citrifolia*, a small tree prized throughout the islands for its medicinal properties; a tonic thought to promote health. Also called "noni."

ñeñe — The length across the breast from fingertips to fingertips; one fathom.

ņok — The midrib of a coconut leaflet.

pako — Shark.

pāle — Dried, braided coconut leaves used as torches for fishing; a coconut frond.

pejpetok — The spent core of a pandanus kernel drifting about in the ocean; a drifter.

Pit — A chain of thirty-three atolls south of Rālik and Ratak; currently the Republic of Kiribati.

Pohnpei — Currently one of the principal island groups that make up the Federated States of Micronesia, located in the Eastern Caroline Islands.

pọljej — Ripened breadfruit filled with coconut milk and baked in a breadfruit leaf.

proa — An outrigger canoe rigged with a sail.

rajraj — A knife or sword-like weapon uniformly edged with shark teeth.

Rālik — The western chain of atolls of what is now known as the Republic of the Marshall Islands.

Ratak — The eastern chain of atolls of what is now known as the Republic of the Marshall Islands.

ri-bōb — Literally, "bones of pandanus"; Pandanus people.

ri-jekjek wa — Literally, "person who hacks hull"; boat builder.

ri-katak — Understudy; apprentice.

ri-kwōjkōj — Literally, "bones that cast fortune"; fortune teller.

ri-Pit — An ancient term for people of Kiribati; literally, "people or bones of Pit."

rojak — The yard or lateral boom of the triangular lateen sail.

rojak ṃaan — Literally, "spar man" or "spar in front"; the vertical boom or yard of the triangular lateen sail.

roñoul — Twenty.

ruo; jilu — Two; three.

sakau — Kava; a drink with anesthetic properties made from the mashed roots of the propagated *Piper methysticum*, or pepper plant.

Tartok im kein liitiō, bwe? Ijañin eoḷōk! Ellok im toto wōt! — "Rush here and yank back at me, because the others have twitched me not! Relax and hang yourself!"

tilaan — Pumice stone: a porous form of volcanic glass that drifts up on island shores.

Tipen keidọọj? Dọọj? — "Piece of what sinks? What sinks?"

Tipen keimera? Mera? — "Piece of what's light? What's light?"

Tūṃur — Antares, the brightest star in the constellation Scorpius.

utak ṇe. — "Utak": the bud sheath from which the composite coconut flower will burst; "ṇe": "that there by you." In the Marshallese language, prepositions are directional, allowing for specificity when barking boat or with fishing commands.

U-waak tak-li! — Answer floats eastward.

Wa jab depet āne. — Literally, "boat does not pierce islet." This proverb means that a canoe's hull does not pierce the sand of an islet without bearing gifts.

wapepe — Literally, "boat floating." The symbol represents the four swells, one from each quadrant, converging upon an island in mid-ocean.

Wōde im ajoḷe! — "Chew it and gnaw at it!"

wōdwōd — To chew on a pandanus kernel with a twisting motion that crunches out the pulp and minimizes the fibers caught between the teeth.

wōjjej — An idiom used to express surprise.

wōr — Spiny lobster: *Panulirus penicillatus.*

Wūj uwaṇ in jān lōḷḷap in! — "Pull this gray hair from this old lady!"

wūnaak — Flocks of seabirds diving for baitfish driven to the surface by tuna.

wūno — Medicine.

wūt — Large-leafed land taro: *Alocasia macrorrhiza.*

wūtak — The bud sheath from which a composite coconut flower will burst.

Place and character names

Aelōñļapļap (aka Ailinglaplap Atoll)
Altair
Anbōd (shark-hunting reefs off Jālwōj Atoll)
Antares (aka Tūṃur)
Aorak (Liṃanṃan's clan)
Aries
Bōkrōk (aka Ļōbōkrōk; Liṃanṃan's brother on the boat; has a scar)
the Chief (frigate bird)
Delphinus
Diaj (immense coral rock on Namorik reef)
Ellep (aka Lib Island)
Epoon (aka Ebon)
Etre (aka Ļāātre; a boy who climbed a coconut tree with Ļainjin)
Idedh (islet given to Paratak by Raipuinlang)
Intertropical Convergence Zone
Irooj Rilik
Jālwōj (aka Jaluit Atoll)
Je (easternmost islet)
Jebrọ (aka Pleiades; constellation; Taknaṃ's nickname for Ļainjin)
Jiañ (Ļainjin's drowned boyhood friend)
Jibke (Lenkar's chosen one)
Jitwa (aka Lijitwa)
Joļọk (aka Lijoļọk; Liṃanṃan's younger sister)
Kalbōk (Ļainjin's fishing, shark-fighting friend for life)
Kāliptak (an eastern-flowing current)
Kāmeto (Liṃanṃan's name for a baby)
Kōkkāļọk (aka Likōkkāļọk; Taknaṃ's niece)

Kōle (aka Kili; bird island)
Konak
Kosrae (a small island)
Kuwajleen (aka Kwajalein Atoll; islets of)
Ļāātre (aka Etre)
Lae (Atoll)
Ļainjin (Tarmālu's son)
Lairi (lived on Wōtto; lives in a story)
Ļajuōn (Lijitwa's infant son)
Ļaluj (an elder who tells the story of Jibke and Lenkar)
Ļani (small boy who makes fishing line)
Lenkar (Jibke's chosen one)
Lijitwa (Ļōtokjān's chosen one)
Likeju (Jitwa's sister)
Likōkkālọk (aka Kōkkālọk; Taknaṃ's niece)
Likoropjen (an ugly spirit)
Liṃanṃan (Irooj's daughter; Ļainjin's chosen one)
Lirukōb (the daughter of Irooj Rilik)
Litaknaṃ (Ļainjin's name for Liṃanṃan's grandmother)
Ļōbōkrōk (aka Bōkrōk; Liṃanṃan's brother on the boat; has a scar)
Ļōbwebwe (a boy liked by Jitwa's younger daughter)
Ļōkajaaj (a reef off Ebon)
Ļōpako (aka Pako; Ļainjin's nickname; man shark)
Ļōpedpedin (aka Pedpedin; the Irooj; Liṃanṃan's father)
Ļōppeipāāt (a huge octopus)
Ļōtokjān (aka Tokjān; Liṃanṃan's uncle)
Ļōkkōkālọk
Lōktañūr (Tūṃur's mother)
Mānnijepḷā (sick bird; mythic bird)
Marshall Islands
Namorik Atoll (where Ļainjin lives; part of the Rālik string of islands)
Naṃo (aka Namu Atoll)
Nan Madol (Ponapen village on the reef)
Nan Samohl (an eel)

Ngalen (splashes Ļainjin with water when he has sunstroke)
Pako (aka Ļōpako; Ļainjin's nickname; man shark)
Paratak (the father of Likōkkālọk's daughter)
Pedpedin (aka Ļōpedpedin; the Irooj; Liṃanṃan's father)
Pleiades (aka Jebrọ; constellation)
Pohnpei (where Paratak is from)
Pohnpeian
Polaris
Raipuinlang (the wealthiest chieftain)
Rālik Chain
Rālik Islanders
Republic of Kiribati
Republic of the Marshall Islands
Satawan (Wisina's island home)
Scorpius
Shark (Ļainjin)
Taknoḷ (apprentice hull maker)
Taknaṃ (aka Litaknaṃ; Liṃanṃan's grandmother)
Tarmālu (Ļainjin's mother)
Tokjān (aka Ļōtokjān; Liṃanṃan's uncle)
Tūṃur (aka Antares)
Ujae (Atoll)
Wisina (Ļainjin's former lover from Satawak)
Wōjjā (aka Woja Atoll)
Wōtto (aka Wotho Atoll)

www.ingramcontent.com/pod-product-compliance
Lightning Source LLC
Chambersburg PA
CBHW030647020726
47493CB00006B/1915
* 9 7 8 1 7 7 1 8 0 2 2 8 4 *